Well-Founded Fear

ALSO BY TOM LECLAIR:

Fiction: *Passing Off*

Criticism: *In the Loop*
                The Art of Excess

Interviews: *Anything Can Happen*
                (with Larry McCaffery)

Well-Founded Fear

Tom LeClair

OLIN FREDERICK, INC.
DUNKIRK, NEW YORK

Library of Congress Cataloging-in-Publication Data
LeClair, Tom
    Well-Founded Fear / by Tom LeClair

    ISBN: 0-9672357-5-8

To and with Antonia Mitroussia, Esq.

For a homeless people

I Letter of Recommended Action

Chapter 1

"Casey Mahan, a 33-year-old citizen of the United States, departed her country of origin on August 15, 1998. She legally entered Greece on August 23, 1998, and shortly thereafter was granted a residence permit and work permit. After several months employment examining applicants for refugee status at the United Nations High Commissioner for Refugees in Athens, Ms. Mahan became a friend of her translator, Ziba Mamozin, a 27-year-old Kurdish citizen of Turkey. On December 22, 1998, Ms. Mahan returned to Cincinnati in her country of origin for the Christmas holiday. It is from her re-entry into Greece on January 3, 1999, that Ms. Mahan dates her fear of persecution."

That's how I'd begin describing myself if this "Letter of Recommended Action" was going to the Director of UNHCR. Summarize facts from the questionnaire, note important documents, identify the compelling event in the narrative. Then I'd analyze the applicant's actions, evaluate her interview, explain why I was recommending status or denial, attach my Letter to the front of the file, and send them to the Director. Because UNHCR has too many applicants, the Director observes the letter of the law and refuses to read a Letter of more than one page. Every applicant is equal in that regard. Now that I'm applying for asylum, I need more space to say why.

With no job to go to in Cincinnati, I felt trapped in my apartment. "Snug as a bug in a rug," Mom used to say when tucking me in. Ants and roaches had disappeared, leaving the apartment like a tomb that's been robbed. My former colleagues at Snow and Fiore were too busy billing and toting up year-end billing statements to show much interest in the non-profit refugee business. As I walked through sleet with other Christmas shoppers, I felt my hometown was like Istanbul, the same shearing of wealth and poverty absent in Athens. A few blocks up Vine Street from the office towers, I drove through Over-the-Rhine, the decaying neighborhood of Appalachians and African-Americans, emigres from eastern mountains and southern fields, Ohio's Kurds, my specialty at UNHCR.

Out in Mariemont, Mom and Dad watched an hour of local news about downtown people abusing their children and shooting their parents, but my parents didn't want to hear the stories I heard, not first-hand, not second-hand. Before the New Year, I missed Greek sun, talking with Ziba, listening to the applicants. I also worried that while I was away the Director might fire

Ziba because we'd become fast friends—both quick and close—outside the
office. I'd helped Ziba get her job, she'd helped me avoid a serious error, and
we helped each other be single foreigners in a new city.

In Athens, I was surprised to find Ziba waiting for me at the baggage carrousel.

"What are you doing here?" I shouted when I spotted her waving to me.
Among the Greeks in Italian suits, Ziba in her pajama pants looked like a child
brought out to meet a late flight.

"You're a translator, not a transporter," I kidded her after we hugged. The
smell of her cigarettes was strong after ten days with pure Americans.

Ziba didn't grin, didn't joke back. Something was wrong.

"The Director didn't call you in, did she?"

"No. I received information about my brother."

Ziba's formal phrasing alarmed me.

"He's not ..."

"No," Ziba finished for me, "he's not dead. But he's in prison in
Diyarbakir."

"Oh no, Ziba. How did you find out?"

"Mother finally got a letter through to me. She hasn't been allowed to visit
him, but she heard from another Kourd," Ziba said, giving her people their
pronunciation.

"What are the Turks charging him with?"

"Treason."

"Jesus, no. Not treason."

In the hundreds of hours that Ziba translated, the word "treason" was
always the sound of a gun cocking. Then I'd hear "torture," "disappearance,"
"corpse." After hours, on weekends, treason was the word Ziba and I tried to
avoid, a reminder of the state she fled.

"Yes, treason," Ziba said. She looked down at the tiled floor.

"Do you know why?"

"Mother believes it was for treating persons also charged with treason.
Two Kourds wounded by the police."

"That's why you were tortured."

"It must be, but the police said nothing about why they were looking for
Osman."

When I'd interviewed Ziba, she'd kept her composure. Now she started to
cry. No sobs or tremors, just some tears running down her cheeks. I dropped
my carry-on and put my arm around her shoulders, but there was little I could

do to comfort my friend. Under the public security laws, a person charged
with treason can be held indefinitely without trial. I couldn't say that her
brother would be okay or that he might beat the charge or even that he'd get
out of prison some day, not if he was tried for treason. We looked straight
ahead at the baggage carrousel. It went around and around and around, but
no luggage came up the chute.

"I'm afraid the police found Osman because of something I told them,"
Ziba said.

"Why do you believe that?"

"Because of things in mother's letter. I didn't know where Osman was.
When I finally gave the police the address of one of Osman's friends, I thought
the man was non-political. Now he's in prison too. I'm afraid Osman must
have been with him."

Ziba quivered under my arm, and I squeezed her shoulder, thin even
under her jacket.

"I led the police to my brother," she said.

"You don't know that, Ziba. Maybe your brother's friend knew where
Osman was and led the police to him. And even if you did reveal Osman's
whereabouts, it was an accident. You shouldn't hold yourself responsible."

Ziba pulled away, turned toward me, and glared into my eyes, as she had
at her interview. "I don't want a defense attorney," she said. "Of course I'm
responsible. I've done the worst thing a Kourd can do, betray a member of the
family. Family and clan and tribe loyalty. It's what we learned as nomads, the
way we survived. And I betrayed it all."

There was no use arguing history with Ziba at the baggage carrousel. "The
important thing," I told her, "is what can be done now."

"Yes," she said, "and immediately, too. Mother is afraid Osman will die in
prison before he's ever charged."

"Can she get a lawyer for him?"

Maybe it was ten hours in the air or ten days in America, but that was a
dumb question, and I knew it before Ziba responded.

"Lawyer?" she snorted. "Lawyers in Diyarbakir are all in prison for treason—for trying to defend Kourds accused of treason. There's only one way for
Osman to get out of prison alive."

"Do you think he can escape?"

"Do you believe those escape stories applicants tell? They're made up
because all of Turkey is a prison. There's no escape from the new military
prison in Diyarbakir. No, Casey, I hate to say this, but I have to." Ziba hesi-

tated, locked on my eyes, and spoke like the Director, slowly, without contractions, "You are the only person who can save Osman's life."

I looked past Ziba. Luggage was now thumping down on the carrousel. Travelers don't have to talk their way back through passport control, sneak out a one-way corridor, jimmy glass doors, and run across the tarmac to the conveyor belt below the plane.

"Me? I can save your brother's life?"

"Only you."

"How, Ziba? How can I do this?"

"You can because you represent the United Nations. You can intervene."

Ziba was back to the formal language of her first statement, of the organization we worked for.

"Intervene? You know how little effect letters have on the Turkish government. Amnesty International has been organizing campaigns and releasing recommendations for years."

"Of course I know this. That's why I'm asking you to go to Diyarbakir and get Osman out of prison."

She wasn't just asking me to run across the tarmac and wait for a passenger to slide down the emergency chute. Ziba was asking me to climb into a smoky plane, grope my way down the aisle, and pull out a person I've never seen. All I seemed able to do was repeat Ziba's statements as questions.

"Go to Diyarbakir and get Osman out of prison?"

Ziba came a little closer, took my elbows in her hands.

"It's Osman's only chance, Casey."

"But how, Ziba? Diyarbakir is not like the detention center at Lavrion. Your brother is not Mr. Kaya."

"We can figure out how later. Will you do it, that's the question?"

I'd examined Ziba for asylum. Now I was being examined. My friendship with Ziba and sympathy for Kurds were being questioned. My loyalty was being tested. Also, I felt, my nationality: an American who would fly Athens-Cincinnati-Athens to visit parents could go to Diyarbakir to save a life. Ziba felt compelled to ask. Two months ago, she'd saved my skin during an interview, but I still needed time to answer.

"I know how afraid you must be, Ziba. This is terrible. And I'll do anything I can. But if there's no 'how' to be imagined, I'll have no reason to go."

"No reason to go?" Ziba asked, repeating my words as I did hers.

"I have to know why, Ziba. You know that. Why it would make sense."

During the cab ride to my apartment, I had Ziba retell the sequence of

actions that led to Osman's imprisonment. He'd been working at a hospital in
northern Iraq, and was back in Diyarbakir visiting family and collecting medical supplies. Ziba hadn't seen him for two days when the police broke down
her front door. I asked her to translate everything in her mother's letter. "How
could I forget?" she said halfway through and rattled the letter. "Osman has
diabetes. He'll never get the insulin he needs in prison."

Pull the passenger down the aisle, shove him down the chute, pick him up
off the tarmac, and shoot him with insulin before he goes into a coma.

In my apartment, Ziba told me what she hoped I could do, use my position to investigate inhumane prison conditions, look into some cases that
would include her brother, and make the authorities recognize that Osman is
not a Turkish citizen.

"How can your brother not be Turkish?"

"When mother and father were younger, they often crossed over into Iraq
to see father's relatives. Osman's birth was registered in Zarkho so he could be
educated in Iraq. Then and even now, education for Kourds in Iraq was better
than in Turkey. When it came time for high school, Osman lived with father's
family in Zarkho so he could go to the university in Baghdad."

My concentration wavered. I thought about my parents sending me two
miles to St. Anthony's. Ziba's parents sent one child to Baghdad, one to
Istanbul. Both went on to universities in Chicago and then returned to
Diyarbakir. Now Ziba couldn't go back and Osman couldn't get out.

"How," I asked Ziba, "will I go about proving Osman is an Iraqi?"

"You can get documents from Northwestern Medical School."

"I'm sorry to be a black cloud, Ziba, but what happens next? What if the
Turks are convinced your brother is Iraqi? They're still going to be angry about
him bandaging up Turkish Kurds."

"The first thing is to have the treason charge removed. If that happens,
Osman will have a chance. If not, we'll never see him alive. With your attention, maybe he can be released on humanitarian grounds."

"Maybe so," I told Ziba, but she was desperate to believe in UNHCR lingo,
believe that a legal technicality and ethical appeal would work. The plane is
burning. It's a long way away. There's no time to waste.

"I'll do what I can," I said, "starting tomorrow. I promise. But right now I
need to close my ears and eyes, sit here in my bunker, and think about the situation. Will you be okay alone tonight back at the Flea Palace?"

"I've been alone there for the last ten days and the last five months." The
proud, tough Ziba of her interview was back.

"I think best when I'm all alone," I told her. I lock my office door, turn off the overhead lights, and turn on the desk lamp. "Rigor almost to 'mortis,'" my legal drafting instructor said the first day of class. 'Mortis' was a distinct possibility, and I didn't want the distraction of another body in the room.

Think like a lawyer. According to the stipulated facts, Osman was found through illegal means, is charged with a capital offense for following the Hippocratic oath, and will be denied both legal representation and a medical necessity. But a UNHCR attorney from Athens marching into Diyarbakir and presenting a habeas corpus writ won't save Osman. I've read the telexes from Geneva. It's martial law out in eastern Turkey. Legal subtleties and moral distinctions have collapsed. Five of the Kurds' elected members of Parliament were charged with treason for mentioning the possibility of Kurdish autonomy.

Think like a "Soldier of Jesus," as we used to call the Jesuits in college. Like the applicants, I'll need "status" in Turkey. I'm a well-connected American, connected to the CIA's secret soldiers. The Turks should believe that because countries with the worst Human Rights abuses all suspect UNHCR is a tool of the CIA. Next, I'll have to extend status to the Turkish soldiers, and affirm their importance as allies of the United States. When we're equals, I can offer the Turks something, maybe some policy changes UNHCR in Athens can enact to discourage refugees. We'll dance around with diplomatic generalities. Then I'll get down to business:

"An official high in the U.S. Government studied with Dr. Mamozin at Northwestern. They remained friends. Since Turkey is a friend of the United States, I've been asked to intervene, officially if that will work, privately if nothing can be done through UNHCR."

This story might play in Diyarbakir. But am I the one who can play it? I took a course in Negotiation and Dispute Resolution in law school, but INS didn't negotiate. My clients, even the pro bono Latin Americans, were never in prison. I've never stood before a judge. I don't know more than five words of Turkish, and I can't bring Ziba along to translate. But I've been on the receiving end of numerous lies. I've seen the signs, heard stories falter at UNHCR. If I can stand tall and act entitled to Osman, he may have a chance.

"Documents are key," the Director told me during my training week. My protection in Diyarbakir will be the letter I'll fax ahead and my UNHCR card. If my story doesn't work, I'll have with me the file of a Kurd, Jalal Kaya, whom Ziba and I interviewed in November. That file was the reason why I decided to go. With documents in hand, I may be able to do more than get the treason charge dropped.

Once I bought my ticket to Diyarbakir, Ziba abandoned official language and prepped me like a war veteran:

"Diyarbakir is not Istanbul. Tourists never came to the city, even before it got very dangerous. Everyone will notice you. If you stay in the hotel they suggest, your room may be recorded."

"You mean 'bugged?'"

"Yes. But if they suggest the Hotel Anahid, you should stay there anyway. Otherwise, they'll be suspicious. Don't let anyone in your room. If you leave your hotel, don't speak to people on the street. Kourds working for the secret police may try to trick you into showing your sympathies. Don't leave the city. The PKK kidnaps foreigners for publicity and money. If they know you're an American, they'll believe you're CIA. Two pilots from Incirlick air base were shot and killed outside Diyarbakir last year."

It was hard for Ziba to imagine a foreigner in her home town. Once she got beyond the worst that could happen, her advice came jumbled together.

"Drink only bottled water. Don't take a camera. Change your money at the airport in Ankara. Maybe they'll let you visit the prison, but I doubt it. If they invite you to dinner, look out for being drugged. Don't ever get in a car alone with a Turk. Be careful never to say 'Kurd' as 'Kourd.' Eat only kebabs or other grilled food. Wear boots. Use bottled water to brush your teeth. Don't stand in front of windows."

"Why's that?"

"Remember Kaya? If a bomb goes off in the street, you'll be full of glass."

Ziba tried to cover every contingency and eventuality, without ever expressing fear that I might back out in the face of so many difficulties and dangers. I took strength from her trust, even as I recognized that she has no choice but to trust me. I have to trust myself, that I can pull this off. I won't have any support from Human Rights law. Out in eastern Turkey, I'll be outside the law. Lawless, like the stereotype of Kurds. If the Turks see through my story, I may be detained, but I know I won't be tortured as Ziba was. If the Turks, like Jalal Kaya, communicate with the Director, I'll be out of the only job I've ever loved and out of Greece, a country I've learned to enjoy. When these fears interfere with my future focus, I remind myself of Ziba's past. I think about Osman's present and future. He's in the kind of danger applicants describe. But their worst fear is over. Osman's fear is now. They have me to tell, a way to hope. In prison without visitors, Osman has no way of knowing that help may be on the way. I picture Osman alone in his cell. The jailers won't have to torture him. Without insulin, Ziba said, his body will persecute itself, will poison itself and double up on itself. His limbs will curl into a fetal position. Damn Turks. Charge a doctor with treason for following his law. Osman didn't have the UNHCR lawyer's luxury of accepting some applicants for aid and refusing others. Now the doctor can't help himself. He can't even smuggle out a letter, tell his story. For some reason, I remember Huck's Jim and other stories I read as a girl, about maidens rescued by heroes. Free Osman from his dark tower or dungeon cell, and I'll reverse those tales of Cinderella helplessness. Even the much older Greek story of Eurydice. "Wide justice," her name meant. "Do Justice" is on the lintel at my law school. "Do right," the nuns said. "Do well," my father used to say. Do something.

This thinking wasn't the risk-benefit analysis I'd have done at Snow and Fiore. I know that. My thinking wasn't even the deeds-needs analysis I did at UNHCR. But the plane was in flames, my friend's brother was strapped in, poisonous fumes were in the cabin, and adrenaline pumped bravery through my frame.

The law you need to know is simple. According to the *United Nations Handbook on Procedures and Criteria for Determining Refugee Status*, a person in flight must demonstrate he or she has a "well-founded fear of persecution for reasons of race, religion, nationality, membership of a particular social group, or political opinion." Fear of Osman's persecution by the Turkish authorities sent me to Turkey. Fear of other persecutions compels me to write this Letter, put together this book organized like the files I read and prepared. In a Questionnaire and Narrative, the applicant documents her background and describes her movements. Few governments issue official bans, like the ancient Greeks' "ostracism" or the present Iranians' "fatwah." The applicant's flight does not prove fright. So in an Interview the applicant must explain why she fled and—most importantly, crucially—why she felt she had to flee. Everything depends on why, so the desperate person is required to analyze our deepest instinct and speak our strongest emotion in reasonable sentences, her own or her translator's. At the Interview, the applicant must tell a story that an objective examiner—a person trained to be detached and suspicious—will believe, accept, and recommend. "Documents are key," the Director believed. That's why I've chosen a documentary style in this Letter, in this book. Laws and rules, facts and acts, grounds. Like the Director, you're the judge. I'm the refugee. This is my file.

II Questionnaire

Chapter 2

CASEY MAHAN

Address: 2805 Digby Ave. # 11
                 Cincinnati, Ohio 45220
                 U.S.A.

Bar Status: Member of Ohio Bar, 1989-present

Education: University of Cincinnati College of Law
                 Juris Doctor, May 1989
                 G.P.A.: 3.705   Rank: 7 of 108

                 Xavier University, Cincinnati, Ohio
                 B.A. in English, Summa cum Laude, 1986

Honors: Cincinnati Bar Association
                 Immigration Lawyer of the Year, 1993, 1995

                 Urban Morgan Fellowship, College of Law, 1986-87

                 Senior Thesis Prize, Xavier English Department, 1986

Experience: Snow and Fiore, Attorneys at Law
                 32 Court Street
                 Cincinnati, Ohio, 45203

                 Associate: 1989-1996
                 Partner: 1997
                 Practice area: Immigration

                 UNHCR Research Intern
                 Latin American desk, Geneva, Summer, 1987

                 Editorial Assistant
                 Human Rights Quarterly, 1987-89

Organizations: American Bar Association, Immigration Section;
                 Ohio Bar Association; Cincinnati Bar Association;
                 Amnesty International; Library Guild

"You'll get the job," Sam Roberts told me after calling the Director, "Christina and I served on a couple of commissions together, and she was pleased with the intern I sent her two years ago. Your resume is strong. Just don't mention your plastic chair guy when you fax her your letter."

I'd billed a quarter-million dollars to move a Canadian manufacturer from Toronto to Los Angeles so he could extend his lawn furniture empire. The application was what INS termed a "national interest" case, one in which the immigrant brought capital and jobs to the US. For Sam Roberts, though, the "plastic chair guy" stood for my life since the second year of law school. Because Roberts directed the Urban Morgan Institute for Human Rights and ran the *Human Rights Quarterly*, the two fellowships he gave each year usually went to former English majors who could help him edit the *Quarterly*. Even with the fellowship, I had to take out a large loan for living expenses. After spending my undergraduate years in my parents' attic, I insisted on a place of my own. But listening to visiting lecturers and talking to staffers in Geneva, I realized that a career in Human Rights was as unlikely as supporting myself doing free-lance writing, my hope while in college. I decided to switch my concentration to Immigration, take out larger loans, and give up the fellowship.

"In ten years, you're the first student to refuse the fellowship," Roberts told me. "Most of my fellows go on to become tax gurus and real estate moguls. You don't have to do this."

"When I was twelve, a priest told me 'God sees all your sins, my child. Put your list in your pocket and open your heart.'"

"Okay," Sam said, "you've opened your heart. Now keep the money."

"You got me off to a good start. I appreciate it, but now I'll borrow my own way and get a job in a firm after graduation."

I did some volunteer editorial work for Roberts my last two years. He steered more pro bono Latin Americans my way than Snow and Fiore allowed me to take on, and we saw each other at Amnesty International meetings, where Internet users pen personal letters to Third World dictators. Roberts knew a chunk of the "plastic chair" money bought stamps for those letters. I knew he had unemployed former fellows looking for Human Rights jobs, but it was me he called when he heard about the position in Athens. Maybe it was because I'd turned back the fellowship, or perhaps "Good Sam" was testing my vow to take some time away from the firm once I made partner.

The founding fathers—Snow and Fiore—and the senior partners called the months following partnership "the baby year." After a woman was off for six months, they suggested she take her computer to her house and give her husband more time to enjoy the kid. I didn't have a house or a husband, not even a condo or a pet, so the managing partner was surprised when I asked for a year of leave.

"If you're not secretly married," Adam Stricker said, "you must be flirting with some other firm."

"No other firm."

"Then you're being wooed by an industrial-park corporation offering nine-to-five hours and six figures."

"Maybe not even five figures, but definitely not in Cincinnati," I told him, "Athens."

"There's no law school at Ohio U."

"Athens, Greece."

Rumored to have once been a lawyer, Adam Stricker was now a CPA, or "Certified Public Asshole" to everyone whose billing lagged behind his elaborate computer models. If Stricker and the old guys ever came to my interior office from their river-view suites, they'd have seen my collection of travel posters from places I've never been except for London and Geneva. After two months looking at the lake and Alps, I knew I wanted—some day—to live elsewhere, not just occupy a hotel room and ride around in black taxis. No weekend getaways or Cancun packages for me. While moving up in the firm, I was saving up—days and pay—to catapult myself outside Cincinnati long enough to forget and then miss Skyline chili and the ATP tennis tournament. After thirty-three years in my hometown, I was sick of home. I wanted to be homesick.

"You'll be back in six months. Those international firms chew up women," Adam said.

"It's the UN."

"That's even worse. You won't make enough to buy food you can chew."

"I'm a vegetarian, Adam."

Athens wasn't a poster on my wall, but the only other opening Sam Roberts had mentioned since my partnership party was in an African country where visitors are advised to bring their own frozen blood in case they need a transfusion. Recent liberal arts graduates, assured of their immortality, and well-meaning retirees, who've had their sixty-five years, can follow the Peace Corps into jungles and slums, and live in tents and teach English. My pragmatic ideal was to work in a country where salads were served and law still existed. I never met an actual refugee in Geneva, but I read field reports and saw telexes from lawyers who were protecting victims. In the multi-volume maze of INS regulations and in the warren of Snow and Fiore, I never forgot the international altruism and elegant simplicity of the Human Rights declaration. It was "universal." It cut below national differences and authorized lawyers around the world to do—not just practice—law. UNHCR would be my baby year, succoring the helpless, caring for the recently arrived.

"Once Christina sees your resume, you may have to get to Athens quickly," Roberts told me. "She sounded harried and understaffed."

"My associate and paralegal can't wait to take over my billing."

"What about your apartment?"

"I'll let the dust gather."

"Maybe you could sublet it to a Tibetan I know."

Roberts thought I was an ascetic. The night I invited him and his wife for dinner, he looked around and asked, "When's your flight?" I had a second-floor, two-room walkup where I slept and breakfasted through law school. I sometimes spent the night on my couch at the firm and downed my coffee and bagel there six days a week, so I had no reason to give up the apartment. I didn't need much furniture, and I didn't want a yard. My paralegal, who surrounds herself with plants, said the apartment looks like the rooms where potential presidential assassins write their journals. My associate, though, understood. She broke off her engagement, gave away her dog, and sold her exercycle after a month in law school.

Dates saw my place and asked what happened to my "nesting instinct." The bare apartment was a good way to rule out men who believed in laying eggs, though to others it might have made me a more eligible bride. While they were filling up the basement with tools and the garage with toys, I wouldn't be demanding a lot of expensive carpets and draperies. My only luxury was a queen-sized bed, a place to stretch out my 6 feet 1 1/2 inches, eat delivered pizza, and watch the eleven o'clock news. For a year, a man named Rick often shared that bed when he wasn't in Wisconsin or California making P & G factories run more efficiently. Or when he wasn't in Michigan or Tennessee rock climbing. Rick lived in an efficiency. Neither of us would commit to a bigger place. Six months before my partnership vote, he gave me back my key and left me the dehumidifier. Still paying student rent, I could afford to use my home as storage space, and with few domestic details to arrange I could spend a few days in Paris and in Rome on my way to Athens.

My only anxiety going to the airport with my two suitcases, laptop, and Greek tapes—an anxiety reinforced in a restaurant on the Isle de Paris and in a bus back from the catacombs—was linguistic. I was a whiz at dead languages: straight "A's" in Latin through high school and an "A" and "B" in Attic Greek I at Xavier, but I withdrew from both French I and Spanish I in the fourth week. Somewhere between my ears and tongue is a chasm. Sounds fall the length of my body and have to be recalled from my toes. That's why they curled up every time I was called on to engage in dialogue, even if the other person was a wrestler or, in Spanish, a girl with a speech impediment. I was a confirmed English major and, as several of my clients later reminded me, an American. A Belgian chemist and a Brazilian biologist told me the same joke:

"What's the word for someone who speaks two languages?"

"Bilingual."

"What about more than two?"

"Multilingual."

"Very good. And the word for someone who speaks only one language?"

In Belgium and Brazil the answer was the same: "American."

It was an American who went to the UNHCR office in downtown Athens. When I turned onto Arahovis Street, the first thing I noticed was a policeman standing in the doorway at the top of five marble steps. No one stood on the last step. The three men on the next step down leaned toward the policeman and with outstretched arms tried to give him sheets of paper and sheaves of documents. Women and men standing lower on the steps jostled each other, shouted to the policeman, and waved papers above their heads. The people looked like crazed autograph seekers outside a celebrity club, but they sounded like mourners, pleading for mercy from someone further away than the policeman. He had his right hand on the half-open door, his left hand on the barrel of the machine gun slung in front of him. With his right hand he pointed to the watch on his left wrist. I looked down at my own watch: 12:50. I was ten minutes early. I stood at the bottom of the steps, hoping to catch the policeman's eye without shouting or waving my letter. Surely he would see I was different: blonde, blue-eyed, taller than the people in front of me on the steps, dressed in a business suit and shoes, not jeans and sneakers or robes and sandals. I was the only person carrying a briefcase. When the policeman's eyes reached me, I saw no sign of recognition. He looked at me and then glanced to my right, where a black man and woman now stood. The policeman's eyes came back across me and scanned the small courtyard to my left. Women in multicolored ankle-length dresses and barefoot children were sitting on cardboard sheets or lying on thin mats, their heads resting on dusty duffel bags. Old men in turbans stood with their hands clasped behind them.

Although crowded, the courtyard seemed lifeless, as if the occupants lacked the energy to compete on the steps. Some of the people in the courtyard were talking, but the shouts and cries on the steps were all I could hear.

I counted the heads in front of me: sixteen. If they all had to present their papers or tell their stories to the policeman at 1 p.m., I'd be late for my interview. If the people on the steps were representing the people in the courtyard, I might not get in the building this afternoon. I had an appointment, but I didn't want to offend the people in front of me. I decided to edge up the steps, using the only verbal wedges I knew: "excuse me" and "pardon moi." Whether or not they understood, the people above me let me squeeze through and approach the policeman. He watched me move toward him, but his dark eyes were blank. On the top step, I said, slowly and clearly, "I have an appointment." He pointed to his watch. "For an interview," I said. He didn't respond. I pulled out my letter confirming the date and time. I extended my document toward the policeman's free hand, and he said, "No read English." He again pointed to his watch and said *Mia*, "one," one of the twenty numbers I knew in modern Greek. I went back down the steps to my place beside the black couple. Four more people, two in robes and sneakers, had joined the line.

At 1:15, after three people were granted entry, a young woman came to the door, spoke to the policeman, looked down at us, and immediately beckoned to me. This time I had more room going up the steps, but the policeman still made me squeeze by him and his machine gun.

"So sorry," the woman said, "we forgot to tell Panos you were coming this afternoon."

I'd come six thousand miles for my interview, but I wasn't afraid out on the steps. Unlike the other people waiting to get inside UNHCR, I had a letter from the Director. I could phone her and explain why I hadn't made it to my interview. And yet, for a few minutes and in some secure way, I felt what being outside the building was like for the others. We were many and the door was narrow. The doorkeeper didn't speak our language. I felt the frustration of possessing documents—my letter, my identifying American passport—I couldn't present. I also felt that my feelings shouldn't matter, not here, not next to the emotions of the beseeching crowd around me.

The receptionist showed me around the first floor. It was the ground floor of Babel, the noise of the steps trapped and echoing. In the entry hall, newcomers shoved and yammered at each other as they gathered around a secretary's desk, where she handed out application forms and they shook their sheets of paper in her face. In the former dining room, applicants emitted a

deep moan as they waited to receive appointment slips or their written verdicts from another secretary. Old people with gnarled canes groaned and
women nursing infants sang in the wooden chairs lining the ten-by-ten square
waiting room. In front of the chairs, sons and husbands crouched on their
heels and muttered to each other or themselves. Children sat on the bare
wooden floor and cried or screamed. Teenagers milled around in the middle of
the room and shouted above the noise. Next door, in a room that was once a
kitchen and was now jammed with three metal desks, refugees or applicants
jabbered at the translators who jabbered back in languages that sounded like
the aggressive German in old World War II movies or the condescending blurt
of televised Viet Cong.

"Is it always this noisy?" I asked the receptionist.

"Except Saturday and Sunday."

To reach the Director's office, we had to wind our way single file through
refugees sitting motionless on the narrow circular staircase, their hands dan-
gling between their legs, their heads propped against the wall or the iron railing, with their eyes closed, perhaps sleeping. Men holding gray files against
their chests or under their arms were leaning against the wall on both sides of
Mrs. Constantinou's door. Silent, they looked like a gauntlet that had been
plastered against the wall by some powerful force, perhaps the Director. A few
feet down the hall, women and men with yellow appointment slips held faces
high like votive candles pressed up against the door of the lawyers' office.
Across the narrow corridor, women holding plastic bags and carrying children
jockeyed for position at the open door of the social workers' office. Down at
the end of the hall, I glimpsed the backs of a woman and man whose heads
inclined toward each other and bowed to something I couldn't see at the time,
the bursar's cubbyhole. The second floor was surprisingly quiet, as if the
applicants respected bedrooms become offices or wanted to catch the murmur
of official voices inside the rooms.

"Is it always this crowded?" I asked my guide.

"No. More people are here in the morning."

UNHCR's hundred-year-old neoclassical building, with enough rooms for
any Athenian family, was like a nineteenth-century American asylum, jammed
with the agitated and the impassive, the impoverished and the eccentric, men
in gowns, women in what looked like pajamas, children in rags, some people
waiting in desert silence, and others contributing to a pandemonium that
didn't sound human. As I walked through the narrow halls in my suit, I felt as
if the scattered street people of Cincinnati—sidewalk-tanned men who draped

themselves in bedspreads, black women who spluttered cracked dialects, pasty-faced kids recently arrived from Kentucky hills—had been gathered up and transported here, jammed almost as tight as economy passengers in a chartered jumbo. I'd heard stories about Cincinnati street people from other downtown attorneys—a woman spit on by a wine-stained panhandler, a man menaced in his car by an astral traveler washing windshields. But the aliens at UNHCR were not threatening. The office was like a homeless shelter to which helpless people come in their time of trouble. Inside the building, I knew I was in the right place.

Mrs. Constantinou talked for a few minutes about Sam Roberts and American immigration law. Then she said, "Aliens are coming from everywhere. Like your 'wetbacks,' they swim across the Evros River or splash up onto our tourist beaches. We need you to begin as soon as possible."

The five-minute interview. I'd been grilled for two days at Snow and Fiore.

"But," Mrs. Constantinou said, "we cannot pay you right away. Now that you are here, we will apply for your work permit, but sometimes the government is slow to respond, even for UNHCR."

Ten minutes earlier I was out in the courtyard with the refugees.

"Money isn't an issue right now," I told her, "I'm on sabbatical."

Mrs. Constantinou wrinkled her forehead. About sixty, with carefully permed gray hair, a formal lady who never used contractions, Mrs. Constantinou didn't want to ask the meaning of "sabbatical." She had studied at the Sorbonne and spoke English with the insistent correctness of a CNN foreign correspondent, but she needed a translator.

"Is this a French word? From 'saboteur?'"

"No, no. It's from Greek, isn't it? From 'Saturday,' right?"

"Ah, *savvato*," she said, restoring the "v" sound to the letter we pronounce as "b."

"Right," I said, "After a professor works seven years in an American university, she gets a year off with pay. I've been saving for my leave from the firm. For now, you can think of me as a volunteer."

"Volunteer" was a word Mrs. Constantinou knew in both French and English. She repeated it, drawing it out, savoring the sound.

"I will give you the *Handbook* and some files to read this weekend," Mrs. Constantinou said, "and you can begin observing interviews on Monday."

Once "volunteer" entered our conversation, I had no more worries. The Director didn't inquire about my knowledge of foreign languages. She didn't need to see any of the supporting documents I had in my briefcase. Mrs. Constantinou didn't ask if I'd ever been arrested, and she didn't care that I'd never litigated. I was thankful that the Director hadn't interrogated the volunteer about her motives. She didn't ask me why I was here by myself or why there was no "personal" category at the bottom of my resume. I didn't have to explain that I wanted to get beyond the personal or extend the personal, I wasn't sure which.

I also wasn't compelled to tell the Director something I'd concealed from everyone in Cincinnati, that three months before my partnership vote I began walking down the seventeen flights of stairs from my office, that I always got to the building early so I could stand tight against the elevator's paneled back wall and avoid the atrium view out the glass door. Flying didn't bother me that much, not even the window seat, because my legs wedged me tight in my space. It was standing near a sheer drop that made my body feel like the leaning tower of Pisa. How it and I remained erect was a mystery because I felt sure I would topple. My size eleven shoes couldn't possibly stay flat on the floor. Whenever I had to be in a partner's river-view office, I sat down as quickly as possible. Standing and wavering, I'd feel myself blush and stammer like a girl, as if my condition made me both highly visible and transparent, a glass statue on a flimsy pedestal.

"Pre-decision stress," a psychologist told me. He specialized in downtown professionals, brokers who couldn't decide which frozen dinner to buy, insurance executives with speeding tickets.

"Post-decision stress," he said when I still had the condition after the partnership vote. The psychologist sent me to a neurologist. No inner ear infection, no brain tumor.

"You're afraid of heights," the psychologist said when I came back with the negative test results. "Consider yourself lucky. It's an illness you can work around. You're a lawyer, right? It could be much worse."

I didn't admit it, but he was right. Lawyers fear lawyers. At Snow and Fiore, associates fear partners. Partners fear future partners. Associates and partners fear lawyers in other Cincinnati firms, and all Cincinnati lawyers are afraid of lawyers on the east coast who have been immigrating recently to the Midwest because they're afraid of their city's streets. Lawyers all over America fear lawyers in Washington who are constantly changing the rules. The Litigation department at Snow and Fiore could sell their excess adrenaline as a scent—Nervosa—if they figured a way to bottle it. Rona Winget says she spends more on dry cleaning each week than on meals, and you can still see sweat stains in the armpits of her suits. Whenever I drop by her area, I always find one of the men with his hand in his pocket, hefting his testicles. The

Trust department is deathly afraid of their clients' minor children, who will sue for malpractice in twenty years when the lawyers have much more to lose than they do now. The three-man International group takes turns staying up all night, six nights a week, to monitor worldwide markets around the clock. One associate confessed to me, after he fell asleep during dinner at his place, that he often sets his alarm for 2 a.m. and logs onto his computer at home because he distrusts the colleague who is supposed to be on watch.

Compared to those departments, Immigration is secure. My second-year associate from Case Western is happy to have a job, any job while most firms are downsizing and using staff attorneys. I'm up against INS, and they're paranoid about the United States becoming an alien nation, but most of my cases have a safe circularity. A multinational corporation—let's call it G and P— wants to transfer a computer programmer from India to American headquarters. I have G and P send me their job description and the "applicant's" resume. I write a want ad for *The Wall Street Journal* and other newspapers, an ad tailored so closely to the resume that no more than five or ten people in the world can reasonably apply. I then figure out ways to rule out all applicants but G and P's inside person. It's all perfectly legal. The "plastic chair guy" spent a quarter million to move to California because he insisted on writing his own ad. He thought he was singular, but I had to invent ways to rule out two hundred fifty U.S. workers who applied. The process was complicated and time-consuming, made for a Jesuit logic-chopper and spreadsheet user. In my practice, there are no contingencies. Whether the transferee wins or loses, the firm always gets its money from the corporation, and I always surpass Adam Stricker's billing expectations.

"So if it's not stress or a brain tumor, why do I have this phobia now?" I asked the psychologist, not really believing I'd believe the answer I thought he'd give: childhood trauma. Or the even earlier explanation I remembered from a Poe story: the womb-snug fetus's fear of the pit, the down elevator.

"You probably won't live long enough to find the cause. It could be splitting with Rick. It still could be your job. There are too many variables. Forget about cause and practice the coping strategies I suggested."

I could have imagined good reasons to refuse the move out to a glass-walled office. Failing that, I could rearrange the furniture and put up curtains. My colleagues would believe I was using the stairs to lower my cholesterol. But before becoming another American coper, I wanted to get out of the building and away from home. Outside my country of origin, I might understand the origin of my acrophobia.

Chapter 3

United Nations High Commissioner for Refugees

Questionnaire

Attach passport size photo in upper right corner of this form. All supporting documents <u>must</u> be translated into English, bear stamps of the Interior Department, and be attached to the last page of the Narrative.

1. Family name _____ Mamozin _____

   First name(s) _____ Ziba _____

   Alias _____ none _____

2. Sex: Male   <u>Female</u>

3. Marital status: <u>Single</u>   Married   Divorced   Widowed   Separated

4. Date of birth: __June 20, 1970__ (if not known, estimate year)

5. Place of birth: __Diyarbakir, Turkey__

6. Nationality/citizenship:____ . Turkish _____

7. Ethnic or tribal group:_____ Kurd _____

8. Religion:_____ none _____

Questionnaire, page 2

9. Education:
   Primary school (place) _Diyarbakir_ (dates) _1976-85_
   Secondary school _Istanbul 85-88_
   Vocational school _____
   University _U. of Illinois-Chicago, Illinois, USA 88-92_
   Degree, certificate, or diploma _B.S., Nursing_

10. Language abilities: _Kurdish, English, Turkish_

11. Military service: _____ --- _____

12. Occupation, trade, or skill: _Registered Nurse_

13. Employment record (starting from last job in country of origin)

Employer	Work	Place, dates
St. Joseph's Hospital	trauma unit	Chicago, 92-93
Halal Hospital	surgery	Diyarbakir, 93-98

14. Where did you last reside? _Diyarbakir_

15. When did you depart from your country of origin? _Aug. 7, 1998_

16. Where and when did you enter Greece? _near Alexandropoulis_
Aug. 7, 1998

17. How did you enter the country? _By crossing the Evros River_

18. Identification and travel documents (make a copy of each for the file)
   Document used to enter country: _none_

   Place and date issued:_____

Questionnaire, page 3

Other identification documents:
Turkish passport
_____
_____
_____
_____

19. Do you or any members of your family belong to any political,
religious, military, ethnic or social organizations outlawed in your country
of origin?_____no_____
_____
_____

20. If you belonged to such an organization, what were your activities and
responsibilities? _____---_____
_____
_____

21. Have you or family members ever been arrested? ___no_____
If yes, answer the following questions below. Date of arrest and charge?
Was there a trial? If so, was sentence passed? Period of imprisonment?
Date released or escaped? If multiple arrests, document each separately on
a separate sheet. _____---_____
_____
_____

22. Were you ever mistreated mentally or physically during arrest? If yes,
please describe details. _____---_____
_____
_____
_____

23. Do you have relatives in Greece or any other country where you might
be relocated? _____no_____
_____
_____

United Nations High Commissioner for Refugees

Narrative

In the space below and, if necessary, on other sheets of paper, describe in your own words the events leading to your departure from your country of origin and your reasons for applying for asylum. Provide specific details of your experience and refer to any documentary evidence that would support your claim.

On the night of July 3, 1998 three Turkish policemen broke down the front door of my home in Diyarbakir. They accused my brother of belonging to the PKK and they wanted to know where he was. When I refused to tell them, they tortured me in my own home. When they were satisfied with me what I told them, they forced me to leave my home and Diyarbakir.

Attach all documents to this page or to the page ending your Narrative.

The files I brought home the day of my interview were as packed with paper as the Commission was with people. From the photo-booth black and white pictures pinned to the top of Questionnaires to the prayers for mercy that often end the applicants' Narratives, the files are cardboard archives of misery. From three different files:

> Ethnic or tribal group:
> This I can not answer. Yes, I am Kourd. But in Anfal, my whole village was destroy and whole of my family was gone. When I return from Persia, no one is left, no one can told me if the Jamalis still exits.
> ***
> When did you depart from your country of origin?
> No know. Long time hide in forest. I go to prison and forget year.
> ***
> How did you enter the country?
> Always we were in the dark. The captain keeped us below the floor. For days he gaved us no food, only water. Then he called us out and pointed at land. 'Swim,' he shouted, 'that is Italy.' My husband drownded. Then we found we are in Greece.

These were answers to what seem like neutral, harmless questions. Those designed to elicit accounts of persecution produce histories of suffering, repeated from blank to blank, file to file. I leafed through the first files with amazement. The reports I read in Geneva were second-hand. The files are primary, raw and bloody data. A man from Sri Lanka was arrested twenty-three times in the last decade. An Iranian Christian took pride in giving the exact name and description of the twelve prisons he'd been in. One Afghan head of household included four separate sheets to list eight family members' arrests and detentions. Overwhelmed by so many facts, I skim names and places, looking for keywords: "kidnap," "torture," "execute," "disappear." I notice cross-cultural patterns. Victims are often last seen in unmarked white Land Cruisers, whether in Somalia, Iraq, or Turkey. Sticking a prisoner's head in a toilet—a bowl, a pail, or a hole in the ground—is popular with police everywhere. When released, detainees express no joy because the release is often as random—as mysterious to them—as their detention. As I skip from one country to another and selectively dip into the files, I realize that my perusal is like the power inflicted upon the applicants: arbitrary, impersonal. I want to be fair to each applicant, so I read the Questionnaires more closely. I organize the files by national origin, locate each case on a map, dig into the background information, try to sort out confusing groups and sects.

The Narratives written on the applicants' own paper—plain sheets longer and wider than the UNHCR 8 ½-by-11, smaller lined sheets torn from a pad, paper that looks like it's made of rice or corn rather than wood—are like biblical chronicles of atrocity and suffering, persecution and flight. Or they are like reversals of the *Arabian Nights*: accounts of nightly deaths instead of stories about holding death at bay. Events are compressed into a few paragraphs or pages, so they seem melodramatic: surprise departures, risky deceptions and secrets revealed, sudden betrayals and narrow escapes. But no matter how unexpected the events, the accounts are always ruled by consequence, by causality. Because an Ethiopian journalist left Eritrea, he was jailed as a spy in Somalia. After he escaped and returned to Eritrea, he was tortured as a double agent. When he finally fled to Djibouti, he was accused of being a smuggler because no one else would have traveled between Eritrea and Somalia.

In the Narratives, applicants assume a specific shape and personal voice. An Iraqi begins, "Like the birth mark on my arm, the Assyrian religion has made me different from my beginning." "For many years, I hear my cousins make the love in the apartment next to ours," a Bosnian writes, "and then one night I hear screams I know are not love. That night I decide I cannot live in my home." From two different Narratives:

> We were held in a garage. We slept on newspapers on the cement floor. We ate soup in motor oil cans and maybe two days a week the guard throw us loafs of bread. We shitted in a barrel by the door. When our women went to the barrel, we all put our heads down to the floor like praying.
>
> ***
>
> Ever day the lieutenant comed to our cell. Every day he told his men to drag my brother and I to a room where they place our feet on batter plate and shocked us. Then they put iron ropes around our chest and hanged us from ceiling. They torture us together to torture each other with scream. One day my brother died and I am released, but our family never was gived Hamid's body. Still they torture us.

I turn back to the photographs on the Questionnaires and try to imagine feelings the applicants can't always express. I review facts and decipher documents to understand desperate actions, to find grounds for panic or paranoia. And yet a few of the autobiographies seem somehow similar, not just in recitations of genealogy and descriptions of homes, and not simply in methods of torture and means of escape, but also in the writers' recall of motives and emotions, a possibly conventional hyperbole. I remember enough about ancient Greek literature to know that oral stories have this formulaic quality.

Some applicants must be dictating their Narratives, speaking in their native tongues to translators who write down the accounts in English. Then I find two very different stories—a two-page account by an Iraqi Shiite who escaped after her husband was killed, the other a lengthy account by a Kurdish man from Akra who witnessed the murder of his parents—but in both accounts climactic episodes of violence are followed by exactly the same English sentence, which I'd never have noticed if not for a puzzling spelling: "After this happened, I fared for my life." The applicants go on to describe their escapes, the woman through Iran, the man through Turkey. The Narratives are personal and persuasive, but a very close reader—a former student of metaphysical poetry, an attorney trained to examine every letter and digit—spots this single word, the foundation of the applicant's claim, and wonders if the applicant was describing motivation— "I feared"—or action—"I fared," a wayfarer who ended up in Athens.

I showed the two files to the Director when I reported in to begin observing interviews.

"Congratulations," she said, "You will be an excellent examiner. Applicants are not content to withhold facts in the Questionnaire or change events. Instead of renting a typewriter, some applicants hire a person to write their Narratives. The writers know what elements UNHCR requires. These components the writer adds to facts supplied by customers."

"If the writer is a professional, why would he make such a mistake on a crucial word?"

"The Narratives cannot all be in the same handwriting, so each creator has—how do you say? —scribes. Of course, there is no spell-checking for this type of word processing. So you read 'fared' instead of 'feared.' It could just as easily be 'fered' or 'geared.'"

"So that's why documents are crucial?"

"Yes, they are objective, public, like UNHCR. The documents are printed, filled in by a typist, signed by an official. But you must beware of 'secret' documents."

Mrs. Constantinou said "secret" as if she resented the word's existence, as if there was no secret police in countries from which we received applicants.

"At a critical stage of their stories," she explained, "some applicants produce from inside pockets or undergarments their secret document. It is so important they refuse to leave it at the government's translation office. The applicants open up these folded or tightly rolled pieces of paper they have smuggled in prophylactics."

Mrs. Constantinou stopped and looked at me, either to check her usage or to apologize for the distasteful word.

"Yes," I said, "condoms."

"Inside their bodies, you see. Applicants direct their translators to translate and then explain the secret power of the document. However, without stamps and seals the special documents can have no official status."

I nodded.

"Nikos and Erica will show you how to discover the applicants' real secrets."

Again the distaste. I'm glad UNHCR is only two storeys high as the Director walks me to the windowless office shared by Erica and Nikos. Their desks face each other, but are separated by a five-foot-high partition. In front of each desk are three straight chairs, for applicant, spouse, and translator. After being introduced, I place a chair facing the end of the partition and listen back and forth from one interview to the other. Applicants speak in different languages, translators sometimes switch between English and Greek, examiners call over the partition in Greek or address me in English. Like the building, the office is a din.

Nikos is about my height and heavy, with prematurely graying hair and mournful dark eyes set deep in a face on which the sun never shines. He leans back in his chair, sympathetically murmuring "yes, I see" like a therapist or social worker. Then he abruptly interrupts the translator to request impossible documentation. He doesn't seem interested in the answer, but peers at the applicant, looking for some physical response, some revealing gulp or nervous twitch. Perhaps because Erica is always nervous—fidgeting with her pen, wiggling her feet underneath her desk, throwing papers around—she looks a little like a refugee: short, yellowish skin, black tightly curled hair. Erica is probably younger than me, but she wears huge horned-rimmed glasses that make her look older. The lenses also enlarge her eyes and make them appear affrighted. Erica sits behind her big steel desk and treats interviewees as if they are challenging litigants. Like a U.S. Supreme Court Justice, she gives applicants a chance to be thirty-minute lawyers. She expects them to answer any factual question she puts to them as she probes for internal contradictions, hoping to make the applicant incriminate himself or herself. She knows the countries' political parties better than most applicants do. Sometimes she argues a fugitive splinter group's ideology with a translator while the applicant sits and wonders what is happening.

At noon Erica and Nikos take me to lunch a block from the office, and I get to interview them. Nikos is overqualified and unhappy at thirty-seven because an LLM from Germany and his fluent English have not attached him to some multinational company. He says he makes "holistic judgments" and "epiphanic decisions," both of which he claims are rooted in ancient Greek law and language.

"In classical Athens," Nikos says, "lawyers didn't exist and citizens were judges. Like us. So you must watch the supplicant for *tremoulisma*."

"I don't know much Greek," I tell him.

"Not 'anxiety,'" Nikos says, "for all the supplicants are naturally anxious. And not 'fear,' because if they are truly refugees they are not afraid of us. This *tremoulisma* is a quality of nervousness that indicates the supplicant is lying. Sometimes I can smell this when he comes into the room."

"Don't listen to him, Casey," Erica says. "Nikos' citizen-judges condemned Socrates to poison himself. This *tremoulism*a method is no method at all."

"The comrade," Nikos says to me and nods toward Erica. "She denies *tremoulisma* because she wants to import only the most dangerous people, political leftists like herself."

"The racist," Erica screeches in her high-pitched voice. "Nikos recommends only people from the north, the Greek-speaking thieves from Albania, the Orthodox murderers of Serbia."

Nikos shrugs and smiles, as if his comment has produced *tremoulisma* in Erica. It's hard to tell if they're engaging in a long-running joke or lobbying for a swing vote in their partitioned office. Office politics at the firm were all about money and hierarchy, not politics. Here there is conflict, ideological argument, ethnic insult. Our talk shifts away from the office, but I wonder about the Director, where she stands.

On Friday of my training week, Nikos went home at four, but Erica stayed at her desk, updating her huge loose-leaf notebooks.

"I'll never know enough," I told her. "Too many countries, too many groups."

"It took me three years to put together these notebooks. If you'll be here only a year, you should specialize."

"Who do you suggest I adopt?"

"You can keep busy doing just Kurds. They're the world's oldest refugees."

"Not the Palestinians?"

"And not the Jews either. The Kurds have never had a homeland. They've been wandering around forever, before Xenophon reported their fighting off Greeks."

"You don't resent them for that?"

"Nikos would, but that was two thousand years ago. Look what they're doing to the Turks now," she said, opening her eyes even wider than usual and grinning like she did when she caught some applicant in an irreversible error.

"So they are your 'dangerous people?'"

She handed me a photocopy from *The London Times* entitled "Viewers of the World, Unite."

You saw us on your televisions, live colour documents from the Gulf War. We were fleeing north toward Turkey, which already had more Kurds than it wanted. We loaded cars and pickups with our possessions, drove dirt roads that became mud holes, slipped into ditches on the steep grades near the border, abandoned autos to walk toward a swollen river we couldn't cross or to a bridge the Turks had closed. Turned back, we camped in our cars and trucks, in makeshift lean-tos. You watched us dig graves for grandparents, dead of exposure, and infants dead from bad water. And you were happy when a few tents and supplies parachuted onto our mud-scapes.

Once your networks had live footage, you saw film from the archives, amateur tape of villagers lying twisted and bloated in their doorways, in the narrow paths between their stone houses, face down in brooks where they tried to breathe water instead of the poison gas the Iraqi government had dropped on their mountain homes. For these Kurds, there were no parachutes. And although they were killed several years before the Gulf War, it took real-time genocide before you gave us a safe haven.

We thank you for your protection. Now we want you to know what was never on your television. For ten years before the Gulf War, the Iraqi government systematically emptied villages in the north and east, dynamited them, and trucked their Kurdish inhabitants to the south, where they were killed and bulldozed into mass graves. In this "Anfal Campaign" more than a hundred thousand Kurds were exterminated. Although we have no videotape, there are living witnesses and documents captured when the Iraqi army left Erbil.

Now your governments are debating the future of our safe haven. If you think our expensive protection has lasted long enough, remember Saddam's "Anfal." And know, too, that Kurds now have video cameras. If the "Anfal" returns, we may not be able to resist, but we will record, and then we will beam mass murder into your homes.

"Do you think this is authentic?"

"Don't you have a television?"

"I mean about this 'Anfal?'"

Erica loaded me with pamphlets, her loose-leaf country notebooks, and a book of photographs. I took them back to the ground-floor studio I'd rented, only a ten-minute walk from the office in Exarchia, a neighborhood near the Archaeological Museum. The studio was beginning to look like my old study carrel at the law library. From my year in Human Rights, I remembered that Kurds were oppressed in eastern Turkey, that the Kurdish language was not allowed in schools or newspapers, on radio or TV. And, of course, I'd seen Iraqi Kurds during the Gulf War, heard the reports of poison gas.

Erica might want to protect Kurds because they antagonize Turks, but the reports she gave me weren't translated from Greek or Kurdish. Published by Human Rights Watch, assisted by Physicians for Human Rights, the reports documented the Anfal genocide with forensic studies and eyewitness accounts. Villages I'd never heard of—Bergalou, Qara Dagh, Askar, Goktapa—were destroyed and replaced by camps I'd never heard of—Topzawa, Tikrit, Nugra Salman. Whole towns looked like an earthquake had struck, tilting cement slabs, twisting structural steel, bringing down roofs. But the damage was done house by house. To hide human evidence, Iraqis followed the Nazis' example and transported their victims—to the south where Kurds were machine gunned in groups or buried alive. Survivors the Iraqis hoped we'd never hear were identified only by first names—Ozer, Mustafa, Taymour—because they are still in danger. When Kurds gained control of the north, individual victims were exhumed, their wounds photographed with color film more vivid than Holocaust black and white. A medical anthropologist stands in a grave like Hamlet, holding a yellowed skull with its red blindfold still intact. Why the blindfold, I wondered. So the firing squad couldn't see the pleading eyes or so the firing squad would remain a secret to the victim. These reports were not propaganda. They were like the files, but synthesized, formalized, translated, printed. I didn't know about the Anfal before. Now I felt I possessed a secret, knowledge of Saddam's secret war. Refugees are by definition and derivation on the move, leaving homes, abandoning homelands. The people in the court-yard and hallways of UNHCR were not all Kurds, but reading the reports and looking at their photographs of dynamited villages I felt that all Kurds are refugees.

After my weekend of research, I reported in Monday morning to begin interviewing. The Commission was using three refugees to translate the Kurds' three dialects. The first two weeks were very slow. Siamand's three hundred words were haltingly and painfully recombined: "The fear of this person is great. He greatly fears return to Turkey. This country makes him great fear." Despite or because of Siamand's limited vocabulary, his translations always seemed extreme, somehow exaggerated. The Iraqi Rena's voice sounded like a lawnmower idling, so I repeatedly had to ask her to repeat her translation. The effect was like conditioning, hearing the same story twice. Aziz the Iranian would hold me up by hanging around and trying to influence my decision. "You're an American. You know how those mullahs in Tehran treat enemies." The interviews often took an hour, and then I'd use another half hour checking my notes against documents and my background notes.

None of my first applicants could have written the letter to *The London Times,* in English, Farsi, Arabic, Turkish, or their dialects. An Iranian had run an underground cinema that Aziz said showed "revolutionary films." The Iranian knew enough English from the movies he'd watched to correct Aziz: "fuckie flic, fuckie flic," the applicant said. Aziz frowned and bailed himself out with "French films." A couple of the Iraqi Kurds had been to technical universities, but were in flight from politics. Turkish Kurds were mostly young uneducated males, former farmers and factory workers who looked like they'd walked all the way to Athens. If they knew any English, it was "I" or "me," which they combined with *peshmerga,* a word they expected me to know. "Solger" was one of Siamand's three hundred words I didn't understand.

I went to ask Erica what *peshmerga* meant. "Literally, 'he who faces death,'" she told me. "Guerrilla is the closest English word. If *peshmergas* are Iraqi, they are denied unless they can prove they're Talibani men in the west of the safe zone or Barzani men in the east. Iranians don't have much of a resistance movement, so they join up with the Iraqis and Turks. If we followed the letter of UNHCR guidelines, PKK *peshmergas* or sympathizers from Turkey should have the best cases. They're persecuted because of 'political opinion,' but Mrs. Constantinou won't grant status to people she calls 'terrorists.'"

"What about 'freedom fighters?'"

"Not them either. If resistance fighters or guerrilla movements become strong enough to be classified as combatants in a civil war, they no longer qualify."

"So what do they do when we refuse them?"

"First, you and I and Nikos don't refuse them. Applicants get their verdicts in writing downstairs, where Panos stands with his machine gun."

Nikos must have heard his name. He came out of his funk, interrupted his interview, and came to the partition: "And if the aliens are denied, they stay in

Greece illegally. If we don't give them the card that provides free social and educational and medical benefits, the foreigners stay here anyway and take jobs from Greeks and steal."

Erica bristled. "That's just the Albanians, your cousins, Niko."

"Northern Epirotes," Nikos said, "not Albanians."

"And he says he's not political," Erica said to me, "claiming southern Albania as northern Greece."

"The Epirotes speak our language. They belong here, just like Cypriots," Nikos said to Erica. Then he turned to me, "If you stay long enough, you will begin to recognize PKK. They keep coming back under new names."

I asked Erica if that was true.

"There's some evidence that *peshmergas* are provided fake documents, come here to put on weight, and return to fight. But Nikos is being hypocritical, like the government that protects Albanians with Greek names so they can go back to agitate against Muslims. The Kurds aren't quite white, and most are Muslims, so Nikos is afraid of them."

"You should be too, Casey," Nikos said. "If we give too many status, we'll be in trouble with the Interior Ministry. They will throw UNHCR out of the country and the police will process applications. Do you know what will happen then?"

"No, what?"

"Then no applicants will be granted refugee status, no refugees will work as translators, and no lawyers will be employed as examiners. For these reasons, everyone here at the Commission has to be afraid."

Erica said something in Greek that she didn't translate. Nikos smiled and went back to his desk. I went back to my office. As Greeks, Nikos and Erica both have a stake in which of their neighbors they recommend for asylum. Perhaps that's why Nikos hangs on to a job he dislikes and why Erica is so passionate. Since Greece isn't my home, I can try to apply the law more objectively. Maybe that's the reason I was hired by Mrs. Constantinou: to go by the book, the *Handbook*; to counterbalance her native examiners, offer them an example of neutrality and due process, make them aware of and perhaps even afraid of their ideological underpinnings. I wonder if Nikos and Erica are afraid of me. Maybe they both worry about their jobs, which are their jobs—not a sabbatical position. My responsibility is heavier than ever—to my colleagues, to the applicants. Trying to be scrupulous, I work firm hours, but am still a volunteer. Do interviews during the day, check background documents in the evening, and write my letters to the Director on the weekends.

After two weeks, I'd recommended about half my applicants. Mrs. Constantinou dropped by my office to talk about my Letters.

"You are very careful," she said. "Everyone is when they first start. It shows you have the right heart for this job. But if you do not reject more, I will have to. I want you to do this because you have seen and listened to the applicants, while I see only the files."

"'Seen,' yes. But not 'listened.' The applicants' stories often seem garbled or exaggerated when they come through the translators."

"You will just have to trust yourself."

"The applicants' lives depend on the stories they tell me, Mrs. Constantinou. I can't trust myself because I don't always trust the translators. Aziz for example. I think he may be distorting stories. And the other day an applicant fired Siamand during an interview. Twice Siamand reversed what the applicant said. Lucky for him, he knew some English. Most of the Turkish Kurds don't. I need someone whose knowledge of English makes him or her transparent."

I told the Director about Ziba Mamozin's application, which I'd just read. Mrs. Constantinou was running about a month behind the interviews, but she agreed to look at the file. The next day she suggested Ms. Mamozin be brought in immediately for an interview. I was pleased, hopeful. Ms. Mamozin would be able to tell her own story without the stumbling of Siamand, the gurgle of Rena, or the interference of Aziz. I wanted to hear that story because in her terse Questionnaire and brief, literal Narrative Ms. Mamozin treated words as if they were documents.

Chapter 4

United Nations High Commissioner for Refugees
Case: 98-V-341
Applicant: Ziba Mamozin
National or Ethnic Origin: Turkish Kurd
Examiner: Casey Mahan
Translator:
Transcript by: TP, 25-9-98

"You don't require a translator, do you?"

"No."

"We don't get many American-educated applicants here."

"I'd rather not be here myself."

"I understand that. We'll see what we can do for you. But before we begin, could I ask how you learned to speak with almost no accent?"

"Mother taught English in Diyarbakir. When it was time for secondary school, she sent me to live with my uncle in Istanbul. And living in Chicago for five years also helped, of course."

"Do you have your passport with you today?"

"No."

"There's no photocopy in your file either. Where is your passport?"

"It was taken by the police in Diyarbakir."

"Do you have any documents with you today?"

"No."

"Many applicants don't have passports, Ms. Mamozin, but they usually have some documents. You know, a birth certificate or marriage license, something which identifies them. Documents that demonstrate the applicant's conflict with the government are also helpful. Some record of harassment. Could you tell me why you have no documents?"

"I thought that was obvious in my statement. The police forced me to leave Diyarbakir in a hurry."

"Because of your brother?"

"Yes."

"Is he a member of the PKK?"

"No."

"Are you a member?"

"No."

"I'm sorry, but I have to ask this next question. If I fax the PKK office in London, the name Mamozin won't show up on their membership rolls?"

"Not mine. Perhaps my brother's name. You know, don't you, that the Turkish police put innocent people on the membership list and then arrest them for terrorism?"

"How would you define that word?"

"'Terrorism?'"

"Yes."

"What the PKK does. What the police did to me."

"Okay, Ms. Mamozin, but we have a problem here. An applicant's file is stronger if it includes some documents."

"I was born in Diyarbakir. You could call Chicago Circle and get this information."

"That's not ..."

"Look, if you don't believe I'm a

Kourd, bring in a translator and I'll speak
Kurmanji or Sorani to him."

"You don't understand. I believe you're
a Kurd. Documentary evidence would help show
that you have a well-founded fear of persecution. That's the crucial test for refugee
status."

"If you're a Kourd in Turkey, that
should be enough evidence that you fear persecution."

"I'd like to agree with you, Ms.
Mamozin, but we can't take ten million Kurds
into Greece. We are required to examine
applicants on a case by case basis."

"My case is simple. I was tortured by
the Turkish police."

"I'm sorry to say this, Ms. Mamozin,
but many applicants claim to have been tortured. Your Narrative says very little about
the circumstances. It would help if there
were an arrest record, for example."

"My home was broken into by three men
in masks. I don't think that will be on any
record, not in Turkey."

"Can you tell me more about what
occurred?"

"'Tell you more?' I was tortured. The
men wanted to know where they could find my
brother and a number of other people. I did-
n't even recognize their names."

"Are there more details?"

"You want to hear details?"

"I realize this may be difficult to
talk about, but the more specific an applicant's account, the more persuasive it is. Is
there something more you can tell me?"

"I have something I can show you."

"My God, how did that happen?"

Let the record show that the applicant
stood up, unbuttoned her blouse, and exposed
her abdomen. It is an unbandaged, raw mass of
sores.

"How did this happen?"

"'We have something Kurdish for you,'
the lead policeman said in Turkish. He held
up a piece of tent rope, which our herders
make from goat hair, a very thick and rough
rope. I thought they would hang me and make
it look like a suicide: woman kills self
because of terrorist guilt. When they ripped
off my nightgown, I was afraid they would tie
me with the rope and rape me. Instead they
stretched that rope between doorhandles in my
bedroom. They hung me over the rope like a
rug put out to air. My hands were held by one
man, my legs were held by another man. Then I
was pulled back and forth on the rope like a
saw, only it was me and not the rope that was
being cut in half."

"Didn't anyone hear you scream?"

"Who would come into a house with three
policemen? Who would help?"

"Yes, I understand."

"'Where's your brother, the animal doctor?' the leader asked me. 'Iraq,' I told
him, but he didn't believe me. They sawed me
some more, and I said 'Hakkari,' but they
still didn't believe me. 'Maybe he's in
America,' the leader said. Finally I gave
them an address in Diyarbakir. 'Cunt,' the
leader said in English, perhaps the only
English word he knew."

"How did you get away?"

"They wanted me to leave. They wrapped

gauze around my abdomen, dressed me in western clothes, gave me money from my pocketbook, took me to the bus station, and told me not to get off until I got to Ankara. From there I went to Istanbul. I don't have any documents, but you can take a photo of my belly if you need to."

"No, no, that won't be necessary. Please sit down. I can describe this wound and your situation in my letter to the Director. Although your lack of documents is rather unusual, I think you'll be granted status."

"How long will this process take?"

"It could be months, I'm afraid. But I might be able to speed it up. Maybe you could do some translating for us. Your English is excellent. Did you say you speak both Kurmanji and Sorani."

"Yes, and I can get along in Guran."

"We don't have a single person who can cover all the dialects. You're not even thirty yet. How did you learn all these languages and dialects?"

"If Kourds are ever to have a country of our own, we need to talk to each other without translators."

That's when I snapped off the tape recorder. The written record should further show that from side to side, Ziba's skin looked like a colored topographic map of Turkey, red mountains of blisters and scabs, yellow rivers of puss oozing down the valleys. There were also white spots, as if the landscape was covered by clouds. Pieces of the rope or remnants of her bandages stuck out like prickles. Although she was thin, I couldn't see her ribs beneath the raised welts and puckered skin. Her navel had disappeared, and the sores seemed to extend below the waistband of her polka-dot skirt. This wound was not the self-snipped finger Nikos warned me I might see. Ziba's torture was original, unbelievable, evident.

Once Ziba exposed her wound, she was able to tell a persuasively specific story. She didn't cast down her eyes like many women from the Middle East. Just like an American, Ziba looked me straight in the face, controlled the anger in her almost black eyes, and told me the facts without flinching or weeping. By the time I interviewed her, I'd heard obviously rehearsed stories and seen their tellers' eyes wander away from me to an invisible script. I'd also heard stories so pitiable that I had to drop my eyes to the desk to keep my composure. Ziba locked on my eyes as if I were one of the Turkish policemen and she was confronting him in a court. With her straight-cut, shoulder-length black hair, uptilted chin, and subtly mocking manner, Ziba reminded me of a law student I knew, a shy tax savant who mysteriously transformed herself into a self-assured advocate at a moot court competition. Ziba was only about five-four and no more than a hundred pounds, but she was fearsome as she stood before my desk, gripped her blouse, and recounted her torture.

Before interviewing Ziba, I'd learned ways of withholding sympathy by watching Erica and Nikos, by talking to the Director. Treating applicants formally protects examiners from responding emotionally to woe we cannot relieve. Treating applicants as unfriendly witnesses allows us to conceal our feelings, prevent any false signals from reaching the applicants. And, we tell ourselves, treating applicants as litigants protects them from using their thirty minutes to vent feelings that don't contribute to the force of their story. At the interview, neither applicant nor examiner can risk being a person, someone with mixed emotions, crossed purposes, internal ambivalences. The interview is like a half hourglass. The applicant reduces himself or herself, that upside-down pyramid of sand, to a thin line of fear that the applicant hopes will accumulate into a substantial mound, the foundation of the examiner's approval. It's not like a job interview. It's a life interview, sometimes a life-or-death interview. Given those facts, I believed my examination of Ziba was well-founded.

After the interview was transcribed, I hand-carried Ziba's file and my Letter of Recommended Action to the Director. She granted Ziba status and asked me to bring her back to discuss translating. On the arranged day, Mrs. Constantinou invited me to her office for Ziba's job interview. The three of us exchanged pleasantries, and Mrs. Constantinou asked some questions about Ziba's knowledge of dialects and her English training. Ziba had acted entitled to refugee status in my office, but with Mrs. Constantinou Ziba was more deferential, a person who needed a job. I heard no grammatical errors or problematic pronunciations in Ziba's short answers. In fact, Ziba's voice was closer to a native speaker's than the correct, but accented speech of Mrs. Constantinou.

But she wasn't satisfied listening to Ziba speak. The Director wanted to hear Ziba answer questions. Mrs. Constantinou picked up the trail I'd left in Istanbul.

"How did you cross the Evros River?"

"A smuggler took me and two other Kourds across in a rubber boat."

"Where exactly did you cross?"

"I don't know the name of the place, but the smuggler told us the river was deep there. For that reason, there were no soldiers on the Greek side."

"Are you saying that Greek land had no protection?"

"No, only what the smuggler said about soldiers."

"And you believed him?"

"We had no choice in the boat. None of us could swim."

"So if there were no soldiers, what did protect the Greek side?"

"Just a few feet from the river was a high fence. The smuggler told us to climb over it, wait for fifteen minutes to make sure we weren't seen, and walk west until we found a road."

"So it was that easy to enter Greece?"

"No. There were signs on the fence. They were in Turkish and English. They warned that the area behind the fence was mined."

"What did you think?"

"I knew the other Kourds couldn't read those signs. The smuggler was a Turk. He thought that because I was a woman I couldn't read. He wanted us to give him our money, wait until he was back on the other side, and then take our chances in the minefield. I pretended to be pleased that we were finally free. But as I hugged the men, I told them in Kurmanji about the mines. Although I was laughing, I said we had to take the smuggler prisoner. He was trying to keep our celebration quiet and didn't suspect. There was a short fight and we had his pistol. One of the men wanted to go down the river and find a place without mines where we could sneak past soldiers. That was impossible because it would soon be light. The other man knew that and said we should go back. The first man and I refused. I told them there was only one thing to do, climb the fence and walk through the minefield."

"You speak English very well, Miss Mamozin, but it is hard to believe you feared persecution so much that you would walk through a minefield."

"I had been told about smugglers, how they sometimes asked for more money to guide Kourds through mines. I believed our Turk knew the way through."

"It is still very dangerous."

"Not for Kourds."

"Why is that?"

"We pointed the pistol at the Turk, he walked twenty feet in front of us, and we followed in his footsteps. Yes, this night worked out well for us. None of us had documents. But we kept all our money. That way we could avoid riding on a bus. In Alexandropoulis, we found a Greek person who brought us to Athens in his taxi. Unfortunately, we had to pay him all our money. We slept in the courtyard and applied the next day."

"I know the place you have described, Ms. Mamozin. There are not really any mines there. The signs are put up to frighten illegal aliens."

Until this point, Ziba had shown none of the toughness I saw in my office. She told her story as if she was doing a literal translation of a documentary film. Now she looked right into the Director's eyes.

"Mrs. Constantinou, I don't believe you are correct."

The cords in the Director's neck tightened.

"Oh. And why not?" she said.

"Because just a few steps into the minefield the smuggler asked us if he could stop to defecate."

Ziba didn't give the Director a chance to ask the meaning of "defecate," her nurse's term, or to question the Turk's fear.

"*Scata,*" Ziba said, as if it were the last word.

"Yes," Mrs. Constantinou said, "I understand."

Perhaps Mrs. Constantinou was secretly pleased to hear about a Turk almost shitting his pants, or maybe she was impressed with Ziba's Greek as well as her English. Whatever the causes, Mrs. Constantinou approved Ziba as a translator. I was pleased to have my judgment confirmed, but Mrs. Constantinou's questioning rankled. I felt she had been reinterviewing Ziba, checking on me.

I had Ziba translate for all the Turks and tried her out with a few Iraqi and Iranian Kurds to see how smoothly she handled their dialects. Ziba sat with her knees pressed together and her hands in her lap, formal, even a little prim. She'd been almost aggressive in her interview. Now she was nearly invisible. With applicants, she was polite, gentle, slightly raising her hand when she had to interrupt and translate. Siamand foreshortened answers and Aziz expanded them. Ziba's translations took the same time as the originals. Her voice was calm, objective. Instead of replicating the interviewees' body language or volume, Ziba would summarize the applicant's emotional state. "Mr. X was very angry. Mrs. Z is still grieving." With Ziba speaking her nearly native

English, the interviews went more quickly, I grew more confident, and I
started to bring down my approval rate. About that, both Mrs. Constantinou
and I were happy.

Now that the interviews were going more smoothly, I could "enjoy" weekend relief from persecution. I went to beaches below Athens and took the
hydrofoil to nearby Saronic islands—Aegina, Poros, Hydra. On Spetses I
stroked through the salt pool Aegean and let the kind September sun tan my
limbs. Altruism and tourism, I thought. This really is a sabbatical, a city job, a
seaside life. Lying on the sand is like reading in bed except the world between
your jacked-up knees is real. The Greek sun is shining on Virginia Woolf's
lighthouse and waves, unfiltered by her sensibility. Water I'm not afraid of. I
might succumb to vertigo, but I'll never drown myself. The purple mountains
of the Peloponnese are far in the distance, harmless. I wonder what was more
fundamental for Greeks, Odysseus's sea or the gods' Olympus. Socrates had
little use for either and considered Athens a refuge from nature, though not
from his wife. My Greek-American secretary at the firm joked about fishermen,
what she called *kamakees*—literally "harpooners," actually tourist scavengers.
Greek men must be sated by a summer of Scandinavian flesh or discouraged
by my one-piece suit and hardcover book. Lying on a mat, I can't be threatening to the mostly short men preening on the sand. With my Hillary Clinton
hair and zinc on my nose, I'm certainly not a Greek, and English, the secretary
told me, is the universal language of aviation and *kamakees*. But none of the
Spetses natives—who advertise themselves with swim suits so skimpy and
tight that olives would create bulges—approach me. On other islands, I was
asked for the time or a light by tourists with pale rings on their tanned hands.
While their wives and kids took late afternoon naps, we talked about the
island, the food, the Greeks.

"They are more sensual, don't you think?" a Dutch man about fifty asked
while I was on Hydra.

"Maybe they're just happy to be on vacation."

"But don't the Greeks make you feel free to do things you wouldn't do in
America?"

I saw where these leading questions were leading.

"Not really," I said, "Five days a week here I listen to stories about atrocities."

"I don't understand."

I gave the Dutchman detailed examples instead of a synonym for "atrocities," and he soon went back to his own mat on the rocks.

I knew exactly what I was doing with the one-afternoon standers, the guys who stood over my mat and me. But looking west across the flat Aegean to flat Ohio, I wonder why I tested even men I knew: with my billing prowess at the firm, with my apartment, with what Rick had once called, behind my back, "bitwit," short for "bitch wit" and, I suppose, alternative to "mother wit." I sent him an email at P & G: "Dear nitwit: Why don't you lift your leg at home if you want to piss on me. Titwit." Isn't it sufficiently difficult to be 6 feet 1 1/2 inches and neither thin like a model nor muscled like a beach volleyballer? Why add distance to the inches that separated me from every woman I've ever known and all but a couple of men? Yes, I fear towers, but I'm not afraid of men. Maybe I fear they'll be afraid of me, my body seeming to tower over them. I don't want to see that in their eyes. My testing of men gives them an excuse to shy away, though it was no excuse for Rick to run away. "Love at first slight," he said of us. He liked to needle and rub the wrong way. Maybe he didn't want to live with a double who wouldn't give an inch, who had an inch on him.

But I didn't come all this distance to conduct a self-examination, to grope around my interior as I feel my breasts every three months. Here I feel interior life is a luxury. The applicants are exterior, are sometimes forced to be ulterior. Besides, ever since I first put a one below another one and added them up, I've been oriented toward the future, a problem solver: the answer below the line, the blank to be filled at the end of the line, the pages left to read and the discussion questions to be answered. It was only inside the confessional box that I had to scrutinize the past. About behavior I was exhaustive. But because my thoughts turned outward, toward the future, books to be read, jobs to be done, I was rarely guilty of all that soul-rotting evil inside that the nuns told us about: envy, sloth, despair. After my growth spurt, there was plenty of me outside, in full view, to keep self-consciousness busy. In high school and college, I bent over books, opened up poems and novels, poured my self-consciousness in, found self-consciousness gushing back, and hunched over further. Literature was about victims, was written by victims. Until my Senior Seminar in Literature and Law. Still victims like Joseph K and little JR, but I did my thesis on Melville's *Benito Cereno*. Literature had a history, but was invented. As I studied the legal background of Melville's slave revolt, the documents he included, I discovered the law was founded, grounded, built up over generations from actual events, real people. When asked "Why?" you could discover the answer, drill through the palimpsests to the ruling precedent, pile-drive down to bedrock. And the law had power. I leaned on it and applied to law school.

"Why are you wearing those vertical stripes now?"

"Wouldn't it be better to let your hair hang a bit around your shoulders?"

"Why don't you get some nice, dressy flats?"

No, I didn't come to Greece to answer those questions my mother has been asking since my second semester at UC Law. Even in this country of short people, I won't go back to bending and hunching and drooping, crossing my arms on my chest and leaning against walls, as I did in high school and college. But lying on the beach mat, I also have to admit that all my success has occurred sitting down. The classroom desks where I answered casuistical exam questions, the fixed seats in law school amphitheaters where I refused to be browbeaten by men or women down in the well, my custom-made office chair where I drafted two-hundred-page briefs, talked on the phone, and rarely had to stand to meet a client. The clients were in other countries, and the corporations that wanted them in the United States contacted the firm by mail. The travel posters were sent to me UPS. My Immigration practice was elaborate play, a global board game like the Risk I'd played as a kid. But no lives were at risk. If a client was denied the chance to make big bucks in the U.S., he'd continue making large lira or prodigious pounds where he was. At UNHCR I'm still seated, but the clients are four feet away and their lives are in my hands. Now I'm doing something worth doing. I don't stand when the applicants come in or when they leave. But when I listen to probable survivors of genocide or to possible perpetrators of terror I'm on the edge of my chair while Ziba is doing the talking.

Chapter 5

While the burden of proof in principle rests on the applicant, the duty to ascertain and evaluate all the relevant facts is shared between the applicant and the examiner. Indeed, in some cases, it may be necessary for the examiner to use all the means at his disposal to produce the necessary evidence in support of the application. While an initial interview should normally suffice to bring an applicant's story to light, it may be necessary for the examiner to clarify any apparent inconsistencies and to resolve any contradictions in a further interview, and to find an explanation for any misrepresentation or concealment of material facts. Untrue statements by themselves are not a reason for refusal of refugee status and it is the examiner's responsibility to evaluate such statements in the light of all the circumstances of the case.

Handbook on Procedures and Criteria for Determining Refugee Status, p. 47

I was interviewing a Kurdish woman who had been living in Basra in the south of Iraq. Her two-year-old son stood beside her and stared at me as if I were speaking in tongues. A baby was on her lap. It was a complicated case because the woman was married to an Iraqi Catholic from Baghdad; she had started passing as an Assyrian when they moved to Basra, where few Kurds lived. The facts were documented with baptism records, marriage license, identification cards. Her husband had a well-paying job with the electric department, also documented with tax returns, but got into trouble when he didn't show adequate appreciation of Hussein's Ba'ath Party. The police looked into Mrs. Haydar's background, which included parents killed during the Anfal. This too was "documented" by a letter from the Iraqi Security Service saying that Mrs. Haydar's parents were probably kidnapped by Iranians. After she was brought in for questioning, she and her husband gathered their documents and prepared to flee to Jordan. Then her husband, Ziba translated, "was disappeared." I repeated the phrase. "Yes," Ziba said. If as Mrs. Haydar's reasoning went, an Iraqi Arab could be disappeared and if thousands of Kurds had been disappeared in the Anfal, she and her children were next. Three weeks after she lost her husband, with no sign of his whereabouts or return, Mrs. Haydar arranged to have her children and herself smuggled into Jordan, where she stayed for six months before coming to Athens and applying for asylum at the airport.

"How," I asked, "did you have the money to fly three people to Athens?"

"My life's savings" was her answer.

To have a husband or wife "disappeared" in Iraq was a common occurrence, though difficult to prove. The timing in Mrs. Haydar's story was unusual. Since she left Iraq only three weeks after her husband was abducted, I wondered if she'd abandoned him. I also wondered why, if she spent six months in Jordan, she hadn't applied to UNHCR there. I didn't think Mrs. Haydar was one of the Director's "philhellenes," lovers of European wages. Mrs. Haydar's hands were delicate, her nails polished. She was well-dressed. I employed the examiner's ironic rule of thumb: those applicants who seem to suffer least are the most likely to fear persecution. People don't leave high-paying jobs and risk their lives for a slightly better life and more television channels. But the timing in Mrs. Haydar's case still bothered me. I asked her to wait downstairs while I faxed an inquiry to UNHCR in Amman. When I got my reply two hours later, I called her back in. The little boy, his eyes downcast, was leaning against his mother. The infant was crying. "Baby year," I thought, and asked the question required of me:

"You applied in Jordan, didn't you?"

"Yes," the answer came back through Ziba, though by now I knew "yes" and "no" in the dialects I heard.

"You and your husband applied, didn't you?"

"Yes."

"What happened to your husband?"

"He disappeared himself."

I squinted at Ziba, the look she knew meant "interpret" as well as "translate."

"That's the way she put it. She means 'He deserted me,'" Ziba said.

"Why did your husband leave?" I asked.

There was no answer. I asked again.

"He just disappeared."

If the man had "been disappeared," passive voice, or if he had "disappeared himself," the transitive case, before Mrs. Haydar left Iraq, she probably would have been granted status in Amman. But the husband left in transit, and Mrs. Haydar had lied, twice. When I told her this, she began to weep. The baby was already crying. The boy began to sob and climbed on his mother's lap.

"Please, please, I beg you," Ziba translated. "For these children. We have no money, no place to live. My children will starve. In the name of Allah, I beg you."

While Ziba spoke, the kids continued to wail and their mother sobbed "Please, please, please" in English.

"Tell her," I said to Ziba, "I'll see what I can do."

After Mrs. Haydar and her kids left the office, I asked Ziba, "Are mixed marriages frequent with Kurds?"

"Not in Kourdistan. When Kourds leave, they sometimes marry others."

"Even Iraqis?"

"More often than Turks."

I asked her for more interpretation: "Do you think Mrs. Haydar was a victim of a mixed marriage?"

"As a doctor in America told me once, 'You're not paid to think. You fill out the chart, and I do the diagnosis.'"

This was the first personal information to pass between us since Ziba's interview. I'd been friendly, reporting whatever Chicago news I gleaned from the *Herald Tribune*, but Ziba kept her distance, like the translators behind walls of glass at the UN in New York. I wondered if she resented having to expose her wound to a stranger, even if that stranger helped her get a job.

"So you don't want to speculate?"

"Who knows what goes on inside—or outside—a marriage? I don't know. I prefer not to judge."

Her oddly formal usage reminded me of pale, helpless Bartleby though Ziba's skin had the reddish hue of Melville's other copyists and Native Americans.

"Even though the applicant is a Kurd?" I asked.

"Isn't that the reason I shouldn't answer your questions?"

Back again was that slightly mocking tone of Ziba's original interview, as if she saw through my question. No, not "as if." She did realize, even if I didn't, that I, like Mrs. Constantinou, was reinterviewing her, now as a translator.

"Yes, you're right," I said. But now that I knew what I was doing, I decided to ask one more question with a slightly different cast: "But what about those little kids? How do you feel about them, Kurdish or not?"

"They're lucky to have that mother, but they will never be Kourds."

"Because of the Iraqi father?" I asked.

"No. Because they won't grow up in Kourdistan."

"So, what will they be, then?"

"Refugees."

I went to the *Handbook* for guidance. Although Mrs. Haydar had lied, she had a well-founded fear of persecution if she was returned to Iraq. She wouldn't be murdered in her first forty-eight hours home, as Saddam's son-in-law and family were, but leaving Iraq was a crime. Leaving Jordan was probably a mistake. Now she was in a country where she'd need a translator for the simplest communications. But if I returned her to Jordan, she might not get status there. With a blue card here, she and her kids won't starve. She can't camp out in Omonia Square like male aliens. One of our social workers can find Mrs. Haydar and her children a room. Their mother lied, but the kids hadn't. Why punish them? They won't fear persecution in the future, but for the rest of their lives they'll hate that word their mother begged to be called. Better refugees here, I judged, than aliens in Jordan or fatherless Kurds in Iraq.

After our last interview that day, I asked Ziba what she'd said to the doctor when he told her not to think. The question brought the first smile I'd seen on a face almost always blank.

"The doctor was a woman," Ziba said, "and I told her that if she read the chart carefully she wouldn't have to think very hard."

"When was your deportation hearing?"

Ziba smiled again, a little wider.

"I wasn't so brave. The doctor was Pakistani and had been in the country less time than me."

"What about American doctors? Did they treat you as badly as they do patients?"

"Actually, I liked them. They were very efficient, very skilled."

"With all the problems in Turkey, did you want to go back when your training was over?"

"Yes. Chicago was too big and too flat. Besides, my student visa ran out. But that didn't matter. I missed home."

"Do you miss anything about the States?"

"The hospital. Our hospital in Diyarbakir is very poorly equipped. And we need more doctors. I saw patients die there who could have easily been saved in a small city hospital in America."

"What will you do in Greece once you're granted asylum by the Ministry?"

"*Matheno* more *Ellenikah*," she said. I recognized the last word, Greek for Greek, and guessed at *matheno* from its root and context: "learn."

"Maybe I can get a job here some day," she went on. "I know that Filipina nurses work in the hospitals."

"I'll be collecting social security before I ever learn enough Greek to be a lawyer here."

"*Kali nichta*," I said, "good night," but also, figuratively, the end, case closed.

"*Ti na kanome?*" Ziba said, "what are we to do?" the favorite refrain of older Greek women waiting in line or complaining about any fate that has befallen them.

Then we both laughed—at our phrase book knowledge and, I felt, to celebrate the unlikely communication of two beginners.

"*Horice kremethia*," I said gravely, as if it were a profound answer to Ziba's question instead of "without onions."

"*Poso kanei isiteria?*" she replied with a straight face: "how much is a ticket?"

We laughed again and exchanged more non-sequiturs. If Erica or Nikos had dropped in, they'd have thought we'd gone mad in Greek. "What time is it?" "I want fresh bread." "Your boat is blue." "My foot is green." "The doctor is in." "My mother has a pencil."

Ziba was already far ahead of me in Greek, yet not so far that I couldn't surprise her when she came into the office. With my knowledge of ancient Greek, literary terms, and Latin derivatives, I could spring some arcane vocabulary on her. She had her medical terms, of course, and was much better with sounds, correcting my American liquid "r's," making me raise the tip of my tongue and roll the "ro." After a few days of hit and run exchanges between interviews, I realized this is the way to learn a language: with another learner, teaching and learning at the same time, playing with words like building blocks or tinker toys, not reciting for a professor. To work in Greece as a nurse, Ziba would eventually need steel and concrete Greek, but where I lived in Exarchia someone in a store or on the street always spoke English if a conversation became functional. My three-word sentences were for politeness in the tavernas, for friendliness in the shops.

That first exchange of non-sequiturs began our friendship—*filia* in Greek, stronger than English "affiliation," not as strong as the ancient Greek "love" in *philologia*. Outside the office, we look as improbable as our first communication in *Ellenikah*. Athenians in flowered housedresses gawk at the tall woman in an Ann Taylor suit walking with the short woman in pajama pants. The usual stares of men seem diffused when I'm with Ziba, my height accentuated, but the lookers' attention shared. I'm a northerner. With her thick black eyebrows, Ziba could be a Greek. Waiters bring salads and potted vegetables to me, chops and souvlaki to her. Sitting in cafes, we turn away from each other while reading our *Herald Tribune* and *Hurriyet*. Ziba can blow her smoke in another direction, and I can—I tell her—pretend I'm not associating with a Turk. We combine our ignorance, west and east, speculating about Greek customs.

"Why do middle-aged women speak in a high-pitched voice?" Ziba asks.

"Why do young men spend so much time looking into shoe-store windows?" I want to know.

"Why do all Greeks repeat whatever we say to them in Greek?" both of us wonder. Ziba's hands support her positions on these matters. I'm the TV talking head. About things American, we often disagree. Ziba exclaims over health care I say is "atrocious." I praise liberal education she calls "a waste of time." She admits a soft spot for Disney animation. My guilty pleasures are period pieces, Jane Austen and Henry James movies. "No action," Ziba says. "No people," I reply about cartoons.

We shared, though, an unspoken agreement that our friendship had to be circumspect. The other translators and their cohorts would suspect special treatment for Turkish Kurds. I knew Mrs. Constantinou would deplore unprofessional involvement. She treated all the translators with a condescending intimacy, calling them by their first names, but prefacing the names with honorifics: "Miss Ziba" and "Mr. Aziz." Ziba and I talked often about Kurds, her colleagues and friends, how they lived, what they felt about Turkey, but also trivial stuff, how Kurds answer the phone, why they celebrate New Year's in March, when girls are expected to marry. In all our conversations, though, we never spoke about individual cases we'd heard. I was frequently tempted, after the interview of Mrs. Haydar, to ask Ziba's opinion of applicants, but I always resisted. She never volunteered information.

Ziba didn't come to my studio, and I didn't go to the residence hotel where she lived with other aliens. On weekends we'd usually arrange to meet at a museum or some other spot refugees don't frequent. One Sunday afternoon we got into a central Athens retreat never seen by tourists and denied to all but a few hundred Greeks: the tennis club between the Plaka and the Olympic Stadium. We spoke our fluent English to each other and walked by the guard at the gate as if he surely recognized two wives of multinational executives who pay enormous sums to play on red clay and meet government ministers. For two dollars each, we sipped iced tea on the patio under the plane tree, watched the doubles games, listened to the gentle pop of business tennis, and pretended that we belonged to a group more exclusive than law partners or surgeons.

I told Ziba about my father's clan, the athletic Irish: "My father never played anything besides beer-in-the-hand softball, but he named me for a batter in a poem. Dad loved John McEnroe's tantrums and started me playing tennis when I was eight. I liked the competition and won some local tournaments. But all the expensive lessons and winter court time went to waste when my growth spurt betrayed me."

"Didn't your height give you an advantage?"

"I couldn't even be sure my service toss would go where I wanted it to. So I waited in my room and inside the Xavier library for my eyes and arms and legs to work together, but they never came around, except for walking and swimming."

"Inside I know about," Ziba said. "In Diyarbakir, I spent most of my childhood inside our apartment, speaking Kurmanji with mother, Sorani with father, reading banned Kurdish papers and books. Learning English and avoiding the Turks."

This was the first time Ziba talked about her childhood.

"That must have hard for outside people," I said.

"Yes, it was. But summers I was free. I went to mother's village in the mountains near the Iran border. In Hakkari, I rode donkeys and dodged goats, picked berries and sheared sheep. My cousins and I built tree houses and played hide and seek in the caves. But it wasn't all play. My parents wanted me to learn about hard work, the old ways, making bread outdoors, washing clothes in a brook, sitting at the loom. Those were happy times. But then no more summers in Hakkari. The Turks put mines in the caves, one of my cousins was killed, young men were arrested, and the people in the village were forced to leave. Then I was always inside, because mother wanted me to get out of Diyarbakir."

"To study?"

"Yes, and to live and marry and have children who felt safe."

"And your father?"

"He wanted me to stay, so I compromised—left and returned."

Even when Ziba went to Istanbul, her uncle made sure she was home right after school. "We were not Muslims, but I was treated like a young virgin. That's probably why I got the grades for a scholarship to Chicago Circle. There I was the only Turk, the only Kourd, the only person from east of Portland, Maine, but I was out. The streets of Chicago felt safe and free after all those years inside, so free I almost flunked out my first year."

Ziba was almost as animated about Chicago as she was about Hakkari.
"Were you in nursing because of your brother?"

I thought this was a natural question, but it seemed to take Ziba aback.
Perhaps I'd insulted her: male doctor, female nurse.

"No, not my brother. I guess I wanted to do something for my people. But
looking back now," she said and smiled, "maybe I chose nursing because I
knew it would get me out of the house. What I'd really like now, though, is a
job outdoors."

She gestured at the tennis players. Greek, English, French, and, I was sure,
Arabic were floating up from the courts.

"Maybe I can get a job here treating sprained ankles and tennis elbows.
You can coach me in some details, and I can pretend I'm an American trainer.
Then I'll use my influence to get you into the club to swim."

I enjoyed seeing Ziba in high spirits, hearing her talk about Hakkari and
Chicago. I knew Diyarbakir was painful for her, but I'd wondered why she
rarely said anything about her parents. Another kind of refugee fear—remembering what you'd lost. Back at my apartment, I remembered the two-person
club my eleven-year-old neighbor and I formed. Joan and I met in the park
behind our house, set up a pup tent, wrote down our club rules, spoke pig
Latin, which we said was Indian, and mocked boys in their cowboy outfits and
Little League uniforms. Our secret society was the product of two only children and one's failed desire. With no brother or sister to spy on, I investigated
my parents. I assumed they had some secret, and I wanted to know it. I lay in
the upstairs hallway and eavesdropped on adult conversations downstairs,
picked through bureau drawers and closets when my parents were out,
painstakingly unpacked trunks looking for old letters, pinched myself to stay
awake at night to hear my parents make love, but what I really wanted to find
was some solid object—a gun, say, or a hypodermic needle—I could touch, a
thing in itself, not speech or writing or noise. What I would do with this thing,
this fundamental fact, I didn't know. Some kind of emotional blackmail? I still
don't know. I never found anything, probably because my parents were so
ordinary, normal, moral—just the reasons I snuck around and searched for
their secret. They had me when they were in their late thirties, but instead of
lavishing attention and anxiety on me like most late-blooming parents they
continued on with their normal routines and assumed I'd be like them—no
odd desires or strange fears, no weird allergies or embarrassing idiosyncrasies.

When I decided my parents had no secrets—or none I'd ever know unless
one of them came to my room late at night and confessed—I focused on

myself and did a quick investigation. I pored over Mom's "Baby Book," went through boxes of old clothes and old toys, inspected report cards, stuck my finger into my orifices, asked my best friends if they didn't find me "odd"— but no uniqueness revealed itself. Fingerprints didn't satisfy me. Genes everybody had. I think I wanted some public recognition. But no matter how well I did on tests at school, I never heard a teacher say "she's special" or "Casey's one of a kind." The closest was my mother's comment when she found me looking out the window of our bathroom one night:

"What are you doing in here with the lights off?"

"Just looking out the window."

"Are you looking into the Krupniks' bathroom?"

"No, I'm just watching them watch television."

"Casey, you *are* a snoop."

My parents gave me a wider world to investigate when they sent me at twelve to a Catholic school. I'd never even been in a church. My father's name was inherited without red hair or freckles or faith. For some reason, I was a total convert, perhaps because the nuns and their rules were so strange to me. The sisters definitely had secrets, some of them in Latin, but even when they wore ordinary clothes they were a mystery to me, far beyond my powers of investigation. They didn't live in homes. Some of them moved from state to state. They never made mistakes. Despite my fascination, I never wanted to join up, maybe because I was certain nuns didn't snoop on each other.

At fourteen I got my wish for uniqueness, the inches that made me literally stand out in every crowd at school, stand above my parents, and leave the tennis court. In college I was big enough to be one of the Soldiers of Jesus—if their logic and Inquisition history hadn't made my faith disappear as surely as my coordination. When my acrophobia appeared, I wondered if it could be some tricky, delayed consequence of my desire to have a secret. Or, I thought, acrophobia could be my uniqueness, even rarer than my inches.

The weekend after our conversation at the tennis club, Ziba and I went to a Woody Allen movie. We were laughing ahead of the Greeks, who were reading the subtitles, or we were laughing alone. During the intermission that gives Greeks a chance to get a smoke, Ziba said they were missing a lot.

"That's one thing I miss about the States," I said, "native speech, recreational English, Woody-wit. Even overhearing blah-blah-blah. What about you?"

"I'd like to talk with my family, hear ordinary news, you know, what's in the pot, who's seeing who."

She sounded a little forlorn.

"Have you started to get homesick?" I asked.

Ziba used a Kurdish word and then tried to translate it: "Folk-sick."

"There must be people around you can speak dialect with," I said.

"Yes, but even in Kurmanji there are old feuds and warring groups here. Away from your home, you don't know who to trust. And besides, all the Kourds in Athens know about UNHCR. If they knew me and where I lived, they'd come around with requests. I hear enough of that at the office, words that Kourds used to be too proud to speak."

"Do you mean the pleading and begging?"

"Not just that. Some Kourds now give their children terrible names. I've heard 'Diel,' for 'prisoner,' and 'Awara,' for 'refugee.' In Iraq, kids were named 'Kimewe,' which means 'chemical.'"

Ziba spread and opened her palms in mystification.

"Why do you think they're doing that?" I asked.

"I don't know. Maybe the names will make the children *peshmergas* when they grow up. Maybe parents think this is the way to preserve the Kourdish language. It's about the only thing we have."

I thought of a question I probably should have asked Ziba earlier.

"Do Kurds hate to be translated?"

"Of course it shows we have no power. But applicants don't expect an American or Greek to speak their language."

"Would you rather not do this job, Ziba?"

"What else can I do? I can't even empty bedpans in a Greek hospital. I miss my patients. I could do things for them. Real things. Change dressings, administer meds, when we had them. I could change people, heal them. Now I just repeat their words, change them into English. And every time I say 'torture'..."

"I'm sorry, Ziba."

"You shouldn't be. If I didn't have this job, I'd be changing sheets in some Omonia Square hotel."

We both looked at the blank screen. The couples around us were discussing the movie in loud, fast Greek. They pronounced "Woody" as "woodee." I asked Ziba if there was Saturday-night itchiness at the Flea Palace.

"Some people hang around the steps and buy themselves an ice cream on a stick. The Chechen and Georgian men—at least that's what I think they are—go up to the roof, drink vodka, and throw the bottles down into the alley."

"Some of them must speak English."

"Not to me. I pretend I was raised by wolves. I'm not ready for men," she said. Then she laughed, "But you don't have any excuse for a white shoe Saturday—unless there's someone back in the States."

"'White shoe Saturday?' Is this a Kurdish expression?"

"Nurse talk. It's what we called a Saturday night out with someone who wore the uniform."

"Rick could have had a Delta uniform, as much time as he spent in the air. But he's been gone for more than a year. Maybe it was a stewardess or someone else in uniform."

"What about here?"

"Do you see anyone sitting behind me, even four rows back?"

"You can't get away with that excuse."

"I've been out a few times, once with a Greek lawyer Erica introduced me to. We had a good time, but at the end of the evening he started asking questions about the high incidence of AIDS in America. I also had dinner a couple of times with an American classics professor I met at a bookstore. He's a nice guy, interesting on almost any American subject, but he can't stand living Greeks. He talks about them in this loud, carrying voice in tavernas, and I cringe. This is a man who actually uses the word 'scoundrel.' There's no stopping him, so I stopped seeing him."

"'Scoundrel?'" Ziba asked.

"It's an old word, found mostly in novels: a very bad person, dishonest. Like 'villain.'"

"'Villains' I know," she said. I could see her hand move toward her abdomen and stop.

"Villains, yes," I said and put my hand on her's. Ziba looked at the blank screen and began speaking in a low urgent tone, as if my word "villain" had opened her wound, as if she worried Greeks would be back and overhear her before she finished.

"They weren't just after information, you know. They were trying to prove something. That's what they were doing. Prove that a Kourdish woman naked was beneath their sexual interest. At least, the usual."

I was surprised Ziba decided to talk about what she wanted to forget. "What do you mean?" I asked. Maybe she'd been raped, but had wanted to conceal it. In Ziba's second of hesitation, I also realized that rape was rarely a fear of mine, not one my towering body recognized, not the persistent fear other women talked about.

"Something I didn't tell you in the interview."

I kept silent, waited for Ziba to volunteer whatever she wanted.

"When they sawed me across the rope, I was afraid of myself, what I was going to do, what I would say. But I didn't tell them what they wanted to hear. I screamed and cried, but I didn't tell. Then the leader said, 'Let's cut this donkey-rider the other way.'"

"You mean ..."

"*Maleesta*," she said, Greek for "yes," the first time either of us had used Greek in a serious manner. Perhaps Ziba wanted to tell the rest in our secret language, but knew I didn't have the vocabulary. "Yes, he was going to pull that goat rope back and forth between my legs. I knew I wouldn't be able to stand it, Casey. I'd seen a girl with almost no pubic hair in a Chicago emergency room. After being raped, she was mutilated with a tree branch. It was horrible. When they took me off the rope, I told them what they wanted."

"You couldn't help it Ziba. Don't blame yourself."

"I spoke out of a future I imagined, Casey. I can't help but feel guilty about that. Kourds are supposed to be courageous. *Peshmergas* face much worse. I was afraid that rope was something I'd never recover from, like a clitorectomy."

The nurse's exactitude. I squeezed Ziba's hand, but didn't look at her. I was afraid I'd see tears rolling down her cheeks. I wanted Ziba to be the woman who stood in front of my desk and dared me to refuse her, maybe a woman who doesn't confess her secret to me.

Ziba took her hand from beneath mine and pinched the skin on the back of my hand. I looked at her then, and she smiled.

"Great Saturday night conversation, huh?" she said. "You didn't come to Greece for six-day weeks of suffering."

Greeks were making their way back to their seats. The lights were going down, and the movie was about to continue. But that was an excuse. I had plenty of time to talk to Ziba later as we walked arm-in-arm like Greek women to our trolley stop. As we argued about the movie—Ziba had no use for ineffectual Woody—I felt guilty about Ziba's apology for spoiling a work-week altruist's Saturday night. But I didn't tell her about my acrophobia or confess my first thought when Sam Roberts called to report the opening at UNHCR: the Acropolis, the high city. What better place to understand the ancient Greek *phobos*, to overcome my fright of heights? Except for pointed Mt. Likavitos at its center and, somewhat lower, the plateau of the Acropolis, Athens is not a high city. Built low to withstand earthquakes, Athens has no skyscrapers. A perfect place to live and work and choose when to take the cable car to Likavitos or walk up the steep, narrow steps to the Parthenon.

I also didn't tell Ziba about my initial attraction to the Kurds in the book of photographs Erica loaned me my first week. Beautiful color shots of the few surviving nomads, their huge, almost-black communal tents, donkeys tethered to the stakes. Sheep and goats graze in nearby pastures that have never been plowed or settled. In the background, always mountains, purple and blue, some snow-topped. A woman wearing more colors than a clown swings a heavy wooden mallet, hammering in a tent stake. Another woman, sinews visible in her neck and arms, lifts wood onto a donkey. Two children in skullcaps play a game with string, a kind of cat's cradle. Men in jackets that look like football players' shoulder pads drive sheep across a white-water stream. In their bright, layered dresses and baggy, sashed pants, Kurds remind me of gypsies, but without the squalor or suffering. The kids are bright-eyed, expectant as they gaze directly into the camera. Over the centuries, Persians, Arabs, and Ottomans forced most nomadic Kurds to retreat high into the mountains, where they built stone and mud villages like Native Americans' pueblos. The Kurds' homes are stacked on each other, one's roof another's balcony, no railings. Preschoolers walk on the edge of thousand-foot drops. A man rides a donkey side-saddle toward one of these villages. He seems oblivious to the chasm he's facing. Two photographs show a wedding celebration, women in brocade dresses and spangled shawls walking to the bride's village home. Above the women, hundreds of arm-linked men crowd on the edge of a ledge. In the background, snowy crags and immense gorges. Since looking at those photographs, I've read numerous documents about the Kurds, examined their files, listened to their stories, and talked with Ziba about why people moved from their villages. Viewing the photographs the first time, though, I wanted to know why people stayed in those villages, how Kurds lived without fear on the edge of those abysses. I also wanted to visit one of those mountain villages more frightening than any skyscraper.

Those are the things I should have told Ziba after the movies. As far as I knew, I was her only friend in Athens. And she was my only friend. I'd gone to one meeting of AWOG—American Women of Greece—but the matrons there were AWOL for a night from their Greek husbands, the former *kamakees*. Ziba had revealed a painful private secret, and yet I concealed my phobia. I was chagrined to have a fear I could, as the psychologist said, "work around" and maybe, as I hoped, "overcome." Ziba was compelled to leave her home, I'd chosen to work in Athens. Perhaps I felt guilty about a deeply personal fear, internal, mysterious. Ziba had scars to prove her fear was public, political. Those scars are still raw. My scares can be avoided by staying low. Lying in bed, I feel low, ashamed. Three men dressed in doctors' white coats come into the room. They are very polite, but I can't understand the questions they're asking me. They apologize when they fold me over a tennis net. They must know what they're doing because I don't feel any pain, mostly anger that they're controlling my limbs. The men seem to know my body, know that talk is close to my skin, that talk is what I've been taught to do. It's what I do for patients when meds don't work. Talk is the drug that can ease future pain. The lies I tell patients don't work with the men. They know their business, their art, the sawing and the stopping. Somehow they know exactly when I don't lie. My voice must have betrayed me because I don't speak their language. A translator might have protected my secret.

"Beasts" I thought when I seemed to be awake, but that was wrong. "Animals" would have fucked me. The men were men, human. They had imagination like the carvers of alphabets and inventors of lasers. They were capable of vicarious pleasure and simulated sex. They were efficient torturers because they'd managed to suppress testosterone or deny an old evolutionary urge. From this came their fear. They wanted me to fear being raped, but they feared doing it. Raping me would have awarded me a certain status, a basic natural connection with them, a human intimacy. The men also knew they could not fuck me for as long as they could saw me. These men were not "beasts." They were thinkers, advanced humans. Their detachment and objectivity and functionalism were, I realized when wide awake, the foundations of law, but turned to cruelty instead of protection.

Chapter 6

United Nations High Commissioner for Refugees
Case: 98-V-256
Applicant: Jalal Kaya
National or Ethnic Origin: Turkish Kurd
Examiner: Casey Mahan
Translator: Siamand Yilmaz
Transcript by: AN, 6-9-98

"Do you require a translator?"

"He say yes."

"Do you have documents to show me besides the ones in your file?"

"No."

"Mr. Kaya, your application states you came here because you were tortured by the police."

"Yes."

"Please tell me what they did to you."

"Police make me lose my head."

"I don't understand."

"Sorry. Mr. Kaya say I lose my hand."

"How did this happen?"

"The police doctor cut off."

"No, no. Police do auto lift. After, doctor do."

"You speak English, Mr. Kaya?"

"Very bad, but this man do mistakes."

"Please add to or correct Siamand if you want. Do you understand?"

"Yes."

"So police crushed your hand with an auto jack and then it had to be amputated."

"Mr. Kaya say this is so."

"Why did the police do that to you?"

"Mr. Kaya say because I do bombs for PKK."

"No, no. This man do too big mistakes. Police says I do bombs. Police says, not I. Understand?"

"Yes, Mr. Kaya."

"I no do bombs, understand?"

"Yes."

"Now I speak for I, understand?"

"No."

"This man go now."

"I see. Yes. You may leave now, Siamand. So, Mr. Kaya, I need to know why you got in trouble with the police. Do you understand?

"No understand trouble."

"A big problem."

"Okay."

"Have you been a member of the PKK?"

"No."

"Why did the Turkish police believe you were a member?"

"I no know."

"Can you think of any reason?"

"Maybe I do something for PKK man. I know police watch I and watch I at work."

"What do you do?"

"Keece."

"Keece?"

"This."

Let the record show that Mr. Kaya held up a key in his right hand.

"Did the police accuse you of breaking into buildings?"

"They say nothing. After watch I, they use machine to make I say I do bombs."

"But you claim you don't understand why?"

"Maybe PKK man have I make key. Maybe some man say I PKK."

"But you don't know for sure?"

"No. No know who is police, who is PKK. Never know. Know only police lose hand."

"After this did you fear the police?"

"Yes. I have now one hand."

"If you're given refugee status in Greece, what job can you do here?"

"I no do work. I no stay here."

"Where could you be relocated?"

"What?"

"Where would you go?"

"Canada. Brother of my father's son live there."

A small, gaunt man of fifty-five, Mr. Kaya was one of my first applicants and one reason Ziba was hired to replace Siamand and the other translators. Only Mr. Kaya's thick black mustache looked healthy. His eyes were dilated, as if he'd been staring at the sun. His stump looked as if it had been sewn up by a seamstress. The skin was puckered, the stitches irregular and raw, the color black and purple. When he showed me his key, he was like a three-year-old unable to name some treasure he'd found. I remembered how my father used to describe his job sorting mail: "Busy as a one-armed paperhanger." After Siamand left, Mr. Kaya leaned forward in his chair, eager to close the gap in understanding between us. Even when mystified, he spoke with a firm, guttural voice.

Although Mr. Kaya had difficulty telling his story, his case was strong. The documents in his file demonstrated earlier problems with the Turkish police. Whether Mr. Kaya was rightfully or falsely accused of helping the PKK, he had been illegally treated. And if the police crushed one hand with a jack, Mr. Kaya was, I judged, logically fearful they might come back for the other hand in the future. The Director approved my recommendation.

I had to review Mr. Kaya's transcript in November when the Greek police caught him inside a grocery store at 3 a.m. Mr. Kaya was practicing his trade after all. Now he was in Lavrion, a small town south of Athens where the police detained obvious "economic migrants"—the groups of twenty and thirty Indians or Pakistanis found in cargo holds—and applicants accused of committing crimes while awaiting our decision or relocation.

"If we send undesirables to other countries," the Director told me, "we harm the opportunities for future refugees."

"Mr. Kaya may have been hungry. His arrest doesn't automatically rescind his status here, does it?"

"No, but when you reinterview him you should treat his original statements with more suspicion and reconsider your recommendation."

"Where will the interview be?"

"The police could bring him up here, but they prefer that we go to Lavrion."

"Mr. Kaya's English is very poor. I assume I can take Ziba with me."

"Of course, but you are responsible for your own transportation."

Even on my law-clerk salary, the ride down the coast of Attiki toward Sounion was well worth the bus fare. In the November sun, the deserted beaches were clean and the Aegean was a dark blue I'd never seen last summer. The scenery was all new to Ziba, who hadn't been out of Athens since her arrival in August. "*Thalassa*," I told her, "sea" in Greek, one of the few words I knew that she didn't. "Look at all those hotels with no one in them," she said.

South of Lagonisi, the bus turned inland and started climbing into the mountains. Ziba had the window seat.

"Just like Kurdistan," I said.

"Anatolia, maybe."

"What about Vermont or Montana? They've got real mountains, and I could get you in," I told her again. "It's easy for nurses and physical therapists. We need you to care for aging natives, you know, do jobs Americans don't want."

"Or aren't qualified for?"

"For those we bring in Pakistani programmers and Indian anesthesiologists and Egyptian pathologists, the Third World's best and brightest."

"I don't want to go back," Ziba said.

"I'd hate to see you go, but there you wouldn't have to live in the Flea Palace."

"Here I'm closer to my family."

"Is this a well-founded desire?"

Ziba laughed. "Probably not. But Kourds can't afford to have strong personal desires, you know, just the desire for change."

"You'll be here a long time waiting for Turkey to change."

"Maybe Kourds will find something that Europeans and Americans desire. Some Kourds say the only reason for the safe zone in northern Iraq is the possibility of oil up near Zarkho. If the streams from Mt. Ararat or the waters of Lake Van could cure cancer, the West might protect Turkish Kourds."

"Then a Kurdistan?"

"That would take more than charity and Western self-interest. We'd have to discover how to cause cancer."

Ziba's remark seemed a cruel thing for a nurse to say. I felt the cruelty was partly self-directed, tribe-directed. Because Kurds ignored property ownership and national boundaries when they were nomads, Turkish Kurds now have no base of power, only movable bases for guerrilla groups like the PKK.

Greeks had lived and mined in Lavrion for four thousand years. With the silver and most of the lead gone, Lavrion was decaying, just the place to put Third World aliens. From the bus station, we walked past boarded-up shops and peeling taverna signs on the way to the detention center, an old brick building that looked like an abandoned factory and smelled like a subway station.

Some families came to the office in Athens. The detainees were all men, six or eight to a cell. They looked like the prisoners Castro sent us during the Mariel boat lift, more ragged than the people at the office and even noisier. The detainees were also hopeless. They shouted sexual invitations to us in English— "Come live with me." "Let me be your slave."—and in languages neither Ziba nor I understood. I knew many of these desperate men left their countries to support wives and children and parents back home, but UNHCR could do nothing for them, would never see them.

Mr. Kaya was brought into an interview room, and I introduced him to Ziba. He looked at her suspiciously and said, "The number one man do many mistakes."

"Yes, I know," I said and assured him that Ziba's English was excellent. He spoke to her in Kurmanji, as if anyone whose English was excellent might not speak his dialect. She replied, he seemed satisfied, and I switched on my tape recorder.

I asked him about personal background in his Questionnaire, the leftist political groups referred to in his documents. With Ziba instead of Siamand translating, Mr. Kaya could supplement his Narrative with details of how the police mangled his hand: "First they put my fingers between the jack and wall.

Then my whole hand flat. Finally, they turned my hand, and I heard my bones snapping like dry sticks."

With Ziba translating, I could also ask more probing questions.

"Did the police accuse you of supplying bomb materials to others?"

"No. They said I made the bombs."

"Why did the police suspect a locksmith of making bombs?"

"How do I know? They said they watched me work. I know nothing about dynamite. I can't make a bomb. Now I can't even make a key."

"If that's true, you should have no fear of persecution from the police in the future."

I wasn't proud of this, but whether or not Mr. Kaya had been making bombs the Turkish police might welcome him back as an example, like Saudi thieves without hands.

A loud and long response came back. Ziba said, "Mr. Kaya is angry. He says that you know nothing about the Turkish police and what they do to Kourds."

"I've seen the lacerations on your abdomen, haven't I?"

Ziba was silent. This seemed to worry Mr. Kaya, as if Ziba wasn't translating a remark directed at him. He didn't understand what I'd said.

"No I, no PKK," he said in English. "You understand?"

"Yes, I understand," I said, "but don't locksmiths have machines they could use for bomb-making?"

Ziba translated.

"No, no," he said in English, and "Not for bombs" through Ziba.

I really didn't have anything on Mr. Kaya—just my unlimited freedom to ask questions, a passing knowledge of the Unabomber case, and the Director's desire to rescind his status.

"Bombs require precision, just like keys. Why couldn't you use your lathe to machine the parts?"

After Ziba translated, Mr. Kaya leaned back in his chair and laughed.

"Locksmiths know nothing about detonators."

This sentence would never have come through Siamand. I asked Ziba if Mr. Kaya used the technical term for detonator in Kurmanji. She said he had.

"Why," I asked Mr. Kaya, "does a locksmith know the word for detonator?"

When Ziba translated that, Mr. Kaya spoke to her in Kurmanji and she replied to him without translating.

"What did he say?" I asked.

"He didn't answer your question. Instead, he asked me why I was translating these questions for you."

"And what did you tell him?"

"That this is my job."

It was hard to tell how much of this exchange Mr. Kaya understood, but he spoke to Ziba in Kurmanji. Then, for my benefit, he said, "She no Kourd." With his good hand, he reached over and tapped Ziba lightly on the shoulder, a condescending gesture of dismissal, something a teacher might do to a student who has performed poorly. Then Mr. Kaya turned to me and held up his stump, "Tourkish police do this. No more keece."

"Please be calm, Mr. Kaya. I have to ask you these questions because you broke into a store."

"No more keece, no more keece," he shouted and lapsed into Kurmanji for a few words as he stood up, leaned over my desk, and shook his stump in my face. I was afraid he was going to hit me. I pushed my chair back away from him, and with the distance realized that Mr. Kaya wouldn't hit a woman. And a millisecond later, that he couldn't hit me, not with his stump, not the way it was sewn up, still unhealed and now looking infected.

After my second of fear, I pitied Mr. Kaya. He was harmless, helpless. Why didn't he deserve refuge?

As Mr. Kaya continued to wave his stump in the air like a hammer without a head, his long shirtsleeve slid down a little, and Ziba said *Kitah kato to haeri* very fast, running the words together. I thought it was some Kurdish expression, like "Oh no" or even "Oh shit." Mr. Kaya paid no attention to her. Perhaps he thought she was translating what he had yelled. He kept brandishing his stump and shouting "No more keece." Then I realized Ziba was speaking Greek: "look down hand" or "look down arm," since "hand" and "arm" are the same word in Greek. I was slow to register—because it was Greek, because Ziba had never intervened in an interview.

On Mr. Kaya's exposed forearm were scars about the size of a dime, but irregularly shaped, most like miniature tadpoles.

"Please sit down, Mr. Kaya," I told him, "I understand 'no more keece.' Please be calm. Just a few more questions."

Ziba translated and he sat down. Brushing his mustache with his good hand, he seemed satisfied he'd made his point.

In formal English I hoped would keep Mr. Kaya calm, I told Ziba, "Please inform the applicant that he is required to answer queries through the translator because he lacks the linguistic capability to respond adequately in

English."

Ziba translated and Mr. Kaya nodded, grudgingly I felt.

"Now ask him what those marks are on his left arm," I said to Ziba.

"What marks?" the answer came back through her.

"The scars on your arm. Roll up your sleeve, please."

He looked hard at Ziba, then at me, and finally rolled up his sleeve. The scars were numerous up to his elbow, more sparse on his upper arm.

"How did you get those?"

"The police did this. They threw some kind of poison liquid on me."

"Please let me see your other arm."

Ziba had to help him roll up his sleeve. There were no scars on his right arm.

"The police didn't do anything to this arm?"

"No."

"Why not?"

Mr. Kaya stood up again, but he spoke in Kurmanji. Ziba translated, "I don't know why not. Ask the police why. Why do you always ask me why?"

I didn't explain that asking why was my job.

Leaving the detention center, I thanked Ziba for directing my eyes and told her I thought Mr. Kaya lost his hand and got all those irregularly shaped scars when a bomb he was making went off. Ziba didn't respond, but I didn't ask her why.

Now I was the interpreter.

Was Ziba silent because she had violated her neutrality as a translator? Or because she preferred not to confirm or deny my conclusion? Was she silent because she felt guilty about betraying a fellow Kurd? Perhaps Mr. Kaya surrendered any claim to loyalty when he accused her of not being a Kurd. It was, after all, his anger at me that betrayed him.

Ziba had no reason to fear this one-handed man, and yet she spoke in Greek. I wondered why and wondered even more why she chose to speak. Had she done this for me, protecting a friend from a bad decision? Despite Mr. Kaya's arrest and the Director's obvious desire, I'd been ready to reaffirm my original recommendation, unduly influenced by Mr. Kaya's rage and my pity. If Ziba was not protecting me, perhaps she'd spoken to protect other Kurds, refugees who deserved relocation more than Mr. Kaya did. Or did she speak for herself, separating the true victim of torture from the imposter?

Why didn't I ask Ziba these questions?

Because I was thankful for her help, because I didn't want to make her

self-conscious about providing it, and, I suppose, because I might need it in
the future.

Although I couldn't be certain that Mr. Kaya had been a bombmaker, I recommended that Mrs. Constantinou rescind his status. Mr. Kaya would not be
on the list of relocated refugees for whom I was responsible.

Three weeks after Mr. Kaya's reinterview, Mrs. Constantinou called me to
her office. She handed me a letter signed by Mr. Kaya and obviously written by
a helper, who was not much better in English than Mr. Kaya. This was a document. In it he accused Ziba of mistranslating and thus making him look like a
member of the PKK when, in fact, Kurds who'd been in our office suspected
that she was a PKK "agnet." He also recommended that she be fired.

"Kaya is not a very pleasant person, is he?" Mrs. Constantinou said.

"No, but he has his reasons."

"I have looked at his file again. I think you made the right recommendation."

"Actually, I believe the cousin in Canada may be relieved by a denial."

"What I am more interested in are these accusations against Miss Ziba."

"Mr. Kaya is confusing Ziba with Siamand."

"So you think this charge about mistranslation is untrue?"

"I think so, yes, but how can I be sure? Except for 'fear,' 'yes,' and 'no,' I
don't speak Kurmanji."

"We could bring in Siamand to listen to the tape."

"There was no tape down in Lavrion."

"No tape? Why did you not bring your recorder?"

"I thought there'd be one there."

"I see. To protect ourselves, we should always take a recorder along for
future reinterviews."

"I understand," I said.

As Mrs. Constantinou wrote a note to herself, I knew the fear Mr. Kaya
must have felt when he first lied to me. What will the next question be? Will I
need to lie again? Sitting in front of my desk, Mr. Kaya had a translator to send
his lies through. I wanted the Director and her desk to disappear. If she finds
out I'm lying, I'll be fired. But she won't find out because only three people
saw the recorder. Mrs. Constantinou has the negative recommendation she
wants from me. She won't call in Mr. Kaya, the Greek criminal and possible
Turkish criminal, to testify against me. I can tell Ziba I lied about the tape. She
said nothing tying Mr. Kaya to the PKK, and yet I didn't want the Director listening to that interview, hearing Ziba's Greek. Initially, I lied to protect my

friend, her job at UNHCR, but maybe it was also myself I was protecting, my reliance on Ziba to see the secret Mr. Kaya had up his sleeve.

"One other thing," Mrs. Constantinou continued. "When I received Kaya's letter, I reviewed Miss Ziba's file."

Mrs. Constantinou paused, as if I was supposed to guess what was on her mind, something I'd missed in my original interview of Ziba. But by now that interview had blended into many other conversations with Ziba, both inside and outside the office. I didn't want to refer to something that wasn't in the transcript. I waited for Mrs. Constantinou to identify the matters she wanted to talk about.

"You know, of course, that the PKK has female recruits, including guerrillas. Do you think Miss Ziba could be PKK?"

Now I was the one being reinterviewed, though Mrs. Constantinou didn't have a tape recorder running.

"I very much doubt it. She was educated in the U.S. She's a nurse. From what Nikos tells me, PKK come in with false documents. Ms. Mamozin had no documents with her."

"This negative proves nothing."

"It's also impossible to prove a negative, that she's not affiliated with the PKK."

"Is there any possibility that her translations are helping Kurds who may be terrorists?"

Now I was silent, as helpless as Mr. Kaya. I couldn't tell the Director that Ziba undermined the case of an applicant very likely to be PKK. I couldn't say that Ziba is a friend I trust and that she dislikes translating.

"I've never seen any evidence," I said.

"But now we must both be alert to that possibility. We would be in serious trouble with the Ministry if they found out we have a PKK agent on our staff."

"I understand."

"One last thing. When you interviewed Miss Ziba, why did you not ask her about fear of future persecution?"

"As I remember, after the police in Diyarbakir tortured her they told her not to come back."

"Yes but earlier in the interview, she mentioned an uncle in Istanbul. Miss Ziba might well return to Turkey, if not to Diyarbakir. I would like to talk with her about that."

"We'd be losing a very good translator."

"Perhaps, but UNHCR cannot afford to depend on a refugee."

I thought my interview was over. But as I was leaving the Director's office, she said, "I have to talk with Kaya. He has a final appeal with me once the Ministry begins deportation proceedings."

Applicants are waiting in the hall. Oh no, oh shit. I feel sick to my stomach. I'm in trouble now. In my four months at UNHCR, I'd never reinterviewed an applicant who'd been arrested. I didn't know about the Ministry's appeal process. The Director won't weigh and balance and decide whether or not to talk with Mr. Kaya. She has no choice. Greek law and due process require it.

I unlock my door, sit at my desk. I'm definitely in trouble. Not like being questioned by the Turkish police or being detained in Lavrion or being interviewed in this office, but still serious trouble. Legal trouble that might force me to relocate. "You have to suppress your emotions," the Director told me in training, "to protect yourself." But not if it's the examiner who's in trouble. I look at the tape recorder. The translator. Ziba is really in trouble. Protecting her job, I'd endangered her life, her status and safety in Greece. Like Mr. Kaya, she can be deported. She may be tortured—again. She could be imprisoned, raped. Scoundrels, villains. I was afraid of what the Director would do to me. Looking at the translator's empty chair, I was terrified of what could happen to my friend. I'd put her in danger. I saw the festering wound on Ziba's belly. I saw Mr. Kaya's criss-crossed stump, then pictured his good hand cuffed to Ziba's thin wrist, two Kurds sitting on the floor of a Turkish prison cell, neither speaking Kurmanji to each other, both forced to speak Turkish to their captors and judges. They wouldn't listen. After judgment was pronounced, Ziba disappeared from my sight.

Chapter 7

"Fear must be reasonable. Exaggerated fear, however, may be well-founded if the state of mind can be regarded as justified. In such a case, facts established in the Questionnaire and documentary evidence are particularly useful to the examiner."

Handbook on Procedures and Criteria for Determining Refugee Status, p. 12

After the Director's interrogation of me, I told Ziba about the trouble I'd caused us by lying.

"*Then vleppo*," she said, as quickly as she'd spoken Greek in Lavrion. "I never saw a tape recorder," she translated and added.

"You don't have to do this, Ziba. If you lie to the Director and she believes Kaya, you'll be in real danger."

We were sitting across from each other in a smoke-clouded café, one of the less appealing facts of Greek winter life. Ziba took a drag on her cigarette.

"Who will Mrs. Constantinou believe? Who does she have reason to believe, a man being deported or her two employees?"

"Us, I hope."

"That's right. Anyway, I'm not so worried about the job. The Greek family I've been talking to has decided to hire me as a live-in tutor to teach their two children English."

This struck me as very strange, the world woven in an impenetrable design. A Kurd was teaching English to Greeks.

"Maybe that's the job I should have. I could moonlight writing Narratives for applicants."

"I'm sorry I caused you this trouble, Casey. I know how much you love this job. You have to keep it. You're careful and fair."

I thanked Ziba for the compliment, then told her the news I'd been delaying: the Director might be asking about her uncle in Istanbul.

Ziba put both her elbows on the table and leaned toward me.

"What does she want to know?"

"She thinks you might return to Istanbul and live safely with him."

This time there was no pause, no cigarette to the mouth.

"My uncle was murdered during my junior year at college."

"Jesus, Ziba, I'm sorry."

"It's okay. How could you know? I never told you."

"Do you want to talk about it?"

"Not with the Director."

"Tell me," I said.

Ziba put out her cigarette and looked me in the face the way she had at her interview, as if only fierceness could get her through the story.

"He was very strict with me, but also kind and a very energetic supporter of Kourdish music. He sold tapes in the back of his bakery. The music wasn't political. Most didn't have words, just instruments. But Kourdish instruments, Kourdish sounds. One night he didn't come home. He was found shot in the back of the head. All the tapes were smashed. Money was in the cash register. Pita bread had been placed in his hands and stuffed in his mouth. The police called it a 'mystery killing,' but it was no mystery to us. Not after hundreds of 'mystery killings' of Kourds in Istanbul, thousands in the country. As my uncle's funeral was ending, someone began playing a Kourdish tape on a boom box. The police smashed it, and a riot started. Two other Kourds were killed. The riot was reported in the Istanbul newspapers as a feud between Kourdish groups. This was a joke, because one thing Kourds agree on is our music."

"I am sorry, Ziba. It seems the more questions I ask, the more pain I cause you."

"Almost every Kourd has this pain. I think you have a saying. Something about skeletons."

"Skeletons in the closet."

"Yes, for us the phrase is real. Sometimes we're afraid to bury our dead, afraid that more will die, as at my uncle's funeral."

Ziba sat back in her chair and took a sip of the tea she always ordered.

"If the newspapers covered this," I said, "you'll have a document to show the Director."

"If she insists, I guess I can have my friend Nurettin get me a copy and send it."

"I've seen the posters up around Athens. 'Tourists in Turkey Support Torture.' How would you feel if I went to Istanbul to look around? If the Director is going to fire me, I want to see some of the country and talk to Kurds there before I have to leave Greece."

"A weekend won't support much torture, but Istanbul is a dangerous city. Not long ago, the PKK bombed the covered bazaar and killed two tourists."

"Why?"

"To reduce foreign money, put the government in trouble. If I were you, I wouldn't go."

Ziba frowned and shook her head. "No, I wouldn't go."

"But millions of tourists visit and come back every year."

"They don't go to see Kourds. If you ask some taxi driver to show you where Kourds live, you could end up at a police station."

"What about your friend? Could he show me around?"

"He probably could, but his English is very basic. You won't learn much from Nurettin. But if you insist on going, I can call him and let him know you're coming."

I wasn't ready to retrace Ziba's route to Athens, but I wanted to see the city through which many of our applicants passed and to which thousands of internal refugees had fled over the last twenty years. Istanbul was also supposed to be the foundation of Turkey's application for membership in the EU, for refuge in Europe. With just my American passport, I boarded an Olympic Airways flight at 2:30 on a Friday afternoon and ninety minutes later landed in Istanbul. I paid twenty dollars for an entry visa, took a taxi to the Green House Hotel in the Sultanhamet area, presented my American Express card, and changed some dollars into lira.

Nurettin picked me up Saturday morning in a car so old and battered that the make was unidentifiable. Since I knew Istanbul was built on hills, and I'd seen high bridges over the Bosporus on my way in from the airport, I worried that Nurettin's car might not make the tour. "Sorry, sorry," Nurettin said as I bumped my knees against the glove compartment. Soft-spoken and quiet for long periods, Nurettin was the definition of bespectacled. His narrow face and old wire-frame glasses made him look like a middle-aged antiquarian bookseller though he was about Ziba's age. He drove and announced. "Here rich Turks live." "Here poor Turks live." "Greeks." "Poor Turks." Nurettin didn't translate the settings that he identified into historical or political stories. Nurettin also didn't want to talk about himself. "Yes," he was from a village in the east. "Yes," his village had been destroyed while he was in school in Ankara. "No, never" could he go back. "My car," he said, "here I have this car." Between his short utterances, Nurettin coughed and apologized, coughed and apologized.

"Are you okay?"

"Yes, in summer. But this city is very bad for us. Water is in the air."

Then there was rain in the air. Maybe it was the rain or Nurettin's smeary wipers, but I couldn't tell Kurds from Turks in Kanarya, a shack-city on the outskirts of Istanbul. The low sprawl of jerry-built shelters looked like a film I'd seen of Mexico City, where indigenous people pick over garbage, use it to build lean-tos, and eat it. The "houses" here were like sculptures made of found objects—sheetrock covered with plastic tarps, plywood propped up with rocks, a few metal roofs, an occasional cement-block mansion, usually without windows. Doors were cardboard or canvas. No electricity. Wood smoke in the air. Water and sewage were running in ditches on both sides of the mud streets. Without foundations, the temporary dwellings looked like they could float away with another day's rain. Sluing along in low gear, Nurettin distinguished between "Anatolians"—peasant farmers—and Kurds, which the Turkish government called "mountain Turks." The few people I saw buying goods under makeshift awnings or avoiding puddles in the streets looked the same. The women tried to keep dry under layered shawls. Men wore thrift-shop bellbottoms and plastic jackets. They all seemed too beaten-down to get to the border and cross the Evros. Racist politics had caused scavenger economics, but UNHCR didn't and couldn't or wouldn't trace poverty back to its cause. The rain also reminded me of the link between international politics and macro economics: both Kurdish and Turkish farmers were displaced when Turkey built huge dams in the southeast to provide energy for western cities and control water to southern states like Syria and Iraq.

"How can you tell Turks from Kurds?" I asked Nurettin. "From what they wear?" Maybe there was some secret code in the scarves and headwraps, the way women cut their hair or men clipped their mustaches.

Nurettin touched his cheek. "By heads. Turks are round, Kourds are like knife. Also by color. We have blood."

Nurettin had sharp features, but I didn't see the red in his skin, not like Ziba's and other Kurds I'd interviewed. Perhaps Nurettin spent too much time indoors or in his car.

"Can a Turk see this color when you talk to him?"

Nurettin chuckled and made a growling sound. "A blind Turk knows my 'grr' when I speak."

Perhaps that's why Nurettin didn't have much to say.

"Yes," Nurettin knew Kurds who lived in Kanarya. "Yes," he could take me to a friend's house, but the family didn't speak English. "Are you sure?" Nurettin asked, looking at my low shoes. "Yes, I'd like to see inside," I told him, even if I had to rely on Nurettin to translate.

His car felt like a flat-bottomed boat as he slipped through muddy corners and dropped into puddled potholes. No street signs, no numbers, no way back without Nurettin. His friend's house had a tin roof, plywood walls, cardboard floor, two windows covered with plastic, and two rooms. An elderly man and woman wrapped in blankets sat cross-legged on beds in the back room. They didn't move as Nurettin explained my presence to his friend, Abdullah, and his wife, Leya, both about forty-five though the dim light may have made them look older. Neither smiled or extended a hand, and Leya didn't look at me.

Why had I come here?

I could have imagined the inside from the outside. I didn't need to force myself into this makeshift home, where someone's parents were waiting to die. For some reason, I thought of Ziba's parents in Diyarbakir.

As Nurettin, presumably, explained my job at the United Nations, I tried to imagine questions I could ask Leya and Abdullah. Not where they slept. Not how they all ate with only two chairs and a small table. Not why they were wearing their parkas inside.

"What jobs do you have?" I asked.

Abdullah spoke for about three minutes.

"No papers, no jobs," Nurettin translated.

"How do you get food?"

After about two minutes of back and forth discussion with Nurettin, Abdullah held out his hands. They were so white they looked bleached.

"Sometimes Abdullah washes dishes in the city," Nurettin said, "and brings home food."

Abdullah waited for Nurettin to finish, then stuck his hands back in his coat pockets. Before I could think of another question, Leya thrust out her hands, still without looking at me. They too were unnaturally white and wrinkled. She quickly put them in her pockets.

"Two days each week," Nurettin explained, "Leya cleans hotel rooms."

"Do they ever think about leaving Turkey?"

Nurettin didn't translate. He didn't even answer me. He just nodded at the elderly couple sitting on the beds in the back room. They couldn't swim. Without working papers, Abdullah and Leya would never make enough to pay a smuggler four or five thousand dollars. I felt my face reddening like a Kurd's. Now everyone in the house, except the old people on the beds, was ashamed.

"Please thank your friends for answering my questions," I told Nurettin. There was nothing more to learn, nothing I could do. I felt like my feet, slimy and cold.

On the way back to my hotel in Sultanhamet, we drove through an old section Nurettin identified as Sulukule, his neighborhood. The rain had stopped and a few people were in the narrow streets between three-storey wood and stucco tenements that may never have been painted. Women were buying bread out of baskets and tea from a man with a giant urn strapped to his back. A boy was selling dresses from a pushcart. Two men were eating some kind of takeaway in front of a storefront "restaurant." Laundry was strung above the streets in a futile attempt to dry in the afternoon humidity.

"Gypsies and Kourds live here," Nurettin said.

Again I asked him the difference. Again he chuckled and said, "Gypsies steal with hands, Kourds steal with feet. The government says this."

"I don't understand."

"Gypsies want only to eat. Kourds want ground."

There was no ground here, only cobbled streets and narrow, cracked sidewalks. Over-the-Rhine, the Appalachian and African-American ghetto of Cincinnati, was upscale housing compared to Sulukule. In a courtyard, though, I glimpsed some people dancing. When I pointed to them, Nurettin stopped the car. There were six teenagers. Dressed in sneakers, jeans, and sweatshirts, they could have been Americans, except their arms were linked and they were circling and kicking like Greek folk dancers I'd seen in the Plaka.

"Are these kids gypsies or Kurds?"

Nurettin laughed.

"These are surely Kourds."

"Do you think they speak English?"

"Probably. This language they learn in school."

"But not Kurmanji?"

"Yes, this is true."

"I'd like to talk with them."

"No, no. You must not leave this car. Not here. Not like Kanarya. Here the police are everywhere watching."

"I'm an American. They won't arrest me for talking with some teenagers."

"Maybe no. But me, and they will take my car."

Nurretin seemed more worried about his car than himself. A thoughtless tourist, I'd considered neither. Before I could apologize, Nurettin got out and yelled at the kids. They gestured at him, what seemed to me signs of mockery, but they stopped dancing. He screamed some more, and the group broke up. One of the dancers scooped up their boom box, and the kids disappeared down an alley.

Nurettin was coughing when he got back in the car. "Very dangerous," he said. "They should be afraid of police here."

I thought of American black kids break-dancing in Cincinnati's Fountain Square in the 80s. The beat cops enjoyed the show, happy the kids in high-tops and baggy pants weren't doing something that required pursuit. In Istanbul, a vast hypocritical system was at work: the Turks knew who and where Kurds were, but did not want to know, did not want to hear or see signs of difference. The Kurds had their refuge in pretending not to be Kurds, in lying about themselves in public. This massive lie inflicted upon Kurds was not, however, a sufficient basis for refugee status. Could Kurds say they feared becoming not-Kurds in the future? Their complexions and accents and names would give them away. To escape lying, Kurds had to risk their lives at the Evros, in the minefields. When they got to Athens, many would have to lie again, more dramatically for the examiners.

The afternoon of my ride with Nurettin and the day after I walked through the famous sites near my hotel—Hagia Sophia, the Blue Mosque, Topkapi—and went to the grand bazaar. Perhaps because it was off season, Turks in the tourist business and on the street were friendlier than Greeks, less hurried, more polite and curious. "Why do you come to Istanbul in this weather?" I was asked by the desk clerk, with an apologetic raising of the eyebrows. When a rug merchant found out I was an American living in "Unanistan," he said he had relatives in New Jersey and asked me questions about Greek people.

"They're not as greedy as our politicians say, are they?"

"Not any worse than Americans."

"What about lazy? I believe Greeks are probably like Turks."

"Greeks do like to sell things to foreigners."

The man laughed. Ziba warned me against asking the man-on-the-street questions, but I was curious what this liberal-thinking merchant would say about Kurds.

"If all your niggers lived on your east coast," he said, "you would know what Kurds are like."

Perhaps the merchant was unusual, but after talking with him—and after my ride with Nurettin—whatever I looked at I saw through Ziba's eyes. The largest church in Christendom is a monstrous waste of human energy, a man-made imitation of a mountain, what every city tends toward. The Islam that provides faucets for purification outside the Blue Mosque has tried for centuries to wipe out the old nature religion of the nomadic Kurds. "Our great-grandmothers and great-grandfathers were like the natives of Australia," Ziba told me, "Because Kourds had to know the land they moved across year after

year, they respected and worshipped it." The jewels and gold stored in the
museum at Topkapi are Ottoman imperial hoarding. Istanbul's caravansary
architecture, its second-floor latticed rooms where insiders could observe outside without being seen, represents the military state's surveillance. Kilims
touted by rug merchants at the bazaar are machine-made imitations of Kurdish
women's handiwork. *Hamals*, little men who tote on their backs huge bales of
merchandise in the bazaar, are like Kurds carrying their life's possessions. Fake
Izods sold on the streets are like the false identities that natives of Istanbul
foist on easterners. When I ordered a beer, instead of tea, at a teahouse next to
the bazaar, I even remembered that Ziba claims Kurds invented fermentation.

Sunday afternoon I walked down the hill behind my hotel toward the
water, what my map called the Gulf of Marmaris. Even in Cincinnati, a very
humid place, I'd never used the word "dank," but that's exactly what Istanbul
was. The moisture seemed to penetrate the wooden houses, stripping paint
and rotting clapboards. Walking through the narrow streets, I understood why
Turks might pretend to be Kurds to get out of here. Dank and rank, I thought
to myself, because this area smelled like sewage. Pipes from toilets added onto
second storeys may have been emptying into the storm sewer if there was one.
The seaside was lined with rubbish, hauled down the hill or cast up by the
water. As I headed back and the afternoon darkened, I realized there were no
street lights. I had trouble reading street signs nailed to the wooden buildings.
If I kept walking uphill, I'd eventually come to Sultanhamet and my hotel, but
I hated wandering and peering with people watching me. Only men were on
the streets at this hour; women must have been inside cooking. The men
stared, but didn't speak as I tried to stride purposefully up the hill. Ziba told
me Islam made streets safe for women, and harsh penalties minimized rob-
beries. "Much better than Chicago," she said. Remembering Ziba's remark, I
slowed down, felt less nervous. I realized this section of Istanbul was like my
first summer days at the office, when I felt the poor and desperate watch me
in the halls. But even on the grayest November days in Athens, I didn't feel
Istanbul's oppressiveness. Greek stucco buildings, however soiled, reflect the
light there is, and on clear days the low sun makes Athens look white, like
some Heavenly City in literature. The late afternoon light in Istanbul was swallowed by the unpainted wood, the pervasive gray. Walking in my first Third
World city, I physically felt—not just understood—why the office was overrun
with unjustified applicants, the "economic migrants." Surely there was pervasive fear of dying without living and there was desire, but what propelled
many of the aliens toward Greece was neither of these primal motives, but

something later in evolution, something aerier and illusory, undocumentable and often lamentable, a special kind of lie about the future, a motive ill-founded by definition: hope.

About Mr. Kaya I had no false hope. The Director finally heard his deportation appeal a few days before the Commission closed for two weeks of Christmas vacation. Apparently the tape recorder never came up because Mr. Kaya used his final interview to spout new accusations. With me standing in front of her desk, Mrs. Constantinou reported one in his own words: "Mr. Kaya says another detainee in Lavrion saw you and Miss Ziba together at the hotel where she lives. Mr. Kaya believes that you are 'slipping in the same bed.'"

I laughed, but the Director was serious. Only Mr. Kaya's phrasing was funny.

"Mr. Kaya thinks you and Miss Ziba are plotting against innocent Kurds who do not share your PKK sympathies."

I refused to be accused. Mr. Kaya lacked imagination: Ziba and I were lesbians. If a woman has power over a man, she must be a dyke. Now there is a universal fear, east, west, and in between. In the Midwest, women partners at Snow and Fiore, even married ones, meet secretly for lunch if their associates are male. A well-dressed older woman without children can make grown men joke about being little Dutch boys.

Mr. Kaya also lied with impunity. I'd never been to the Flea Palace.

"I didn't realize hearsay was admissible here at the United Nations High Court for Refugees," I told the Director.

"I would not take his word for this, but someone else has told me that you and Miss Ziba may be closer than an examiner and translator should be."

"Let me guess who your informant is. The three-hundred-word man Siamand, right?"

Mrs. Constantinou sat more erectly in her desk chair. She was surprised to be questioned and, probably, by my identification, but I was sure about Siamand. He'd been around doing occasional work for Erica and Nikos when they had to review old cases, and he always gave me a surly look when we passed in the hall. Ziba had cost him money and possibly even influence. For all I knew, Siamand was faking his ignorance of English and thereby helping his cohorts. He wouldn't mind betraying another Kurd. While slipping around the hall, he might have heard Ziba and me exchanging Greek non-sequiturs behind my office door. To Siamand, the joking probably sounded like plotting.

"I explained to you before that examiners must be independent of translators."

"That's just an illusion and you know it, Mrs. Constantinou. We're dependent on good translators or bad translators, but we're always dependent. As far as I can tell, Ziba is a very good translator."

"But UNHCR should not be dependent on any one translator, particularly someone in so sensitive an area. When you return from your holiday, Miss Ziba will do Iranian and Iraqi Kurds. Mr. Siamand will do Turkish Kurds until we find someone better."

Standing in front of the Director's desk, I thought of Kaya shaking his stump in my face.

"Reward the informant," I said. "It's just the way things work in Turkey and Iraq and Iran."

"You are not a refugee, Miss Mahan. You are an employee. Let me remind you of that."

Mrs. Constantinou stood up, my cue to exit. Case closed. I stood my ground.

"The translators are employees," I told her. "Erica and Nikos are employees. They do this job for the money. I get paid now, but I'm here to 'work for refugees.'"

"Perhaps that is your problem. We all work for UNHCR. If you cannot accept the organization's conditions, you will have to find some other way to 'work for refugees.'"

Yes, I thought in my office, I lied about the tape, and yes Ziba and I were friends outside the office. But neither the lie nor the friendship affected Kaya's application. His charges were false, the process unfair, the punishment—using Siamand as a translator—unjustified and ridiculous. The Director's threat, however, is real. Ziba is willing to lie for me, but won't get the chance, not now that the tape is no longer an issue. If the Director asks Ziba about her uncle, she has her document. Ziba also has another job. She's in the clear. I'm only half-way through my "baby year." The firm reminds me of a staff attorney whose computer was disconnected and whose office locks were changed when she went out to lunch. No notice, no appeal. When I get to Cincinnati, I may find a fax from Mrs. Constantinou: "UNHCR no longer requires your services." Suddenly I fear leaving Greece, fear I'll never return. I haven't climbed the Acropolis yet. I won't be able to plead my way back into UNHCR. Ziba won't be able to help me. I'll be like a refugee with no place to go. My legs begin to tremble. Remember the *Handbook*. "Fear must be reasonable." Be objective. Like the Questionnaire. I have facts and information. Mr. Kaya and Ziba's uncle were watched at work by the police. The police in Istanbul are always watching Kurds. Mrs. Constantinou has at least one informant at the office. The evidence adds up, the applicants' files, their stories, my experience. Surveillance, not severance or deportation, will be next. The Director will be watching Ziba and me. This is a reasonable fear, justified, not exaggerated. I can go home and return.

In this case, my confidence was well-founded and can be documented.

III Narrative

Chapter 8

I departed my country of residence for Ankara on January 7, 1999, four days after arriving from my country of origin. After a two-hour layover, I got on a small jet to Diyarbakir. "The mountains are our only friends," the Kurds say. As we descended, I had a good view of snow-covered crags to the east that protect Kurds from the tanks parked at both ends of the runway. The plane taxied close to the terminal, and we went single file down old portable steps. The wind blowing down the valley made my tights feel like tissue paper. I wished I had one of those ski masks football fans and bank robbers wear. The man waiting for me easily identified his guest among the other twenty arrivals, all men, half in uniform. My escort must have been important because most of the arrivals saluted him first. He had red cheeks, but he had to be Turkish, maybe from up by the Black Sea because he was tall, rangy, but trim in his uniform. His words came out like his snappy return salutes: "Welcome to Diyarbakir. My name is Demirsar. I will drive you. Do you have bags?"

"Just this carry-on."

"Please give it to me."

"You're not going to search it, are you?"

"I beg your pardon."

"I'm sorry," I said, realizing that Demirsar just wanted to carry my bag. "It's not heavy. I can handle it."

Demirsar led me outside, where two soldiers with rifles were leaning against his car. I was a little nervous getting in because Ziba said not to ride alone and because the car was a white Land Cruiser. Though it was unmarked, Demirsar's uniform made him a target if the PKK had come down out of the mountains. Between the driver's and passenger's seat was a submachine gun that looked newer and better than Panos's.

"For safety," Demirsar said, "please cover yourself."

I looked down at the gun. Did he mean cover myself with it, as cowboys and detectives did in movies? Or cover myself with a shawl, like a woman I'd seen in the terminal?

"Like this," Demirsar said and fastened his safety belt. When I was covered, we started as abruptly as Demirsar's sentences. Although the airport road was full of potholes, Demirsar drove fast and let the bumps punctuate his speech.

"General Silay is my superior. He ordered me to show you the old city. We will go first to the wall. Civilization is beginning here."

I didn't know Demirsar's rank or even if Demirsar was his first or last name, but I refused to engage in small talk or ask any questions. I was on a mission, not sightseeing.

Civilization may be beginning in Diyarbakir, but it looked a lot like news footage I'd seen of the West Bank during strikes—rutted streets, low cement-block or stucco or mud buildings, shop windows covered with plywood or metal shutters, few signs advertising what was within. Piles of snow every-where. But no stone-throwing Palestinian youths. In fact, few people not in uniform. Soldiers sat in jeeps and armored cars parked at intersections. The civilians I saw were mostly women carrying plastic bags. Although they hunched against the cold, walked close to shop walls, and didn't look up as we passed by, the women were not veiled or half-masked. Their hair was cov-ered with scarves, but their faces were exposed to the cold and to men. I expected to see the bright colors and mismatched patterns of traditional Kurdish dress in Diyarbakir. The pedestrians wore long dark coats. Only a few striped pants legs poked out beneath the coats. Not a single child accompanied the women. "Inside," I remember Ziba saying, "my childhood was inside." The second-floor windows of buildings that looked like residences were shuttered like the display windows. I couldn't see inside. I wondered how inhabitants did because only about half the houses were connected to the electric lines that ran above the streets. I also wondered if I'd be seeing a different Diyarbakir if Nurettin or Ziba were driving.

Demirsar said nothing about the streets we drove through. He beeped his horn at soldiers manning checkpoints and went through every stop sign. I didn't know—and refused to ask—if it was too dangerous to stop or too much trouble when there was no traffic. Our non-stop twists and turns were taking us uphill. Now some of the streets were paved, and the buildings were higher and more substantial, but still very few people and almost no men were out this January day. Demirsar began to drive more slowly. Perhaps this was where Turks lived, looking down on Kurds huddled below. "Large sight soon," he said. A minute later we parked facing a gap between two high, thick stone walls. Ziba told me Diyarbakir was known for its black basalt walls, ten feet thick in some places. Up close, the walls made the city feel like a prison. The notch between the walls was a window from which detainees could see home, the mountains to the east.

"Please come with me," Demirsar said. Before I could say, "I can see the walls right from here, they're a very impressive sight," he was out and walking through the opening in the walls toward a railing. This had to be an overlook to the valley I knew was below. He waved to me to follow him. I pretended I didn't understand, and he walked back to the car. Now his cheeks were really red.

"Come," he said at the window, "civilization is beginning here." I still had no idea what he meant. Did Turks think that the beginning of civilization was walls? I held up my gloveless hands, rubbed them together. Inside, I'll stay inside.

"General Silay ordered me," Demirsar said and opened my door. I got out and again Demirsar walked ahead. I went toward the overlook and stopped between the walls, about eight feet short of the railing.

"Very nice, a beautiful view of the mountains," I shouted through the wind to Demirsar, who had his gloved hands on the railing. I did not want to put my bare hands on that metal railing.

"No, no, you must come closer," he shouted back.

Never for a second did I suspect that Demirsar was going to solve a Human Rights problem by throwing me over the railing. But the wind was blowing at my back, the footing looked uncertain, and I refused to get any closer to that overlook.

"I can see fine from here," I hollered.

Demirsar walked back to me. "Please, lady," he said, though I was ten years younger than he. There was a note of pleading in his voice. "General Silay ordered me. You must see the river Tigris."

So that's "the beginning of civilization." I have to see the Tigris. It was in Turkey that the Tigris and Euphrates had their origin. Civilization thus began here, not in downstream Babylon or any of those other walled cities Diyarbakir imitated. General Silay insisted I know this fact. It's part of our negotiation. Turkey is an ancient and proud land. For some reason, I thought of Nikos, his belief that Greece is the foundation of civilization. Again Demirsar walked up to the railing, and I took another couple of small steps forward. I stood on my tiptoes, craned my neck, and told Demirsar, "Yes, the river is very beautiful."

Demirsar smiled as he walked back to me. I wondered if he could see me shivering.

"You are lying to me, no?" he said.

"Yes," I replied.

"You are afraid. Of a high place, no?"

"A little."

"Not a problem," he said and put his hand on my elbow. "I will hold you. Come. Really not a problem. You must see this Tigris."

He held my elbow like a tuxedoed escort would hold a debutante. We walked slowly up to the railing. The Tigris wasn't "very beautiful," as I'd said, at least not in the winter. The river seemed too small to have begun civilization, a brook in the snow compared to Cincinnati's Ohio.

"It's beautiful," I told Demirsar.

"Look down," he said, again smiling. I put my hands on the railing and glanced down. Ten feet below the railing was a five-foot wide ledge of scraggly bushes. To commit suicide here, surrender to the pull from below, one would have to get a running start. To commit murder, one would need to wrestle the victim in the bushes. I realized why Demirsar was smiling earlier and now. He looked directly at my face. I wanted to grin, I really did, but caught myself. By a goddamned accident, the Turks had uncovered a secret and discovered an advantage in our negotiation. The woman is afraid. She's a joke. It won't be enough to act entitled to Osman. I'll have to be a bitch, beginning now. Instead of smiling, I turn my head to the left and then to the right, pretend the wind isn't pushing at my back, and ask, "Where's the Euphrates?"

"I want to see the Euphrates," I tell Demirsar.

"This river is far away. Perhaps in two days time."

In two days, I'll be in Athens.

"And those mountains, can you take me there in your Land Cruiser?"

"This is not possible."

"Why not?"

"Too much snow," Demirsar lies to me. Even against the snow, his white Land Cruiser would be an easy target.

"But you have a four-wheel drive."

"This is not for the mountains." It was Demirsar's turn to shiver, my turn to smile, though I knew this exchange would never be reported to General Silay.

As Ziba predicted, I was taken to the Hotel Anahid. I followed all her directions: ate alone in the hotel restaurant, which was not difficult because no one else came to the dining room; hung on the door handle a bell she'd loaned me; and tried to sleep with the lights on. Ziba had not warned me that I would have to wear my coat and boots under the covers to keep warm. For breakfast, I ate a Greek apple and orange, unavailable in Diyarbakir. Waiting in the cold room for Demirsar, taking quick peeks out the shuttered window, I had plenty of time to wonder why the Turks wanted Diyarbakir. Who would be willing to

police such a godforsaken and god-remembering place? Across from the hotel
was a mosque built of black and white stone blocks; it looked like a checker-
board with dome. Only a few men, some in traditional Kurdish jackets that
made their shoulders look like wings, answered the shrill call to prayer. I wondered if the mosque was heated. Perhaps in the summer Diyarbakir was more
appealing. The valley might be fertile. The shops must have vegetables, if not
fruit. Or maybe nothing drew Kurds here. Instead they were driven here by the
destruction of their villages. Yet Diyarbakir existed long before either Turks or
Ottomans dared persecute the Kurds. This settlement where plains and mountains met was evidence of a much more ancient feud, a conflict about land
itself, the fundament. On flat space you could grow crops, dig foundations,
raise cities, invent writing, make laws. Angled space was for herding animals,
occupying caves, living in tents, telling stories. In January, inside my barely
heated room, neither side of the argument was attractive.

At nine, Demirsar drove me to a building I'd never have guessed was a
prison. It looked like an American warehouse, a two-storey sheet-metal building with no windows. And only one door I saw, the front. If the prison ever
became the burning plane I imagined, a lot of people would die. Inside the
door, the reception area looked like a law firm: dropped ceiling, men and
women sitting at desks typing or talking on the phone. Not a gun in sight.
This couldn't be where Osman was held. Demirsar showed me to General
Silay's office and spoke to the receptionist, who spoke to me in Turkish. When
Demirsar translated her welcome, I realized he is not just my escort. He's
going to be my translator. Whatever General Silay has to say, I'll hear it in
three- to five-word sentences, as if Demirsar learned his English reading
Hemingway. And me? How will I sound in Demirsar's Turkish? I should have
talked more with him, found out what will pass through him. He's got to be
better than Siamand. But waiting for General Silay, I felt new trepidation. I'll
be a lawyer represented by a man the client can't understand, a man allied
with my opponent. Kurds were translated by Kurds. I had Demirsar.

Just like an American professional trained in office hospitality, General
Silay came out to the reception area to meet his guest. He reminded me of an
estate-planning partner at the firm, the same pear shape and dainty walk, even
the same half-lens glasses.

"Wall-come," the General said and switched to Turkish, which Demirsar
translated, some staccato apologies for the unfortunate weather here in beautiful Diyarbakir. The General showed me into his office, and Demirsar followed.
He'd seen me quivering up at the wall, but he also called me "lady." Maybe
this deference and General Silay's elaborate politeness entitled me to some-

thing more than official consideration. After we exchanged pleasantries, the
General told me the early history of the Tigris, which Demirsar now called the
Dicle. Copper was worked near here nine thousand years ago, bronze six thousand years ago. After complimenting the General on the area he ruled, I
launched into a formal description of our shared predicament as officials
involved with "transient populations." I never used "refugees" or "Kourds." In
long, vague sentences, I described mutual concerns that might be remedied
with fuller cooperation, repeating and developing the solicitation in my letter
to the General. Demirsar's translated sentences were equally long-winded. So it
was only English that Demirsar broke up into salute-length units, sentences
that made the General's response sound like a primer version of security.

Once I'd established my respect for the General as an official, I lamented
that we often had to serve distant authorities. General Silay must know what
it's like to have someone in Ankara countermand an order or suddenly revise a
policy. Yes, that is unfortunately true, the chain of command and all. Anyone
above the rank of private would see these preliminaries were the equivalent of
Istanbul rug merchants serving free tea to tourists.

It was time to change from global official to American emissary.

"Since we agree on so many large issues, General Silay, I'm hoping you
can help me with a small matter. I want to put this delicately."

I looked at Demirsar. I repeated "delicate" with eyebrows raised. He shook
his head. "Like a lady," I told him, and he passed that on in Turkish. The general nodded.

"It's about a prisoner named Dr. Osman Mamozin." I paused to see if
Osman was important to the General. He nodded slightly. "An official in the
American government called Geneva to see if UNHCR could help get some
information about Dr. Mamozin. Geneva called me in Athens."

After Demirsar translated this, the General picked up his phone and spoke
a few words that included "Mamozin." When I tried to continue, the General
held up his hands. A minute later his secretary came in with a file. General
Silay opened it and looked at the top sheet.

"He is arrested for betraying Turkey," the General said through Demirsar.

"Yes, we understand the charge. But we have information that Dr.
Mamozin is an Iraqi citizen." I pulled out documents from Northwestern that
Ziba had translated into Turkish. I handed them directly to the General. He
didn't question their authenticity. He just had Demirsar repeat the charge of
"betraying Turkey" and specified it—"assisting bandits."

I explained to the General that doctors trained in America had to treat

anyone in need. I didn't mention Hippocrates, a Greek. I also said I knew that
medical ethics might be different in Turkey. I wasn't here to dispute this.

"I came because the American official is very high in our government and
is a good friend of Dr. Mamozin. They went to medical school together. Since
Turkey and America are also good friends—valuable allies in this region of the
world—I was asked to secure the release of Dr. Mamozin as a gesture of good
will from Diyarbakir to Washington. It would be a great favor to me as well."

The General's response was much more detailed and polite than mine
would have been to an applicant, but this request was impossible. I didn't
think posing as a ladylike petitioner would work. An emotional appeal was out
of the question.

"Do you mean you don't have the authority to grant such a request?"

The General's reply was made for Demirsar's English: "I have authority."

It was time to do some business.

"If you have this authority, I have something you will want to see."

Demirsar looked at me, expecting more. I told him to translate. No more
long diplomatic sentences and fuzzy abstractions. General Silay had to ask me
what I had. I reached in my briefcase and pulled out Mr. Kaya's file, at least
some of it, the part Ziba translated. Before I handed over the file to the
General, I mentioned recent events not in the file: although Kaya is a member
of the PKK, he has just been given refugee status by Greece, he will be leaving
for Canada soon, the U.S. can intervene, all of which the General should
believe. Turkey thinks Greeks will do anything to anger Turkey and please the
West.

General Silay took five minutes to look at the file. I knew he was interested, but I waited for him to question me. Maybe the General said something
diplomatic, such as "what do you propose," but the question came through
Demirsar as, "What do you want?"

I ignored the "you" and the "want," which made my proposal too personal. I decided against conditionals, the "if … thens" of logic and contracts.
No causal linkage.

"You release Dr. Mamozin. We deport Jalal Kaya to Turkey."

Again Demirsar didn't believe I was finished. I wanted the terms stark,
unarguable, forgetful of Greece's possible dissent. The General's response
came back as a cloud of possibilities, reservations, qualifications.

I stood up, stepped to the General's desk, and took back Mr. Kaya's file.

"Stop," General Silay said in English, and I thought of all the stop signs
Demirsar had driven through. The General's next words through Demirsar

were more polite, "Please let me photocopy. I need some time. Perhaps we will reach an understanding."

The plane is burning. Fumes are filling the cabin. Osman needs insulin. An understanding is not good enough. Just like the Istanbul rug merchants with one chance, I have to close this deal now. I hold onto the file, remain standing.

"Dr. Mamozin is very ill. We're afraid he'll die."

Stop, translate, underline the necessity.

"Dr. Mamozin must be released immediately." And to Demirsar, "You do know 'immediately,' don't you?"

"Yes, of course," he said.

"Tomorrow I go back to Athens."

Stop, translate, force the urgency.

"If Kaya leaves Athens, it will be too late."

Then I ask the General my first question.

"Do you want Kaya or not?"

He's not expecting this. It's impolite. The General squints up over his half-lenses at me.

"Yes," he finally says, "he is criminal."

"Release Dr. Mamozin."

Again hesitation, a sign of lying at UNHCR. Maybe a better sign here.

"I will inform you tomorrow."

"Tomorrow morning."

I'd bluffed the General as far as I could. Suddenly my armpits felt clammy, and I was afraid I'd start shivering again. I thought I'd suppressed any questions about practical matters, but the General couldn't avoid expressing his fear. He probably wished his question was phrased more subtly than Demirsar managed in the longest sentence I'd heard him speak: "How can I know this you will after arrange Turkey for Kaya?"

I wasn't going to stand on a bridge over the Evros and push Kaya toward the General when Osman started walking toward me. I refused to get in a discussion of facts, events, arrangements. I also wasn't about to put anything in writing.

I extended my hand over the General's desk, and he got up out of his chair to shake it. His hand didn't feel particularly warm, so mine probably wasn't cold.

"Because we are friends, Turkey and America," I answered his question, "because we are friends. *Müttefikler*," I said, "friends" in Turkish, a word taught me two days ago by Ziba.

The General smiled, and this meant Demirsar was allowed to smile. Listen to this horsetrading CIA bitch tell us we're friends, the smiles said.

"Yes, good friends," Demirsar lied back for the General. "Today you must see what we done for America. Colonel Demirsar will take you." Demirsar hesitated and pointed to himself, confused by the General's reference to him.

"You will see the city of refugees."

"Yes, please," the General added in English. He was the friendly citizen and generous host again, using his English, arranging a tour for the visitor. This, too, was part of the negotiation, saving face, pretending noblesse oblige or its military equivalent after the American bitch gave him twenty-four hours to barter prisoners. I couldn't chance offending the General any further. I'd have to see the city of refugees even if it was up on Mt. Ararat with Noah's Ark. Now there, I couldn't help thinking, is the beginning of civilization, the mountainside origin of all life for fundamentalists, both Christian and Muslim.

"This will be my pleasure," I said to the General.

To Demirsar, I said, "Are we going soon?"

"Yes, yes, right now," Demirsar said, "before more snow."

And just as a pleasant reminder, I asked the General, "And tomorrow morning Colonel Demirsar will drive me to the airport?"

"Yes, certainly, tomorrow," Demirsar said.

It was the best I could do. I'd hoped to see Osman, but I didn't dare force that issue. After all, I wasn't supposed to be personally involved. I was just here to do a deal. If the General wanted Kaya, I might see Osman tomorrow before I left.

It was trying to snow when we left the building. Fog in Istanbul, snow in Diyarbakir. The bottom of hell was ice. This time Demirsar's Land Cruiser didn't climb. In just a couple of minutes, we were out of the city, in the valley. The mountains were hidden by the spitting snow. We joined a wide two-lane road with tractor-trailers, mostly oil tankers heading south toward Iraq. Except for an occasional military vehicle parked just off the road, the flat landscape was blank, desolate. I didn't see another car. No people or livestock. Perhaps five miles south of Diyarbakir, Demirsar turned off the highway onto a dirt road and slowed down.

"This is the city of refugees," he said and motioned with his left hand to both left and right. A burned-out car covered with snow was about thirty yards to my right. Out about the same distance to the left was a cement block building the size of a bus shelter. It was riddled with holes, as if the masons had laid the blocks on their sides. What looked like telephone poles stood at irregular intervals. Looking more closely, I could see under the snow regular lines of almost square humps extending in both directions. Graves, I thought, the Turks have brought me out here to see a mass burial ground, the place they keep refugees.

"Thousands of tents were here," Demirsar said. "Over there. Everywhere tents and refugees."

The lines of humps were tent platforms, not graves. Now I recalled the tent cities UNHCR and other agencies built for Iraqi Kurds, the ones who escaped gassing and got across the Habur River in 1988. General Silay sent me here to remember that Turkey had once been a refuge for its enemies, a huge favor to the United States. I owed him. He wanted to remind me. Perhaps this little tour was a good sign for Osman's future. But looking out across the snowy ruins, I also felt the site could be a threat. If the UN wanted to avoid these camps in the future, we'd better continue the safe haven in northern Iraq. If UNHCR continued to encourage refugees, we to the west of Turkey would have to build camps in our own lands. These were the messages the emissary was supposed to take back, with or without Dr. Mamozin.

Back on the highway heading north, thankful for the heat on my cold feet, but resenting my politely menacing hosts, I thought this is as close to mountain villages as I'll ever get. I'll never visit Ziba's Hakkari, ride donkeys up treacherous paths, stand with her relatives and their goats on the edges of their pueblos, and understand my fear. Donkeys, goats, I thought. Maybe acrophobia comes from too much understanding. In Greece I'd learned that the most fundamental meaning of "acro" was not "high," but "edge." Every edge presents a decision, a chance to make a mistake. Maybe that's the fear, not heights, I have to overcome. I'd begun by making this trip. I'd come over the length of Turkey and lied to a General. No one was overwhelmed. I didn't litigate, but I made a pre-trial deal, possibly cheated the General out of a prisoner. That—not some show of macho bravado at the overlook—has to be my satisfaction.

As the city wall loomed up before us, I saw that Demirsar was mistaken about the abandoned camp. Its flat, almost non-existence represented all those Kurdish villages Turks had razed—burned, dynamited to the ground, bulldozed into gorges—to make black-walled Diyarbakir the city of refugees.

Chapter 9

The Hotel Anahid didn't serve lunch. "If you leave your hotel," Ziba told me, "go only to the bazaar. Walk. Do not take a taxi. Don't talk to people. Definitely do not speak to anyone who tries to talk with you because you'll be followed by the secret police." It would be a long afternoon and evening in my room until dinner at nine. The bazaar is not the mountains. And not that damned wall either.

My round-faced, olive-cheeked, twenty-something guard was waiting for me in the lobby. I turned in my key, and he turned in a key. His overcoat looked like military issue, and I wondered why General Silay or Demirsar was not more subtle. I disliked being followed, but I also remembered what Ziba said about the PKK kidnapping foreigners. Although I had a map Ziba drew, walking away from the Anahid I couldn't tell narrow streets from alleys. Since most of them had no identifying signs, I was supposed to count streets and turn left at the fifth. After fifteen minutes of tracking and backtracking in the snow, I wished I could walk the thirty feet back to my guard and turn him into a guide. But I didn't want to scare off my not-so-secret soldier. He might have a submachine gun under that overcoat. Like the uniformed soldiers manning checkpoints and like the General and Demirsar, my guard was clean-shaven. The few civilians I met on the street all had mustaches. In Diyarbakir, Kurds didn't even try to pass as Turks.

I went into a bakery and asked "bazaar?" The old woman behind the counter looked past me to the front window, came around the end of the counter, took my elbow, and ushered me out. She said nothing, and didn't point in either direction. Out on the step, I heard her throw the deadbolt. She was mute or she didn't understand "bazaar." Or I was a tourist collaborating with the Turks. Or I was a clever Turk pretending to be a tourist. I'd seen blonde models in Ziba's *Hurriyet*. Now I felt like a Turk, suspected, hated, feared. I was thankful for my guard, protecting me from everyone, not just guerrillas.

I finally found the street where I needed to turn. I expected to see a miniature version of the covered bazaar in Istanbul. But the Diyarbakir bazaar was just a block of closely packed one-storey shops with glass windows and electric lights, no roof. I went into a carpet shop. The rug salesmen in Istanbul sounded almost like native speakers of English. "Restaurant?" I asked the mustachioed young man sitting in the back. There was no response, not even the raised eyebrows Greeks use for disdain. I tried "Eat?" No response. I mimed putting food into my mouth. He then got up, went to the door, stepped outside, glanced in the direction of my guard, mimed putting food in his mouth, pointed to the right, and then gestured a right turn. "Thanks a lot," I said. With his back to my guard, the young man softly replied "Thank you."

"Thank you" for not making me speak English, for not asking any more questions, for not staying in my shop any longer.

The "restaurant" fortunately had a glass window because I'd never have read its sign. Inside was a small room with eight tables and a counter in the back. I sat at one of the two free tables and scanned the room. The women and men sitting at the tables all looked like Kurds, white kerchiefs and turbans, ruddy sharp faces, mustaches on the men. As I scanned them, they looked furtively at me, quick glances or heads-down, peripheral scrutiny. I tried not to look at the other diners, but I felt I was being watched minute by minute. And there were plenty of them because no one came to take my order. I'm being shunned, I thought, denied sustenance. Then a man came in, went directly to the counter, and took a plate of food to his table.

"Kebabs only," Ziba said. But at the counter no kebabs were to be seen, so I pointed at a heaping bowl of rice and beans. The counterman dished me out a plateful, wrote the amount I owed him on a slip of paper, and I paid him. "I'm from the United Nations," I wanted to say to him. "Here's my ID card. I came to help one of you," I wanted to say to the other diners. But they wouldn't have understood, and I had no translator. I took my beans and rice back to my table.

It's almost warm inside, but, like the others, I keep my coat and toque on. I'm inside and frustrated, but not ashamed as I'd been in the home of Leya and Abdullah in Istanbul. I'm an outsider, but I don't feel like a Turk. My guard is outside. Eating beans and rice, I no longer feel like an American. I feel like one of the diners. Like them, I'm under surveillance. Eating together, we might be plotting together, planning an escape. My bodyguard can turn into a prison guard at any moment, come through the door any second. No place is safe for Kurds. I can avoid heights and edges. For Kurds, no room is private, not even Ziba's bedroom. How to describe how I feel to an examiner? Not fear. Anxiety is too therapeutic. Unease too weak, paranoid too loaded. Keep your head down and eat your beans and rice, I tell myself.

Outside I was afraid. My guard had disappeared. I looked in a couple of store windows, waiting for him to get back out into the cold. He didn't appear,

but two men, one in his thirties, the other in his fifties, both mustachioed,
were leaning against a door in the direction I had to go. Snow had collected
on their turbans. They weren't window-shopping. After I passed them, they
fell in behind me. I wasn't afraid they were PKK. These were the collaborators
Ziba told me about. Hurrying back to the Anahid, I imagined how Kurds in the
restaurant would feel if these two men trailed them. The diners never know
who is watching and listening, waiting to betray you, saw information out of
you, throw you in prison. In the city of refugees, I realized all Kurds are not
just refugees. They're also all secret-keepers, secretly collaborating with Turks
or harboring secrets against the Turks. All the Turks in Diyarbakir are jailers,
and any Kurd may have a shiv secreted on his or her body. For this, Kurds are
constantly and subtly tortured, deprived of business, of speaking a foreign
tongue, of ordinary safety. Keep the psychological pressure on, and the Kurds
may give up, flee, or reveal their secret. Cold as it was, the Hotel Anahid was
a refuge. No one watched me in my room. My only secret was in my head,
and Silay wanted Kaya too much to come bursting through my door.

The next morning, on the way to the airport Demirsar announced,
"Osman Mamozin was sent to Iraq this morning." The General was showing
off his authority or pretending to.

"Good," I said, the official emissary suppressing her personal joy. I'd be a
bitch until I was in the air, heading west.

Like an applicant, I now had to wait for a result. It could be a month or
two before Ziba receives word about her brother, if she receives word, if
Osman was really deported to Iraq. In the plane, I pictured him riding in an oil
tanker to the Habur bridge. "Welcome to Kurdistan" says a hand-lettered sign
on the Iraqi side. But Osman's welcome will depend on what color controls
the highway this week, the green of Talibani's PUK, the yellow of Barzani's
PDP, or some plaid rogue element charging entry fees. With a dozen parties,
it's as difficult to be a neutral in Kurdistan as a Kurd in Diyarbakir. Doctors are
rare, a valued commodity as the factions snipe at each other, but political tol-
erance is even rarer. Osman will be examined like a foreigner at the border. He
won't have any documents, just Turkish prison clothes. He may be taken for a
spy. He'll have to talk his way into the country where he lives and works.

And if he isn't allowed in? I didn't consider this. I'd never interviewed
anyone who tried to get *into* Kurdistan. If Osman is turned away, he'll be able
to sneak back over the border. Iraqi Kurds have to worry about Turkish military incursions, not individual smugglers or spies. And when Osman gets in?
Ziba never told me what party he belongs to. For all I know, Osman could be

patching up PKK guerrillas in Iraq. According to the Geneva Conventions, combatants have the right to medical attention. This is not a case I'd want to make to the Director, but what Osman does out on the frontier is his business. Erica believes the PKK is a reasonable response to Turkey's war of terror against its citizens. After two days in Diyarbakir, I felt the same way. When Osman recovers from his stay in prison, he may even return to Turkey. If so, he'd better not be caught. There's only one Kaya. If the Interior Ministry decides not to deport him to Turkey, General Silay may contact me. Flying high above Turkey, I felt that possibility was remote, not a future to fear.

Ziba didn't know when I was returning, and I couldn't call her at the hotel. I took a taxi to the Flea Palace, walked up three flights of dark stairs, and knocked on Ziba's door.

"*Pios einai?*" she said, "Who is it?" in Greek.

"*Ego*," I replied.

"Casey?"

"Yes."

As the chain rattled, I could hear Ziba say, "What are you doing here?"

"I was told that Osman was deported to Iraq this morning."

Ziba grabbed my elbows and pulled me into her room. She stood there, holding onto my elbows, looking at me, afraid to respond until she heard more.

"That's what I was told by the Turkish authorities today. I never saw Osman. I don't know if it happened, but I think so. I'm pretty sure, Ziba, but I can't tell you for certain."

Instead of pulling me toward her, Ziba straightened out her arms, pushing me slightly back. She looked me up and down like a recruit.

"You did it, Casey. You did it."

Then she wheeled me around and around, still holding onto my elbows. I remembered the circle-dancing teenagers in Istanbul. I wanted to celebrate, let go and let out the elation I felt when Demirsar told me Osman was free. But I'd had time to worry about who was telling me. I couldn't be sure our joy was well-founded. When Ziba stopped spinning me, I told her the Turks might be lying. She had me replay the whole interview with General Silay.

"If they haven't released Osman, they will," Ziba concluded. "If you were a man, the General could lie to you. Turks think women are not worth lying to. If the General lied, he would lose face."

A second retelling of the interview didn't lessen Ziba's enthusiasm. Then she asked how I felt about Diyarbakir. I told her it was not a place I'd want to live.

"No," she said, "but if you could only have seen the inside of my parents' apartment." She gestured at the bare walls of her room. "Nothing like this or those black city walls. I wish you could have seen our wall hangings and rugs and tablecloths." She pointed at a small orange and red kilim on her bed. "Colors like these all over the house."

We'd been standing this whole time. Ziba sat me on her bed, took the only chair in the room, and made me tell the whole trip again. Reciting my movements through her country of origin and the forbidden city of Diyarbakir, I realized Ziba's room was another place I wasn't supposed to be. Except for the kilim, it was like a cell: bed, end table, chair, sink, single bare bulb hanging above. The toilet and shower were down the hall. If I'd been living in this room for six months, I'd want to be relocated. Now, though, I was in no hurry to leave.

A month later Ziba brought a letter from her mother to the office. Osman was in Iraq and recovering his health. He was anxious to be working again for the good of Kurds. Ziba translated two sentences directed to me: "We can never repay the debt we owe you. Since only in families are debts unpaid, we welcome you as our daughter."

I don't know if it was confirmation of Osman's safety or those sentences, but tears came to my eyes. I told Ziba to thank her mother and to tell her that I hoped to meet her one day. That night we went out to celebrate, purge our ill-founded anxieties about General Silay. In a basement taverna in the Plaka, we both ate grilled fish and drank retsina in water glasses. No one with guidebooks or postcards was in the taverna, yet it was full of customers, Greeks enjoying the underground heat and sentimental bouzouki songs.

"*Yeimas*'" we toasted each other in Greek, "to our health." As we were working on a second copper carafe of wine and eating our halvah, I told Ziba I was proud to be considered her sister.

"And that makes you a Kourd," she said and raised her glass again. "*Ba silamati*," she said, "'to our health' in Kurmanji."

"*Ba silamati*," I replied. My face felt flushed with the heat, the retsina, the emotion. I could almost believe that the temporary redness was my skin color, that I would some day say more than "*ba silamati*." I did believe in the more intimate bond, the power of adoption, a foundling gaining a sister—and brother—by action rather than blood. Until I was adopted, I forgot I wanted a sibling when I was a kid. A little sister and I would have whispered secrets under the covers. I wouldn't have been so obsessed with my parents' doings. I'd have been sharing space and clothes and genes. I'd have had someone to protect other than my beanpole self. I might have felt differently about having babies, who always struck me as alien because my parents' friends, as old as they, had kids older than me. A sister would have been the first to know about my acrophobia. I could have called Ziba when Rick and I split. I told her some of the details as we finished up the retsina.

"Let it go," she said and raised her hands, as if releasing a partridge Kurds keep in cages, "lovers and husbands are always from another family. Kourdish women don't expect them to be loyal."

"What about faithful?"

"Loyal is more important for us."

"Why's that?"

"Because men didn't make us slaves, not like Arab women or Turkish women. As shepherds, Kourdish women were more like equals, moving together from grazing ground to grazing ground. That's why husbands could sell their loyalty as mercenaries. When they did, women found it's only your own family, your brothers and sisters and cousins, you can depend on."

"To the Mamozins then," I said and raised my glass.

"To the Mamozins," Ziba said and clinked my glass. Surrounded by Greeks—who seem to have only about a dozen last names, most ending in *poulos* or *akis*—we toasted a name as odd in this country as "Mahan." In the United States or in Turkey, the toast might never have happened. But here between our two homelands we felt the kinship of aliens, the refuge of kinship.

During the next few weeks, Ziba and I saw less of each other than usual. It was too cold for Kurds to cross the Evros or swim up onto island beaches. Ziba was still translating for the few Iraqis and Iranians who came in, but she'd moved into her Greek family's home and was busy as a weekend nanny and English teacher. With more time to conduct interviews and think about them, I was bothered by two recent cases, one that of a fifty-six-year-old Kurdish widow from a small village on the Armenian border. She had lived in Ocakli her whole life, had walked past the police station to the village well for forty years. About six months ago, a very light-eyed young police recruit came to the station. When the applicant passed, he stared at her. At first, she was slightly bothered. "She open her mouth and close her eyes," Siamand said and mimed a yawn. Then the woman grew weak, sick without symptoms. There was only one route to the well, so she had to pass the policeman almost every day. One day she fainted in front of him. She was sure this light-eyed man from far away was inflicting the evil eye on her. She had believed in the power of hex from her girlhood; all of her friends believed in it and thought that indeed the policeman had hexed her. She became so ill she couldn't go for water. When others brought water to her, she believed it might be hexed as well. She arranged to be carried on a stretcher to a cousin's house in a neighboring village. She got better, but then the policeman in question was transferred to the new village. After the woman became ill again, she came to Greece with the hope she could join her son in Germany.

The applicant was sure her future had been cursed. After I heard her story, I consulted the *Handbook* about subjective and objective fear. I was inclined to recommend the old woman. The Director certainly couldn't suspect her as PKK, but I first talked with Nikos.

"Even after six months on the job you still want to protect every Kurd who can get here," he said.

"I've read that northern Greeks and others in the Balkans also believe in the evil eye. Would you respond differently if they were applying?"

"You and I and the Director and the Interior Ministry know the Declaration doesn't exist to protect superstitious old ladies, wherever they come from. The Declaration was invented in 1951 to shelter anti-Communists from Eastern Europe. It was all politics."

He took a pamphlet out of his desk and read the first preamble of the Declaration: "Whereas recognition of the inherent dignity and of the equal and inalienable rights of all members of the human family is the foundation of freedom, justice, and peace in the world."

"Citizens," he said, "have no fundamental rights because they're human. Roving bands of humans were killing each other long before law. Even in ancient Greece, citizens feared the democratic state. If the state breaks its own laws, okay. Then we can step in."

"The Turkish police stepped into her village to deprive Kurds of rights other Turks enjoy. The old woman never wanted to leave her home. She cries every time she mentions it. I know she's not lying, and her case fits the *Handbook*."

The strict constructionist was through arguing. "Tell it to the judge," Nikos said and nodded at Mrs. Constantinou's office.

I went to the giant English-language bookstore on Panepistimiou Avenue to do some cultural research. The essays in *Anthropology of Fear* were almost as amazing as the files. Although the Maasai and Sukuma are neighbors in Tanzania, the pastoralist Maasai have very different fears than the agricultural Sukuma. According to samples in Human Relations Area Files, the Tlingit fear the dead, but not death itself. The Dogon fear the disapproval of an aging man, error in ritual performance, and the magician. Serbs fear vampires, graveyards, and the nationalization of farm lands. An essay entitled "The Transformation of Fear in Urban Life" compared the avoidance techniques of city dwellers to those of bathers on a crowded public beach, but didn't measure their fears. One scholar concentrated on etymology. In Old English, he wrote, "fear" was used to describe an external event, a catastrophe, but through the centuries "fear" became an internal state, a response. In some languages, "fear" is not even a separate word, but part of others such as "fear-shame" or "anger-fear." Another contributor analyzed different fear responses of tribal peoples to the investigator herself. But there was nothing on the evil eye.

I decided to deny the old woman's application. After my experience on the streets of Diyarbakir, I hated to do it, but I didn't want to cross the Director, not now. Since I have blue eyes, the old woman probably thinks I too have hexed her.

The second case that sent me to the bookstore was not even a Kurd, but a Syrian accidentally assigned to me, I supposed, by area. Professor Malik was a sixty-year-old psychology teacher who could have been mistaken for an ambassador. He wore a three-piece suit, had a carefully trimmed beard, and spoke an old-fashioned, formal English. He had taught at the University of Damascus for twenty-five years and had published several books in Arabic. Professor Malik belonged to no banned political or religious groups. He had never objected to Assad's rule, and no students or colleagues had falsely informed against him. He could trace his family in Syria for at least three hundred years. Reading Professor Malik's Questionnaire, I thought he had no possible case, but his story was ingenious.

"So until two months ago," I asked, "you had nothing to fear in Syria?"

"That is correct."

"Not even when you began, let's see here, 'tidying up' your affairs?"

"That is correct, Ms. Mahan."

"You didn't have any problems getting a visa to come to the Conference in Athens?"

"It was routine."

Professor Malik was not a refugee when he left Damascus on a round-trip ticket on January 19. A day later, at the "Mideast Conference of Psychology" he gave a paper entitled "Syrian Totem and Taboo" on the cult status of Assad's dead son Basil, whose pictures were everywhere and about whom no one spoke. Breaking the taboo, Professor Malik had insulted the Father of the Nation. At the lecture there were no more than fifteen people, none of them identifiably Syrian. But Professor Malik had guaranteed his fear of future persecution by posting his lecture on the Internet where anyone in the world could see it.

More than anyone I'd interviewed, Professor Malik's fear was well-documented. He was obviously telling the truth and yet, like the woman afflicted by the evil eye, Professor Malik was also not a person for whom the Declaration was intended, not even in Nikos' interpretation. Professor Malik had never been fearful in his country, had not suffered, had not earned the status he sought. He wasn't political. He'd studied UNHCR guidelines—probably on the Internet—and constructed his air-tight case.

"This is off the record," I told Professor Malik and shut off the recorder, "but I have to ask why you did this. You've given up a great deal: your home, your position, your salary."

"And my library. I will miss my library."

"So why?"

"Disgust."

"'Disgust?'"

"Yes, but in its technical meaning. Perhaps you are aware that psychologists have recently done experiments on the phenomenon of disgust. For example, some persons are not disgusted by the idea of drinking their own urine, but would never swallow their own sputum after expectorating it into a glass."

"And you couldn't swallow Assad's son anymore?"

"Precisely, Ms. Mahan. I could accept Mr. Assad's grooming his living son, Bashar, to succeed him. This is a familiar practice in dynastic Arabia. But this cult of the dead son has no precedent. It is almost Christian, if I may say so without insult. I have visited churches where the mournful eyes of Jesus look down on the congregation. The cult of Basil is also like worshipping some young dead movie personality, for Basil did nothing in his life to deserve his status. I do not wish to offend you, Ms. Mahan, for you are clearly a person who can influence my future, but I must say that Syria is coming to resemble the United States."

"I hadn't realized. I don't wish to offend you either, Professor Malik, but could I ask you this: did you gag when you saw Basil's picture?"

"On many occasions. I kept a small notebook recording the times and places I gagged, what kind of picture stimulated the response, how powerful it was, whether or not it led to retching."

Professor Malik's notebook was a document I didn't ask him to produce. Anyone with Internet access could read his lecture.

"Very clever," Erica said when I told her about Professor Malik. He was not one of her dangerous people, but her appreciation of his lawyerly skills overrode her political agenda. "I'd recommend him. He's the kind of applicant Mrs. Constantinou likes. But if you do, you should stipulate him and relocate him fast."

We stipulated the identities of applicants, like Ziba, who could not prove their identities. If they were accepted for relocation, UNHCR gave them one-time, one-way travel documents.

"Professor Malik says he might be able to get a job at the University of Maryland branch here."

"People like Professor Malik tend to have tragic accidents. They fall off fifth-floor balconies despite high railings or choke on corks they've somehow jammed into their throats."

"Assad might send someone for Professor Malik?"

"That 'someone' is already here, at the Syrian embassy. Or at the Iranian embassy or the Libyan embassy. Perhaps you spoke to him at that reception you went to at the Austrian embassy."

Erica's remarks clinched Professor Malik's case for me: he had a well-founded fear of future persecution—assassination—in both his country of origin and his country of asylum. And yet I was dissatisfied with my letters recommending Professor Malik and rejecting the old woman. If the motive of the Declaration was to honor different cultures, not just documents and legalisms, the old woman should have been granted status. If the Declaration was actually intended, as Nikos claimed, to protect anti-Communists during the Cold War, then Professor Malik should have been rejected. The Universal Declaration was short and simple, two pages of profound moral values. In their treatment of Kurds, Turkey and Iraq violated almost all of them. But the *Handbook* was complicated, and doing Human Rights law was becoming complex, a morass like interpretations of Camus' lying lawyer in *The Fall*, like the muddy streets of Kurdish shanty settlements in Istanbul.

I went back to the bookstore and bought a biology text. It went all the way down to the bottom, to cell level—the amoeba's capacity to contract and the paramecium's ability to dodge a bright light—and came back up through reptiles to the amygdala, the little almond-shaped part of the brain that controls emotion. Designed to make quick survival decisions, the human nervous system struggles to calculate because this little nut still exists at the footing of gray matter. The book reported the effects of fear—changes in endocrinal releases, heart rate, skin conductance—but all tests required subjects be hooked to monitors in a laboratory, impossible at UNHCR. Though the author made subtle distinctions among fear, anxiety, dread, panic, anguish, and fright, the term "well-founded" was nowhere to be found. "Raw" and "respectful" were suggested. But "strong," "average," and "weak" were the operative terms, vague, as relative as anthropology.

The more I thought about law and knew about fear, the more I felt UNHCR needed more than fear as a foundation. I decided to use some of my free time to work on an essay for Sam Roberts and his *Human Rights Quarterly*. I'd argue that the most fearful—the traumatized victims—are the ones granted status. If UNHCR rewarded applicants who demonstrated a well-founded desire to change victimizing conditions in their countries, we'd be supporting legal changes in states like Turkey. Repatriation, not relocation, would be the goal. And an office like ours, I thought, should be more proactive, not waiting for the persecuted to reach us, but creating outreach missions with examiners going to prisons and camps. The essay was for the distant future. Eventually, journals and law reviews have an effect on the law and government officials. In the meantime, I was writing letters to embassies, trying to relocate the victims we'd already granted status.

I had my laptop in bed with me one night when my doorbell rang at 11:30. When I answered the intercom, Ziba yelled, "Do you have a man in there, Casey?"

"Not right now."

"Then buzz me in."

Waiting for her knock, I wondered if Ziba had been out celebrating again. She had never been to my apartment. If not for her tone, I'd have thought this was an emergency. She thumped on the door, and I opened it.

A man stood in front of the door, with Ziba off to his side. He was smiling, but his forehead was creased and his eyes round, as if he were an applicant who didn't understand all this loud English. Bent over laughing, Ziba couldn't translate.

"I'm Osman."

He stretched out his hand as if we were meeting at a cocktail party and I had on my black dress, not the baggy gray sweats I wore as pajamas. His hand was soft, like a dermatologist's.

"I asked her not to pull this, but she wouldn't listen," he said, still holding my hand.

Osman could have been British or Ivy-trained. His English was slightly nasal, pitch rising at the end. He wore a brown suit, but no tie, and the top half of his body bent toward me, as if apologizing.

"I hope we're not disturbing your work," he said, releasing my hand and nodding toward the laptop on the bed.

I couldn't seem to get out a word. I was the one who needed a translator. All I could think to say was, "How did you get here?" but some part of me knew that interview question was inappropriate, impolite. Ziba was giggling, enjoying my embarrassment.

"Aren't you going to ask us in?" she said.

"I'm sorry," I said to Osman. "I had no idea you were coming. I'm Casey, as you know from the giggling fool to your left. Please come in. You, Miss Ziba, can wait outside since it appears we don't require you."

"If it wasn't for me, Osman would never have found this place. He can read Arabic, but not Greek signs."

"I'm sorry about the late hour," Osman said. "I wanted to thank you for saving my life, and Ziba said it would never be too late for that."

"I'm glad I wasn't too late. It's wonderful to finally meet you. Come in, come in. You too Ziba. I want to hear why you didn't tell me Osman was coming."

"I've known only a couple of days, and besides I wanted it to be a surprise."

"You got your wish," I said and pointed to my sweats and bare feet. They were pure white, but I felt pink in my cheeks.

To put me at ease, Osman gestured at his own clothes and said, "I just got in from the airport. I only wear a suit to travel. This one isn't even mine."

Ziba plucked at the shoulders of his coat to show how loose it fit him. Osman smiled, unruffled by his clothes. His skin didn't have Ziba's reddish hue, but his curly hair did. His face was all angles, the Kurdish high cheekbones, his own sharp chin, perhaps accentuated by his months in prison. Unlike Kurds in Diyarbakir, Osman had no mustache. He was also taller than most applicants, perhaps 5 feet 10 inches. For someone wearing a borrowed suit into this awkward situation, he was remarkably unselfconscious. Like several doctors I'd visited, Osman seemed oblivious to his own body and unsurprised by others,' no matter what they might be wearing or not wearing.

Even in my robe and slippers, even when we were all sitting and drinking ouzo, I was still disoriented by the Mamozins' visit. I couldn't help but ask, "How did you get here?"

"I flew Olympic from Cyprus. I got there from Lebanon by boat."

"No river crossings for Osman," Ziba said. "He even has a visa."

"But only for thirty days and on a Lebanese passport," Osman said. "I'm supposed to be buying olives."

"To the export business," I said and raised my glass of ouzo.

"Yes, to export," Osman said. "Please tell me how you transported me out of Turkey, Casey. In the States, I used to be afraid of malpractice lawyers. Now I owe my life to you."

His sincere directness was slightly embarrassing, pleasing, but embarrassing with Ziba in the room.

"There was some legal malpractice involved. I pretended I could deliver a PKK bomber. I guess the military wanted a terrorist more than they feared a doctor."

"You make it sound too easy. I know it must have been difficult. I have to know this to know how to thank you." Osman leaned forward in his chair, waiting for my answer. I noticed his eyes were green, and for some reason the phrase "green-eyed lady" from an old song came up from the depths of my youth.

"Actually," I told him, "the negotiation was easier than I thought it would be. But Diyarbakir was difficult, frightening."

Ziba said something in Kurmanji. Osman laughed and immediately translated, "'Cold as an Arab's heart.'"

"'Honest as a Kurd,'" I said. "Isn't that what Arabs say?"

Ziba laughed. "So you remember that," she said.

"But only in English."

"And only some Kurds," Osman said. He glanced at Ziba, but I couldn't decode the look. It was Ziba's unintended honesty that—eventually, after her attempts to lie—put Osman in prison, according to her. I doubted Ziba told Osman this at the airport. If she had, she wouldn't be kidding him about his roomy suit and easy entry into Greece.

"Did the Kurds at the Habur bridge give you any trouble?" I asked him.

"No. I know enough people in Kurdistan to get in. But the KDP and PKK were fighting over the road from Zarkho to Duhok. I was too weak to help the wounded."

Osman told us about recovering his strength in Duhok and traveling south to Erbil where he'd left his passport, his Iraqi passport. When he was strong enough, Osman crossed into Iraq.

"But why would Iraq let you in?" I asked.

"Because they think he's *jash*," Ziba answered, using the Kurdish word for "collaborator."

"This is the advantage of a Baghdad education," Osman said. "I give the Iraqis just enough information so that my Iraqi passport remains good. In Baghdad, I pick up information about poison gases the Iraqis still have. That helps my work on the antidotes."

Osman paused and asked, "Do you know about Halabja?"

"Yes, of course."

"Good. Many lives could have been saved at Halabja with simple masks and basic chemicals. If the safe zone collapses, Saddam won't hesitate to use gas again. Not from the air this time, but from agents."

"Agnet," I thought, Kaya's word. Double agnet. Or magnet, attracting both sides. Even the way Osman told his story was magnetic, an offhand recitation of facts and prediction as if he were dictating a medical record. Ziba dared me to deny her status. Osman dared to not care how his listener responded. When he spoke about Halabja, he sat back in his chair and crossed his hands in his lap, like an old man who no longer needs to impose his presence because he has been present at some historic tragedy.

Nothing on Osman's Iraqi passport indicated he was a Kurd. His Arabic was fluent. He darkened the red in his hair and flew from Baghdad to Damascus. Some Kurds smuggled him into Lebanon's Bekka Valley, where he washed out the dye, shaved off his mustache, and bought a Lebanese passport. This got him easily to Cyprus, though the ferry made him slightly seasick.

"But those Greek-speakers in Larnaca," he said, shaking his head like an irritated tourist, "The Turks in Northern Cyprus would have been easier. First, the Cypriots didn't want to let me in, not even when I told them I was going on to Greece. Then the Greek consular official was very suspicious. Maybe it's the shared language. He asked me why I wanted to go all the way to Athens to buy olive oil."

"'Not Athens, Tripolis in the Peloponnese,' I told him."

"'Yes, but Cyprus has very good oil.'"

"I showed him some phony documents from my 'business' in Bekka. Then I told him, 'I thought you consular people were employed to help your country's trade.'"

"'Your business is impressive, Mr. Mamozin, but sometimes economic arrangements between countries require a facilitator.'"

"Fortunately, I've heard a lot of bureaucratic English. I realized the official was asking me to grease his palm. Isn't that what you say in America, Casey?"

"That and 'oil the deal.'"

Osman laughed, pleased with the pun. "That's even better. I oiled him $300 and got my visa. At the airport here, the Greek in the booth didn't even look at me or my businessman's suit. He saw the visa his fellow Greek had glued in and stamped my entry date. Using that Lebanese passport, I felt like a citizen of the world."

"But a refugee in Greece," Ziba said.

"Perhaps that wouldn't be so bad," Osman said, turning from me to smile at Ziba.

That's when I changed from sweat-suited listener to underdressed examiner. If Osman wants to be a refugee, his story is all wrong. He left the safe zone of Kurdistan. He had documents that protected him in Iraq. He left the safe haven of Lebanon, traveled through Cyprus, and entered Greece with a false document.

"What's the name on that Lebanese passport?" I asked Osman.

"My own."

"Oh oh," Ziba said.

"And your Iraqi passport?"

"The same of course."

I looked at Ziba. Osman turned back to her, and she got my hint. She should be the one to tell him the bad news.

"'Mamozin' is suspect here. Casey and I had some trouble with an applicant, who accused me of being PKK. If you apply at UNHCR, the Director will never approve someone named Mamozin."

The news didn't seem to worry Osman. To Ziba, he said, "I just arrived. We can talk about that tomorrow." Then he turned to me, smiled, settled into his chair, took a sip of ouzo, and said, "Right now I'm just happy not to be afraid of some official."

I was happy Osman felt comfortable in an official's apartment, but after he and Ziba left I thought that not being afraid was Osman's second mistake. The wrong name, the wrong emotion if he decides to apply. First, he'll have to throw away his documents. Then someone can advise him to make up a name for his Questionnaire, invent a new route for his Narrative, and recall his fear in Diyarbakir. An official or friend will want to hear about Osman's months in prison. He said it left him "weak." I wondered if there was evidence of torture under that baggy brown suit. Cigarette burns on limbs, abrasions on his abdomen, prison "stripes" or welts on his back, or something worse.

Chapter 10

To be safe from Mamozin contamination, Osman got a room in Vathia Square, what Greeks call "Muslimistan," ten blocks away from Ziba's hotel. To be extra cautious, the three of us took separate subway cars to Piraeus when we went to dinner a week after Osman arrived. There would be no refugees at the high-end fish tavernas in Mikrolimino, a yacht harbor Osman compared to a marina on the North Shore of Chicago.

Ziba and I pronounced the Greek names for cod and halibut and swordfish, but Osman read the English menu.

"Thank the dollar and pound for English," he said, "we don't even have words for some of these fish in Sorani."

"Greeks catch fish we don't have in the States," I said. "You'll need to learn the names if you stay here."

"No more languages," he replied. "I'm sick of some I already know."

"But doesn't *sifias* sound better than 'swordfish?'" Ziba asked him.

"The Greeks may be selling the sizzle rather than the steak."

Osman was more colloquial than Ziba, perhaps because he'd been in the States longer. As for Greece, his first experience with Greek-speakers in Cyprus seemed to put him off the language or the country or both, though he did admit that the yachts showed that some Greek doctors knew how to live. During his days in Athens, Osman had learned the consequences of his fake documents. He visited the Center for Rehabilitation of Torture Victims in Kolonaki. "They're doing great work there, particularly the orthopods and dermatologists," he said, but the Greek Director had trained in Austria, so he and Osman could talk only in the Greek's pidgin English. This was adequate for Osman to understand that to be employed at the Rehab Center he would need to gain residence on his real credentials, which he knew was impossible.

"My credentials are good, now, only where I received them, in Illinois."

"Your medical credentials, yes," I said, "but you'll never get back into the States on the Iraqi passport."

"I told him that," Ziba put in, as if my opinion had just settled an argument. "I also told him that west of here the Lebanese passport will be worth nothing."

"Pure Kurds, aren't we?" Osman said to me while nodding at Ziba. I didn't understand, so I waited for him to explain: "Quarreling between ourselves about where to go, what to do."

Ziba also spoke to me, as if I were a translator or intermediary in this dispute: "I suggested Osman see Kourds here under the table, like a Ukranian doctor does at the Flea Palace."

"Every doctor's ideal practice: no overhead, cash payment, no taxes," Osman replied. Then he said to me, "I was contributing more than that at the hospital in Erbil. I've become very good at reattaching feet blown off by mines."

I thought of Mr. Kaya, how his stump appeared to have been sewn up by a seamstress. Kurds missing feet rarely made it all the way to Athens.

"Why didn't you stay?"

"It was only triage medicine. The job supported my work on antidotes, but even that research was response doctoring, preparing for a future plague. After being in prison, I decided not to wait for it to happen. That's why I left Kurdistan. I want to attack the causes of the plague, its foundations."

Ziba interrupted in that mocking tone she'd used in her interview: "Osman wants to be like the doctor who wrote *ER*. No more scrubbing, no more bloody hands, just communicating."

"Please, Ziba," Osman said, "If I wanted to be Michael Crichton, I'd at least do *Jurassic Park*."

There was something between Ziba and her brother that I wasn't getting—maybe a quarrel that went back to their childhood or to their different rungs on the medical ladder—so I tried to reduce the tension: "In your version, who gets trampled?"

"First the Turks," he said, taking my question seriously. "Not just for their 'mystery killings' and other atrocities, but for their support of Saddam's genocide. Then the Arabs. Before the Gulf War they allied with Saddam to prevent the spread of shiaism. It was during the Iran-Iraq war that he began gassing Kurds with no objections from the Arabs. Next the Iranians should be trampled. Under the Shah they were in bed with Saddam because his Ba'ath Party was secularist. That was before every Middle East leader had to be Muhammed's successor. In that period, the Kurds were persecuted as a deviant religious sect."

Osman recited dates and treaties and betrayals of the Kurds by their neighbors. Ziba intensely hated Turks, the people who'd murdered her uncle and tortured her. Osman was more animated in a different way. He seemed pleased to be given the chance to rattle off Kurdish history. He was like a litigator making an opening statement, citing precedents and principles, the reasons why religions, peoples, and parties were tangled in the fertile crescent. His voice rose as he went on, and I felt he would like to rise from his chair and address the other diners.

"Don't forget the Greeks," I told Osman as he started skipping centuries of Kurdish persecution.

"The Greeks? What did they do?" he asked, anxious to hear my contribution to his angry litany.

"'Mesopotamia,'" I said. "It comes from the Greek, 'between rivers.' Naming the valley, the Greeks insulted mountain people."

"*Kala Ellenikah,*" Ziba said.

Osman groaned and looked to me to translate.

"'Good Greek,'" I told him.

"Between," he said, shaking his head only partly in mock frustration, "between Greek speakers, between rivers, between countries, between major powers. It's the Kurd's fate. Always between."

We all looked out at the yachts. I thought about Ziba between the three men who sawed her on the rope, about her and the other Kurds on the Evros between Turkey and Greece. Then I was reminded of Ziba's phrase, "Always inside." I wondered if the difference was personal or gender. The woman inside—her home, her hospital, her country—until she was chased out. The man outside, "between," but freer to range and decide what he called "fate." Between this woman and man at the square table was me, looking over the empty chair in front of me. A fourth at the table might have balanced us. But there was no fourth, and I felt tugged between Ziba and Osman.

I asked Osman if he felt "between" when he was training in the States.

"Far from it. The States were the end, the final goal when I went there in 1985. Any other training—Cairo, Rome, London—would have been between what we had in Iraq and the States. But I mistakenly specialized in trauma. I should have been preparing for gas. But even if I could have predicted what I needed to fear, there were probably no research facilities—outside the military—investigating the effects of chemical warfare back then. Now, with the Gulf War Syndrome, the States would be an exciting place to study. A young Kurdish doctor could learn a lot there."

"But you're no longer young," Ziba said, deflating Osman's excitement.

Osman replied to Ziba in dialect and apologized to me, "It's hard to translate, Casey, but it means 'Kurds are born a thousand years old.'"

In the hundred hours since Ziba and Osman were in my apartment, Ziba's giddiness had changed to pettiness. Had she told Osman about her part in his capture? Was he unwilling to believe in Ziba's fear and forgive her? These questions were too personal. When Osman went to the toilet, perhaps to avoid the unpleasantness of Ziba's comment, I felt I could ask her if they differed about what Osman should do. After all, if he decided to seek refugee status I'd be involved.

"After only a week here, he says he needs to go back to the States," she said with a note of disdain.

"Does he want you to go with him?"

"No, that's not it."

"Why are you against it then?"

"I think Osman's being unrealistic. He can't get in with his credentials. If he gets in some other way, what can he do for Kourds there? If he really wants to be useful, he should go back to Kourdistan."

"It's a dangerous place."

"Bah," Ziba said, imitating Greek women, their response to foolishness. "Osman's not afraid. He chose to go there before. He'd be safe as long as he doesn't return to Turkey. So now he's decided to apply for status here."

"Did you tell him what he'll need to do?"

"Some of it," she said, and I wondered how much, what Ziba might conceal if she felt Osman didn't belong here.

If I'd been "between" when leaving a table, I'd have felt eight feet tall walking back to the other two people. Osman returned speaking a jaunty toilet Greek, "*Gynekon* gives us gynecology, the study of women. *Anthron* must be the origin of anthropology, the study of humankind. Aren't you women insulted when you go to toilets here?"

"We're thankful priests here don't make us wear long skirts," Ziba said, "so we can crouch down and urinate privately when there are no toilets for women."

"Is that true in Iraq?" I asked.

"I don't know," Ziba replied. "It's an insult Kourdish women in pants use against Iranian women in their chadors."

Ziba was in better humor after our short talk. "To women who wear pants," Osman said and raised his glass of retsina, which he said resembled one of Saddam's tastier poisons.

"No more poison tonight, okay?" Ziba said to Osman, and he nodded. This gave me a chance to ask Osman what, besides research, drew him to America, the country I'd wanted to leave. Conversation moved west—to Chicago—and then to westerns, which Osman discovered in medical school.

He mentioned titles of films I'd never heard of, and did some dialogue from *Dances With Wolves*. Osman knew the names of nearly extinct Native American tribes. He and Ziba described a summer camping trip to New Mexico and Colorado, and both were surprised that I'd never been west of Chicago. I was amazed that they knew more than I did about my country of origin and its original inhabitants. Ziba and Osman told funny stories, misunderstanding western accents, Ziba's being mistaken for a Sioux, getting lost on back roads. I told them about my mixups in Geneva trapped among four languages I couldn't speak. We drank some more wine. We told other stories. This, I felt, is what narrative should be for, not torture and fear, but mistake and recovery, enjoyment and the desire for a new life. Not one-to-one transmission or one-to-one-to-one translation, but collaboration in the telling and in the listening, a group, no matter how small, celebrating itself with interruptions and commentary and response, listeners providing words the teller can't remember, the teller uniting listeners in attention, the ancient Greek way, before documents, below writing. Talk, this kind of talk, is what I missed in Greece. When Ziba and Osman told stories about America, they were like a long-married couple supplementing and complementing each other, and I wanted to be a part of their talk.

A few days later the three of us met at McDonald's in Syntagma Square, another place refugees don't frequent and the Director would never go. It was four o'clock on a Sunday afternoon, so even the staff was sleeping as they stood in front of their silent registers waiting for an off-season tourist searching safe food. We sat in a back booth on the mezzanine level, where only the security camera could see us. The seating had changed. Now Osman was across from Ziba and me. Between us was the Questionnaire.

"What family name will you use?" I asked Osman.

"Alpdogan."

"Does it indicate where you're from?"

"No, it's a common Kurdish name."

"Okay, fine. But we have to be careful on every detail. A background and story that will almost automatically get you approved here may make it difficult to be relocated. Greeks like enemies of their enemy, Turkey. But Turks are very hard to relocate."

"The United States gives billions of aid to Turkey," Osman said. "It's third behind Israel and Egypt. Why would I be denied as a Turk?"

Osman had been in Kurdistan too long. He was informed about factional political matters and he'd crossed numerous borders, but I had to explain immigration to him: "For refugees, it's closing time all around the western world, even in Denmark and Sweden which used to be havens. Not even item 8 on the Questionnaire—religion—is much help. Muslim countries don't want any more Muslims, and Italy and Ireland aren't taking Iranian Catholics. If you happen to be one of the five Seventh Day Adventists in Turkey, a church in Auckland, New Zealand, might sponsor you. Or if your religion has exotic appeal, such as Sufism, I might place you in Melbourne or Toronto or some other large city where you can count on a few people believing anything, believing everything."

"What about a Yezidi?" Osman asked.

Ziba laughed, and so did Osman. They now seemed in agreement on Osman's plans, or Mamozin loyalty had reasserted itself.

"If Osman claimed to be a Yezidi," Ziba explained, "you might find him a sponsor in New York or San Francisco. Yezidis are called 'devil-worshippers' by both unbelievers and Muslims."

"To INS, all aliens are 'devil-worshippers.' The States rejects immigrants from Turkey even if they have a family member in Columbus. We used to support 'family reunification,' particularly if it was an anti-Communist family, but current 'family values' don't extend beyond the seven-mile limit."

"But there are a lot of foreign doctors in the States," Osman said.

"Not from Turkey, not from Kurdistan."

I told Ziba and Osman about my conversation with the U.S. Immigration Officer at a reception given by the Austrian Embassy. My fellow American was brushing filo off his tie when I walked up to the buffet table and introduced myself.

"The food is too good here," he said, "I've gained twenty pounds in a year."

I hadn't gained or lost a pound since I was eighteen, so such remarks always make me self-conscious. Was I supposed to say, "I sure wish I could?" Or "You certainly don't look it." Instead, I said, "My clients don't complain." I guess this was insulting because he said, "Then they should stay right here."

Although Joseph Costa had either an Italian or Spanish name, he was now the doorkeeper. A little taller than me, eighty pounds heavier, and thick-handed, he might have been a bouncer when he was my age.

"Some of my clients from Kurdistan," I told him, "risked their lives when Bush encouraged them to revolt."

"If you get a cousin of Saddam or a high-level defector from Iran, let me know," he said and started moving up the table toward the main dishes.

"How about one of the Barzanis?" I asked.

"Who are they?"

"The Barzanis? They're the Kurdish Kennedys."

"Ms. Mahan, have you lived in the United States recently? Don't you know that a third of our fellow citizens would vote to deport all our Indians, Afro-Americans, and Hispanics? Elderly Greeks die waiting to join a son or daughter in Astoria. If you turn up some very special case, you can try me."

Osman shook his head at this story. For the first time, he looked worried, maybe irritated. He began rubbing his upper lip, as if he missed his Kurdish mustache.

"Too bad you chose Talibani," Ziba said to him.

"Too bad Barzani betrayed us and lined up with Saddam," Osman said and twisted his Coke in his hands. I thought of him sewing legs back onto Kurds and felt sorry for him, his betrayal by Barzani.

"What about a composite figure?" he asked, "maybe a defector from the Great Satan Saddam, someone who knows about his poison gas program?"

"This might help get you into the States," I said, "but pure Iraqis don't get in here. Greeks think they should go to Jordan or some other Arab country."

Again Osman twisted his Coke. He was "between," nowhere.

"Instead of making up a refugee," Ziba said to me, "why not work with the facts we have? Drop the Turkish origin. Osman becomes an Iraqi Kurd, a Talibani man working on antidotes in, say, Dohuk. Then you've got Barzani's people harassing him and Saddam's secret police trying to assassinate him."

Osman looked at me. He seemed surprised that Ziba would make up a story for him, or he wondered if I thought it would work.

"Ziba's been listening," I told him. "The basic story should be okay, but we're still lacking documents."

I hesitated and described Mr. Kaya's lost hand, its initial effect on me, how physical evidence could substitute for documents. I avoided Ziba's wound; I still didn't know if she'd told Osman about her torture. He saved me the embarrassment of a direct question.

He put his right hand on his shirt and pulled it away from his chest.

"I was tortured all right, but the Turks in Diyarbakir were professionals. Very clever. They left nothing to show except this gap between what I used to weigh and what I weigh now."

"I'm sorry, Osman, but could you be more specific?"

"The Turks have an ingenious way of shrinking your body. It's like the reverse of Chinese water torture. I'd rather not go into it."

That old man's or survivor's diffidence had returned, as if the victim was the Osman whom Ziba had postulated, not the man in McDonald's. What had the Turks done to him? But I couldn't ask, not directly. Ziba knew what I needed, what she'd given me.

"The Turks gave Osman a series of injections," she said, "but the marks don't show."

"What did they inject?" I asked Osman.

"That's something I'd like to know. I expect it was some kind of truth serum at first. I had the usual after effects, nausea and lethargy. They hooked me up to an IV a couple of times. And, of course, there was just enough insulin to keep me alive and thirsty. I'm most worried about the last puncture. They did it the morning I was released. 'Dogs need their shots when crossing borders,' they told me. Then they pulled down my pants and held me down on my cot. Like a veterinarian, the guy in charge jabbed me in the buttock. I'm afraid they injected some kind of toxin."

Osman's hands on the Coke were still. The only sound was McDonald's Greek Muzak. Like Ziba, Osman had been stripped, violated, figuratively raped. But Ziba could feel her wound. Osman had reason to fear his body, what it might be harboring. He was like a Bosnian woman waiting to see if she would bear a Serb baby. No, worse, for Osman couldn't abort his injection. His whole body was at risk in the future.

"I've never heard anything like this," I said, breaking the silence, trying to stay professional, official. "Transferred to Iraq, this kind of torture confers a special status on you. But it still may not be enough. Is there any other way you can demonstrate your fear of future persecution?"

Osman tapped his head, "With what I've injected up here over the last couple of years. All the technical information I have on poisons and their antidotes. It's the reason the Turks tortured me."

"Make this stuff look documentary in your Narrative. Go on for pages and pages, list minute details of your research. Then at the interview I'll ask you how the information you provide can be corroborated. What would you say?"

"Scientists in Greece might be able to corroborate some of the details, but the CIA would probably be needed to corroborate others. I'd also say that I know some things the CIA may not."

"Is this true?"

"Honest as a Kurd," Osman said in Kurmanji and, in English, "I think so, at least about ricin."

"What's that?"

"A very deadly poison made from beans."

For the second time, Ziba swerved Osman from the subject of poison: "Do you require a translator?" she asked him.

Some of his new confidence went out of his face, and he looked to me, hopeful, I felt, that I could restore that optimism.

"It's the first interview question. If you're Iraqi, Ziba would do the interview. She might 'correct' any false steps, and that would be an advantage. But being in the room would implicate her if your relationship ever surfaces. Anyway, I think you should know English. When it comes to relocation, that will be a large plus. But you've never been to America. That's a detail that's easy enough to check."

Osman Alpdogan: Born in Zarkho in 1963. His family was killed in the Anfal. Their ancestral village was bulldozed and its well poisoned. Caught in Dohuk when power shifted between the KDP and PUK, he was tortured by Barzani *peshmergas*. When they were done with him, they turned his name over to one of Saddam's hit squads. Walking home one night, Dr. Alpdogan was shot at. He played dead in the street and never returned to his apartment for his papers. He borrowed money from a fellow doctor and that same night headed north to Turkey. A smuggler walked him across the border near Silopi, two days and two nights through the mountains. During the day, they hid in caves from Turkish helicopters. At night they walked paths without a flashlight. Dr. Alpdogan had only the loafers he was wearing when shot at. When he got across the border, his feet looked as if they'd been beaten by the police. Dr. Alpdogan then made his way to Bodrum on the west coast of Turkey. There he hired another smuggler to transport him to Rhodes. Before dropping him in the water off Lindos, the smuggler robbed Dr. Alpdogan of his wallet.

"How will you get to Athens?" Ziba asked.

"So I keep my money?"

Ziba and I both nodded.

"Don't write the way you speak," I told Osman. "No slang, no figures of speech."

"Say you I no should use you computer for to print?"

Now Osman was smiling again.

"This is hand work," I said.

"Doctors have very bad handwriting."

"But it identifies who you are. Your Narrative will be your only document. Once I see a draft, we'll do a mock interview. Ziba can play the Director."

"If Mr. Osman speaks Sorani, he should be the replacement for Miss Ziba as a translator," Ziba said, imitating the Director's speech while reminding us of Mrs. Constantinou's suspicion of Ms. Mamozin.

Walking back to my apartment, I think about Ziba's remark—"replacement"—and ask myself why I'm not afraid. If I'm caught inventing a refugee, I'll be fired, replaced, but not deported. I'll be detained by the Justice Ministry. But I won't be caught. Unlike the experience with Mr. Kaya, Ziba and I know what we're doing. Osman won't write a letter betraying us, complaining that he's been recommended for status. Since the Kaya episode, I've not agitated to replace Siamand, and Mrs. Constantinou mostly rubber stamps my recommendations. But there is something more: if I could get Osman out of a Turkish prison, I should certainly get him through Greek offices.

Without fear interfering, the jump from "could" to "should" is not so difficult. Although Osman doesn't exactly fit UNHCR guidelines, he's been tortured by the Turks. When in doubt about an applicant, like Mr. Kaya, I've always denied him. Osman is the first applicant for whom I'm bending the rules. He came in with false documents. But he also has no intention of staying in Greece or returning to Kurdistan, so he doesn't fit the PKK profile. As a doctor, Osman won't pose a danger to public order or health. In the long run, his political commitment, his urgent desire to publicize the Kurds' plight, may even help reduce the flow of refugees into Greece. Did the Canadian "plastic chair guy" deserve to be in the United States because he had a quarter million dollars to spend on himself? The law said so. Osman's motives are altruistic. Justice lies with the Kurdish doctor.

Back in my apartment, checking my hair and looking at my walk-reddened cheeks in the mirror, I have to admit it: from his first night in my apartment I felt a niggle of attraction to Osman. Then I couldn't come close to explaining why. Something about the way he held his body, as if he hadn't thought about it for twenty years. That odd combination of professional confidence and personal diffidence, as if he'd been through an exacting test and come out the other side. He was also the first man to be in an apartment of mine since Rick, so maybe my body was doing some thinking I didn't know about, hormones rather than adrenaline circulating through my brain. The best evidence I had then was waking up the next morning and wondering where Osman was sleeping, what one might find under that brown suit. Now I confess to myself that I'd like Osman to live in Muslimistan, not Kurdistan or America. Not a replacement for Ziba, but an addition, a second person to talk with, another informant about Kurds. And yes, maybe another secret to keep. There's something gentle and genteel about Osman, unusual in both the Kurds I've questioned and the American men who asked me out. Since I'm already committed to risking more than my job for Osman, I don't want to examine myself any more than necessary. I know I can't be diffident, but I don't want to sound guilty. I want to have Osman's relaxed confidence when the tape is running.

Chapter 11

Osman was Ziba-literal and uncannily distant at his interview. Although only the two of us were in my office, he gave no sign we'd ever been on the same continent. Like Rena, my former Iraqi translator, he rumbled his English "r's." Unlike amateur-rehearsed applicants, who avoided hard questions, Osman answered each of mine directly, but not too quickly, just as he'd been rehearsed by a professional. My Letter of Recommended Action recited the facts, objectively evaluated his interview, noted his lack of documents, and strongly supported Osman Alpdogan for status.

While we waited for the Director's decision, Osman did volunteer work two days a week at the Rehabilitation Center and tried to pursue his research at the National Medical Library, which received a few English-language period-icals. It was May and warm enough for cold-climate foreigners to eat outdoors at night and swim on weekends. One evening when the three of us were hidden behind the walls of Xynos, a Plaka taverna, I asked Ziba and Osman if they'd like to go to the beach some Sunday.

"I would," Ziba said, "but I doubt you want to speak Greek to my children."

"I used to like walking on the beach in Chicago," Osman said, "but I don't know how to swim."

"This is the place to learn," I said, "the salt holds you up and the water is calm."

"Maybe you should learn," Ziba said to Osman, "in case you have to cross the Rio Grande."

"Or worse yet," Osman said, "one of the Great Lakes. If I try it, will I have to wear those inflatable water wings I used to see on little kids?"

I assured him he wouldn't, and we arranged to meet the next Sunday at the bus stop for Vouliagmeni. The ride down the coast reminded Osman of his years in Chicago. We talked about living near water, how it gave one a sense of freedom, if only the freedom to cross the Ohio River into Kentucky.

When Osman came out of the changing room at Vouliagmeni, he was wearing cut-off surgeon's pants he said he'd "liberated" at the Rehab Center. He was thin, but his abdomen was rippled like a body-builder's.

"Have you been helping others or working on the Nautilus machines at the Center?" I asked.

"These are prison muscles," he said, tensing his stomach. He flexed his arms, and I could see the muscles in his shoulders. "Sit-ups and push-ups. They're all you have room to do in solitary. I got into the habit and still do them in my new cell." He pointed to his downright skinny legs and shrugged.

"Walking everywhere in Athens," I said, pointing to my own legs, my newly defined calves. "Put us together and we'd make a real specimen."

The truth was I also had strong shoulders from swimming. Together, then, two good backs, which made me think of the beast with two backs. And four very white legs. Maybe Kurds weren't really reddish, just sun- and wind-burned on the skin I got to see at the office. Walking toward the water with Osman, passing the olive Greeks, I didn't feel self-conscious about my fair skin.

The only other person I'd taught how to swim was a six-year-old cousin. I put my arms under her chest and hips while she flapped her arms and pedaled the water. That would be a little too intimate for Osman. I had him stand in chest-high water and practice breathing before I demonstrated the crawl.

"You have to relax and trust the water," I told him.

"And you."

"Yes, and me."

Osman tried it and swallowed some of the Aegean. "It's okay, it's okay," he said. He tried again with the same result. "No problem. I need the salts." Again he thrashed and came up spitting and smiling.

"We mountain people are too highly evolved," he said. "It'll take some time to remember gills."

As Osman practiced, I tried to think of some other man who would let me teach him how to swim. Rick welcomed information about the law and advice on his service motion and the secrets of a woman on top, but he'd never let me show him how to rappel (if I'd known how) or stay afloat (if he hadn't known how). Lawyers are sharks. They can swim and rip at the same time. Maybe not Nikos. His spirit is so heavy he'd give up and force me to rescue him. I pictured Erica flitting above the water's surface. I put Ziba in a one-piece bathing suit, her scars covered. No, as good friends as we were, Ziba was too proud to do what her brother did.

Lying on a mat under a beach umbrella, Osman and I joked, as Ziba and I used to, about the people around us. Without Ziba to interrupt or deflate him, Osman was more relaxed. He spoke freely about everything until I asked him how he and Ziba felt about being sent away from home to be educated.

"Personal history," Osman said, as if the two words didn't belong next to each other. He picked up a handful of sand and threw it ahead of him.

"I don't bother remembering anything that happened before med school."

He dug deeper into the sand and threw away another handful.

"As far as I'm concerned," he said, "my life began in Chicago."

"You had the good fortune to move. My whole life was spent in Cincinnati."

More sand.

Ziba and I made up a personal past for Osman, and now he wasn't interested in his own or mine. But Osman asked me numerous questions about my job—the people I'd interviewed, what I thought about their lives, how I felt about UNHCR. "Not nearly enough aid to dispense," I told him, and he spoke bitterly about his job in Erbil, the difficulty of doing normal medicine in a civil war zone: "Women were having babies at home because the beds were all filled and obstetricians had to be surgeons. Kurds killing Kurds in our 'safe zone.' It was sickening. Between the UN embargo and Saddam's embargo, we couldn't get antibiotics. Infection killed as many as wounds. Women and children were dying of simple pneumonia."

Well-founded fear of disease, I thought, another ground for flight not covered in the *Handbook*.

"The beach lets me forget the nine out of ten I can't help," I told him.

"I hope it will work for me," he said and threw some more sand. When we were leaving, Osman asked if we could do it again the next Sunday. "Sure," I said. "Maybe a beach without the sea," Osman said. "I liked the talk, but really don't need the water."

Osman most enjoyed talking about the States, a long-time resident comparing notes with a short-term exile. Eight years in Chicago, he had learned a lot about American culture—present and past, Madonna and Shirley Temple—and enjoyed quizzing me, as if he were administering a citizenship test. The following Sunday, after I swam and he waded, Osman asked, "Do you know why white people defeated the Indians?"

"High technology."

"Nope," he said.

"By introducing the liquid banned in strict Muslim countries."

"Nope," he said, beginning to sound like John Wayne.

"Because Indians had their ghost dance and weren't afraid."

"I hadn't thought of that. Guess again."

"That's it. Fear is my final solution."

"Because Europeans used biological warfare," he said in a way that reminded me of Professor Malik's disgust. "Americans gave Indians blankets infected with smallpox."

"I do remember that now."

I didn't mention syphilis, which came back with the smallpox story. And I know why: my Greek date who quizzed me about AIDS in America. I reached over, touched Osman's red-tinged hair, and said, "You'll never be mistaken for an Indian."

"Better dead than red," he said. "I wonder if Americans said that about the Irish."

Like some of my immigration clients, Osman knew the negative history of America. Foreign universities must teach courses in the subject: old, old evil, but great new science and indispensable English.

I told Osman about visiting Mrs. Haydar and her two children in their one-room basement apartment. Litsa, the UNHCR social worker, kept delivering invitations, so finally I went with her on a monthly call. The kids were kicking a soccer ball around the below-ground cement courtyard outside Mrs. Haydar's glass door. She insisted she serve Litsa and me some lunch—pita bread, hummus, and tea. Mrs. Haydar wanted to return the favor I'd done her. She also invited me to show off the English she was learning. "Thank you very much." "Children are happy." "This is good place." "Please eat more." So few words, such a small place, and yet better, I supposed, than the shack I'd been in outside Istanbul. Still, not much to assuage a well-off American's guilt.

"Even Mrs. Haydar's English made me feel ashamed," I told Osman. "She should have been learning Greek, like Ziba, not the language of hope."

"I don't know about Ziba," Osman said. I asked him what he meant.

"Learning Greek, working for Greeks—it's like she wants to change her skin. Sometimes she doesn't seem like my sister anymore."

Osman picked up sand, tossed it on my legs, and changed the mood by starting another quiz: "Why did your people build skyscrapers in Chicago?"

"Because ground-level space was so expensive."

"For once, money's not the answer."

"To get away from the smallpox."

"Be serious."

"Okay, here's one you'll like. Because they were afraid of a future flood and wanted their own Mount Ararat."

"You're getting closer. With your specialty, you should know this."

"Tell me, O Oz," the name I called him when he was questioning me.

"Because their genes missed living in mountain caves, humans' original refuge."

I didn't really believe him, but I enjoyed being quizzed, the tables turned, no table or desk, just a beach mat and two people partly dressed. Both serious and ironic, Osman had the almost nerdy charm of a boy I dated in high school, until it came time for the prom and he calculated just how much taller I'd be in heels.

The next Sunday it was overcast and cool when we met at the bus stop. I asked Osman if he'd rather come to my apartment and use my Internet connection. In Kurdistan, he'd used a computer to run numbers, but not to surf the net, and he was anxious to see what was out there. I showed him how to use Alta Vista, and while he clicked and scanned I read files. They were piling up again, the warm weather bringing Kurds over land and sea, now in groups of fifty and a hundred. The more applicants I had, though, the less I worried about the Director somehow hearing about Osman in my apartment. Anyway, Osman is not a translator. He's a researcher, making good use of my computer now that I was too busy to work on my essay. I told him he should finish it. He read it and agreed that current law responded to symptoms, but he felt it would take a lot more than revised UNHCR guidelines to have any effect on Turkey.

Like me reading files my first month, Osman was amazed at the information on the Internet, the up-to-date, almost daily reports he could get on events in Turkey, Iraq, and Iran. He bookmarked several Kurdish sites, and got himself onto two lists, one in a language I couldn't read. For my purposes, the information was always too detailed, but Osman couldn't get enough of it. After a couple of hours, he complained about the speed of my provider and then my modem.

"Too many damned pictures on the Internet," he grumbled while waiting for some images to load.

"Pictures are what first drew me to the Kurds," I said and showed him Erica's book of photographs, the tented hillsides and cliff-hanging villages.

"The old way of life," Osman said, turning from the screen to leaf through the pages. "What attracted you to it?"

"Movement, I guess. Freedom of movement. When the weather changed, those nomads packed their tents and moved. No fields to cultivate, no houses to clean. Home on the range. And always in the background beautiful snow-covered mountains. Maybe I spent too much time in Ohio."

"The mountains are still there, but now we're nomads without tents and animals."

Osman closed the book and hefted it, as if measuring how much truth it contained.

"Would you like to visit Kurdistan?"

"I wanted to when I saw those pictures, but it's a dangerous place for an American passport."

"I could disguise you as a Kurd."

I ran my hand through my blonde hair.

"Dye," he said.

I stood up on my tiptoes. He laughed and said, "You'd just have to keep your head down. You know, like army recruits."

I batted my baby blues at his green eyes.

"I don't think so," I said.

"I'd love to take you there and show you the real thing, what's left of it, not just a bunch of pictures."

He handed the book back to me, turned to the screen, and said, "The trouble is these images aren't even pictures. They're just filler, the people who manage the site showing off."

I moved behind his chair and leaned over his shoulder to work the mouse, open up options, click on "disregard images," and speed up the data. Because it was hard to see the screen from my angle, I leaned closer and brushed against Osman's shoulder. I clicked and the image disappeared.

He turned his head up toward me and asked, "Can you do that again?"

"I don't need to. I've just set it to not load images."

"I don't mean the command. I mean, can you brush my shoulder with your breast again?"

I could and I did.

"Like that?"

"Exactly," he said and stood up. Then there was brushing of hands and other body parts. There was the meeting of lips and the rapid meeting of minds. There was the rushed unbuttoning of clothes. Having swum together, we didn't hesitate for visual inspection. On my bed we moved like sidestrokers, stroking each other. Neither of us, however, had remembered to let down the blinds, so I got up to do it. In the dark, Osman realized the computer hadn't been put to sleep. I welcomed these comic interruptions because that awkward safe sex moment was near. Osman fumbled in his pockets, held up a condom, and said doctors have to be prepared for any health emergency. Although I hadn't intended to rub Osman's shoulder with my breast, I was very happy he was planning for the future. Osman's penis wasn't made fearful by its protective sheath.

The rest is a secret, two bodies' almost silent secret that shouldn't be translated into words. No Narrative or Interview requires the description of sex. It's an action no Letter can adequately recommend. Not even video can document it, the sub-skin communication of blood and chemicals and electrical charges obeying natural law, the foundation of life. In less than a minute we'd both come. Two ascetics, I thought, too long. The suddenness didn't bother me, but I worried Osman might feel bad. He'd kept his head in the water longer than this.

Osman pushed himself up with his prisoner's arms and put the tip of his nose against the tip of my nose. "Can you do that again?" he whispered.

"Can you?"

He could and I could, I did and he did, and lying beside Osman in artificial dark was softer and sweeter than lying on sand in Greek light. Released from solitary, I found joy in this single-bed asylum.

It was only when I stood up that self-consciousness kicked in. That's you, Casey, the consummate yuppie, romanced while bending over a computer. I didn't care. Lying down, we were a great fit. Walking arm-and-arm down the street to lunch, we made a great pair. I felt like one of those leggy models on the arm of a tall, red-haired Italian designer. I leaned into Osman as I had at the computer, and he said, "Voracious. I've heard about you American superwomen sucking old wealthy doctors dry."

"You're only a year older than me, Osman."

"Ah, that's right, and you're wealthier than me."

"I'm going to spend it all on condoms."

"A loving, humanitarian gesture."

"Humanitarian" made us both realize where we were, what we were doing: walking together down an Athens street a few blocks from UNHCR. Not just together, but arm-in-arm, no space between us, refugee applicant and his examiner. We let go of each other, separated a little, walked quickly back to the apartment, and ate everything I had in the refrigerator. We lay our heads at opposite ends of my bed and stared at each other. We pondered the distance both of us had come to this intersection. "Intercourse," Osman said. "Interlacing," I replied, tangling his legs in mine. We drowsed and dawdled, made love again, fell asleep. I used my Greek to have a pizza delivered. The laptop stayed closed, files went unread.

Though my ground-floor apartment felt like a mountain cave where we might hibernate, and although my bed, with its solid wooden footboard and headboard, was perfect for making love, it was not made to sleep two. At midnight Osman told me he had to go to his hotel for his insulin. He'd be back in the morning with more food and condoms.

Putting on his shoes, he said, "Maybe we shouldn't tell Ziba about your rubbing against my shoulder."

"My brushing, your asking that I do it again."

"Okay, but however it started it's still incest."

Incest? I thought of Oedipus. I'd taught Osman to swim, but he wasn't my son. Had I violated a Kurdish taboo regarding adopted siblings? Or was Osman giving a free translation of some Kurdish word?

"You're kidding, right?"

"Yes, it's what Turks say about Kurds, that we marry our sisters and brothers. You know, like gypsies. It's an old prejudice against people who stick together and move around. But seriously, I think Ziba might feel even more isolated than she does now. You're her only friend. I'm her only family here. If she knows we're swimming in the sheets, I'm afraid she'll feel left out."

"Left out? The bed's too small for us. How could Ziba feel left out?"

"A poor choice of words. How about 'hurt,' maybe 'betrayed?' Ziba does think of you as her sister. For us to be lovers may somehow spoil that. I don't feel that way, but Ziba could. She might conceal her feelings from you, but punish me somehow."

Osman hesitated, as if he didn't want to say what was really on his mind.

"What is it?" I asked.

"Ziba has changed here. I know she was tortured, but that doesn't explain why she's so unpredictable. I used to rely on her. Now I don't feel that I can trust her in some situations."

Our first day as lovers was no time to ask Osman about Ziba's betrayal.

"Don't worry," I said. "Ziba won't be calling her big sister at this hour. We can talk about her tomorrow if you want to commit incest again."

"I'll be here at nine."

"I have to be at work at nine. Don't you have an alarm?"

"Okay, seven."

I hadn't thought about Ziba all day. I had a college classmate who never stayed overnight at a man's place because she wanted to get on the phone to do play-by-play with a mutual friend of ours. I've never felt like talking about intimate details with anyone. With a sister I might have discussed a new lover, in general terms. But not if he was her brother. If sex is a secret, something to be hugged close and silently savored, incest is the deepest secret, even if it's only figurative. The ultimate clan infolding, the worst familial offense. If discovered, I can plead ignorance. I can blame it on Ziba: she's the one who delivered Osman to my door. I remembered the old high-school reluctance to admit falling for a guy introduced to you by a girlfriend, as if he were somehow second-hand or you were unable to pluck boys out of the air. Really, though, I was more concerned with the incest continuing than with Ziba's feelings. Altruism had reached its limit. I'd be selfish and guiltless for a while, do what I desired. Well-earned, well-founded pleasure. Ziba had betrayed Osman once. I didn't want to be the reason she might punish him here, and if Osman thought telling her would affect our incest, I definitely wanted to keep it secret. It had to be a secret from everyone else. Although the *Handbook* said nothing about sexual intercourse with an applicant, I knew it was more dangerous than friendship with a translator.

When Ziba, Osman, and I were together, we maintained our usual seating arrangement. When Ziba and I were together, neither of us mentioned Osman very often. I feared betraying my feelings. She seemed satisfied to continue our friendship as if Osman was still in Kurdistan. Ziba knew I'd given him a key to use my Internet access when I wasn't home. She thought he was busy on weekends with some Kurds he met at the Rehab Center. One of them worked for a magazine that was published here, printed in both Greek and English, and sold on the street to Greeks and tourists by young kids. Though printed on glossy paper, *Kurdistan News* must have been a low-budget operation because Osman asked me to show him how to download Internet items onto disks from which the editors could print, magazine journalism's equivalent of "rip and read" radio news. As with Greek, Osman was impatient with computer instruction; he wanted to know only enough to do what he wanted to do. I liked this impatience because we could rub and rut whenever I was asked some new question.

In my apartment, Osman and I had no fear. We were "inside," not "between." On the rare occasion that the phone rang while he was there, I didn't answer it. He never called me at the office. I didn't try to hurry his application through Mrs. Constantinou. In fact, the longer she took getting to it the longer Osman and I would be together. Though he didn't often mention his application, he was frank about his desire to get to the States as soon as possible. Waiting for the Director's decision was also bringing me closer to a decision about my future country of residence. I was happy with the work at UNHCR. I was very happy about my part-time life with Osman. If he was in the United States, perhaps working at the firm would be more tolerable. I asked Osman where he might go. Chicago, he thought. It was a long way from Cincinnati, I thought to myself. Maybe I should ask Mrs. Constantinou to return Osman Alpdogan's file to me for reconsideration.

Waiting for Mrs. Constantinou brought even better beach weather, but we spent most of our free hours in the apartment. Without air-conditioning, our love nest and refuge was very warm, and we couldn't open the street-level shutters. One Saturday afternoon in early June, we were sticking to each other. Bonded by sweat, our chests spoke love's noise-language. Suddenly Osman pulled away and sat up on the edge of the bed.

"I'm sorry," he said, "I seem to have liquefied." He held his flaccid penis with two fingers. There was no sperm in the condom.

"It's okay," I told him, "is this another one of those lowland problems Kurds have?"

He smiled and said, "I wish it were true. We could rent a room up near the Acropolis. But it looks seasonal. Or maybe a syndrome, the doctor's usual excuse for anything mysterious."

Something about his tone, the way he said "mysterious," implied I shouldn't try to kid around this.

"Could the problem be related to what the Turks injected?"

"Dear, dear, Casey. Who else but you would ask that question, give me that escape?" He leaned over, kissed me on the nose, and said "Can you do that again?"

"Could it be related to what the Turks did to you?"

"I'm afraid it might. Not the injection. I'm still losing weight, but I think the trouble is much older, much less scientific than injection. Association. The nervous system that connects head and penis."

"Tell me," I said. Not a question, but the command you can give someone you love.

"The Turks had medical expertise. I think they were also afraid of harming me, for what reason I don't know. They certainly couldn't know Ziba and you were here in Athens planning my release. Anyway, they didn't beat my feet. Maybe they were worried a doctor would find that crude. They didn't rape me or shock my genitals, if that's what you're thinking."

Osman had lapsed again into that professional tone. I didn't want him to cover all the Turks' options and methods.

"Tell me what they did to you."

"Did you ever know a New Ager who sat under or slept in one of those metal pyramids?"

"No, but I've seen pictures of them in magazines."

"Okay, now add plexiglas to three sides, leaving one side open. Tie a prisoner's hands and feet to ring bolts in a cement courtyard. Around eleven a.m. place the pyramid over him and wait for the sun to do its work. Gradually the temperature rises and you start to sweat and sweat and sweat. You don't know how hot it is in there, but you know how much temperature the body can stand, how much water and how many salts you're losing, what damage dehydration can do to the organs and brain, and you know, if you're a doctor, that the Turks know you know what's happening and what could happen to you in that pyramid. They were literally, repetitively, gradually sweating information out of me. It was the perfect torture for someone with diabetes. I went days without urinating. Maybe my penis got trained to disuse. My body's toxins were coming out my pores. The Turks wanted out of my mouth what I knew about unnatural toxins, man-made poisons. They shouted at me in Turkish, but I refused to answer. Then they brought in a collaborator, one of those *jash* village guards. He'd scream at me and then get up close, breathe in my face, and whisper to me in Kurmanji. If I gave him a little information, he gave me a little water. It went on for weeks, slowly, slowly. When they or I miscalculated, they gave me an IV, just enough liquid and just enough insulin to keep me alive so they could wring me dry. When I got back to my cell I was so cold I had to do exercises to keep warm."

"This pyramid works in the winter, in Diyarbakir?"

"It works all right, on the same principle that lets Greeks heat their water with solar collectors. I could barely walk when they jabbed me in the ass and told me I was being deported to Iraq. My information might have lasted another month, but I think I'd have been comatose in two weeks if you hadn't shown up. Now I'm comatose down here." He gestured to his penis.

I sat up with him, pulled the sheet up around him, and put my arms around him. Then with the sheet I wiped the sweat off his face and arms and body. I cracked the shutters for some air. Fucking Turks, those fucking Turks. Tortured Kurds and made sex difficult for both Ziba and Osman. Get the information and stop the natives from breeding. No wonder Mr. Kaya risked losing a hand and arm. Osman didn't appear to be a victim. His wound was invisible and deeper. No prosthesis could fix it. Every time he sweats, he'll think of the pyramid. Every day the sun comes up, he'll be afraid.

Osman stared straight ahead, drained of his story. He was as motionless as he'd been in the pyramid, as alone.

"Slowly, slowly," I whispered his words back to him. "Slowly, slowly we'll

make you forget the pyramid, destroy the association. Slowly, slowly we'll
make love and show those bastards what slow can be. We'll get a fan. I'll buy
an air-conditioner. We'll move to a penthouse for the sea breeze."

"Dear, sweet Casey," Osman finally said, "I hope we have the time."

Chapter 12

The Director approved Osman's application. I called Joseph Costa at the American Embassy the same day. I reminded him that we'd talked about Kurds.

"Ah yes," he said, "the Barzani lady. I've been reading about Barzani lately, his alliance with Saddam."

"That's why I'm calling. I have an Iraqi Kurd who's an enemy of the Barzanis. They tortured him in Dohuk because he has secrets about poisons."

"What kind of secrets?"

"Inside information about Iraqi chemical weapons. I'm no scientist, but the information is very detailed. The man is a doctor asking to be relocated in the States. I thought you'd want to read his file and talk with him."

"Send over the file. I'll show it to our agricultural attache and get back to you."

"I'm not talking about pesticides, Mr. Costa. This refugee has knowledge of Saddam's poison gases."

"I realize that, Casey. But we can't have a 'chemical warfare' expert here at the embassy. Our 'agricultural attache' is the man to look at your doctor's information."

I assumed Costa's inflection of "agricultural attache" meant that, like other attaches, he had a dual function, one other than advising Greek farmers how to grow olives. In the States, I'd spoken with plenty of bureaucrats like Costa. They preferred the phone to email because they loved insider talk, keeping secrets and giving them away at the same time. Costa's desire to show off his status bred a cynicism I might somehow exploit. For now, though, I was the model of decorum and procedure.

I faxed the file to Costa. My cover letter quoted passages from INS regulations on national interest. Osman was just like those scientists Snow and Fiore moved to America, except for the urgency of his health. He'd had a blood test and didn't like the numbers. But we had to wait.

And while waiting, I saw where new boatloads of Kurds waited for UNHCR to process their applications. Everyone at the office was invited to a festival at a camp run by Medicins du Monde north of Athens on the slopes of Mount Pendeli. Erica said she was going and encouraged me to come: "It's an amnesty from office politics. Maybe even Mrs. Constantinou will be there."

Osman wanted to see the camp. He and I talked Ziba into going.

Riding the bus toward Pendeli, gouged white by two thousand five hundred years of marble mining, I was reminded of the mountains east of Diyarbakir and the snow-covered tent platforms that Demirsar showed me. At the Pendeli camp, the tents were white, made of canvas that looked like very old military surplus. They were pitched among pine trees in an abandoned campground where Greek children had once learned about nature rapidly disappearing from Athens. Now Kurdish children occupied the ten by eight-foot tents with their parent or parents, perhaps a grandparent, maybe an uncle or aunt or cousin. In tents that once slept four kids for a week, six or more adults and children spent months—sleeping on cardboard sheets or plastic bags, eating from tin plates resting on their laps, sponge bathing behind sheets hung from tent poles, waiting for their half hour with an examiner.

This examiner knew from the Questionnaires and from the first-floor waiting room that children accompanied applicants. But I hadn't registered the number, not until I heard babies crying inside the tents and saw preschoolers standing listlessly by the flaps staring at the visitor. They didn't point at me or question their parents about me or wave to me. They just watched me try not to stare at them. Every child I saw was barefoot. Their clothes were too large or too small, pants held up by strings, tee shirts exposing ribs. No chubby, overfed kids like the Greeks I saw. No running or jump-roping or shouting kids. The Kurdish children looked stunned. Not just impoverished like the kids peering out of ads for UNICEF, but shocked and hopeless. They would never tell me how they felt about their country of origin or their new home. But it was easy to imagine their fear. In the past, present, and future. Of their parents, neighbors, and me. For their lives.

This encampment, not Diyarbakir, was the city of refugees, homes utterly transient, completely insecure. No platforms or slabs. The tent flaps rippled in the breeze. The old canvas would soak through in a heavy rain. Residents had to carry with them whatever objects of value they still possessed. In front of one tent, a man had stacked a few canned goods and some candles. I saw no customers approach the store-keeper squatting on his heels, smoking a hand-rolled cigarette. Next to some tents were piles of small sticks, preparation for next winter. The tent city was a pitiful mockery of Kurdish nomad life, an extended family's huge skin tent, vibrant carpets inside, goats and chickens outside, a few of these tents grouped near mountain streams and grazing land. Here water for a hundred tents came from a single standpipe surrounded by mud. Food came from a trailer turned into a soup kitchen. Instead of a hundred people living off land they loved, the camp was a thousand densely packed people living off charity. Pride had become humiliation. Medicins du Monde was doing the best they could with volunteer effort, but the Greek government would not help. Anything more than ugly subsistence, the Interior Ministry believed, would bring even more Kurds in smugglers' boats. With a UNHCR card, camp dwellers could do day labor and move into a run-down hotel like Ziba's or a cellar like Mrs. Haydar's. Where the children would be better off I couldn't judge. Where their parents would go I couldn't predict. Those who didn't receive cards might die here or walk back to Kurdistan or start committing petty crimes as Mr. Kaya did.

"How," I asked the Medicins du Monde representative, a Greek-American woman about my age, "can there be a festival here?"

"Not here," Susan told me. "When other Kurds and guests arrive, there'll be some speeches. Then we'll all walk up the mountain together."

"Don't you have fights here? If Kurds are all mixed in together, Iraqis with Turks and different political factions, there must be conflicts."

"Most of the people here are sick. They're too exhausted to feud with each other. And when they chose what to carry, they left weapons behind."

A boy about seven, barefoot like the rest, grabbed onto Susan's leg and spoke in Greek. I caught the word for "party" and, from Susan, "wait."

"This is a resident?" I asked.

"Certainly is. We start teaching them Greek as soon as they arrive. Just in case," she said and let me finish.

"In case they're lucky enough to receive status."

"Right."

After Susan moved away to greet other guests, I walked around, looking for Ziba and Osman. On a tent in back of the speakers' stage, I spotted a sign that said "Art Exibit." Inside, charcoal drawings and finger paintings lean against the sides of the tent. Suspended from one pole is a large piece of cardboard. At the top, in carefully printed letters is the sentence "Please Open Your Eyes." I go closer. Tacked onto the cardboard are Polaroid snapshots of dead women and children, slumping in doorways, lying in streets. Outside. The photographs alternate between full-body shots and extreme closeups. Documents. These photos are documents. No red from wounds stains the yellow and white and blue and orange clothes of the dead. All of them are facing the camera, all with their eyes open, open wide in bloated faces with open mouths, strings of vomit hanging from their lips. The camera is so close I can see the eyes are bloodshot, reddened by poison gas.

I want to vomit. I have to look away. Nothing Amnesty International publishes is this graphic, this horrible. Greek-speakers approach the photos and turn away. I force myself to stand there. I make myself look at the eye-level photos and be horrified. I want to be terrified by the bloodshot eyes of dead children. I feel I owe this to the "lucky" ones, the kids who watched me from their tents. Looking into the eyes of dead children is my torture. The photographs are like injections jabbed into my eyeballs. I should have come to the camp earlier. Here instead of Lavrion, here in place of Istanbul. But if I'd seen the camp in winter, I'd have been fired for too many approvals. Fucking Turks, fucking Iraqis. For too long, I've responded to refugees as if they were a Greek tragedy. Pity and fear. As if fate and not politics brought Kurds to Greece. As if morality and law could do anything for Kurds left behind. Anger is the emotion I should have been suppressing in the interviews, releasing elsewhere, somewhere it would have an effect. Wide-eyed, bug-eyed anger. Articulate anger like Osman's attack on Arabs and Persians.

Greek on a loudspeaker called me back outside. On the stage a man addressed fifty or sixty Greeks and foreigners sitting in plastic chairs. In front, listening intently, were Erica and a man I assumed was her husband. Residents of the camp stood behind the chairs. Between the guests and the residents were Ziba and Osman, Ziba speaking into Osman's ear. Since I too needed a translator, I walked back to them. For the benefit of any watchers, Ziba pretended to introduce Osman to me. In a low voice, she translated the Medicins du Monde speaker. Winter was coming. The residents had to get out of the tents. Next a Swedish Human Rights official spoke in English, confirming what I'd told Osman about emigration, pleading with the Greeks to do more. Then a British man railed against land mines, how they blew off the limbs of unsuspecting children. Most of the guests seemed to follow the speeches and applauded the speakers. Ziba and Osman clapped. I couldn't. I was still angry. Osman asked me what was wrong. I told him I'd just seen photos from the poison gas attack on Halabja. "See?" he said. "Yes, now," I told him.

The Kurds around us intently watched the speakers, but I doubted they understood much of what was said. They didn't talk among themselves. They just stared at the speakers, as if the people on stage were magical figures. When a Kurdish man took over the loudspeaker, though, the people became animated.

"We're going for a hike," Osman said and pointed up to Pendeli. From here the mountain looked like the white cliffs of Dover.

"How far?" I asked.

"Far enough so we won't have to see these tents," Ziba said.

"Maybe I'll wait for you down here."

"You should come," Ziba said. "That dancing you saw in Istanbul was nothing, some kids playing."

"Yes, you have to come," Osman added. "It's a guest's responsibility. We insist."

"I want to, but I'm not feeling that well. Maybe it's standing in the sun listening to the speeches," I said.

Neither Ziba nor Osman accepted that excuse. They knew I spent hours on the beach. They also knew I did a lot of walking and had on rubber-soled shoes. I couldn't think of another excuse. I didn't want to admit my acrophobia. Here in the camp it would sound ridiculous, maybe even another invented excuse to mountain-climbing Kurds. I also didn't want to insult Ziba and Osman by simply refusing.

"I'm afraid of heights," I told them. "And this climb looks pretty steep."

"We're not going all the way to the top," Ziba said.

"If it's too steep for you, we'll come back down," Osman said.

Up we went, falling in behind Kurds and guests. Hundreds of people were on the move, many singing, several beating the drum-like *daf*. They looked like a migration, not a panicked exile but a high-spirited journey toward some promised land. At first the land was like the camp, dirt and small pine trees. After a few hundred yards, the pitch increased and the surface was mostly rock and scrub brush. I held onto the bushes to steady myself and didn't look back. Then the brush thinned out and the rocks became larger, craggy. The Kurds were far ahead now, as the guests lagged. I stopped, sat on a rock, put my head between my knees. I was feeling dizzy and nauseous. Ziba took my right hand. "Come on," she said, "it's not much further."

"This is far enough."

Osman took my other hand. "Don't be a sissy," he said. "Between two Kurds you can't fall."

Ziba led us up the slope, picking the easiest way among the boulders. I looked at my feet and the ground. Osman was humming behind me. I wondered if, despite the wind up here, he would get sweaty on this climb. I tried not to think about future fear, coming back down, when it would be harder to avoid looking at the drop below. I wondered if I'd have to back down the mountain, like a baby going down stairs. I remembered an experiment I ran across when reading about acrophobia. Kids were placed on a glass floor above a drop. The crawlers were not afraid of falling, but the toddlers were.

After fifteen more minutes of climbing, we caught up with the rest of the people gathered on a grassy plateau the size of half a football field. Guests and Kurds were sitting on small rocks, enjoying the oxygen in their lungs, drinking out of water bottles and wineskins, celebrating the climb, admiring the view. Athens stretched out below us, a city of five million made small. From our height, the Acropolis looked unthreatening. The mountains are our only friends, I thought. Even I found Pendeli friendly, comforting in its perspective on puny lives below—as long as I was sitting and not standing near the plateau's edge. In Diyarbakir, I'd been mistaken. Acrophobia was not a fear of making a mistake. My fear was body deep, brain-stem fundamental, natural for anyone on two feet. My fear was a phobia because my eyes were too far from my feet and the ground.

After the wineskins were passed around, someone turned on a boom box and Kurds got up off their rocks. Three men ran to the center of the flat space and formed a line by linking their arms at the elbows. As they began to dance, a slow left-over-right, right-over-left step, others ran to link arms with them. Women, men, and teenagers, in groups of five and six, joined in to form a huge arm-linked semi-circle. The music whined its repetitive beat and the dancers chanted in unison.

"Come on," Ziba says to me.

"I don't know the steps or words."

"The steps are easy, you don't need words," Osman says and tugs at my hand.

We join the semi-circle as it begins to close. Across from us are Erica and her husband. She grins and winks at me. The circle closes, maybe three hundred people, and we all side-step clockwise. Ziba and Osman join the chant. Tightly linked at the elbows, we bump shoulders and hips. Around we go, a closed circle of women and men and youths, of Turks and Iraqis and Iranians and Greeks and an American. I'd seen Greek folk dancers in the Plaka. From a similar, but much smaller circle, someone always broke away, went to the center, and soloed. Not the Kurds. We go around and around, all united in a closed circle. When the song finishes, another comes on, we clasp hands, and move counterclockwise. Every few seconds we raise our linked hands above our heads, and Kurds ululate, a yodeling sound they make with their tongues. No amount of excitement breaks the circle. With the third song, we grip each other at the waists and shoulders, keeping the circle tight, but connecting other body parts. We stamp the ground. As Ziba grips my shoulder and I grip

Osman's waist, I feel bonded not just to them, but to the whole circle of flesh. Translation is not required. Language is not needed. Not even the steps have to be followed. The only law is physical contact, all fused to all.

Only dancing, only while dancing on a mountain that reminds them of home can these tribal people forget the camp below, forget their anger and despair, the children left behind with elders, the dead left in the east. Welcome to Kurdistan, a Kurdistan without fear of Iraqi planes or Turkish tanks, a Kurdistan where speakers of Kurmanji, Guran, and Sorani unite in song, where PKK, PDP, and PUK circle in step. I squeeze the shoulder of my Kurdish friend Ziba and the back of my Kurdish lover Osman, stamp with them on the high plateau, and put out of mind the walk back down to the camp.

Tuesday after the celebration on Pendeli, the secretary downstairs put through a call while Siamand and I were interviewing a man from Mardin. "It's a Mr. Oroglou from the Turkish Embassy," she said. "He says it's impor-tant."

"Ask him if I can return his call," I told her.

Thirty seconds later, the phone rang again.

"Mr. Oroglou says it's very important."

"Tell him I'll pick up in a minute."

I asked Siamand to take the man from Mardin down to the translator's room with him. I didn't want Siamand lurking outside in the corridor. Kaya, this has to be about Kaya. I never heard from General Silay, so I assumed Kaya was deported by the Ministry. Since it's legal to record calls in Greece, I flicked on the tape.

> "Casey Mahan speaking."
>
> "I am Dogan Oroglou from the Embassy of Turkey in Athens."
>
> "What can I do for you, Mr. Oroglou?"
>
> "There ees nothing to do. I just am calling to tell you that we will be seeing you."
>
> "You want to see me about some matter?"
>
> "No, no. We sees you. We sees you dance with thees Mamozin and all thees others."
>
> "Those others are refugees, Mr. Oroglou. From your country, from Iraq and Iran."

"These are creemeenals. We see you
dance with creemeenals. We ask you to understand thees."

"May I have your number, Mr. Oroglou?
I'll call you back and talk about refugees
when I'm not so busy interviewing them."

"We talk no more. We just am calling to
say we sees. Goodbye Mees Man."

Surveillance. Not by the Director. By Turkey. Maybe. I asked the secretary to call the Embassy, check if Mr. Oroglou's was the voice we heard. A Mr. Oroglou worked in the visa section, but he did not take calls. So said his secretary. Anyone could know this and impersonate him. Or Mr. Oroglou could be delivering a message from General Silay: "We have the bomber, but we're still going to watch you and Mamozin."

I brought Siamand and the applicant back in. While Siamand struggled with his English, I paid close attention to how he pronounced words. "Does the applicant see the problem I have with him?" I asked Siamand. "Yes, he see well this," Siamand said.

At lunchtime, I listened to the phone tape. The caller made the "i" in "this" and "criminal" and "Miss" into a long "e" the way some Greeks do. But the way he said "Athens" wasn't Greek-influenced. Colonel Demirsar and General Silay were the only Turkish officials I'd spoken to. The caller's syntax was a little like Demirsar's, but he said "criminal" and "bandit." The vocabulary was like Siamand's. He was dancing on Pendeli. He could be keeping up the personal vendetta against Ziba, or the call could be part of some Kurdish feud I know nothing about. Maybe the caller was an Iraqi or Iranian Kurd, jealous of special treatment given Turkish Kurds. I thought again about the Director, then Kaya. The Ministry could somehow suspect my relation with Kurds and could be using some Turk at their disposal to deliver a warning.

I listened again. "Mamozin," singular. Okay, if it referred to Ziba. But only Silay and Demirsar know Osman is also "Mamozin." If the name referred to Osman Alpdogan, he could be in trouble. Maybe someone other than the Turks in Diyarbakir and Ziba knows Alpdogan is a false identity. No matter how many times I listened, the tape wouldn't cough up the secret of the caller's identity. Repeated, the words took on ever more threatening possibilities: "we see you," "we see through you," "we seize you," "we seize thees," antique plural you. We cease you, your freedom. We seas you, throw you overboard to drown like the Kurds who never made it to Greek beaches.

After work, I looked into Siamand's file. He was awarded status by the Greek lawyer I'd replaced. Siamand's application claimed he was persecuted because a person he knew was a PKK member. His documents were almost too good—too clean, too pat—to be true. Siamand could be *jash*, a Turkish stooge given persuasive documents and planted in Athens to inform on Kurds. Though his language was garbled, Siamand was right about Kaya. Maybe Siamand only pretends to mangle his English, a way to control the interviews he translates. If that's the case, the caller, Siamand, and General Silay could be in cahoots. If the caller really was Oroglou from the Embassy, he might well have contacts in the Greek Interior Ministry. Separate threats wove together, in my mind if not in reality.

I asked Erica if she got a phone call from the Turks, and she just laughed. I tried for several days to get Mr. Oroglou on the phone, but he wouldn't take my call. Just in case the call was only Siamand's vendetta, I wanted to wait a few days before telling Ziba and Osman. Then the mystery call was pushed back in consciousness by another call, this one in clear, American English.

"Nothing can be done for Dr. Alpdogan," Joseph Costa said. "He probably deserves asylum here, but it would take serious security interest to get a guy like this into the States."

"You don't even want your 'agricultural attache' to talk with him?"

"He said the information doesn't look that promising."

"What about humanitarian grounds? Since I interviewed Dr. Alpdogan, he's had blood tests in a hospital here. He's been losing weight, and he believes he was injected with some timed-release toxin that can be detected only in an American hospital. If he's right about the injection, the government will have some great propaganda stuff on the bad guys in Iraq, and you'll get credit for discovering the source."

"To me, he looks like a risky investment. I bet he's not insured, is he?"

"Probably not."

"An obvious welfare case. We just let in Third World dictators who can pay their own way. Your guy runs up thirty thousand in hospital bills, and I get the blame."

"But that's what 'humanitarian' means, 'welfare.'"

"Not any more, Casey. Now it means 'publicity.' Like that African girl who was going to be clitorectomied. Your guy's injection, if it ever happened, if it ever kills him, is too slow, not dramatic enough for 'humanitarian' effort.'"

"So you won't do anything for Doctor Alpdogan?"

"I can't."

This was the phrase I knew was coming, the words I wanted to hear: Costa admitting or pretending that, despite his power, he was powerless, embarrassing for a guy who enjoys revealing secrets. If he didn't always play strictly by the rules, he might respond to a personal appeal.

"I know it's tough over there, Joe. But Dr. Alpdogan is the only favor this American has asked you for. You remember telling me I could bring you a 'special case,' don't you?"

"I remember. I'd like to help an American out, but I can't do it. We're afraid of this guy."

With the "we," Costa was weaseling out of the personal promise.

"Why are you afraid of him? He's a physician."

"He probably is, but he has a stipulated identity. To you, he may be 'special,' but we don't know who he really is. You don't know who he really is."

For some reason, Ziba's remark at her interview— "I have something I can show you"—occurred to me.

"I know who he is. But you don't have to believe what I'm telling you. Let me bring him over and you'll see. He's about 5-10 and weighs maybe one hundred and fifty pounds. He doesn't scare me at all."

To this, Costa wasn't so quick to reply. For a second, he even sounded apologetic: "I'm sorry I can't help you out. The only way your guy can get in is piggy-back. Get him a job as ship's doctor on one of those love-boat cruises the Greeks run to the islands. Some old lady might take your baby back to Omaha as her live-in physician."

"Without credentials, he can't get a work permit."

"He can go into homeopathy. Those people don't need credentials."

Nothing I could say was going to change Costa's mind. All I could think of was bouncing back his cynicism, testing its limits.

"One last thing, Joe. I've been out of the country for ten months now. Will I have trouble getting back in with my passport?"

"What's the seventh-inning stretch?"

"How many hits did Pete Rose have lifetime?"

"You'll be okay. Just don't try bringing in any of that Kurdish heroin."

Costa knew just enough about Kurds to be dangerous. Lately the European and American press carried reports that the PKK was financing its operations by using its cadres to move heroin from Afghanistan to Western Europe. Ziba didn't believe the reports. "We didn't even have enough morphine at the hospital. Besides, the Turks have that business locked up." Osman had laughed at the reports. "The usual slander, though interesting. Heroin would be quiet chemical warfare, but the PKK is committed to making loud noises with bombs. They put on a show that makes the terrorists feel large, important. At first the show frightens, gives the public a sense of persecution. But soon terror becomes entertainment. When the effects of these terrorist actions are visible, they are automatically past. Public events are studied, analyzed, understood. They don't really inspire future fear. Only mysterious events create fear of the future."

"That's not what I found," I told Osman. "The actions that bring Kurds to Athens aren't mysterious. Applicants know why they're afraid."

"You're thinking only in personal terms, Casey, the individual cases you see. Sudden gas from the sky is mysterious. Watching centuries-old villages dynamited is mysterious. Inexplicable actions like these are the basis for all individual acts of persecution."

Osman wasn't diffident about the effects of secret events. "Gas or the Anfal even makes torture tolerable," he maintained. "Those who know about the mystery are secretly thankful that only the police—and not gas or the army—have descended upon them."

About torture I didn't argue with Osman, not when he still hadn't solved the mystery of his blood test.

When I told Ziba about Costa's refusal, I didn't mention heroin or the cavalier way my fellow citizen treated Osman's application. I whispered the news to her between interviews.

"I'm not surprised," Ziba said quietly, rather flatly I thought.

"And not disappointed?"

"I never thought Osman had a chance to get in, so it's hard to be disappointed. But he will be. I think he was counting on it. I tried to tell him it was very unlikely."

Osman was on the computer when I got home. He could tell from my face what I'd heard from Costa.

"I'm screwed now," he said, standing up. "I'll never know what shit the Turks pumped into me. I'll be dead for ten years before the Greeks catch up to American medicine."

"We can try Canada."

"And wait six months? Besides, Canada doesn't give a damn about chemical weapons."

"We could try Israel. They've got good medical facilities."

"Right, I'll change my name again, this time to Alpstein. Let's face it,

Casey, I'm fucked unless I can get into the States. You'd think I was a fucking 'Islamic fundamentalist' your press goes on about. Christian fundamentalists, now they have status in your country. All other fundamentalists are demons. Examine your famous 'well-founded' and you'll find it's an empty concept. Below every foundation and before every fundamental is some belief, and that fucking Costa believes every raghead in the world wants to pollute Christian America. What did that bastard say, anyway?"

Osman started pacing my twelve feet of floor. I stopped him with a hug and said, "Maybe the weight loss is psychosomatic. You know, produced by fear of the injection rather than the injection."

"Costa said that?"

"No, I'm saying it."

Osman blurted something in Kurmanji into my ear and stepped back from me. I waited for him to translate. He didn't, so I asked him.

"Roughly, in American English, 'get your head out of your ass.'"

"I think I preferred the Kurmanji."

"I'm sorry, but this isn't impotence, blood flowing away from the penis. This is weight dropping off my body."

I remembered Ziba's plucking at his suit the first night here. I wondered if Osman suspected all along that he was ill. Disease, another ground for refusal by INS.

"I was hoping, huh?" I said, trying not to cry.

"Afraid so. Everything isn't caused by fear, Casey. Sometimes actual things and external actions cause fear."

"I know."

"The States was my only chance. Our only chance. Why did Costa deny me?"

"Money," I said, offering Osman what I thought was the least painful of Costa's reasons.

"Money?" Osman spat out. "Your government gives billions to Turkey for arms to kill Kurds. I have a way to stop that. And that fucking Costa is afraid I'm going to cost the U.S. too much money. How can you live with the hypocrisy? I wish I could go somewhere else, but those other countries will never take me."

Now Osman's face was red, flushed. He started pacing again, stooped forward as if searching the floor for a lost object. A nomad, I felt, a caged nomad.

"I'll take you," I said.

"In your suitcase? If I keep losing weight, you can take me in your carry-on."

"You don't understand. I'll take you as my husband. I'm asking you to marry me."

I'd seen Osman angry and desperate and remarkably casual, but never surprised. With his saucer eyes, round mouth, and hands stretched by his sides, Osman looked like the cartoon version of surprise or, it flashed into my head, fear.

"You want to marry me?"

"Yes. And I want you to marry me."

"Right, right," he said, smiling now. "Just like in Kurdistan: the man marries the woman, the woman marries the man."

"That's right. It's done the same way in the United States. And, as far as I know, here in Greece."

"Yes, yes, but ... but ..."

I bailed Osman out. "But why am I asking you right now?"

Though I didn't tell Osman this, my offer to take him as my husband wasn't a sudden decision. I'd been thinking about it since Costa mentioned marriage to a matron. Though I was neither an old lady nor an old-fashioned girl, I was uncomfortable asking Osman to marry me. Not because of our speedy courtship or because I doubted my love for him or his love for me, but because I'd already done a lot for or to Osman: gone to Diyarbakir, made up his identity, gotten him status, welcomed him into my apartment, even rubbed against—he said—his shoulder. I worried that he'd feel "stipulated," a constructed refugee deprived of even the power to propose. Given his health and his urgency and the recent call from mysterious Mr. Oroglou, I felt we had to forego that nicety.

"To be honest," he began to say.

"Don't ever begin a sentence that way when you talk to the INS. If you're married to me, you'll be talking to them soon, in the States."

Osman started pacing the floor again, more slowly. I stood my ground in the center of the room.

"I can't do it," he said. "What if you don't love me?"

"Now you sound like a nineteenth-century maiden. I do love you. And you must do it."

"I can't. You can't. You'll be fired."

"Not if Mrs. Constantinou doesn't know. Even if she does find out, it's legal. I'll tell her our relation developed after your interview. I consulted you for this gynecological problem I was having."

"Which was?"

"Maidenhood. And if she doesn't buy that, so what. My sabbatical is almost up."

Like Mrs. Constantinou, Osman didn't know "sabbatical." Explaining it to him, I remembered the Director's confusion with French: "saboteur." I explained that to Osman, too, and he laughed. Then he asked, "What if it doesn't work? What if you marry me and the people at the Embassy rule it's a marriage of convenience?"

"They won't. Costa owes me one fucking favor, as he might say. He even suggested it."

"But nobody knows how long we've been seeing each other."

"Seeing" reminded me of Oroglou. No reason to tell Osman now, not now of all times.

"That's true," I said, "but we have the computer with all that stuff on your lists I can't read. The downloads will all be dated. But don't worry. This time it'll be easy. I promise. As a last resort, we can be examined in separate rooms and recount every one of our sexual interfaces."

"Your medical condition made them necessary," he said with mock medical gravity.

"That's why I won't be embarrassed to recount them."

He stopped pacing, stood in front of me, looked up those three inches into my eyes.

"Will you marry me?" he said, as if he'd been rehearsing the question for weeks.

"Yes. I'd love to. And you?"

"I love you."

He put his arms around my waist, pulled me close.

"And in Kurmanji?" I whispered in his ear.

"English only. Kurmanji is for fear and anger."

As the newspapers say about the weddings of celebrities, it was a "private ceremony," very private, without a translator, no witnesses and no circle dance. The Greek official knew English and let us say "I do" rather than *kano*. The certificate, though, we had translated and stamped by the official translation center of the Greek Government. On the 29th of June, I called Costa. Keep it casual, buddy-buddy, off-color, a done deal, entitled by the documents, facilitated by our shared roles as insiders and cynics. To General Silay, I had someone to trade. To Costa, I had only my dignity to give up.

"Do you remember that Iraqi doctor you passed up a while ago?"

"The poison gas guy."

"That's the one."

"I can't..."

"You don't need to. He has papers now. There's something I didn't tell you before. I've been giving him refuge in my sheets for the last few months and now we've tied the knot."

"So 'love' is the 'special case.'"

With his inflections, Costa made both words sound like "agricultural advisor," fake, but allowed by international practices, if not protocols.

"Very special. Listen, I'm going back to the States soon. I want to make sure Osman and I can sleep together in London on the way home. I sure would appreciate it if you'd expedite my husband's visa."

"That's the trouble with letting you babes work over here. Lucky for INS you get just one souvenir a posting. Messenger over the certificate, his UNHCR card, and a copy of your passport. I'll fix up his visa and send you a toaster. STP."

"STP? Isn't that some kind of drug?"

"'Sooner Than Possible.' But if you ever start doing drugs and overdose, you've got the right guy. Congratulations and many happy returns."

"Thanks, Joe. It's nice to deal with an American. If my man turns out to interest the CIA in the States, I'll never tell them you once turned him away."

"Not me, Casey. I always make sure someone else's name is on the paperwork."

Chapter 13

"Turkish Embassy Gassed" read the huge headline of *The Athens News* of July 9, 1999. "Eight Persons Killed" was the subhead. The story had the details: five Turkish employees at the embassy, one Greek, one Saudi, and the young woman who managed to smuggle poison gas into the building. She'd been shot and killed in the building. The seven men died on the way to the hospital or in the hospital. Found on the woman were two sets of papers. She was Kiffah Ahmad, an Egyptian applying for a Turkish visa; she was Zeynep Kinali, a twenty-four-year-old Turkish Kurd. Also found on her was a typewritten statement that claimed to be from the PKK: "Forced from our land, we take our war against the occupiers outside Turkey. No place is safe for Turkish Kurds. From this moment, no place will be safe for those who persecute us. Iraqi Kurds are protected by international law. Until Turkish Kurds are allowed our rights, we will attack internationally."

The attack was like a refugee's life: an event occurs and then you find out why. How could she do this? Walk into the Embassy without trembling, sweating, shaking. Chemicals. Like the Turks injected Osman, Zeynep Kinali shot herself with tranquilizers. Why would she do this? Had she been raped, tortured? Her parents gassed? I remembered the "mystery killing" of Ziba's uncle. Zeynep Kinali's death was a mystery to me. What family or clan loyalty could produce suicide? I peered at her photograph. I didn't recognize Zeynep Kinali. My mind jumped to the office. I hoped she was not someone UNHCR had given status before I started processing Kurds. What will Ziba and Osman think about this use of gas against their enemy? I didn't know what to think. It was war out in eastern Turkey. I knew that. I'd listened to survivors and talked with two officers at the front. I remembered Oroglou and checked the Turkish names. He was not among the dead. He and the other employees at the Embassy worked for a government that was waging an unjust war against its citizens. The conflict was also one-sided. That was proven by the Kurdish woman's suicide mission. But the Embassy employees weren't in uniform. Then again, neither were Ziba or Osman or thousands of other Kurds who'd been killed in their homes, destroyed with their homes. Or been tortured and turned into guerrillas.

But what about the innocent bystanders, the Greek and Saudi businessmen who happened to be in the Embassy? Did "the friends of our enemies" principle cover them just because they were doing business with Turkey? *The Athens News* treated the Greek differently than the Saudi. Vassilis Tikopoulos was in his own country, minding his own business; Habib Aref, it was implied, might be using Greece as a go-between. In fact, under international law an embassy is considered part of the country that owns it. Both bystanders were in Turkey. It was a dangerous place. They must have known that. Again, the Kurdish woman proved it. Security at the Embassy had to be very tight if only a suicide mission could penetrate it. Turks in less secure positions all over the world must live in fear now.

I wanted to talk with Ziba, but this—of all days—was no time to be seen or heard with her at the office. When I got there, the receptionist said the Director wanted to see me immediately. I took two minutes to make sure Zeynep Kinali wasn't in our database. When I got to Mrs. Constantinou's office, Erica and Nikos were already there.

"Have you read the papers this morning?" she asked me.

"*The Athens News*," I said.

"I've already had calls from the Greek press," Mrs. Constantinou told all of us. To me, she said, "You may get an interview request from *The Athens News*. You know our position on the PKK."

"We deplore this event. UNHCR refuses refuge to terrorists from any country or ethnic group."

"Unless they're war criminals who share our Orthodox faith," Erica said.

Both Nikos and Mrs. Constantinou jabbered in Greek at Erica. I caught the Greek word for "joke."

Going back to our offices, Nikos said, "This Kinali must have been absolutely fearless to commit suicide. Was she one of yours?"

"Not unless she applied under a different name and different face."

When Siamand came in, I pointed at the headline to see his reaction.

"Very bad for Kourds," he said. He could be lying, and he could be right.

Between interviews, I tried to call Osman at the apartment. The line was always busy, a sure sign he was burning up the Internet. I could have reached him with email, if UNHCR had it. Anxious to talk about the attack on the Embassy, I took a taxi home at lunch. Osman wasn't there. Neither was my laptop. The phone was off the hook, sending its alarm. Under the receiver was a note in Osman's hand, worse than his usual scrawl: "I'm sorry about this. I'll call and explain as soon as I get a chance."

What was "this?" Borrowing my laptop?

Why leave the phone off the hook?

Why not take time to write another sentence to explain?

I got a dial tone and called Ziba.

"Have you talked with Osman today?" I asked.

"No."

"He was here using the computer, but now it's gone."

"Maybe he took it to the magazine."

"Maybe, but he also left the phone off the hook."

Ziba was silent. I was afraid of the next question, but had to ask it: "Do you think this has anything to do with the attack on the Embassy?"

Again Ziba was silent. I wished I could see her face, but the phone was like an utterly neutral translator, a pure transmitter of information.

"I don't think so. Why don't you call the magazine?"

Osman wasn't there. I called the Rehab Center. Osman hadn't been there in two days. I called his hotel, but they wouldn't give information on residents. It was that kind of hotel, lodging people who didn't want to be contacted. I could have walked there, but I didn't know what room he was in.

Back at the office, I thought about calling Ziba again. Osman said he'd come to distrust her here in Greece. I turned on my tape recorder and dialed her number.

> "Ziba, I can't locate Osman. Do you
> think he might have been somehow involved at
> the Embassy?"
>
> "I doubt it."
>
> "It was gas. Have Turkish Kurds ever
> used gas before?"
>
> "I don't think so, but I don't know."
>
> "I helped Osman get status here. I need
> to know if he might have been involved."
>
> "He was researching antidotes, not
> gas."
>
> "He'd have to know how to make gas to
> find an antidote."
>
> "It's possible he's somehow connected,
> but I doubt he was directly involved. I've
> heard him talk about Palestinians. He thought
> this kind of suicide attack was a mistake,
> not productive. Just a way to get publicity."

"Are you saying Osman wouldn't be involved because of strategy?"

"I'm just trying to see the situation objectively. Maybe he was afraid people who knew he was researching gas—people like you and me—would suspect he was involved."

"So what? Are we going to report him?"

"I don't know what's in Osman's mind."

"Where do you think he is?"

"If he's afraid, he won't stay in Greece. He'll feel vulnerable here because he doesn't know the language. He may have gone back to Lebanon. He really wanted to go to the States, but knew that was impossible."

"It is possible now."

"How?"

"I fixed it for him."

"How could you do that? You said Costa turned Osman down."

"Costa changed his mind."

"Why?"

"Osman and I got married."

"You can't be serious. You can't be married to Osman."

"Why not?"

"Because he's my husband."

"What? That can't be true. He's your brother."

"He's my husband."

"You said he was your brother. He said he was your brother. I don't believe you."

"You don't want to believe me. Mamozin is my married name. Ziba Alpdogan met Osman Mamozin in Chicago, two Kourds far from home."

"This is unbelievable. Why did you tell me Osman was your brother at your interview?"

"I didn't know you were new at inter-

viewing. I felt I had to make the strongest
case I could. It would take an overwhelming
fear to make a Kourd betray a brother."

"But not a husband?"

"Perhaps not so strong if the husband
has betrayed the wife."

"So you betrayed me."

"I didn't know you then, Casey. After
we became friends, I couldn't tell you. I
felt terrible about misleading you, but I
couldn't tell you."

"Not if you were going to use me to get
Osman out of prison."

"I can imagine how you feel, but think
through the steps. When we became friends, I
didn't know Osman was in prison. And besides,
wouldn't you have helped me get my husband
out of a Turkish prison?"

"So Osman came to Athens to take you
back to Kurdistan with him?"

"I don't think so. In Diyarbakir he
helped out the PKK. We argued about this.
Then he left me in Turkey and went to Iraq to
treat PKK guerrillas. He returned to Turkey
to persuade me to come with him, but I
refused. I felt he'd betrayed me by leaving
our work in Diyarbakir."

"You're telling me Osman is a PKK member and you're not."

"What's 'membership?' UNHCR believes
too much in documents: names on membership
lists, membership cards. I did some things in
Diyarbakir that could have gotten me ten
years in jail. Osman was more active, put us
more at risk."

"Is that why you didn't go back with
him to Iraq?"

"I thought he wanted a nurse more than

a wife. And I realized that in Iraq Osman had fallen in love."

"With someone in the PKK?"

"No, with poison."

"Poison gas?"

"Poison in any form."

"And so when the police came to call, you betrayed him, got your revenge by telling them where Osman could be found."

"That's something I'll never know for sure. Not intentionally, I know that. But the fear was like I told you at the cinema. If Osman was my brother instead of my husband, maybe I would have let the police run that rope between my legs. I told you before. I betrayed myself that night. I haven't trusted myself since."

"Did Osman come here to find out if you'd betrayed him?"

"He said not. He said he wanted one last chance to make our marriage work. That's why I was so happy to see him the night we came to your apartment. We did save his life, you know. But he wouldn't consider staying in Greece, so I knew right away we had no future together."

"But you agreed to help him get refugee status?"

"Yes. He was my husband. He is still my husband, and he is a Kourd. You can trust me on that. Osman is a Turkish Kourd."

"You've lied to me before, Ziba."

"You concealed your marriage to Osman. How could you do that?"

"I didn't know he was married to you. If you'd just told the truth at the inter- view, this never would have happened."

"He'd already betrayed me. I no longer

believed in him. I felt no one else could believe in him either. If you'd told me what you were going to do, this never would have happened."

"Osman said you couldn't be trusted with a secret."

"Would someone hang me over a rope to find out about your marriage?"

"Osman thought you'd feel it was like incest."

"Not incest. There's a word in English for what you did."

"'Bigamy.'"

"That's it. From Greek, 'two fucking.'"

"Not really, Ziba. Just on paper, a document."

"Then I don't understand. Why would you do that for Osman?"

"I don't know, Ziba. Friendship, altruism, politics. I went to Diyarbakir for you, didn't I? I thought he was your brother. He really needs to be in the States for treatment. Hasn't he told you how much he worries about that injection?"

"Yes, but Osman sometimes exaggerates. I don't always trust his judgment."

"He's the doctor, Ziba. He needs help. Marrying me was the only way he could get there. Also, he really believes he can do more for Kurds in the States than anywhere else."

"Then that's where he's gone. This is terrible for you, Casey. If Osman was involved at the Embassy, he'll be more dangerous in the States than in Greece."

"Why do you say that?"

"He'd say gassing Turks and Greeks is useless. Do you remember his comments on attacking the foundations of Kourdish persecution?"

"Yes."

"'Without the support of the United States,' he told me, 'Turkey couldn't suppress our people for two months. If Americans were terrorized in their homes like we are, the government would have to change its policy toward Turkey.'"

"When was this?"

"When he first got here. He was telling me about his questioning in Diyarbakir. The Turkish police were mocking his American education. 'We're the real friends of America,' they told him. 'America gives us planes and helicopters and bombs to kill Kourds.'"

"He never told me about this."

"You can see why, can't you? Osman always knew about America's aid to Turkey, but after he was tortured he became obsessed with those who supported the enemies of Kourds. You remember what he said about trampling Arabs and Persians?"

"Yes."

"Well, I didn't think much about Osman's rage against the States because I thought he'd never get back there."

"He may feel differently now. It's been six months since he was tortured."

"That's true, Casey, but Osman is like you. He wants only fundamentals. When he learned about 'well-founded fear,' he told me in English, 'Turkey's power is founded on and funded by America.'"

"He could be right, but how do I know you're not lying to me again? This could be yet another betrayal of Osman, punishment for marrying me, keeping it secret from you."

"It could be, but it isn't. You are my
friend, even if you don't feel that way any
more. Now, like Osman in Diyarbakir, you're
in danger."

"I don't know, Ziba. You could be setting me up once again with this story."

"Casey, listen to me. If Osman is as
dangerous as I think he may be, you could be
implicated through his documents."

"I don't trust you any more, Ziba. I
concealed information from you. But you lied
to me. I just don't know. There have been too
many surprises. I need to think about this,
untangle the knot I've gotten myself in with
you Mamozins. I wish I could thank you, Ziba,
but I can't, not right now. Maybe I'll feel
differently in a couple of days."

I hung up the phone. This interview was recorded. I couldn't pretend it
never happened. I pretended to Ziba that I didn't believe her. But what she
said was plausible. When Osman arrived, I pretended his fake passport was
irrelevant, something a doctor could buy. But if Osman was affiliated with the
PKK, he could be directly or indirectly involved at the Embassy. Why else
would he leave in such a hurry? He has my computer and "my" documents. If
he's apprehended at the airport or some border crossing, the Greek police will
be interviewing me. If he escapes, the police may still come to call on Mrs.
Alpdogan.

That son-of-a-bitch, emphasis on son. How could he do it? Not "why?"
That was obvious. He wanted documents, any documents to get him out of
Greece. But three months pretending to be my friend and my lover? How could
he manage that under his wife's nose? The same way men committed incest in
their own home, by blaming the victim, blackmailing the victim. This is a man
whose life I saved, whose life I was trying to save. How could he put my life in
danger?

Fright, fight, flight.

I have no weapons. I don't know where to go. I can pretend nothing has
happened and hope Osman calls to explain before the police arrive. Pretending
doesn't work for refugees, not in their countries of origin. The police come, put

them in the Land Cruisers, and shock or beat or squeeze pretense out. But Greece is a country of laws. I'll be able to call a lawyer. He'll see the documents connecting me to Osman, and I'll have to plead temporary insanity. Love. If the judge refuses that plea, I'll be in a Greek cell for a long time. I'll know what Zeynep Kinali felt when she walked into the Embassy. Oroglou. If he was the caller, he could right now be telling the Greek police to find me at UNHCR.

I take the cassette and my tape recorder and go home. Saturday and Sunday I wait for the phone to ring or the police to knock on my door. Now I know what it's like to be in solitary, to be under the plexiglas pyramid. In my box of an apartment I'm sweating from the July heat, from my fear, or both. I urinate once an hour, drink water, urinate again. I don't call anyone and the phone doesn't ring. My mind circles like fluids in my body: Osman will call, Osman said he'd call to keep me here, Osman loves me, Osman was using me, he'll call. On Saturday I eat up most of my food, and on Sunday feel I'm losing weight like Osman. I listen to my taped conversation with Ziba, searching for some reason to trust or distrust her, my only connection now to Osman. What an idiot I've been! Ziba says "Kourd" on the tape. Osman always pronounced it "Kurd." They're not siblings. Why didn't I hear this evidence before? Because I was an idiot, because I didn't want to hear. Ziba speaks literally, like a document. Osman often spoke figuratively, figured his audience and adapted. I can't blame translation for this terrible oversight. Just myself, my one outstanding talent, my ability to analyze language, listen to people speak. And this failure makes me even more fearful. Like Osman before I offered to marry him, I pace round and around, back and forth, trying to make my legs stop twitching.

I won't try to narrate two days of waiting and indecision. Sunday night I finally judge I have a well-founded fear of prosecution. Right here, right now. To find out if I have a persecution complex, I'll have to find Osman and re-interview him. When I reinterviewed Mr. Kaya, I got in trouble. With Osman, I put myself in danger. Ziba said so, and now I believe her. But the danger isn't just personal, isn't just mine. If Ziba's fear of Osman is well-founded, the danger is public. For that kind of future threat, the word "fear" won't do. To public danger—to peril—the reasonable response and right word is "alarm."

Monday at nine a.m. I called a travel agent and booked a flight the next day to my country of origin.

Chapter 14

I went to the office and told Mrs. Constantinou that I'd received a call from the States: my father was in the hospital and needed open-heart surgery. "*Po, po, po, po,*" she said, Greek for "what a shame," the number of *po's* representing the seriousness of the problem. As an older woman, Mrs. Constantinou sympathized with diseases of the elderly. I think she bought my story, but maybe she just pretended to. After all, I had only a month left, and she knew I didn't need the UNHCR salary or her recommendation. From me, she needed letters on people I'd interviewed. I told her I'd fax them from the States.

It was too late to figure legalities or moralities. Now I was calculating the quid pro quo. When I was first learning Latin, I thought the phrase meant "what for whom." I'd already done too much for several "whoms." In the future, I'll remember this for that. And tit for tat, if it doesn't hide a sexual reference.

Nikos didn't say so, but I could tell from his voice he thought I'd been spooked by the attack on the Embassy. I saw it in his eyes: if a Kurd can get into the Turkish Embassy, someone can certainly walk by Panos and kill us all for denying him or her status. Nikos was probably pleased by my *tremoulisma.*

Erica said I'd be back after my father's operation.

"Maybe so," I told her.

"You have to come back," she said, fluttering her hands in front of her. "The Kurds need you. Because you're a neutral, you've gotten applicants approved that the Director would have rejected if I'd recommended them. After the Embassy, it's going to be even more difficult for Kurds here."

"You know I'm not a neutral."

"I do, but Mrs. Constantinou was never sure. You always had the facts in your Letters. What if the Director hires someone like Nikos?"

"Then you'll have to train him as you did me. Give him the documents— and the pictures to see what's been lost."

"No, no. You'll be back. I saw you arm in arm with Ziba and another Kurd on Pendeli. Now, it's your father's heart. Your own heart will bring you back."

Erica and I exchanged Greek ceremonial kisses on the cheeks, and I hugged her tight. I swear I could feel her heart beating fast like the bird I'd always associated her with.

Only Ziba remained. I called her, told her I was leaving, and asked if I could stop by her house for a few minutes. She'd been angry about my revelation, but also concerned for me by the end of our taped phone conversation.

At the front door, Ziba's charges seemed to swarm around her. She was different with them, all reserve down as she corrected their English and they corrected her Greek. I wouldn't have mistaken Ziba for their mother. More like an older sister, one secure in her family, her home, and her country. Watching the boy and girl tug on her arms and clothes, I suddenly realized this is a Ziba who never existed until she got to Greece. Maybe no Kurd could be this defenseless. Where Ziba lived, the police could come through the door at any minute, without warning, without a warrant. From what I'd read and heard, the police would have sawed Ziba in front of her children. Though I'd vowed to be distant and had rehearsed my wariness on the way to her house, seeing Ziba with the Greek kids reminded me of Mrs. Haydar.

After Ziba quieted the kids down and formally introduced them to me, she and I went into the back yard and sat on metal patio chairs, angled both toward and away from each other. We sat silently, half facing each other, as if we didn't share a language. Ziba spoke first.

"I have something for you," she said. From underneath her tee shirt, she took out a small air mail envelope. A letter for Osman? My name was on the envelope.

"For your flight," Ziba said. And then, "I know why you came. But first I want to thank you for getting me started in Greece, for giving me the translator's job."

"I needed a good translator."

"And I needed a good friend."

"You didn't seem to."

"I couldn't seem to."

"I guess I could."

"It was a good thing for me. And now you're leaving."

We were rapidly moving away from each other. I pulled my chair around to more nearly face Ziba.

"I have to find Osman. If you're right, I have to change his mind."

She turned her head and looked at me.

"You won't be able to do that. All you can do is protect yourself."

"I can't protect myself without doing that. He's traveling on my documents."

"Husbands," Ziba said and shook her head.

"You probably didn't feel that way when you met Osman in Chicago."

"I was even more alone there than you were here. I didn't know any

Kourds. I didn't have a friend. No, that's an excuse. That's rewriting the past. We were in love, there and in Turkey, but conditions at home separated us. Even Kourds in love can be split by politics."

This last sentence was matter-of-fact, as Osman might have delivered it when talking about his torture. There was no quaver in Ziba's voice, no blinking back tears. But she had reversed herself, what no applicant ever did, not voluntarily. Maybe her "no" was true, maybe it was a clever tactic she'd learned from months of translating.

"Between, always between," I said.

"Yes, always something between Kourds."

"And now between friends."

Ziba was silent.

"Look, Ziba, I don't know if we were ever friends, but you don't have to be afraid of me. If Osman has done something that leads back to you, I won't be able to help you. But I won't endanger your life here because you lied to me about him. I still believe you deserve your status."

Ziba looked down at her hands in her lap.

"Something more to thank you for, Casey."

Now.

"Where can I find him, Ziba?"

"I don't know."

"He's talked a lot about Chicago. Where would he go there?"

"We didn't have many friends. Maybe he's still in contact with some doctors."

"Ziba, please help me."

"It's been years since we lived there."

I reached forward and took her right hand in mine. "I'm not asking you to betray Osman again. Just give me a chance to find him and find out why he's there."

Ziba pulled her hand away: "I can't help you, Casey."

"You have to help me. I'm in love with Osman. I need to find him, help him through this illness."

"Next you'll tell me he's in love with you," she said in her mocking tone.

If friendship didn't work, maybe anger will.

"Yes, Ziba, I hate to admit this, but we've been lovers for a month."

"You're lying," Ziba said, as if I were a Turkish policeman.

I was silent. Give her time to process the clues she overlooked, the weekends Osman and I spent together. Give Ziba's pride time to work along with her anger. Keep my dignity and keep quiet.

"If you're not lying," Ziba finally said, "describe the marks on his ass, Miss Casey."

So now Ziba was examining me, like an INS officer testing a suspicious marriage with a trick question.

"Osman has no marks on his buttocks."

Ziba stared at my face, looking for any sign of *tremoulisma*. "He's all yours," she said, "look for his ass and cock at St. Joseph's Hospital. Dress yourself up as a nurse."

Ziba got up, walked into the house, and closed the patio door behind her. I found a way out through the back of the yard. In the street, I was crying. I thought that with my suspicions and fears, I could hold myself back, practice Ziba's reserve, but the months of intimacy, the hundreds of hours we'd spent together listening and talking, translating and being translated, couldn't be suppressed by the former interviewer.

A Greek woman on the sidewalk looked at me, but didn't speak. I was a foreigner. I wiped the tears off my face and started back to my apartment, but I couldn't stop crying. No one I met tried to comfort me. Goodbye Ziba, goodbye Greece, goodbye UNHCR. Walking along, hearing an occasional English phrase from passersby, I realized I wasn't even a responsible tourist. I used the beaches—the rocks of Hydra, the sand at Vouliagmeni and Spetses, the pebbles of Evia—but never climbed to the country's high points—the Acropolis and the chapel on Likavitos in Athens, Delphi and the monasteries at Meteora, Mt. Olympus. Though I lived here for eleven months, I never treated Athens like a home. I doubt I cooked five meals for myself. I ate in the tavernas, used my flat to read and sleep. I was like an urban nomad. Except that, obsessed with the homeless, I spent more time than most natives at my desk. Until today, I've never been in a native's home. Greeks were no more hospitable to me than to refugees.

Despite Ziba's help, I didn't learn more than three hundred words of Greek. I didn't need to. I had a hundred translators, natives happy to speak English to work with me, to sell me goods and services. Without the language, I couldn't know how natives lived, not with each other. Except for my trips to Lavrion and Pendeli, I didn't know much about how applicants lived while they were here. I didn't really live here, not until I met Ziba and Osman, my Kurdish friends. But they're not really Kurds. They're "educational migrants," Americanized semi-Kurds, special cases, people who didn't require translators to talk with me.

Wrong again. Not semi-Kurds, but super-Kurds, people made doubly conscious of their identity by their education in America and exile in Greece.

Wrong yet again. Ultra-Kurds made triply conscious by their torture. Not all Kurds have the Mamozins' secrets, but every Kurd who didn't collaborate had to conceal his or her rage against everyday fear in Turkey. Osman had practice concealing his rage against Turkey's ally, my country of origin.

So many wrongs I committed and didn't right.

I failed to be even singly conscious with Osman, maybe because I was far from home. That should make one more suspicious. Or more susceptible? Osman was also far from home. He felt as harmless as Mr. Kaya. Him I've deported. Osman I've relocated. I'd saved his life. Why would I need to fear him or test him? "Baby year." I'd have done better to volunteer at a Cincinnati orphanage or adopt a crack baby. Maybe my fear of a twenty-year future, two decades devoted to the upbringing of a child, was why I tested men so carefully. Except Osman. I never considered what would happen if his condom failed. Maybe failing to test Osman was my success: giving the trust I've denied every other man, every other person except Ziba. I trusted myself enough to bestow that trust. Ziba could be right about Osman's danger to me. I'm clearly a danger to myself because I have to find out if I was wrong about Osman, about myself.

One last Greek test. Standing in line at the Delta counter, waiting for my boarding pass, I watched policemen with machine guns walking around the terminal, just like they do in Istanbul's airport. I kept my head down, face averted. Tall blonde, blue eyes. I was thinking like a Kurd. The police are watching for any different-looking person trying to leave the country. I feared being apprehended by a man like Panos at the office.

"Come."

"Is there some problem we can discuss, sir?"

"No speak English."

Suitcases checked, boarding pass in hand, sitting in a chair and holding *The Athens News* in front of my face, I realized applicants weren't usually afraid when leaving Turkey. The country wanted Kurds out. How else could they row across the Evros, get loaded fifty at a time into cargo holds? Border police are on the lookout only for "creemeenals" like Kaya, like me. Trying to work up courage to go through passport control, I examine myself one last time. I have all my limbs. I'm not carrying explosives, just some tapes from UNHCR. My passport is my own. These are certain. Look right into the policeman's face, as Ziba did mine at her interview. No *tremoulisma*. No reason for the examiner to look at the name on the passport. Match my face and photo. That's me, no lie. I'm entitled to leave. No translation required, no quid pro quo.

The young policeman sitting high in his control booth looks down at my face, glances at my photo, doesn't puzzle out the English letters of my name.

I'm out.

Then he runs my passport through a scanner. Worrying about fear on my face, I forgot how travelers are examined—by utterly objective, completely trustworthy, possibly infallible electronic scanners. The policeman looks at a monitor I can't see.

"How long have you been in Greece?"

I know he already knows the answer, but "Mahan" must be clear. I feel my shoulders slump just a little.

"Eleven months."

He speaks to me in Greek.

"*Ohi*," I say, "no. I don't speak Greek."

"Do you have your documents with you?"

"What documents? You have my passport."

"Your residence permit."

"I'm not coming back. Why do you need to have this?"

"If you stay in Greece for more than six months, you must surrender this document when you leave."

"Here, here it is."

Nothing to implicate me there.

The man behind me in line starts talking to the policeman in Greek. He stands up inside the booth and shouts at the man. Yes, this policeman also has a gun, a small pistol.

"And your work permit," he says.

UNHCR. Refuge for terrorists. This is the alarm. I won't be getting out. I rummage around in my purse, and the man behind me again says something in Greek. The policeman laughs now and replies in Greek.

"Here it is."

He looks at it, compares the name and picture with my passport, looks back at my face.

"You must surrender," he says.

I put both my hands on the booth to steady myself. Done for, but I don't raise my arms. One last question.

"Why?"

"Like the residence permit. You must surrender the work permit."

Yes, yes, of course. So I won't sell it to some refugee who really needs it to survive. Sure, certainly. By all means, keep my documents. I don't need them. Just please give me back my passport.

As I watch the policeman push my passport toward me, I feel him staring at me. When I look up at his face, he smiles and winks. I take the passport, shake my head, hold up my left hand, and show him my wedding ring. Two months I spent alone on beaches and not a single Greek approached me. Leaving the country—that's when a policeman sitting above me in his booth decides to flirt. "You must surrender." To me, to my Greek-speaking, pistol-packing, joking charm. Too late. I've surrendered to someone else, and now I'm compelled to find him.

IV Documents

Chapter 15

Document: (noun) 1. a written or printed paper furnishing information or evidence, as a passport, deed, bill of sale, bill of lading,
etc.; a legal or official paper. 2. any written item, as a book, article,
letter, etc., especially of a factual or informative nature. 3. a file in
certain word processing programs. 4. (archaic) evidence or proof.

American Heritage Dictionary of the English Language

In a refugee file, Documents are appended to the Narrative. The first was
hand-written in very small letters on the back of a UNHCR telex dated January
13, a few days after I came back from Diyarbakir. It's the letter Ziba gave me
at our last meeting. I've retyped it here because of its length. The second was
scrawled on a scrap of map. I've duplicated it here to preserve its authenticity.

Dear Casey,
    "Short letters, short words" mother used to write when I was in
Chicago. There were many things she couldn't say because we suspected
Turks opened mail. And because writing is a poor translation of speaking.
Some of mother's letters I never received. I hope you never receive this
one. If you're reading it, you know I lied about Osman. If you know, I may
never talk with you again. This may be my only chance to tell you why—
why I'm writing it, why I lied.
    You went to D. for me, but I can't thank you, not really, because I can't
tell you how much I loved Osman, what he meant to me once. I won't try to
write down all those emotions here. You will want only the facts. "No gift is
enough" we say. Because when we're not betraying each other we're giving
gifts—things, loyalty, ourselves. You have laws. We have gifts. But I have nothing to give you for saving Osman's life. Just this letter telling the truth.
    I had a brother, two years older. It was Anarada who was killed by a
mine in the Hakkari cave. He was 13. He said he was never going to grow a
mustache. One minute he was running ahead of my two cousins and me
and the next second the ground flew apart and Anarada was lying on the
ground without legs. I ran back to get father while my cousins stayed with
Anarada. I think I've been running ever since. Back to the cave to find
Anarada dead. West to D., Istanbul, Chicago. Until I ran into Osman in the
hospital. Bumping up against Osman stopped me from running and brought
me back to D. After Osman slipped away from me, it was Anarada that I felt
closest to. So I told you it was my brother the police wanted to find. Maybe

because I want to find him. When the jash learned he'd been killed by a mine, they took his body away. We don't know where he is buried or if he is buried. Anarada doesn't even have his small piece of ground.

Now that I've written this, I don't believe you'll ever read it. If you do, you probably won't believe it. So, written to you, this letter may be written for me. And maybe for Anarada, who now has a place in my file as well as in my mind.

Ziba

This is your written release. You were always innocent. You knew nothing of my plan. Don't be afraid. You'll never need to use this document. Mobility is my refuge.

V Interview

Chapter 16

Do you require a translator?

No. No more translators.

What do you know for sure?

1) That a woman called Ziba had a wound on her belly.

2) That a man called Osman was fucking me.

Was Ziba ever your friend?

Probably. If not, it was a long impressive charade. It certainly felt like friendship before Osman arrived.

Did Osman love you?

I don't know. It felt like love, but from the beginning Osman had more to gain from me than Ziba did. She had her wound; she didn't want to go to the States. Maybe he decided to marry me the night he and Ziba came to my apartment. Perhaps Ziba and he planned the seduction before Osman came to Greece. Ziba could have known at her first interview that Osman was in prison and needed outside intervention from an idealistic, romantic woman. Ziba might have faked her torture and fled Turkey to get Osman out of prison. Maybe Ziba and Osman are Turkish agents undermining the work of UNHCR and the Kurdish cause.

Are these reasonable conclusions?

It was reasonable to be afraid of surveillance after Mr. Kaya's final accusations, but I was mistaken. It seemed reasonable to be unafraid of Ziba and Osman, but I was wrong.

Why?

Because I failed to examine myself.
They kept secrets from me, but I kept secrets
from myself. Emotions got me in trouble and
put me in danger. Now I have to erase any
unfounded assumptions from the past. I'm
afraid of the future. I need to start from
zero, be an objective examiner of others, an
unemotional interviewer of myself.

What do you want to do?

1) Avoid being charged as an accessory
   to any crimes Osman has committed or
   might commit.

2) Do justice without revealing my complicity in his movements.

3) Get answers to some of the questions
   above.

4) Understand why I got myself into
   this tangle.

In that order?

I'm not certain about the order.

And the individual items?

I'm not sure about all of them either.

Why?

Because I can't expunge the feelings
that put me and others in peril.

These were the questions and answers I wrote on my legal pad during the flight from Athens to New York. My computer was gone, but I could still force myself to think objectively the old-fashioned way, the Jesuits' catechistic method, paper and pen. I suppose I could have been lying to myself on the pad. As the Director said, applicants routinely lie in their Interview, their last chance to tell their story, make a listener believe that their fear of the future is personal, intense, and well-founded. I have the hand-written document to introduce into evidence at the appropriate time, but your judgment of me will depend on, I believe, the interviews I conducted, the judgments I made, the actions I took, the story that follows.

Looking at the phone on the seatback, I feared electronics. Not the pilot's computer and controls. Wedged in the middle of the plane, far from the windows, I never felt the plane would plummet. I was afraid of electronic communications, the phone or fax or email connection between the Greek Interior Ministry and INS at JFK. I made it through the Greek scanner, but I could be in the American scanner by the time I got to New York.

I was spending a lot of time in the toilet.

Rip my passport to shreds and flush them down the toilet. I'll say, "I had it in Athens. I don't know where it could have gone."

"I guess we'll just have to wait for the plane to be cleaned."

"Maybe my pocketbook was picked when I went to the bathroom."

"If your passport doesn't show up, we'll have to detain you until we get some evidence of your identity."

What to do? Try to walk through the scanner or give the Ministry even more time to communicate with INS?

Throw away all identification and ask for political asylum?

Maybe that's what Ziba did. I could be Swedish or Norwegian or even Irish. Speak one sentence and the agent will know I'm an American.

Pretend to be deaf and dumb or under the influence of drugs?

More delay. "Casey Mahan" will come to the surface sooner or later.

Test the scanner and bribe the agent.

With about thirty dollars worth of Greek drachmas and my credit card?

Run like hell.

On my heels?

Databases have ended airport chases. Zero or one, yes or no, A or B. Just like the Jesuits taught me. In or out. In the country or in jail. Heading home, I feel like an illegal alien. Not just a Kurd, anyone trying to get into the United States. Not just a "creemeenal," but a "devil-worshipper." After days in a moral vacuum, I feel the nuns and my parents rushing into my empty head, what used to be my soul. I should be caught. I ought to walk up to the INS supervisor, surrender, and confess. To mistake, error, wrong, sin.

Standing in the passport line with fellow citizens, listening to them joke about the goods they would try to smuggle past customs and the years they might spend in jail, my urge to tell all to Father INS disappeared and good, old healthy self-preservation welled up. I'm a repeat offender: I smuggled Osman into both Greece and the United States. I thought about federal sentencing guidelines and started to sweat. I tried to think of an excuse. Dysentery, malaria. But I'm coming from Greece, a civilized country not the Third World. The scanner. I keep forgetting. Fear is irrelevant to the scanner. It's what I wanted to be, processor of information, Erica not Nikos. And still want to be. But better programmed, wiser. Remembering the scanner's objectivity makes me relax. Waiting at the stripe on the floor to be called forward to a booth, I don't feel at all self-conscious. I hand the young Hispanic woman my passport, she passes it through her scanner, and says, "Welcome home."

Maybe five seconds of relief. "Home." My address is on record at UNHCR. The Greeks and FBI know where to find me. I get my suitcases and throw away my connecting ticket. I won't push my luck any further. The police could be waiting for me when I step off the plane in Cincinnati. I'll rent a car and drive home. Not my apartment, but my parents' home. There's something I need there that I'm afraid I can't easily buy, not in America, not in every state.

In Cincinnati I put my wedding ring in my purse and drove around my parents' block a couple of times before I pulled into their driveway. Dad's car was gone. Good. I spent an hour with Mom before I told her I had to leave right away. I was supposed to meet this guy in Nashville, he was in transit, I couldn't get hold of him, the plane delay meant I might miss him.

"But you haven't even seen your Dad."

"He won't be back from golf for another two hours. You don't want me to miss a date, do you? I'll be back in a couple of days and tell you all about it."

"At least let me make you a couple of sandwiches. You don't look well."

While Mom was mixing the tuna, I went upstairs to the bathroom and lifted Dad's 22-caliber pistol from the closet shelf, where he kept it under some towels. It was easier to drive here to get the pistol than to check Pennsylvania and Ohio laws governing gun sales, waiting periods, proof of identity. Being home also gave me a chance to lay down a false lead, just in case the FBI wanted information from good old, trustworthy Mom and Dad.

One more test by electronics. I went to my bank and withdrew five thousand dollars. Then I stopped looking in my rear-view mirror. I was in and in the clear. As long as I observed the speed limit, made sure my brakelights worked, drove defensively, and didn't use my credit card, nobody could find me. Like Ziba and Osman in Greece, I had no identity.

In Chicago, I checked into a cheap hotel in Greektown. No telling how long I'd have to be here, and maybe eating Greek food would bring back some clue to Osman's whereabouts that he dropped in an Athens taverna.

I called St. Joseph's Hospital and said I was from the Child Protection Agency of Chicago Welfare: "We have a five-year-old child badly injured in an auto accident. He apparently speaks only Kurdish. His mother was killed in the accident, and we need a Kurdish doctor who can speak to the child. Do you have any Kurdish-speaking doctors on your staff?"

I had to ask this question of three different people, but was finally transferred to a woman who knew something about the hospital's doctors.

"Not Kurdish," she said, "I don't know of any Kurds on our staff."

"What about doctors from Iraq or Turkey?"

"No one from Turkey. I believe Dr. Hoseini is from Iraq, or it could be Iran."

"Close enough," I said, "Do you have his extension?"

Quick change of identity now. "My name is Cheryl McArthur, and I need to see Dr. Hoseini as soon as possible."

"He's booked this week. Would next Thursday be okay?"

"Actually not. This is an urgent personal matter, and I have to speak with Dr. Hoseini right away. You see, I just found out that I'm HIV-positive and I need to notify all my sexual partners as soon as possible."

"Would you like to leave your number so Dr. Hoseini can call you?"

"No, I'm not sure he'd recognize my name, and this is something I need to talk with him about in person. It will take only a few minutes if you can squeeze me in between appointments."

"Come at nine tomorrow morning, Ms. McArthur."

AIDS—the death threat that requires people to find their former lovers. I thought of using it when remembering my beach-mat conversation with Osman about different kinds of plagues. I didn't believe Dr. Hoseini would make me show him medical documents, not if I played as dumb as I was about Osman's injection. And not if I presented myself as the altruist I used to be.

The next morning I wasn't asked to fill in a new patient form, so at least the receptionist knew this was no ordinary visit. I wondered what would be written in the file the nurse leaves on the waiting room door. "Former lover." "Current lover." "Kurd lover."

Dr. Hoseini looked puzzled when he came in. He also looked more like a bald Indian computer programmer I'd imported than a Kurd. The doctor had cut his hair down to a stubble, had very dark skin, had a beard rather than a mustache, and was wearing a wedding ring. Probably about Osman's age, Dr. Hoseini appeared older despite the presumed ease of American life. He was not my kind of guy, but I had a role to play.

"I have no chart for you, Ms. McArthur. Why are you here to see me?"

"Oh, Dr. Hoseini, I'm so thankful you agreed to see me. I've just recently found out that I'm HIV-positive, and I'm trying to contact former lovers. I'm hoping that you know how I can reach one of them."

Come on, Dr. Hoseini look me in the face. It's not you, but I want to see if he's talked with you recently.

"And who is that?"

"Dr. Osman Mamozin."

"Osman? Osman is back in the States?"

Dr. Hoseini seemed genuinely surprised. Shit.

"Yes," I said, "but he doesn't want people to know it. It's something hush-hush, political you know, and that's why I can't locate him. He'd be so upset with me if he knew I was here. But you're a doctor. You know what a terrible thing AIDS is. I need to tell Osman."

"Yes, yes, of course. But I haven't heard from him for at least a year."

"If he calls you, please don't tell him I came to see you, okay? I guess we have doctor-patient confidentiality."

"Certainly, Ms. McArthur."

"But if he does contact you, would you call me and give me some idea of how to reach him? I'm not asking for his address or anything. Just a phone number, if you have one."

I wanted to cry, but couldn't. I tried thinking of the kids at the Pendeli camp. But the most I could do was pretend to snuffle and say, "I feel so guilty. I didn't know I was infected. And Oz is such a wonderful person. If he's positive, I want to see him get that new cocktail. He has so much to do in his life. You know, for Kurds."

"Yes, of course, but I never understood why he went back to that hospital in Turkey. If he contacts me, Ms. McArthur I will certainly find a way to let you know."

"Thank you so much, Dr. Hoseini. I'm sorry to take up your time this way, but knowing you're a friend of Osman I knew you'd want to help. Maybe you know some other friend I might contact."

"No, I'm afraid not. Osman and Ziba kept to themselves after they met."

I wrote my telephone number on one of his prescription pads, and he wished me the best of luck with my treatment. Now he could tell his wife about this strange woman who came in search of Osman, poor Osman mixed up with some blonde American bimbo. Should have stayed in Turkey with his Ziba. She'd never have betrayed him with another man, unless it was a policeman.

I went back to my hotel, and the combination of failure and jet lag put me to sleep for three hours. When I woke up, I walked to a Greek restaurant for lunch. Too bad Osman isn't Greek. I could cruise this strip of restaurants, Astoria and Athenian diners in the Loop, Greek Orthodox churches on Sunday. But Osman disliked Greece and Greeks. Eating my salad, I felt I should go back to Cincinnati and try to forget about Osman. But then I'd never know what

Osman's motives were, and I'd still be fearful there, waiting for the FBI to call. Just thinking about more waiting sent me to the toilet. Not just urination now, but loose bowels.

On the way back to my table, I asked to use the restaurant's Yellow Pages. There must be some reason why Osman and Ziba came independently to Chicago. Every known religion but Yezidi.

The cook was shouting at my young waitress in Greek. I recognized the words for "slow" and "school," and wondered if she had come here to study as Ziba and Osman did. Back at the hotel, I called Northwestern and asked for the Office of International Students.

A woman who sounded like a Chinese geneticist I'd imported while at Snow and Fiore answered the phone.

"I'm doing research for a book on international students in the United States. I was wondering if you keep statistics on countries of origin?"

"Yes."

"Perhaps you could tell me how many Kurdish students you have."

"One moment please."

I heard her on the keyboard.

"I'm sorry," she said. "Kurd is not in our database. There must be some mistake because I know we have Kurdish students."

"Do you have any idea why they'd come to a place as flat as Chicago?"

The Chinese woman was a believer in America.

"For the quality of education, I'm sure."

"Of course," I said. "I didn't mean to insult Northwestern. Can you think of any other reason?"

"Perhaps there's a community here. I believe there's a library or cultural center downtown."

No Kurdish Library, no Kurdish Cultural Center. Reverse the terms. Cultural Center of Kurdistan. I called to get hours and directions.

The voice that answered "Kurdistan" sounded like "Bastan."

"You better get down here soon sweetie, because I won't be here long today."

"Maybe there's someone else I can speak to."

"Not here. I have the keys, clean the toilet, shelve the books, and keep the tapes locked up."

"And you are?"

"Augusta Khan." Or "Can" or "Con."

A Kurd with a Roman first name and a Boston accent? I told her I'd be there right away.

Chapter 17

The Cultural Center of Kurdistan was a two-storey shotgun house with dirty aluminum siding south of the University of Chicago. Lots of African-American teenagers with low-riding baggies on the street, but nobody with pajama pants. Inside, another surprise. Though Augusta Khan sounded about fifty on the phone, she had white hair, deep wrinkles in her cheeks, and old-lady wire-rim glasses. She looked seventy—but also forbidding behind her desk eight feet from the front door. She and the desk blocked access to the bookshelves behind her and some ratty stuffed chairs in the next room. High above the bookshelves were dusty photographs of mountains and Kurds in native dress.

"I hope you don't want to take anything out," she said before I could introduce myself, "because our materials don't circulate. Not unless they're stolen."

"Do you have a card catalog?"

"I'm it. What are you looking for?"

"I'm doing research on medical practices in different cultures. I hoped you would have something on medicine in Kurdistan."

"Do you read Sorani?"

"No."

"I have something on folk cures in Sorani."

"Anything in English?"

"Just a few pages in this little collection of proverbs I translated."

She gestured to a pile of thin paperbacks on her desk. I picked one up, looked at the table of contents, turned to a section entitled "Health," and skimmed some items. "There is a medicine for every condition except stupidity." "A sick man is God's guest."

"I'm selling those for ten dollars apiece," Augusta Khan said. "To help keep the Center open."

I gave her ten dollars, cheap if she could answer my next question.

"Would you know any Kurdish doctors or nurses I might interview?"

"Look, sweetie, you can't learn anything by interviewing Kurds." She pronounced the word like "Kads."

"Why do you say that?"

"The Kurds who give interviews are chiefs like Barzani and Talibani, the warlords. They'll talk forever, but they don't care about their people. They'd betray their own brothers, if they were still alive."

"I was told that family loyalty is central in Kurdish culture."

"Not any more. Now it's rage. You're a professor, you must know about displacement. Every Kurd is tortured by powerlessness, self-hate. With no political hope, rage seeks some victim, any victim, near or far. Kurds have become like Zohak in their origin myth."

She looked at me for a sign of recognition and went on.

"Zohak was a gigantic tyrant that required young men's brains for break-fast. When calves' brains were substituted, the survivors were smuggled to the mountains and begat Kurds. Now they're eating each other."

Deceptive as a Kurd, I thought, from the very beginning.

Augusta Khan nodded at the proverbs and said, "'A brother is a brother, until he has a rifle.'"

I asked her a question I knew the answer to, at least part of the answer: "You're not Kurdish, are you?"

"Me?" she laughed. "No, sweetie, I'm Jewish."

Augusta Khan couldn't help me, so I could ask her the next question.

"What are you doing here, then?"

"I'm a librarian. Years ago, I got interested in Sufism and learned to read some Sorani. When I was hired a year ago by the two Kurds who began the Center, they said, 'We want a professional.' But I think they really wanted someone who could feel for Kurds from far away." She waved her right hand at the shelves in back of her. "You know, from reading. Years ago I guess students used to come here to read the newspapers, but nobody does that any-more. Now they get everything off the Internet."

She pointed to the back room. I had to walk around her desk to see a computer, which was not visible from the door.

"We provide free access," she said. "It's about the only way we get anyone to come to the Center now."

After posing as a researcher, I couldn't very well ask Augusta if a red-haired man about five-foot-ten had come in to use the computer.

"Free access? Is that for anybody? I'm here from Ohio. The hotel I'm stay-ing in charges an arm and a leg, and I need to do some email. I'd get off if anyone else came in."

"Help yourself. You're the first person I've seen today."

I went back and fiddled with the computer, read *The Athens News* online. The Greek police had no further leads on the embassy attack. Hoping to hit the lottery, I typed both of Osman's names into a search-engine. Nothing. I searched Kurds, hoping that something would pop up as I waited for Osman to come through the door. I typed in Kurdish doctors. Nothing. Poison gas. Lots of entries, but no address for Osman. I exited the computer, thanked Augusta, and exited the Center. I went to a diner across the street. Not a single person with a mustache. I sat in a window seat, drank tea for my bowels, and watched the Center until Augusta closed up. Osman had my laptop. He spent a lot of time online. Without Dr. Hoseini's help, I had no other place to go.

The next day I watched the Center from my car and from the diner. I didn't feel like a cop. More like an applicant waiting for the only person who can help me, an Aziz or Ziba. Two old men who didn't look Kurdish to me were Augusta's only customers, and for all I knew they were just friends or former lovers. This waiting is crazy, I thought, driving back to the hotel. I need some reason to stay here.

The following morning I called Dr. Hoseini's office and told the person who answered that I thought he would take my call. He did. "No, Osman has not called me," he said. He could be lying, but I had no way to pressure him short of going over there and threatening to kiss him on the mouth.

"Can you give me any idea of where he might hang out if he's back in town?"

"Not really. He used to live in student housing, so there'd be nobody he knew there. When he had a car, he and Ziba used to go down to the Center once in a while."

"What Center is that," said the dumb blonde.

"The Cultural Center of Kurdistan near the University of Chicago. It's gotten dangerous down there now, but I think the Center is still there."

I was back there an hour later. At lunch, I brought Augusta a sandwich from the diner and asked her where younger Kurds, doctors or otherwise, might be found.

"You're really desperate for first-hand information, aren't you?" she said.

"My research requires it," I replied, thinking of my second-hand husband.

"I don't know any young Kurds," she said. I went back to my car.

The next day at lunchtime, I went back in to use Augusta's computer, which was less boring than sitting in my car or the diner. A half hour later, I heard the door open and Augusta say hello. Then Osman's voice. Something in Kurdish, I assumed, maybe a greeting. Then, "I'm the person who talked to you on the phone about newspapers."

"Oh yes, the man with a laptop. I don't know if you can plug it into our line, but you can try. Right now, though, someone is using the computer."

Get up and go out? Risk Osman running out the front door or let him come back here where I can corner him?

Augusta solved my dilemma. "Just go back and ask her how long she'll be. She's never on very long."

I stand up and think of Osman sitting at my laptop, me leaning over him. I don't know him any more. He might hit me in the head with my laptop. His steps creak on the old linoleum floor.

He says something in Kurdish when he sees me. His eyes flick around the small room, as if looking for policemen hidden among the dusty books.

"What...," he starts and thinks better of it, maybe remembering Augusta ten feet away.

I don't say anything, just point at my laptop. He hesitates, then hands it to me. "A peace offering," he says. "You know, like Indians before a pow-wow."

"It's going to take more than a laptop to make peace with me."

"I know."

Be the aggrieved wife, I felt, angry and realistically curious. But don't spook him.

"Why did you take it, anyway?"

"I wanted to get it out of your apartment."

"And why was that?"

"Because of what was on it and because it was yours."

"What was on it?"

"Would you like to get a cup of coffee and talk about this across the street?"

"That's fine. I want to hear what you've done about that injection too."

"What a coincidence," I said to Augusta as we walked past, "this man is a doctor who can tell me about Kurdish medical practices."

I doubt she believed that, but I didn't care. I wanted Osman to believe I hadn't told Augusta why I was there. He shouldn't feel she'll be dialing the police while we're at the diner. Out on the sidewalk, I told him that I was posing as a researcher, hoping he might show up.

Waiting to cross the street, I thought about other roles I'd played: the CIA bitch in Diyarbakir, the cynical babe with Costa, the bimbo blonde with Dr. Hoseini. They looked easy compared to playing myself, the role I need to be not to scare off my husband. Duped idealist. Or was it gullible romantic? Unmarried woman over thirty? Any person in a tight spot? Or some combination of them all? I'll just have to trust myself, even though doing just that got me into this tangle.

"Let's sit in the corner booth away from the other tables," Osman said.

I took the seat across from him, put the laptop on the table between us. Although he hadn't shaved recently, I could see haggard creases in his cheeks. His eyes looked jet-lagged or worse. I tapped the laptop. Stick with it, something inanimate and neutral, then move to motives, fears and desires.

"So what was on it that you had to leave in such a hurry?"

"Information about poison gas."

"You have that on my computer?"

"Yes. I wanted to record what I remembered from my research in Iraq."

"Who besides Ziba knew you were using my computer?"

"The editor at the magazine."

"Did he know my address?"

"No."

"Then what was the rush? Why didn't you write more than two sentences when you left? Or call me?"

"I guess I panicked," he said.

I looked up from the computer, tried to catch Osman's eyes, but he was still looking down at the computer, as if it were the translator between us.

"Panic? Osman, it's me, Casey Mahan, former examiner at UNHCR. I was interrogating applicants there long before I became Mrs. Osman Alpdogan. You have to tell me what happened. I can't accept panic."

Osman glanced up at me. Looking at those sleepless eyes and scraggly beard, I suddenly realized the meaning of panic—fear of Pan, god of shepherds.

"The editor knew about my research. Kani is visible, very involved in Kurdish support. He was afraid of the police. After the Embassy attack, he said he was disappearing. But if the police caught him, I was afraid he'd give them my name."

I felt relieved. If Kani escaped, the connection between gas and Osman was broken. Even if Kani didn't escape, he might not give up Osman's name.

"This doesn't sound like a well-founded fear to me."

"You think the Greek police don't torture suspects who aren't Greek?"

"You're the husband of an American citizen, someone with a position in Human Rights. The police weren't going to torture you."

"First Kani, then me. You know what Ziba did. I didn't want to do that to you. I wanted to protect you. That's why I left Greece."

Betrayal. Osman knew Ziba was involved in his arrest and has a compelling fear of betrayal. I'll need to be very careful.

"You left Greece for my sake?"

"Mine and yours. I wanted to break the connection, put as much distance between you and me, the police and me as possible."

"Osman, you know I have to ask this. Were you involved at the Embassy?"

"No. I told you, I panicked. I've been in prison once. I wasn't taking any chances. I would have been a suspect, but I wasn't involved."

Be trusting, Casey, or gullible. Either one will do for now.

"If you panicked, why didn't you go to Kurdistan?"

"No more Kurmanji for me."

"Honest as a Kurd," I said in Kurmanji.

"Please don't, Casey. It's as bad as sweating. I hate the sound of Kurmanji."

"Your mother tongue?"

"When the Turks sweated information out of me, they had their Kurdish collaborator pour Kurmanji into my ears. I hated him for betraying us, and I came to loathe the language. Every time I hear it, I remember my torture, how I was betraying my people by giving Turks information about poison gas. Now Kurmanji disgusts me."

If Osman was telling the truth, he had logophobia. Ziba hated to translate. Osman hated his language. It was one thing to fail at learning a new language, another to fear the tongue you first heard as a child, to despise the words you once spoke to your wife.

"Does Ziba know this?"

"No. I couldn't tell her. I was the only person she could speak Kurmanji to without fear."

"Why did you keep it a secret from me?"

"Don't I have enough problems? I didn't want you to pity me."

And yet Osman's eyes ask for pity. Careful, Casey.

"No danger of that, not after running off without explanation. Now what about the weight loss? Why haven't you checked into a hospital?"

"I can't."

"Why not?"

"I don't have the money. A homeless man can't walk into a hospital and demand expensive treatment."

"Not a homeless man, no. But your name is on my insurance. I called the States the day after we got married. You're covered."

"Oh no," Osman said and hunched forward over the table between us. "You shouldn't have done that, Casey. Now there's a documented connection between us here in the States, not just in Greece. I can't check into a hospital on your policy. You've got to worry about yourself."

"Now you're being paranoid. There are thousands of undocumented aliens in Greece. The police will never find Kani. You're in the clear."

"No, Casey, there can't be any official connection between us here."

"Osman, I saved your life. I can't let you sacrifice it because you're paranoid. Look, I've got money. We can pay cash, up front. If you want, we'll check you into the hospital under an assumed name and find out what's wrong."

"That would be a waste of your money. I've started to get diarrhea. I had some more outpatient tests when I arrived. I'm afraid it may be too late for a hospital."

Our common diarrhea threw me off for a second. What was Osman afraid of. Then I registered his last sentence, "What do you mean 'too late?'"

"The Turks injected me with thallium. I don't believe there's any treatment."

"'Believe.' That's no basis for a decision. You have to check into a hospital. I'm going to give you the money. Do with it what you want."

I reached for my purse. Maybe Osman married me for the money. I didn't care.

"You're a hard negotiator, Casey. Something like this I'd have to consider carefully."

Before these last two sentences, everything Osman said was factual, earnest. Here was a sign of his old ironic diffidence. I felt encouraged.

"I'll give you time to think. Where are you staying, anyway?"

He didn't answer.

"Look, come back to my hotel with me. Maybe it has a house doctor who can write you a prescription. Maybe the diarrhea is just from something in the water. If not, maybe the concierge will know an old-fashioned country doc, one who still makes house calls."

"I have to go," he said and started to slide out of the booth.

I slid out more quickly and stood before he could. "I can't let you go, Osman. We need to get you into a hospital."

He looked up, far up, at my face and grinned. "The men's room," he said. "I have to go to the men's room."

He slid the rest of the way out of the booth and walked slowly to the nearest waitress. She pointed to the left. I waited five minutes. The diarrhea must be serious. I waited ten minutes. Osman needed to be in a hospital. At fifteen minutes, I walked to where the waitress had pointed, knocked on the men's room door, opened it a crack, and called, "Osman, are you okay?" There was no answer. I poked my head in. Two sinks, two stalls, no men. I went in and looked under the stalls. No feet. I opened up each stall. No Osman. I'll be damned.

I checked the women's rest room. One woman, no man.

I went back to the booth and understood why Osman chose it. From there, I couldn't see the entrance to the toilets or an exit to the street. Osman had been in this diner before. The computer was on the table. I wished it were a tape recorder. I wanted to listen to our conversation again, discover what I'd done or said that spooked him. Osman somehow sensed or I somehow gave away motives beneath love: keep him under surveillance, under house arrest in a hospital if possible; bind him so close in marriage he won't consider committing a crime that will implicate his wife. Maybe I'd overplayed my trust.

Then I thought, what if the diarrhea isn't a cover story, one that got him out of the coffee shop? What if his suspicion is true: what if he is now too ill to be treated?

Osman might be dying. He seemed to believe it. I had tried not to. I couldn't. But what if it's true? The primal fear, below all others, reason for the amoeba to contract, the paramecium to dart. Has he fled to save me from the torture of watching the man I still love die? Did he run to save himself from seeing pity in my eyes?

My questioning mind goes blank. Osman dying. My stomach is in my head. Now I need to use the toilet. Dying. The final fall, six-foot plunge into the abyss. No matter how wounded or traumatized, applicants are survivors. Maybe patients, but still survivors. The doctor dying? This can't be true. My new husband dying? It's like a tabloid headline: "Couple Falls Into Grand Canyon On Honeymoon." It's too much to believe. I can't trust Osman's word. Disbelief is my only defense.

I drove around the neighborhood. Osman would be easy to spot among all the black faces. But his story had pinned me in the booth just as his promise to call in Athens. I drove back to my hotel. In Athens I knew the two-dollar eateries and four-dollar hotels where you might find a refugee. Osman knew Chicago, where he could hide with no effort now he knew I was looking for him. Or he might leave the city. I turned on the TV. People were winning prizes with knowledge of trivial information I lacked. I looked out the window at the building across from me and thought of another hapless soul, Bartleby the scrivener, the slowly dying legal copyist. I remembered my essay.

The laptop. Why didn't I think of it sooner? Jet lag and despair. The laptop might lead me to Osman.

I checked the email. All the boxes had been emptied, the trash cleared. Osman was hiding someone or something. Unfortunately, I knew from experience that double-trashed email was gone forever unless I called in the FBI

I checked the regular files, most of them downloads from the Internet. He didn't use directories, just letter and number codes. TU was, predictably, for material about Turkey. IR was Iran, IQ Iraq. I checked TH. There were about fifteen files on thallium. Two were about a Kurdish dissident poisoned with thallium by Iraqi agents in London. The man's flesh fell off. English doctors could do nothing to save him. Did Osman suspect thallium all along? Was thallium identifiable only west of Greece? Or was thallium a deeper cover story?

I looked into other files. Material on sarin and ricin, the one he'd mentioned, made from beans. The files seemed innocent to me, scientific recording. I assumed they had to be or Osman trusted me not to snoop into his files in Athens. Or he didn't know how to create a password. Maybe Ziba was wrong and I could go back home. To read all of Osman's documents for information that would help me locate him, I'd need a stable of paralegals. There was no OA file. No ZM or Z file. No CM or C file.

Jet lag, despair, and idiocy. Check to see if Osman tried to delete anything besides the email. One file. It was named HOMEO and was dated July 7. Osman was an Internet addict, but a cybernetic amateur. He didn't know my laptop had an automatic backup system.

To: The Editor

If my wife has given you this disk, I've died or been killed in the United States. I'm asking you to print the open letter below in the magazine. If Kani has gone back to Turkey, you are my only chance to explain what I did and why.

"I, Osman Mamozin, from Sirnak, Turkey, provided the PKK with information about making the poison gas used to attack the Turkish Embassy in Athens. I regret the deaths of the Greek and Saudi Arabian nationals. I intended and the PKK representative promised that the gas would not be wasted in killing Turkish functionaries."

"My betrayal by the PKK represents the Kurds' fate and the PKK's interest in local action. Kurds will be safe only when nations far away from Turkey understand fear and reverse their terror-supporting policies. My mission in the United States has been to use mystery killings and to report them secretly to government officials. My purpose is not public terror, but private fear, officials' fear of revealing my presence in America and their fear of keeping it secret. Only this fear can change foreign policy in the congressional committees where Kurds' fates are decided."

"My method has been copied from Turks and Iraqis: poison wells for long-term effects. In America land is what laws protect, what Kurds don't have. My action shows Americans that documents like deeds don't protect them, no matter how many acres they own, no matter how they fence them off, no matter how deep they dig their bunkers and wells. Death can come anywhere, at any time, like poison gas, like police breaking down a door. Kurds know this, and now Americans will learn it if their government does not change its policy. Americans will never trust their homes again. Always in the bottom of their minds will be the fear of death from water. Americans will distrust their faucets. Drinking water will become a phobia. People will leave their homes and live in RV's or trailers or tents. Others will leave the country. Americans will no longer fear the water in other lands. Americans will be aliens. Like betrayed Kurds, Americans will live in refugee camps."

Dysentery, this is what dysentery feels like, I thought in the toilet. Washing my hands made me nauseous. The betrayed American tottered out into her cheap hotel room to read the rest of Osman's letter. Fortunately—fortunately!—it was like the thallium in Osman's system, a poison he couldn't purge from the computer.

The file went on for another three pages, describing the history of American betrayal of the Kurds. In 1975 Ford and Kissinger encouraged a Kurdish revolt in Iraq and then withdrew support, which forced Barzani into exile. In the 1980s the U.S. talked Human Rights, but aided GAP, the giant dam project that displaced Turkish Kurds. During the Gulf War, Bush encouraged another Kurdish revolt, never delivered support, and caused thousands of Kurds to die. In 1995 the CIA supported a Kurdish plot to assassinate Saddam, pulled out, had to evacuate thousands of Kurds to Guam, and pushed Barzani into a treaty with Saddam.

This computer file was a sorry history, but not an official document, not like the stamped documents at UNHCR. Technically, I told myself to stop my hands from trembling, the letter could have been written by anyone with access to my computer. Fingerprints on the keys would prove nothing. The letter was neither handwritten nor signed like my Letters of Recommended Action. I could discount the file as a document and I could delete it, but no matter what I did with it—in my examining mind, with my shaking hands—I knew that I'd never see Osman again and that I have to see him again. He is my husband here, in my country of origin. If he commits this crime, he'll be caught. The police will trace back his documents and I'll be caught. For all I know, accessory to mass murder is a capital offense. And if Osman has been emailing his information about poisons around the world—the probable reason why he wiped his email files, the even more probable reason why he was bringing my laptop to the Center—there was no country that would give me refuge. Like gas at the embassy, Osman's poison diffused across the net. But thallium or ricin was no file-eating virus. The information was a people-killer.

"You're in danger," Ziba told me. "My life is in danger," I tell myself back in the toilet. Like the Turkish smuggler in the minefield. My mind veers again. Of all the terrified people I interviewed, why did none ever use diarrhea as evidence? Because they were safe compared to me in my home country. Think like a lawyer. I have to find Osman. Osman has to be found. If I panicked a little in Athens, my jump to the States is reasonable now. If I over-reacted by borrowing a pistol in Cincinnati, I have grounds now. But past motives are irrelevant. Now I have a well-founded fear of future persecution, Osman's persecution of Americans.

Chapter 18

Who could I call?

A lawyer. Snow and Fiore doesn't practice criminal law. None of my clients went AWOL, not even the pro bono Latin Americans. They trusted my ability to keep them in the States legally. I didn't trust anyone at the firm to help me and keep their assistance secret. In my eight years there, I hadn't made a friend to call in the middle of the night. Maybe that's another reason why I applied to UNHCR.

Sam Roberts. His Human Rights contacts in this country are mostly other professors, theorists inexperienced in finding lawbreakers. Academics like Sam argue against prior restraint and unfounded searches and seizures. Osman's theorizing about poisoning Americans is protected speech, as long as Osman doesn't shout it in a theater and panic the crowd.

Speech. Panic. My innocent remark about "something in the water" must have chased Osman out of the diner. Osman is the house doctor, the person who plans to make house calls in reverse, not to cure, but to kill. How can a doctor do this? His job is saving lives. I'd saved Osman and somehow felt he owed me, the ultimate quid pro quo. He'd probably saved hundreds or thousands of lives in his career. Perhaps he feels he has some coming, a few quids for many quos. But Osman isn't just his job, his profession. How can the man I found so gentle be so cruel? Like the proud Ziba who showed me her wound, perhaps the Athens Osman was not the doctor who trained in America or worked in Diyarbakir or researched in Iraq, but a creature humiliated and temporarily gentled by his torture. Or a skilled impersonator of passive victims he'd treated. Or a homeopath become a psychopath.

I could call my psychologist. "Practice coping strategies."

What I need is anger. Ziba, Osman, and I are all in flight, but they have reasons—personal and familial and tribal—to fight. Ziba resisted the safety and ease of America to remain close to home. Maybe, as the Director suspected, she was surreptitiously helping Kurds other than her husband at UNHCR. Osman is taking the fight here, not resisting, but striking first, preempting. What anger could I draw on to even this conflict? They'd used me, put my life in danger. I'm mad, but still not enraged. Because I sympathize with their motives? Because I loved them both? Or because my torture is still in the future, figurative, hypothetical? Osman's was hypodermic, deep in his system. Ziba's was dermic, but more than her skin was abraded. Both were guilty about betraying others, angry at themselves as well as others, perhaps guilty about leaving Kurdistan and surviving, shamed and enraged by betraying land and people. I don't hate myself, can't use that emotion to help dilute my fear.

To find Osman, I'll need to imagine my way out of this knot tied by emotions. I can call Costa:

"I've just discovered that Osman Alpdogan is actually Osman Mamozin, bigamist."

"Tell me something new," Costa will say.

"I think he may be dangerous."

"That's what you all say when your exotic lovers find people their own color."

Even if Costa believes me or pretends to believe me, notification of the INS would trickle back through bureaucratic channels. INS grabs illegals at airports, where it's easy, and chases wetbacks along the Rio Grande, where it's exciting, but only a few agents are slogging middle America. They're looking for group arrests and good television: twenty or thirty Latinos caught making salads or cleaning hotels, then whisked to the airport for deportation.

The FBI might listen to an anonymous phone tip. But even in the wake of the Trade Towers, the FBI will want some evidence. Osman's letter to the editor won't be enough. They'll want to interview me. I'll have to confess how Osman got here.

Official upholders of the law and protectors of the public won't do, not now. I require private assistance, secret-keepers like my Kurdish intimates. Skip-tracers advertise in law journals. But Osman hasn't skipped bail and left behind a record of places lived, jobs done, and crimes committed. There's no mug shot of him, and I don't have a photograph.

I can hire a private detective. But Osman hasn't kidnapped his own easily identifiable children or run off with another woman and his wife's car, both of which could be traced. Osman won't have a driver's license or a Social Security number. He has no home or relatives in the United States. He won't be making telephone calls to Kurdistan. Locating him will be harder than finding a serial killer before he begins to leave a trail of evidence.

I'll put an item in the Personal columns of Chicago papers. "Dear Osman: I know you plan to kill and want to be with you anyway. Please call home. Your loving wife, C.M." Osman isn't the type to read the personals. Like C.M. interviewing applicants, this personable man has a knack for the impersonal, the extra-personal. His mission statement mentioned only his birthplace and ethnic group. The rest read like a summary judgment.

Once I imagined the absurd, I could no longer avoid what I knew all along. I have only one possibility of finding and stopping Osman. I waited until Ziba was at the office, called there, and asked that she be put on the secretary's phone so she wouldn't hang up on me.

"You were right, Ziba. Osman has terror in mind."

Silence.

"I talked with him, but he disappeared on me. I found a file he tried to delete from my computer. It describes his plan. He has sent you a copy on a disk."

"Why me?"

"He wants you to make it public if he dies in the States. Was Osman born in Sirnak?"

"Yes, why?"

"He mentions it in the file."

Sirnak was my authentication, something I couldn't know without reading the file.

Now what I hope is a shocker: "Osman plans to poison wells."

"What?"

Ziba sounded sincerely surprised, shocked. But I couldn't see her face.

"Yes, he's going to kill Americans, the people who trained you to be a nurse."

"He said that on the computer?"

"Yes. You'll probably get your disk in a few days."

"He's not going to attack the government?"

"No. He plans to kill private citizens."

"Not government officials?"

Ziba's follow-up made me wonder if Osman had lied to her.

"No, people in their houses. I doubt he'll stay in Chicago. Can you tell me where he's gone?"

Again silence. Maybe Ziba believes I'm taping this call. Perhaps that's why she begins to cooperate.

"If Osman plans to poison wells, he's probably heading back out west."

"Why?"

"I remember him pointing out well-houses next to homes and barns. He said the wells reminded him of home. Also, he'll feel safer out there, more like Kourdistan."

"The west is a big place, Ziba. Give me cities, the names of people."

"I really don't know where he would go."

"You have to know. I'm not asking you to betray him again. I don't want to turn him in to the police. I just want to stop him. Stay with him and prevent him from doing this."

"Even if you find him, you won't stop him."

"I can delay him, bring him to his senses. Osman needs medical treatment. If he gets cured of whatever is making him ill, he may give up his plan. You're his wife. You loved him once. He and I are afraid he's dying. Won't you help him now?"

"I can't."

"Your letter, Ziba. What about your letter? You said you wished you had a gift for me."

"I don't have anything I can give you, Casey."

I'd anticipated that Ziba would refuse every role I offered her: nurse, wife, friend. That's why I called her at the office. In Athens, I promised Ziba I wouldn't reveal her secret, but circumstances had changed. Nothing from our past or her past could matter now.

"You have to help me, Ziba. If Osman is caught and I'm implicated, I could be looking at the gas chamber or a lethal injection. Legally, you're as guilty as I am. I'll plea bargain and give up your name. It's on the computer."

"That doesn't frighten me, Casey. America is a very large country and Osman is very clever. You know that."

Her mocking gives me the anger I need.

"So conspiracy to murder doesn't frighten you? How about this, Ziba? If you don't tell me where I can find Osman, I'll call the Director right now. You may not be able to get out of the building. You'll lose more than your status. With your position, you'll be deported to Turkey. They're very clever in Turkey. You know that."

Kaya started my trouble. Maybe he could help me out of it. There is a slight sizzle in the fiber optics. Ziba has to decide. In thirty seconds, I'll have the Director on the line. Panos is standing at the door with his machine gun.

"I can give you two cities. Our best man in Chicago was an Iraqi Kourd, a doctor named Kamran Dizai. He was living in Chula Vista, California, the last I knew. When Osman and I were traveling, we met a Kourd in Denver. He and Osman used to write, but I don't remember the man's name. All I know is that he had a restaurant and towing business, was wealthy, and was interested in Kourdish politics."

"That's all you can tell me?"

"It's been five years since we were in the States."

"Think some more about this."

"I have nothing more to tell you."

"Does Osman have a bank account in the States?"

"Not that I know of."

"A credit card."

"No."

"If this information doesn't check out, I'll be calling the office again."

I let the fiber optics sizzle for a few seconds.

"I'm sorry, Ziba, but I have to stop Osman."

The connection closed. The phone buzzed in my ear.

I didn't really expect Ziba to accept an apology.

Now that every secret and every threat at my disposal has been used, I wondered if I could have pursued this interrogation if Ziba were in the same room. If she looked up into my eyes and said, "You promised not to inform on me," would I have pressed on? I can't answer that. Would I have been willing to stand behind a one-way mirror and watch Greek police threaten her? Could I have stood by in her bedroom and watched Turkish police saw this information out of her? I don't have to answer these questions. They're irrelevant ethical hypotheticals. Ziba is seven thousand miles away and I'm desperate.

Now, what do I have to fear from Ziba?

If these leads are authentic, will Ziba, enraged by my betrayal, call the man she named and warn him that I'm searching for Osman? He can politely put me off, and Ziba's status will be safe. Does she know the other man's name, and will she call him? Trying to imagine Ziba's motivation, her combination of anger, guilt, fear, and, possibly, love is worthless. Since her leads are my only ones, I have to assume they're worth pursuing.

I went down to the hotel gift shop and bought an atlas. Although I didn't have a name in Denver, it seemed the more likely possibility. Chula Vista is outside of San Diego, near a desert. No wells there. It will be a hot, sweaty place. Outside of Denver, Osman can find plenty of targets, Americans living on ranches or in trailers far from the random violence of seaboard cities. These self-reliant natives may belong to militias and have guns. They'll be prepared for home incursions by the FBI, the CIA, and the United Nations, but not for a stealth bombing of their water supply by a man who admires Indians. If there's a light over the well-house or a barking dog, Osman gets back in his car and moves on. With no personal connections to the victims, he has a million targets and a one-in-a-million chance of being caught.

Maybe I should just drive back to Cincinnati, withdraw all my money, sell my furniture in a yard sale, fly to Mexico, make my way to Cuba. Castro might welcome a refugee who helped an enemy of the United States. I'll have to learn Spanish. I remembered my difficulties with the language in college. I'll probably have to hire a translator.

It occurred to me that a translator might help me reduce the odds here in Chicago. After months of "why?," why not? Act first, think later, the lesson of a nervous system that evolved from daily desperation. I called Berlitz. Arabic and Turkish they could cover, but not Kurdish dialects. I called the Municipal Court and got the names of several public defenders. I called back and impersonated one of them: "I've been assigned a Kurdish client that I can't communicate with. How can I get in touch with a translator?" The Court couldn't help me. Kurds in America must be law-abiding or quick learners of English.

I went to the Chicago Public Library and looked up a book on kilims. Ninety percent are red. It's probably a matter of available dye, but I wondered if the reds represent Kurds' complexions and their bloody past. After two hours of research, I returned to my hotel, got out the Yellow Pages, and called Oriental rug shops that advertised kilims. I said I was particularly interested in carpets from Van and Hakkari. Was there a Kurd on the staff to whom I could speak? I found two, an old man from Iraq and a woman from Turkey. She was impressed that I'd been to Diyarbakir. She came from Bitlis thirty years ago.

I was glad to find the shop small and poorly lighted, authentic in Istanbul, but not a sign of prosperity in Chicago. The carpets on the walls and in piles were mostly, my library session told me, machine-made imitations of kilims. I was also happy to see a wedding ring on the hand of the fiftyish and overweight Mrs. Gursel. Mr. Gursel was nowhere to be seen. In the bazaar, haggling over carpets made by women was a man's job. It was the tourist woman, her husband silent and hopeful he wouldn't have to get out his credit card, against the native man. Perhaps Mrs. Gursel and I had something in common: left to our own resources by our husbands.

I picked out a small double-diamond Hartushi and an intricate red and blue Jalali. Mrs. Gursel praised my discernment. I told her I'd seen ones like them in Diyarbakir, but was too distracted to buy them at the time.

"Why was that?" she asked, sympathetically.

"I was there looking for my husband. I thought he'd been kidnapped by the Turkish security forces and taken back to his home city."

She made a sound like the Greek *po, po, po,* something I'd never heard

Ziba or Osman articulate.

"We were living in Istanbul. Do you know the Kekule district there?"

"I have heard of it, yes."

If Mrs. Gursel didn't know Kekule and Istanbul, my story may sound plausible.

"My husband was practicing medicine at the American hospital and helping Kourds on the side. Then he disappeared. After months of investigation, I realized he had only faked a kidnapping. Now I think he abandoned me and my three sons to run off with a nurse. You know this story?"

She made the sad, pitying sound again, louder and longer. Depend on the personal, the predictable. Why not?

"I thought I'd find him in Chicago, but I haven't. Now I think he may be in California, but it's a long way and my money is running out. I'm really desperate. Maybe I should just buy some carpets and give up trying to find him."

Mrs. Gursel was in a difficult position now. She was, I judged, truly sympathetic, but she also wanted to make a sale. She chose to say nothing.

"I think my husband may be staying with a doctor friend of his in Chula Vista. He's a Kourd, so you know how he'll feel about me calling him up."

"The men stick together like Turks smoking the same hookah."

"Smoking and talking about women in the streets."

"You're right ..."

Before Mrs. Gursel could finish, I raised my hands to convey surprise and lied, "I just realized how to save a trip to California."

"How?" she asked.

"What dialect do you speak?"

"Mostly Kurmanji, but I know some Sorani. Why?"

"You could talk to the doctor in Sorani and pretend to be calling from Athens. That's where my husband thinks I'd go, to stay with my sister. You'd tell his friend that I have been hit by a car and am in the hospital. I may not live. 'Dr. Mamozin is traveling in the States. Do you know where he might be?'"

"I would like to help you, but I don't think I could do all that. Why don't you call?"

"The doctor might recognize my voice. Someone speaking in Sorani will sound authentic. 'Honest as a Kourd.'"

Mrs. Gursel laughed. She'd probably been lying to customers in English about her carpets for thirty years. This little translating job in Sorani shouldn't be so hard for her. For me, insisting was easy. Like applicants, Mrs. Gursel is a stranger.

"I'll write down the whole message," I told her. "You can say you know nothing beyond the message. You're just the translator and transmitter for Dr. Mamozin's wife. The doctor will know how undependable international phone connections are. No matter what he says, yes or no, you hang up. That way my husband will have to wait there for another call. He can't possibly call all the hospitals in Athens."

"I'd be afraid to do this."

"Why? There's no risk. It will take you twenty seconds. I'll write the message, you translate it into Sorani, you read it, and hang up. It could save me a lot of money."

"I don't think so."

"How much are these two carpets?"

"Together, for you, $400. A little less if you pay cash."

I reached in my pocketbook and put four hundreds on her desk.

"If you make the call, the money is yours."

Mrs. Gursel pursed her lips. She was tempted, but I could tell she was going to refuse.

"The money is yours, and you keep the carpets."

Ziba would have refused. But this was a deal no carpet seller in Istanbul or America could pass up. For $400, even the young man in Diyarbakir might have spoken English to me. Whether or not Mrs. Gursel bought my story, she asked me if I had the number. I gave it to her and asked her to turn up the Kurdish music wailing away in the background. After she translated the message, I suggested she lock the shop door for a minute. I didn't want Mr. Gursel or some English-speaking customer to walk in and waste my $400, a good investment if it saves a trip to Chula Vista or pins Osman there for a few hours.

I dialed Doctor Dizai's office and pretended to be an AT&T operator. "We have an emergency call from Greece for Doctor Dizai. We're having trouble keeping this connection open. Could you tell him that and get him on the line immediately?"

Twenty seconds later, Mrs. Gursel read her piece, paused for a few seconds, and hung up.

"How did he react?"

"He was shocked."

"What did he say?"

"He hasn't heard from Osman in years."

"Do you believe him?"

"Yes."

"Why?"

"From the way he spoke Sorani."

"Are you sure?"

"Yes, I'm sure."

"I really appreciate this, Mrs. Gursel."

"I'm glad I could help you. And it was good to speak Sorani again. My husband and I speak English."

I pushed the money toward her. "Thanks again."

"Take the Jalali," she said, "you should have something beautiful to remember from Kourds."

It was a nice gesture, splitting tribal pride and personal profit. I took the carpet. Mrs. Gursel was right. It was beautiful and in its creation uncomplicated by the motives that had been my job and that I was now exploiting in my search.

Chapter 19

Denver is 1023 miles from Chicago and $1,189 if I wanted to fly without seven, fourteen, or twenty-one days advance purchase. For some reason I couldn't explain to myself, I felt that Osman would be traveling cheap. Rarely did refugees fly into Athens. I knew that Osman had—or said he had—and I knew he was neither a refugee nor an economic migrant in the States, and yet I pictured him buying an old car and driving to Denver or taking the bus with the poor and crazed. Without a credit card, Osman will be saving his cash for his mission. Perhaps this analysis was rationalization. With the pistol, I had no choice but to drive. And think.

As fearful of detection as Osman is, he won't have brought poison with him. He'll have to acquire the materials here. If he wants "mystery killings," he'll use something unusual, hard to trace. From Osman's files, ricin, the one made from castor beans, seemed the most likely for him to use and the least likely to show up in a well. Since ricin is cheap and easy to make, I need to find him "STP," as Costa said. And since beans can be grown anywhere, I have even more to fear from Osman's use of my computer and Internet connection.

So what was the worst case? The doctor in Chula Vista and the restaurant owner in Denver are red herrings. Osman stays in Chicago and dumps poison into the Water Tower on Michigan Avenue. Or he heads east or south, where Ohio and Kentucky farmers have wells.

What would Osman believe about me after our talk? He might assume I'd try to locate him, and if so would see me calling Ziba. I'd be desperate, but wouldn't know about the disk. Neither would she, not yet, not with the delay of international mail. If I was going to do anything, I had to overlook my own doubts, depend on Ziba's fear of me, and believe Osman would consider his two wives too law-fearing to worry him. Ziba wanted her law-abiding life in Greece. I'd bolted out of Greece. Yes, I traveled to Diyarbakir to save a life, but then Ziba was leaning on me. Now alone, I'd be angry at Osman's betrayal and pity his condition, but these would cancel each other. Even if I had a lead from Ziba, I'd calculate the odds and give up because I was a reasonable woman, not some love-obsessed girl. I'd collapse like an American wife, not stalk him like a Turkish policeman or a feuding Kurd. Osman had miscalculated. He should never have given up the computer. Inside its black box was the secret that sent me toward Denver.

After two hours of silence and two hours of radio, I stopped at a Radio Shack and bought a miniature tape recorder. I couldn't drive and make notes. I had only the tape to talk to. After a night at the movies with Ziba, I'd dreamed my way into her body. On this daylight drive, I tried to speak my way into Osman's mind, his feelings. While my Taurus went straight out I-80 at seventy MPH, my words swerved at the speed of association:

So, Osman, a serial killer? If I'd snooped into your files, I'd have known your passion for poison and politics. But not your secret mix. Your aim was research, not testing human subjects, victims and congressmen. "Truth lies at the bottom of a deep well," Poe said. How could I have gotten to the bottom of you? Deep secrets, deep thinking, deep trouble. By showing you less sympathy, by feeling more rage against Turkey, by confessing my anger against the United States. Why didn't you test my feelings about my country of origin? Because you loved America once? Because you loved me? Or because you had your mission in mind in the pyramid? Maybe no love of mine could inject into you what the Turks wrung out. Or I lacked imagination. I still can't imagine that water torture, the hourly, daily dripping away of life. Like life, but conscious. The words of villains and their mouthpieces. "America funds us. The country that taught you to save lives is betraying you, helping us take your life." Well-founded hate? Maybe so. More conscious than most murderers. But more distant. Without some sexual thrill or intimate contact, will you be able to maintain that hate, repeat the killing? Maybe you'll be afraid of what you've become, your serial self, a serial killer. What translation will let you continue? A nomad murderer. A wandering execu-

tioner. A refugee avenger. Far from home,
uprooted, homeless, unrooted. The root of
'fear' in English: to be in motion. I looked
it up. Like translation: transporting meaning. But probably not in Kurmanji, Sorani, or
Guran. Maybe it's only we agrarians and city-
builders who insist on foundations, the
unmoving, being grounded. But the roots of
words aren't the bottom. Not even amygdala.
Greek for almond. Inside the shell shaped
like a Cycladic head is the nut of human
behavior. That protects us and drives us
nuts. That drives me down this road. Well-
founded insanity. You'll refuse that term
too. Guerrilla warfare, cunning negotiation,
justified blackmail. I refuse those terms.
But plead temporary insanity. Except for my
phobia, I was fearless. Of you, of Ziba, of
Kurds. Now I know about being away from home,
in motion, in the middle of nowhere. I'm in
my right mind, fearful, crazed, wide-eyed.

But it's through your eyes I see my
country. Hear your voice in my inner ear.
States say goodbye to and welcome travelers.
No barbed wire, machine guns, helicopter
patrols. No mountains to divide until the
Continental. In the middle of your land, you
Americans are not between. You travel freely,
speak your language openly. Dialects don't
separate you. Out here on the plains, in
small towns and modest cities, natives feel
safe, protected from immigrants and urban
violence. Americans can forget facts—most
murders are committed by a person related to
or known to the victim—and enjoy the illusion
of immunity. No longer dreading the bomb,
citizens can safely worry about Mexico and
safely ignore lands across seas. Refugees

can't cross the oceans. The New World Order
is like the reservation system: land masses
of power, small pockets of resentment.

    And revenge? I'd ask.

    Not revenge for the past, but sacrifice
for the future.

    Aztec politics, Oz?

    Not to placate gods, but protect Kurds
from your godlike power.

    Godlike? Our troops can't even pacify a
few thousand Serbs.

    Because the troops are visible. It's
the almost-invisible flow of money—no
lives risked, no equipment wrecked, nothing
televised—that establishes your power.

    Fight money with money. Apply to foun-
dations, raise funds, make a documentary
movie.

    Power is secret, Casey. Secrets are
power. You should know that by now.

    I should. I do. That's why I have a
pistol in the trunk.

    You're going to kill the man you love
to protect yourself?

    I don't know. The pistol is my secret,
the only undeniable power I've ever had. I'll
keep it.

    So you're in the west now. Sheriff and
outlaw. Cowboy and Indian. You know how these
stories come out.

I pulled over on the shoulder, got out of the car, and vomited on the grass.
Osman will do what he says. I'm sure of it now, feel it in my stomach, see it
in the vomit. When I look up, it's America as far as I can see in every direction. I'll never find Osman. I'll never have to point the pistol. I walk over to
the chain-link fence, think of Lavrion and Mr. Kaya. He never believed the
bomb would go off in his hand. If it hadn't, it might have gone off in a tourist
bus, blowing off others' hands and feet, separating their limbs. I have to find

Osman. I may have to fire the pistol. I feel dizzy and put my hands on the chain link. I lean my head up against the fence and start sobbing. I'm in the immense prison of America. My torture has begun. Like Osman, I'm leaking fluids. Like Ziba's, my abdomen registers the pain of decision. I want my feet to be beaten, my fingernails pulled out, my hair burned off my head. Not this internal sawing. But I'm alone, in the cell of my head, assaulted only by emotions. Which, after thirty-three years, I cannot evade, avoid, or suppress. The victim I pity is me. The torturer I fear is I. Casey Mahan may unlearn recent disinformation, but will never shed her nun-tattooed skin or excise her reptile-based nervous system. No matter how much vomiting and weeping, it will be Casey Mahan who gets back in the car.

I check my map. Colorado is a state of 103,000 square miles. Denver is a city of 467,000 people. Discouraged and encouraged by those large numbers and long odds, I keep driving west. Still trembling from throwing up, still afraid of being stopped for a traffic violation, I mope along at 60. American, Japanese, and German cars go flying past. Women in the passenger seat glance over at the old maid alone in the right lane. Kids in the back seat wave or make faces. Americans, my fellow citizens. The people passing me may be speeding home to their deaths. These are the Americans Osman plans to kill. Talking with and listening to natives, I told Ziba in Athens, were what I missed in America, were one reason I fell for Osman. Except for Mom, I haven't spoken to one native, not just to talk, to listen. Instead I've been requesting or squeezing information. I need food, I need contact. Maybe they will give me courage to save Americans as I once saved Osman.

At a truck stop, I take a booth between two occupied booths—Mom, Dad, and two boys, maybe 10 and 12 in one; a man and woman about forty-five in the other. The couple behind me:

"We just papered that guest bedroom two years ago," he says.

"The green doesn't match the comforter."

"Well, then change the comforter."

"Lucy gave me that comforter."

"Find another room for the comforter."

I tuned out and listened to the tow-headed kids across from me. They argued about the food, who would sit on the shady side, and some toy they were supposed to share in the back seat. Then the older one says, "Do you think we'll ever go back, Dad?"

"I don't know, Austin. It's a long way."

"I don't want to go back," the younger boy says, "I thought they were going to cut our heads off in that dark building."

"Fraidy cat."

"It was dark in there. Those big guys were swinging those big swords."

"They're lasers, not swords."

"Lasers can cut too, you know."

"Those weren't real lasers."

"But how did you know that, Austin?"

"Because it's just a haunted house."

An amusement park. The family was returning from an amusement park, not escaping from some torture chamber. They weren't refugees. They were on vacation, going home. They may live on a farm, drink well water. Innocent bystanders, on their own land, not in some foreign embassy. The unjust, one-sided war is now Osman's. State, national, and international law would condemn him, then me, for treason. Get back in the car and pick up the pace.

Like an escapee or refugee, I checked into a run-down motel on the outskirts of Denver. I called my parents and told them I'd decided to stay in Nashville for a while. Dad hadn't needed his pistol to defend against a home incursion, so they weren't worried. Next I called a shooting range to make sure I wouldn't be arrested if I walked into the place without a permit. "No, ma'am, you're in Colorado." I drove to the range, bought a box of fresh shells, had an attendant show me how to load the gun and set the safety. Like policewomen on TV, I held the pistol with two hands. I was glad to find it didn't try to jump out of my grasp. If I could fire this .22 with one hand, it wasn't likely to kill anyone. I never came close to the center of the target. That was fine too. If I find Osman, I'll be very close to him, stealthy as an Indian, not a cowboy firing from horseback. I thought of Ziba in the minefield, wondered if she or one of the men pointed the pistol at the smuggler.

Back at the motel, I got out the Yellow Pages. No advertisements for Kurdish food, but lots of Middle Eastern restaurants. I started making calls.

"This is Gina Giordano from the *Denver Post*. I'm doing an article on how politics in the Middle East affects the restaurant business. Could I please speak with the owner?"

It was tedious business. I talked to bus boys, cashiers, managers. When the call got passed high enough, I repeated my purpose and got more specific.

"I'd like to talk with people from as many ethnic groups as possible, and I've been told your owner might be Kurdish."

The most frequent answer was "What?" Then "No." A couple of "He no say." I talked with a man who turned out to be a Greek from Egypt. He didn't know any Kurds. A surplus in Athens, a paucity in Denver. I kept calling while wondering if there was some better way to find Osman's friend. He could be out of the restaurant business. He might be serving food in Atlanta. He may not exist. I was getting near the end of the listings. I looked at the last item— Zaza Cafe—and cursed my alphabetical method. Zaza is a minor Kurdish dialect spoken in southeastern Turkey and a catchy name for a cafe, particularly if someone is working backwards through the Yellow Pages. Zaza was the one, but for the sake of legal rigor or delay I called and eliminated the four restaurants before it.

A voice that sounded more Spanish than Kurdish answered at Zaza. I did my bit. Yes, Mr. Nazar is from Turkey. But he isn't in.

"Could you give me his home phone?"

The voice laughed and laughed.

"Did I say something funny?"

"Nobody knows where Mr. Nazar lives. If the restaurant burns, we call an answering service."

"What about his tow company?"

This was the corroboration that made the secretive Mr. Nazar Osman's friend.

"He wouldn't be there now."

"What's the name on that?"

"AZA. It's on West 38th Street. Do you have the Yellow Pages?"

Nazar didn't waste letters, liked his name. I looked up AZA Towing and checked my Denver map. Nazar's two businesses appeared to be within a couple of miles of each other, and not more than five or six miles from my motel. There were no listings for Nazar in the white pages. I wondered just how secretive he was, how he'd respond to Gina Giordano, the *Denver Post*, and a multicultural gesture. Maybe I didn't want to talk with him about politics and food. He might think I was the INS setting up a sting. I decided to ride by Mr. Nazar's businesses before making any more calls.

AZA Towing was an abandoned gas station, a parking lot enclosed by a high chain-link fence, a few cars, a German Shepherd, and no tow trucks or people to be seen. I imagined mustachioed Kurds roaring around Denver, hoisting the cars of American law-breakers, criminals of the no-parking zones. I couldn't think of a reason for Osman to be in the office, out of sight.

The Zaza Cafe was no livelier than the tow shop. There were only two cars in the "Free Zaza" lot, about twelve spaces wedged between the two-storey brick building that housed the cafe and a cinder-block office supply store. In the few minutes I stopped across the street from Zaza, no one went in or came out the front door. I looked at my watch: 11:17. I could come back at mealtimes and park in the metered lot next to me. Get a spot in front, bring plenty of quarters, scootch down in my seat, and watch for Osman. AZA wouldn't tow me, and there was no attendant to wonder why I was sitting in my car instead of eating at Zaza or shopping in the stores on both sides of the street. From food critic to investigative reporter in one hour.

Eating an early lunch three blocks from Zaza, I watched the Spanish-speaking bus boys and wondered if they felt watched as I had in Diyarbakir. The prospect of staring at Zaza made me unnaturally attentive to my surroundings. The waitress spoke with an accent I couldn't place. A black-haired, olive-skinned couple two tables away could be recently arrived Guatemalans or descendants of immigrants who crossed the Bering Strait. When the kitchen door swung open, I noticed the two men back there were African-Americans. Safe, all these people are safe. Osman won't murder ethnics or minorities. He'll want to poison white people, like those in Congress, like most of those in law firms.

The kitchen door opened again and I looked more closely. One man had symmetrical scars on his cheeks. The other one wore a hair net and stirred a large pot with a wooden spoon. Another mistake: unless Osman is dead broke, he has no reason to eat at Zaza. If he comes there at all, it will be to process his castor beans. He'll be in the cafe long before it opens or after it closes. If he comes there at all. He could be working on the beans in the basement of Nazar's house. I could cross off the tow shop, but I decided the rookie reporter needed an experienced private detective to find Nazar's home and watch it.

I went back to my motel and Yellow Pages. From INS regulations in Cincinnati, to the UNHCR *Handbook* in Athens, to the encyclopedia of Denver services, thank the Lord of Laws for texts. The first two detectives I called were busy investigating fraudulent insurance claims, videotaping workman's compensation recipients doing day labor or whiplash victims playing touch football with their kids. Easy pickings at residences in the court record. The next detective specialized in, his secretary said, "intimate surveillance." Mr. Lyle was free and could see me immediately.

Donald O. Lyle had his office in a strip mall on Brighton Boulevard. Driving there, I rehearsed my interview, the questions I wanted him to answer. But "Don-O," as he asked me to call him, began examining me before I could question him. "Before I find the louse," he said, "I have to know the spouse." I wondered if Don-O had watched too much of the OJ trial. He had the fidgets, habitual squint, and mournful eyes of a person most comfortable with one-way scrutiny or a computer monitor. Sitting across from my desk in Athens,

Don-O would have looked like a liar. I wondered if he got into his business because people up close made his skin crawl. At sixty or so, Don-O wouldn't win any footraces, but I felt he should have the experience and patience for this delicate job.

"Do you violently detest your husband?" he asked.

"No."

"Would you call yourself insanely jealous?"

"No."

"Are you unspeakably envious of his freedom?"

No again. Why was Don-O putting every question in such extreme terms? He reminded me of Aziz, always exaggerating for his Iranian friends. Who would answer yes to Don-O's questions? After two or three more, he explained himself.

"I can't risk a spouse bludgeoning or carving up a mate on the basis of information I supply," he said. "I want you to think of me as a family therapist, putting marriages on a bedrock of truth. Many times spouses find their mates are completely innocent. If that's the case, we'll talk through the feelings that made you suspicious. Sometimes they're just fantasies. How old are you?"

"I'm thirty-three. Why do you need to know that?"

"Some of my clients are going through menopause. Several have threatened me when I didn't dig up some dirt to confirm their nightmares."

I wondered about Don-O's squinting eyes and his own mental health.

"Don-O, this is a very straightforward case. When my husband left me and my kids in Ohio, he agreed to pay child support. I want him alive and able to work, so you have nothing to fear from me. The court in Ohio said they couldn't locate him. If I can find out where he's living, maybe I'll get the money he owes me."

"How much is that?"

"About fifteen thousand dollars."

"I see," Don-O said. "Did my secretary explain my retainer and hourly rate?"

Yellow Pages America, I thought. Rely on the invisible hand: the power of cash for Mrs. Gursel in Chicago, the security of a retainer for Don-O. Maybe the whole "family therapy" business was Don-O's client-friendly way of getting to the bottom line.

"I can pay the retainer. It'll be a good investment if I find my husband."

After I described Osman and Nazar's businesses, Don-O agreed to take the case. He assured me he'd have no trouble finding where Nazar lived and staking out the residence. I asked how the professional would do the surveillance.

"I have several vehicles I use, depending on the time of day. For night watch, I have this old Plymouth with garbage bags piled on the passenger's side. I lie down in the back like a guy living in his car."

"That sounds good, but how do you keep watch?"

"I use a mirror on a stick."

"What about the day shift?"

"I use a Chevrolet with a fake county sheriff seal on the side. I put my bus driver's hat on, tip the seat back, and pretend to snooze."

"You do surveillance from a police car?"

"A fake sheriff's car. Everybody out here knows sheriffs spend most of their time cooping on some side street."

"I doubt my husband would know that."

"Doesn't matter. Even wetbacks have seen so many American movies you can't use those vans with the interchangeable magnetic signs any more."

I laughed and laughed like the voice at Zaza's. I couldn't stop laughing. Hysteria, a symptom of extreme fear. And, I remembered, of the sarin gas that Iraq dropped on Kurds. They ran around the streets laughing and then fell down dead.

I told Don-O that it had been a long time since I'd laughed, that my husband had commented on just those vans Don-O was talking about. That last wasn't true, but Don-O believed me. He had a point about vans. Osman had seen plenty of movies and might suspect a van. This absurd Don-O Lyle was the right man for the case.

Chapter 20

The hourly beep beep beep of my watch reminds me of the sound my laptop makes when booting up. Castor beans. Ricin. More powerful than thallium. Almost as toxic as plutonium. Causes immediate death. No known antidote. The information keeps me hyperalert and extra cautious, bouncing my alertness off my rear-view mirror at the Zaza lot and front door.

Chances of surviving a minute ingestion of ricin: zero. Throughout the night these odds keep me calculating the chances of Osman showing up. Good between 11 p.m. and 1 a.m. Any one of the cars driving home could be Osman coming to work before Zaza closes. At 1:47 the odds climb when a man carrying a small paper bag walks to the Zaza door and hammers on it with his fist. Damn little mirror. The odds dive as the man walks away and throws the bag into the street. At 4:10 my tea-soaked brain spikes the odds when a car turns into the Zaza lot. I pull up in my seat. Two seconds later the car heads in the opposite direction and my chances look as bad as an ingester. Daylight shoves me down in my seat, but evens out both the odds and my moods. Traffic is moving. I can't jump at every vehicle that approaches.

At 7:45, a blue car pulls into the Zaza lot and parks at the rear. A short man, short even for a refugee, gets out and walks to the front door, reaches into his pocket for a key, and opens the door.

At 8:13, a rusty white station wagon turns into the lot and parks next to the blue car. A black man with a shaved head gets out, walks to the front door, and knocks. Shorty lets him in.

At 11:00, a tall blonde man about twenty-five walks up to the door, knocks, and is let in by Baldy. A minute later the venetian blinds on Zaza's windows open and I close up shop.

Back at the motel, I phoned Don-O's office. He'd called in to his secretary. Nazar lives in Englewood, but no lights went on in his house all evening. He may be out of town, she said, reporting Don-O's undoubted wish. I had no such delusion. I felt Nazar and Osman were pulling an all-nighter, boiling beans in Nazar's darkroom.

When I woke up, I drove to the nearest mall and did some shopping. I disliked parking backwards and looking in the little mirror. If I could get out of the car and stretch once in a while, I wouldn't have to drink so much tea. This is Colorado. I'll look less conspicuous in Nike hiking boots, some of those

quasi-military pants with the pockets sewn on, and a gray sweater to keep me
warm with the window down. With a sash around my waist, I could be a
peshmerga. I also bought a cheap black wig, good enough for the distance
between my parking lot and Zaza's. If Osman glances at my car during daylight, he can easily assume the dark hair showing above the steering wheel
belongs to an Asian or Mediterranean man getting a blow job before work.

I report in early—at 9:30—to help the odds. And because I have nothing
else to do in Denver. At this hour, people are getting their cars out of my lot or
walking past my car. I feel noticed. Glancing into instead of staring at the
mirror, I also feel silly. I've never even tinted my hair. Now I'm wearing a
forty-dollar wig that makes me look like an illegal alien. Late-night and early-
morning solitude don't help. My eyes focus on Zaza, but my mind occupies
the mirror. Sitting here, like Don-O, is absurd. I'm ridiculous. Osman is in
Chicago. I should be in Athens. Osman could be in Athens, Georgia. Don-O is
home sleeping. I feel my eyelids drop into the space between on and off. This
night starts to dissolve into other nights without men. Turn on the tape and
talk to stay awake.

> Awake, await. A woman's way: not fight
> or flight, but stillness, quiet. Sitting
> still on my ass, my fundament, ancient base
> of desire. Desire. More mysterious than fear.
> Desire. Intrinsically unfounded, inescapably
> personal, uniquely compelling. More frighten-
> ing than a Greek-named phobia, identified by
> the name of the desired, whether invented or
> inherited. Osman. Now a double obsession,
> doubled and contradictory. A pheromone-driven
> attraction to, an adrenaline-charged repul-
> sion from, a conflict so balanced I'm motion-
> less. Only tape and mouth running. And the
> mind moving in the mirror, the undermining
> mind.
>> Why are you waiting?
>> Why are you doing nothing?
>> Why are you asking yourself these ques-
> tions?
>> Why can't you answer that last question?

Why do you feel guilty?

I'm a woman, a man in waiting. A mistake from the beginning. Guilty without being
charged. Never founded, always ready to fall.
The fall gal. Self-punisher, self-betrayer,
do-gooder. Always falling short. A waiting
woman's trap-door thinking, the bottom
falling out, mental ground giving way. The
self-examiner's pratfall. Every woman must
fear falling for. More perilous is falling
in, falling down and through. The self-accus-
ing mind's bottomless well, bathophobia.

Falling and falling and falling.

Beep beep beep.

Bootstrap mind up out of the mirror,
force mind to think about others. Applicants
waited outside and inside my office. Women or
men, they were female in front of my desk,
submitting their pleas and waiting. Even
Osman had to wait. For the Director, for
Costa, for me to marry him. Perhaps he hated
waiting and me as much as I loved doing and
him. Only Ziba didn't plead and wait. She
demanded her status. One more night of waiting for me. Then I'll get more aggressive.
Like Ziba at the minefield. Like those archaic huntress goddesses who took on qualities
of animals. The predators that caused humans
to fear being alone in the dark. Walk in with
Sven at 11:00, wave the gun around, force
Zaza's workers to get Nazar down here. I'll
be Don-O's nightmare client, foolhardy. As
foolish as woman waiting. Wait some more,
make myself imagine others. Kurds in tents at
the Pendeli camp, waiting for their interviews. Americans in their kitchens, waiting
for lethal water from their well. Well, well,
well. A sign of disgust. Or pleasure, not

well-said. Weelll. A sign of indecision,
waiting.

7:42: Shorty parks his blue car in yesterday's spot, walks to the front door, puts his key in, and opens up.

8:15: Baldy pulls in, parks his junker next to Shorty, walks to the front door, knocks, and is let in by Shorty.

8:22: A brown pickup with matching brown cap on the back pulls in the lot and parks next to Baldy's wagon. Could be Nazar or an early customer or someone unlawfully using the lot. A man with reddish hair gets out. It's my husband, I think first. Then Osman. Well-found. He walks slowly, stiffly, as if he'd been sleeping in the camper. He knocks on the front door, and is let in by Shorty.

Watching the lot, I'd always pictured Osman carrying something, what, I wasn't sure. Maybe a garbage bag of beans or a knapsack or a cooler. Empty-handed, he may be picking up something from the Cafe. He could be back out in thirty seconds. No time to maneuver the car out of my lot, across the street, and into Zaza's lot. Fallback to feet. Run across the street and hide behind the corner of the building. To get to his pickup, Osman will walk within a foot of me.

8:25: Only fifteen feet from the door, I'll hear it open.

8:27: If he's carrying poison, Osman will be extra alert. But he can't see around corners or through this brick wall at my back.

8:30: Yes, the safety is off. Forward on, back off.

8:33: Whatever you do, don't scare Shorty to death or kill an innocent pedestrian.

The door opens. Give him half a second to walk by. Red hair.

"Osman," maybe a little louder than planned.

He acts like he's been hit by the .22 in my purse. He lurches a half-step sideways, but holds onto the paper grocery bag in his left hand. His face looks more amazed than frightened, like a superstitious old woman dazed by a TV-sized evil eye.

"Casey. What's that on your head?"

The son-of-a-bitch is either preternaturally quick to recover his cool or says the first thing in his eyes.

"It's a wig."

Then not "What are you doing here?" or "How did you find me?" but, "Why are you wearing a wig?"

"To surprise you, like you surprised me in Chicago. I never got to ask you all my questions."

"You need a wig to ask me questions?"

Osman's interest in the wig is either a great pose or he believes I know nothing about the "deleted" file.

I ignore his question. I'm the examiner. But I don't ask "What's in the bag?" Not now. I don't want to chase Osman down the sidewalk.

"I want this to be private," I tell him. "Let's get in your pickup."

"Okay."

Ever polite, Osman unlocks the passenger door first. I think of Mr. Kaya, the one-handed locksmith. I don't get in, not until Osman starts getting in his door. He puts the bag on the floor under his legs and looks at me.

"I kind of like the wig," he says. The night I met Osman he was oblivious to my appearance. Now he can't take his eyes off the wig.

"It's yours," I tell him. I pull off the fool wig and put it on the seat between us.

He looks down at it and asks, "Did Ziba call you?" as if the black wig reminded him of Ziba's hair.

But not, "Did Ziba call you about the disk?"

"I'm asking the questions, Osman."

"What do you want to know?"

"Everything."

"That could take some time."

"That's why I want to get out of this parking lot."

"Where do you want to go?"

"Out of the city, out where our conversation won't be overheard or inter-rupted. Someplace where there are no toilets for you to use."

"Now I'm having trouble breathing," he says and points to an inhaler on the dashboard.

"Why did you come to Denver, then?"

"I have a friend here, as you know." He reaches out for the inhaler and sucks on it.

"You've never been here have you?" he asks.

"You know that."

"There's some great scenery to the north, up around Arapaho Park."

So far, so good. But Osman's relaxed compliance and tour-guide concern are too good to be true. I don't trust them or him. Before he can start the engine, I say, "I want this to be a safe drive."

Then I open up my purse and show Osman the pistol.

"What are you doing carrying a gun?"

"For protection. Didn't you tell me in Chicago I should protect myself?"

"Yes, but a gun?"

"I drove out here. Some pretty lonely road."

I close the purse, rest it on my left leg with a pistol aimed at Osman's right leg. I keep my right hand in the purse. Sometimes, I realize, it pays to be a woman, to carry a bag.

"Osman," I say, "I want you to use your right leg to nudge that bag under your legs over here."

Osman's hands are together at the top of the steering wheel. Now he drops his head on his hands and closes his eyes. His pose collapses. He's amazed again. Like one of those horror-movie lovers who keep returning from the dead, I'm next to him. I have a gun. The wig between us looks like a dead animal. How did it get in my camper? How the hell did she find the Zaza Cafe? Why does she know I have poison in the bag?

I wanted that gesture of defeat and, I suppose, the fear that accompanied it.

Osman raises his head and looks at my purse.

"You're not going to shoot me," he says.

"I don't know," I say, "I really don't know."

He waits a few more seconds and nudges the bag toward me. I bring it the rest of the way with my left leg, careful not to disturb the angle of the gun in my purse.

"Now lift up your shirt," I tell him.

The stomach muscles are gone, but no gun fills out his waistband. I won't have to kill Osman. I hope I don't show my relief.

"Please give me your wallet."

No credit card, but his travel documents and six new hundreds. I put the wallet in my purse.

"Okay, let's go."

Osman starts the pickup and pulls into traffic. I open up the glove compartment. His insulin kit. Two more inhalers. These aren't props. No gun and no registration.

"Who does the truck belong to?"

"I don't know."

"You're lucky to have a friend who steals cars with his tow trucks."

"You were lucky to have Ziba for a translator, weren't you?"

I remember Ziba's silences. Let Osman wait. Make him sit and sweat, like applicants in the waiting room, like me in Athens, Chicago, and Denver. Except we're in motion with no destination, no promise of home. The fundamental state of fear. Holding the gun in my hand, I feel the punishing wait is worth the time I'm giving Osman to think.

I consider the initial questions I've rehearsed in the Taurus.

I can begin, "Why did your Questionnaire say you were single?"

Or I can ask, "Why did your Narrative state you wanted to do medical research in the United States?"

Or, "Why did you lie to me in your Chicago Interview?"

But instead of asking, I tell him about the laptop, finding the undeleted file, reading his letter to the editor, calling Ziba in Athens. I want to reduce his room for lying, head off stories he may try to make up.

"Poor Ziba," Osman says.

"You're calling Ziba 'poor?'"

"She could never get beyond nursing, patching up what was already done, nursing her own wound."

"It was some wound. Did you ever see it?"

"No sister would show her brother the evidence of rape, not even if it were visible, not even if he's a doctor."

"Ziba was raped by the police?"

"So she told me."

"But she's not your sister."

"No, she's not."

Osman isn't surprised I know this. He keeps his eyes on the road and continues as if I'd known it for months, "And that's what made the wound worse. Because her husband got her tortured for information and then raped as punishment for marrying him, Ziba no longer wished to be a wife."

"That's not what she told me."

"You didn't try to make love to her, did you?"

I thought I knew everything I needed to conduct this mobile reinterview. The wig amazed Osman. I'm stuck on Ziba's rape. I need time to process this. I look at the faces of drivers and passengers coming toward us. They're mouthing lyrics or talking on cell phones or discussing last night's Rockies game with each other. In the camper, getting an early start on a weekend camping trip, the redhead and blonde are discussing rape. The revelation came naturally, almost spontaneously out of Osman. It could be the truth. It could also be a diversion, an item from the personal past delaying questions about the public future.

At a stoplight, a woman across from us is checking her lipstick in the mirror.

I foresee the story that leads from Osman's revelation. If Ziba refused to be his wife, he could respond to my brushing his shoulder and accept my marriage proposal, a marriage document in Chicago notwithstanding. I won't let Osman tell that story, make that argument. I refuse to believe he had the right to let me fall in love with him. That belief would make even more difficult what I have to do: stop him from poisoning Americans.

But I also resent Osman's "poor Ziba," as if some past wound—rather than her desire for a future, a normal life in Greece—directed me to Denver and the Zaza Cafe. "Poor Ziba" also implied "poor Casey," our shared band-aid response to suffering: wait for it to come to us, then nurse and nurture, provide comfort and refuge, actions less heroic than Osman's lonely male adventure, his experiment in preventive medicine.

"I threatened Ziba," I tell Osman. "She told me you might be in Denver only after I threatened to expose her at UNHCR. Leave Ziba out. This is between you and me."

"So now you're threatening me with the gun."

"That's right."

"You're not a Kurd, Casey. I still don't believe you'll shoot me."

"And I still don't know. If you stop the truck, get out, and walk away, maybe not. If you try to get your bag back or force me out of the truck, I probably will. But I'm not threatening you with exposure, not yet. I need to know some things."

I wait a few seconds, take my hand off the gun in my purse, fake a cough, and turn on the tape recorder.

"When did you decide to kill Americans?"

Osman says nothing. I ask him again, and still without looking at me he points to the purse. Then he makes a circular motion with his hand. He heard the click or doesn't trust an interviewer. He points to the floor. I don't need a translator for this sign language. I take the tape recorder out, switch it off, and put it on the floor.

"Collecting evidence?" he says.

"Data," I tell him.

Some more minutes of silence, both of us staring at the road. Like Nikos, though, I can look at Osman without him looking at me.

"So when did you decide?" I ask.

"When an American doctor in Chicago said there was thallium in my system. The day I found out I couldn't be cured, I mailed the disk to Ziba."

We were back to Ziba.

"That's not what Ziba says. She told me you'd been talking about terrorizing America for a long time, long before you met me."

"Thinking about and talking about and giving away information to others, yes."

"You could do this even while on your honeymoon with an American?"

"America is not the name of a clan or tribe. I wouldn't attack a Mahan. In fact, it wasn't until I read my results that I felt I could do what I believed for a long time was necessary. Maybe I wouldn't kill if I weren't dying."

Osman's eyes are on the road. He doesn't need to look at me. He knows that my eyes will water at this sentence, that I won't be able to speak after hearing "dying." Osman drives and I look out the side window.

Sloopy's Car Wash. Rocky Mountain Animal Hospital. A woman lifting a stroller out of her trunk.

Do I ask Osman for the results of a test I didn't administer, the document that proves he's dying? Or do I stipulate that, trust my perceptions of his body, the way he walked like an old man into Zaza's, the inhalers, his passivity now, the affectlessness of his speech? The man I love says he's dying and all I can do is ask myself questions. I'm almost as affectless as Osman. Maybe my eyes are watering at that sadness, what we've come to, what we've lost, this mutual torture chamber on wheels.

A stretch of open land, a few houses in the distance. Mailboxes on wooden posts.

Five minutes later, like Nikos coming at an applicant from left field, I ask Osman, "Do you love me?"

"Yes."

"Then don't do this to me."

"I was going to destroy those travel documents you have. If I'm caught, I'll be dead before anyone can trace me to you."

"I'm not talking about the law. I'm talking about me. Show me I didn't fall in love with a murderer. Don't make me fear myself for the rest of my life."

"I'm sorry, Casey," he says and reaches for his inhaler. With the oxygen, some affect comes into his voice.

"It's what Turks do to Kurds. Make them fear themselves. Fear they will lose their pride. I've lost everything. I've lost my land, my people, my wife, my profession, my language."

He stops and goes on, angrily now as at the fish taverna, "I'm what Turks want to do to Kurds. Turn us all into refugees, disperse us, make us disappear. Everything lost. I've lost you. I'm losing my body. I don't have much time to lose. This mission is all I have left. It's keeping me alive."

Grief, I think, well-founded grief, personal, tribal, cultural. But this is no time to join Osman in mourning.

"Killing innocent people is keeping you alive? This mission is destroying everything you are, everything you've been. Talk about Kurds and betrayal. You're betraying your profession. You were a doctor, Osman."

"I still am. You're the linguist. From the word meaning 'to teach.' The same root as 'document.' My actions and letters will teach a lesson."

Like Ziba said, Osman wants to communicate, instruct, be a Kurdish Crichton. I look at the mountains in the distance. America's Kurdistan. We're getting closer. Already the two-lane road has steel guardrails protecting us from ravines. I think of the drive Demirsar never took me on: up into the mountains where Kurds' villages were blasted down into gorges.

"You're also still a Kurd. You're betraying your people, your tradition. Poisoning a well or an oasis is the unpardonable sin. What Kurd would do this?"

"The Turks threatened to poison the Euphrates. The Iraqis used helicopters to drop poison into springs when Kurds tried to escape to Iran in 1991."

"You're not Iraqi or Turkish."

"No, but I'm a Kurd far from home, one without any other weapon."

"This sounds like the 'burning bed' defense, a woman's excuse. 'I was powerless, helpless. I had to kill him in his sleep.' It's cowardly, unmanly."

Osman shakes his head. I see what I think is a smile, one that sees through me. What can I do? I push on, press deeper.

"What you're planning is like suicide. A form of punishment, yourself and others. You're displacing your hate of Turks onto Americans."

"Never mind the psychology. Kurds are displaced enough."

"You'll be caught. You want to be caught. You want those who betrayed you to feel guilty. You're also persecuting yourself for betraying others. I understand why you want to do this. I still love you. Just tell me you won't go through with it. I'll believe you and stay with you. We'll live in this camper if you want. We'll travel anywhere you want to go. Maybe you misread the tests."

"Forget the personal appeals, Casey. I'm beyond them."

Beyond the personal. It was one of my reasons for leaving the United

States. Leaving life, Osman is beyond law and morality, detached from pride and honor and guilt and love. Like Denver, like us snaking up this mountain highway, Osman is in thin air—of his obsession, his desire or wish or hope to alter the future for Kurds. I have no Kaya to trade for this tortured, self-destructive Osman. I'll have to take action, like the day Costa refused Osman.

I look out the side window. Guardrail beside me, mountains in the distance, deep, rocky ravines between. I think about my near future, what I'm going to do, what Osman will do in response. I have to wait, look ahead. Big sweeping curves, a red four-by-four coming toward us, no other traffic. I glance in the side mirror. No one behind us.

I spot a scenic overlook and tell Osman to pull in. Nobody else is parked there. A sign next to the low retaining wall says "No Littering." Chained to the sign pole is a metal garbage can. Off to the east are the flat states I've just driven through.

When Osman stops the pickup, I grab the bag, open my door, and jump out. Osman stays behind the wheel. I look back and see just the slightest frown between his eyes. He still doesn't know if I'll shoot him. I walk sideways toward the can. Osman watches me through the door I've left open. I walk up to the can and look down over the retaining wall. A sheer drop of thirty feet, then a more gradual slope of rocks and scrub. No person, animal, or evidence of either anywhere I can see. I don't feel dizzy at all. The mountains are our only friends. I take a step back, then a step forward, and heave the bag over the rail and out into space. A faint sound of glass breaking. I look down, far down the slope, and see the bag. I don't feel nauseous at all. I take the pistol out of my purse, step back, and throw it overhand. The pistol goes further than the bag, but makes no sound when it hits. That safety really works.

Now I turn and look to Osman. From twenty feet away, I can't read his face inside the camper. Tick, tick, tick, the old engine goes as I stand still and wait. All the possibilities I considered the last few minutes flash through my mind. Osman can take a pistol from under the seat and shoot me in well-founded rage. He won't. That's my trust. He can get a gun from the back and try forcing me to climb down the cliff. I won't because I don't believe he'll shoot me. He can't climb down the cliff himself and let me get a ride from a passing car. He can't drive away, leaving me to report him to a passing motorist with a cell phone.

Osman turns off the engine, opens his door, and walks around the back of the camper. He has nothing in his hands. He has a quizzical look on his face.

Then I do something I haven't planned in the passenger's seat, an act I'll never understand, a mysterious action, a spontaneous test.

I hold onto the sign pole and climb up on the four-foot-high wall. I'm no wire-walking daredevil or fearless Kurd. I hold onto the sign with my left hand and face Osman. He stops walking.

"What are you doing?" he says.

This time it's my turn to be silent.

Osman walks toward me. My mind in the passenger's seat was secure, but my body on the wall doesn't trust Osman. Although he's walking slowly, not racing like a four-footed predator, I feel my breathing quicken, my stomach muscles tense, my left hand grip the sign. My mind tells my body adrenaline isn't needed, not yet. This is a test Osman will pass. My mind trusts Osman. He won't try to push me off the wall. He keeps coming toward me.

My cerebellum says from above that I'm 165 pounds and healthy. Osman is 145 pounds and dying. From below, my amygdala asks, How much distance is a test? What's too close?

Osman stops five feet from me. Maybe he knows I won't let him get close enough to make a cliff-hanging fight fair. Maybe he's pleased that he's not a wife-killer. Or he could be admitting to himself what I want him to feel: I don't physically fear him. Finally, here on this wall, I'm glad to be 6 feet 1 1/2 inches tall.

Osman smiles. Deep in gray matter, my amygdala—no scanner it—mistakes Osman's smile for bared fangs and betrays me. I jump down, not at Osman, but still down off the wall.

Osman doesn't move. Only when he speaks, asks me a question, does my amygdala decide adrenaline should subside.

"Will you get in the camper again?"

So ill-founded this amygdala, confusing a smile with a snarl. So foolish this mind, associating this invitation with another question that ended with "again." But it's what I want, neither fight nor flight, but stand-off.

"Yes," I tell Osman, "I will."

He turns and walks back to the camper. I follow him to my door.

"Just a second," I say at the door. I reach in, pick up the wig, take it to the wall, and drop it in the trash barrel. I take Osman's wallet out of my purse, tear his documents into tiny pieces, and drop them in the barrel. Then I walk back and get in the camper.

"What now?" Osman says.

"Let's keep driving. Far away from here. Out of the mountains."

"Okay," he says and releases the emergency brake.

Chapter 21

Peshmerga: one who faces death. Not me, not on the wall, not really. My back was turned to the fall. I was holding onto the sign and leaning toward solid ground. Osman is the *peshmerga* now. Not a mercenary who can be bought like earlier Kurds, but a freedom fighter, sacrificing himself to a political ideal like Zeynep Kinali on her suicide mission. Osman is a one-man splinter group, his own PKK. Personal arguments didn't work on him. Facing my gun wasn't going to stop Osman. Eventually, there would have been a struggle for the pistol and one or both of us would have been shot. I refuse that cowboy and Indian climax.

Now I'll have to argue politics with Osman. No file to show, as I did in Diyarbakir. Like Erica and Greek citizens at the origin of democracy, I'll need to be an advocate. I'll have to litigate, what I've been avoiding all my life. It will be my knowledge and fear against his knowledge and fearlessness. Osman will be both opponent and judge, like I was for the applicants. They had to persuade me to give them a chance to live. I have to persuade Osman that his reason for living is a mistake, not illegal or immoral or a personal betrayal, but unproductive, counter-productive. Impractical, not pragmatic.

Throwing away the poison and gun gives me a few hours. Riding in the camper, Osman and I are like an old, unhappily married couple who can't afford a divorce or like a brother and sister who can't apply for a divorce. Osman doesn't dare leave me to inform on him, and I don't dare leave him to make more poison. He can't walk away from the camper, his means of escape. I can't let him escape in the camper. I won't kill Osman. He won't try to kill me, not unless I give him a better chance than I already have. I won't. He might try to tie me up—control my limbs like Ziba's—long enough to make his getaway. I'd like to lock him up in the back of the camper like Kurdish suspects in Turkish Land Cruisers. I can't handcuff him to me. I also can't count on sticking to him very long, delaying and postponing his action, preventing it.

"Between." Talk is all we have left between us.

Either I dissuade him or I inform on him.

For the next two hours, we ride east and talk. If I could have flicked on the tape recorder, I'd document this Interview. I won't pretend I remember everything we said. Some things were said several times in slightly different ways. Other things said now seem trivial, possibly the personal reasserting itself, as in a marriage, as in a sibling rivalry. What follows is like a selective transcript, accurate in its elements, but without the rigor of a Questionnaire or the continuity of a Narrative:

"I'll just have to buy some cyanide," he says.

"It won't work."

"It'll work, just not as quickly, as painlessly. Now people will be sick and tortured before they die."

We talk about torture: his, Ziba's, mine now that he's making me responsible for the slower, painful death of his victims. He speaks about an ironic balance of torture—Kurds and Americans—he'd never intended. He savors torturing Congressmen with his letters.

"Letters?" I ask. "Do you think anyone in Washington is going to read your handwritten letters? You don't know anything about big bureaucracy, Osman. A Foreign Affairs Committee isn't UNHCR. In Washington and all over America letters aren't read. They're scanned for keywords by a machine that sends an appropriately vague reply—'Thank you for your opinion.' 'We regret we no longer have a position.' With no return address, you won't even get scanned. Nomads and the homeless don't carry on a correspondence."

"The scanner won't work on my letters. Some human will have to read them because stapled to my letters will be documents, photos from the local paper. These documents will prove the letter is believable. And in the letter I'll cite facts, such as the poison used, to demonstrate my claims are authentic."

Documents. I wonder how much Osman has learned about letter-writing from me. Ziba learned about stories by translating hundreds of them. Has Osman learned about lawyerly persuasion from talking with me about files and the Letters of Recommended Action I wrote to the Director?

Osman turns briefly toward me, as if he were addressing one of those officials, lobbying in some Washington corridor: "You have to understand, my mission isn't seeking publicity for Kurds. We don't need the world's sympathy, public pity and a few gifts. Iraqi Kurds enjoy the protection of international law. Turkish Kurds don't. Therefore, we need a change of American policy, a reduction in the flow of money and arms to Turkey. Then we will have a fairer fight."

Osman is confident and calm, like a TV judge. To shake him, I let Costa speak through me: "You can't blackmail Congressmen. Besides, they aren't going to worry about your victims. People are dying every day in America because of governmental neglect. You know about Indians on reservations, blacks on the South Side of Chicago, children born on the north side of the Rio

Grande. Do you think Congressmen in Washington care about a couple of farm families dying way out in Colorado or Nebraska? Representatives and Senators all have bodyguards and security systems. They drink bottled water. They just won't give a shit, not really, about some crazy serial killer who claims to be a Kurd."

Osman is silent. He hasn't lived in America for a long time. Maybe he believes this story—if it is a story—of a government as distant from its citizens as the Turkish government is from Kurds. A few minutes later he says, "We need gas" and pulls into a two-pump station. He takes the keys out of the ignition and gets out to pump the gas. I get out to stretch my legs.

"No Smoking" a hand-lettered sign says. "No Littering." Signs of the law are everywhere. If I had matches, I could spray the camper with gas and burn it up when he goes in to pay. That would certainly cause him a problem. If I had a handful of sand, I could sneak it into the fill pipe and make him some trouble.

"I need some money," Osman says.

"I'll pay. I have to go in and use the toilet."

Osman won't drive off and leave me with a phone.

"We'll go in together," he says.   .

"Into the toilet?"

"No, just in where that kid at the cash register might believe a kidnapping story."

"If I wanted to turn you in, I'd never have thrown away the gun."

"Maybe you didn't believe my plan would work when you threw away the gun."

So Osman thinks he's winning our debate. The more I try to litigate, talk him out of killing, the more confident he feels. Not only do I bring him to the United States, I support his plan by trying to undermine it. Litigation is failing. Or so Osman implied. But he hasn't addressed my mock cynicism. Maybe I'm winning and Osman is faking. It's difficult to judge because Osman is like the Director, the final arbiter, no appeal.

We go in together. Osman waits outside the door while I use the toilet. I buy some soda and sandwiches and get back in the camper. About a half mile down the road, he stops and we eat in silence. He takes his insulin kit out of the glove compartment and injects himself. Poison. I realize Osman knows about chemicals the way I know about heights, body deep, toes to eyes, all over. Osman takes out the keys, walks in front of the camper, turns his back to me, and urinates. Of course, he didn't want me telling secrets at the gas station while he was in the toilet.

"I never believed Congressmen would act out of altruism or concern for citizens," he says when we're moving. "My plan is to set a trap. At first, 'Do what I say or I'll kill more.' Like you say, these letters will be ignored. Then I'll send more letters, 'Do what I say or I'll send letters to the press.' That's my torture. Instead of demanding information, I'll threaten to be an informant. That's my real danger, exposing the Congressmen, showing that they did nothing about me."

"That kind of blackmail may have worked with me, but it won't work with Congress. They'll lie to the press." I put on a bureaucratic voice, "'We've been investigating behind the scenes. We can't give in to terrorism. The American people will have to trust that we're doing all in our power to bring this heinous criminal to justice.'"

"I expect better from you, Casey. You're the expert in fear. As a country, America is now fearless. Russia is in shambles. The Chinese want refrigerators. But American officials are still bureaucrats. They want to keep their jobs. They'll be deathly afraid of this secret getting out. They know what goes on in Turkey. They've learned that the power of a repressive government is its secrecy. They'll understand the secret action I'm demanding. As long as no one knows, Congressmen won't mind betraying Turks with silent committee votes."

I think for a minute. This camper is not a movie courtroom. I'm sitting down. I don't have to be quick on my feet.

"You're depending way too much on betrayal," I tell him.

Deny. It's what I did to nine out of ten applicants. Denying the power of betrayal, I know, will be poison to Osman, but I have no other argument.

"Betrayal is our history. This we know well," he says, sounding like Ziba, sure and curt. Then, more passionately, "Congressmen will have no choice. If this secret leaks, it will be like gas diffusing. The media will spread it. There will be public panic. Like I said in my letter, Americans will stampede out of their homes. They'll live like Kurds in the Pendeli camp." Then, scornfully, "Like me in this camper."

"This future will never happen, Osman. There's one of you and 260 million Americans. You're crazy if you believe you can cause a panic or mass migration."

Osman pushes his back against the seat. He's insulted. "No panic, Casey? Maybe you're right. Then I'll induce mass hysteria. I'll publicly threaten to dump ricin in some small town's water supply."

Halabja, the wide-eyed dead Kurdish kids I saw in photographs.

So, like Erica litigating with her applicants, I'd goaded a secret out of Osman, his back-up plan. I let his threat seep into my synapses. From fear to hysteria. The politics of mass death. It worked for Saddam, Kurds streaming out of Iraq, an ancient exodus on foot. In Athens Osman mocked the PKK's conventional terrorism, but he has come around to it. Now I know what I have to do.

Like Kaya, I decide to lie. Like me interviewing Kaya, I'll use Osman's rage: "You're lying to yourself, Osman. You've built up the arguments, but when it comes right down to it, you won't drop the poison. You'll be afraid. Standing over the well, you'll be the one with a phobia. Thanatophobia. You'll be powerless."

"No, Casey. You know I can do this," he says, calm again.

Osman slows the camper. For only the second time in our long debate, he turns his head toward me, looks at me as he speaks, "You believe what I'm telling you."

"Telling" reminds me of Ziba's interview: "I have something I can show you."

"I don't believe you, Osman," I lie again, adopting Ziba's mocking tone, the kind you might use on a younger brother. "You'll have to show me. I want you to drive us past some isolated house, one that's close to the road, close to you. Then you'll have to point out the well, a real one, not some speculative, imaginary well, not one you're speeding past. You'll have to stand on the ground, lean against the rancher's fence, and tell me, 'About 2 a.m., I'll walk over to that wellhouse, open up the lid, look down, and drop poison in the water.' I don't believe you can do it. And if you get close to it, stop and rehearse it, say it aloud, you'll admit you can't."

Osman thinks this over. I wonder if Ziba ever spoke this way to him. I have to wait, again. At the first dirt road he sees, he turns off the highway.

Good, but why is Osman accepting this test?

Maybe he wonders himself if he'll be able to kill.

Perhaps he believes he can overpower me if he gets me away from the highway and passersby. He can't. I know that. I also know I can't pummel this dying man into submission. I'll defend myself, but not attack him.

Why not?

I don't know, but I just can't.

He drives slowly on the bumpy road. Good, good. We go about a mile without seeing anything human. Then a small white house, not much bigger than a trailer. Nobody visible. No cars or trucks. Next to an independent shed is a little well-house. And a swing set.

"Too close to the highway," Osman says and keeps going.

He drives four or five miles down the road, but it comes to a dead end at a gated fence. This is perfect. On the right are some trees. Osman pulls up to the gate to turn around. As he puts the camper in reverse, I touch him for the first time. I put my left hand over his right hand on the shifting lever.

"Wait a second," I say.

Osman takes his hand off the lever, turns his body toward me. I'm still holding his hand on the seat.

"Did you see the swing set?" I ask, looking into his eyes.

"Yes."

"And?"

"Yes."

"I believe you now," I say, "and that's why I'm telling you this." I take my hand off his. "I hate to, but I have to. I'm sorry if you find it cruel. Maybe it would be possible to induce a panic or turn secure Americans into fearful Kurds, but you're forgetting bureaucracy, procedures, channels. I know about these things. Delay, wasted time."

We're staring at each other across a great distance, growing every second. I force myself to finish, to explain.

"Your plan won't work because you don't have enough time. I'm sorry, Osman, but it's true. You'll take some lives, but you won't save Kurds' lives."

The final why.

"You won't live long enough to follow through with the letters."

Osman doesn't flinch, shows no sign of *tremoulisma*, responds immediately.

"I know. That's why I need you, Casey. You wanted to help Kurds. We're dying. This is your chance. Help me."

One last shock. Maybe two seconds of thought. Osman is waiting for my answer. Through this whole day, he's allowed me close to him because he wants help. He didn't come too close to me on the wall because he needs my aid. I took his mission seriously. While I was trying to dissuade him, he was trying to persuade me to join him, to betray Americans, commit treason. He believed he's won and believed my lie when I said he couldn't kill. He welcomed this test. He felt he needed to convince me he could be a murderer before asking me to become his accomplice. Osman wants me to be his nurse and letter-writer, his attorney. Osman requires a translator, someone who will make sure his idea is translated into action. This will be my gift to him. Like a woman, Osman has waited and waited. Now he's proposing. He mocked "well-founded," but his appeal is fundamental, primal, visceral. Help a dying people, help a dying man.

"Help me," he says again.

I don't answer Osman. No parting words. I jump out of the camper. No showdown, no grappling until death do us part. I proposed his test for just this chance to stop the camper and get away. I back away from the camper.

"Please," Osman says.

I can't listen. I turn tail and run toward the trees thirty yards away. No sound of gunfire, no gunfire. He can't catch me. I know that. No fear of him. No fear of me, not now.

In the trees, panting, I look back. Osman is still in the camper. He backs it into the road and starts back the way we came. About two hundred yards down the road he stops, gets out, and looks in my direction. He can see I'm watching him. He gets back in the camper, but it doesn't move. A minute later, he gets out again with a piece of paper in his right hand. He waves the paper over his head, lays it on the road, and puts a stone on it. Then he gets back in the camper and drives away. Dust. Osman turns into dust.

I walk over to the paper he has left behind. It's a document, my document. It doesn't need to be translated. But in case you couldn't read it earlier, here it is in print:

This is your written release. You were always innocent. You knew nothing of my plan. Don't be afraid. You'll never need to use this document. Mobility is my refuge.

Chapter 22

The document was fake. Osman pretended to believe I'd wait for him to be caught and myself to be exposed.

The document was true. I was innocent. I didn't know of Osman's plan when I sent him to the United States.

The document was worthless. I'd already finished gathering information and interviewing. My judgment was instantaneous. My actions were immediate: run and walk and run to the house we'd passed. Report Osman before he disappears into the refuge of America. Call the police and recommend actions. Go on radio and TV, warn citizens that a random killer is in the area. Anyone with an exposed well should guard it and drink bottled water. Reminded of his time running out, Osman may buy rat poison and kill people tonight. Keep running. He'll have to spend his last days or weeks in prison. I can visit him if I'm not in a correctional facility myself. That thought doesn't slow me down. Run to, not from. Run to make people fear persecution, execution. Run to prevent a future.

Walking and panting, I think about the recent past, the last few minutes. Did I jump to escape Osman or myself, his new conception of me—a fearless wall-climber, but defeated litigator, a hard-hearted accomplice? Did I run because I feared betraying what was left of myself, fallen-away Catholic girl and malpracticing "officer of the court," American in America? The answers don't make any difference, not now. Did Osman bring me down this dirt road to let me out, let me escape? I refused to grapple with him. Maybe he refused to grapple with me. This dead end road might be the best he could imagine for both of us. He has an hour to flee, I have an hour to think about what I'll do. I don't want to. I refuse to grapple with that question.

Run some more. From desire, not fear. Run toward, not away like a maiden in distress. Don't think of the distress you'll cause yourself. Minutes are crucial. Use that adrenaline. In forty minutes Osman can be in a hardware store thirty miles away. Run faster. Feel those endorphins stream. Communication is faster than transportation. I have the information I need: his license plate. The police will radio far and wide, set up checkpoints like those in Kurdistan. Driver's license, please. No license? How about your registration? No registration? Do you have any identification? Not even a wallet? Please step out sir and place your hands on the hood of your vehicle. Osman won't use his dialects to talk his way through American police. "Barzani" and "Talibani" aren't talismans here. He'll have to produce documents he doesn't have.

I see the house ahead and slow to a fast walk. A few more minutes. I'll need breath to tell my story. My sweat will demonstrate its urgency. But what if the homeowner doesn't own a gun and fears I'm being pursued by a maniac with a weapon? I'll explain right away I'm not seeking refuge. Just need the phone to report a serial killer. But what if the owner thinks I'm a maniac or a serial killer? I'll wait outside while the owner calls the police. Yes, that'll work. Even a kid left home alone will do that for me. Just pick up the phone and hit 911.

I wipe some sweat off my face, hunch over a bit, and walk up the front steps. A large dog barks inside. Good. The house is protected. They'll open the door. No doorbell, not out here in nowhere. I knock on the door, and the dog barks louder. Who can be sleeping at this time of day? I pound on the door and I hear the dog jumping against it. It's Saturday. Whoever lives here has gone into town.

I walk across the front porch and look in a window. A Rottweiler looks back at me. He's in a frenzy. He's a predator. I'm afraid the dog will jump through the window.

Osman is lucky. These dog-owning Americans fear home incursions. If they weren't so paranoid about burglary, I could break in the window and use their phone. Or if they trusted those electronics I was touting, instead of the Rottweiler, I could set off their alarm and wait for the police to drive up.

Another mile to the main road. Ten more miles for Osman to put between himself and me.

Two trailer trucks and three cars pass me by. Business and fear still rule, even if the person waving beside the road is a woman. I should have on a dress and heels. The fourth car slows down and stops, two middle-aged women in a beat-up Dodge. The passenger rolls down her window and asks, "Car trouble?"

"Man trouble," I tell her and she laughs.

"Get on in the back," she says, "and join the club."

I climb in the back seat.

"Do you have a CB radio or cell phone?" I ask.

"Don't need them out here as long as you don't travel alone," the driver says. They laugh at some inside joke I don't try to understand, something between them, something between natives and an obvious outsider.

"Can you take me to the nearest police station?" I ask.

"Sure can," the driver says.

"Your man try to beat you up?" the passenger asks.

"My husband's threatening to murder some people, and I have to tell the police."

"Why didn't you say that in the first place?" the driver says and accelerates. "I'll get you to the station in ten minutes."

Ten more miles for Osman.

"What's the matter with your husband?" the passenger asks.

"He plans to kill people to influence Congress. He's been persecuted and wants to do something for his people. He's a Kurd."

"Worse than a cur," the passenger says, "It's a mean dog that beats his wife. But murdering people, now that's something else again."

"Not 'cur.' Kurd. He's a Kurd."

"I'm afraid you'll have to explain that one to me, miss."

"He comes from Turkey. He belongs to a persecuted minority called Kurds."

The driver says, "You know, Emily, one of those A-rabs we fought in the war against Saddam."

The driver asks me, "So he came over here for revenge, did he?"

"Something like that," I say, "It would take longer than we've got to explain it."

Emily persists on the personal angle, "How did you get hooked up with this fella anyway?"

"I met him in Chicago. He's a doctor. I didn't know he was political. He was charming."

"Rich, too, I bet," Emily says.

"Right," I agree, "but it's kind of painful to talk about right now."

Seven more minutes to the police station. I don't care if these women believe my story. They're just transporting me. Like translators delivering a message. But what about the local police? I can't take twenty minutes explaining Kurds to a small-town dispatcher. Keep it simple and believable, like Ziba's story. A story to put Osman in jail and keep me out.

"You better stay away from that Kurd of yours," Emily tells me as I get out.

I thank her for the advice, thank the driver for the lift, walk into the station, and find the dispatcher sitting behind a counter. He can't be more than twenty-three, but looking down on him I notice he has a bald spot. He's in no hurry. I tell him I have an emergency. Officer Green speaks some code words into his microphone and says, "Shoot." I tell him what I worked out in the car:

"I was sitting in my car in Denver, when a red-haired man with a gun approached and forced me to get in his camper. He held the gun on me while I drove. He seemed to be on drugs. He had this crazed look in his eyes, and he spent the whole time haranguing me with paranoid stories about persecution. He was also drinking the whole time. When he finally passed out, I slowed down the camper and stopped. He didn't wake up, so I jumped out and ran. From my hiding place, I saw him drive away. I did manage to get the license plate."

"Are you injured, ma'am?" Officer Green asks and removes his microphone headset.

"No."

"Do you want to go to a hospital?"

"No."

"If you were raped, we need to get you to the hospital for evidence."

"I wasn't raped."

"That's good. Did the perpetrator make any sexual advances?"

"No."

"And he didn't take your purse or anything else?"

"No."

"And he made you drive his camper instead of stealing your car?"

"Yes."

"So the perpetrator just wanted to talk to you?"

Looking up at me, the kid has a strange expression on his face, as if his tie is too tight.

"I don't know what he wanted, but that's all he did. I didn't know what he was planning to do with me."

"Please tell me more about how you got away."

"It was about ten miles back up the highway. He made me drive down a dirt road. After about five miles it deadended. While I was slowing to turn around, he slumped against the door and passed out."

"So he's awake and talking for hours on the smooth paved roads, but he falls asleep after getting bumped around for five miles on a dirt road?"

"He'd had a lot to drink."

"Weren't you afraid he'd hear you open the door and shoot you?"

"Of course, but I was also afraid he was going to kill me out there. I felt it was my one chance to get away."

"You said you jumped out."

"I got out as fast and as quiet as I could."

"After you ran, he woke up."

"That's right."

"But he didn't come after you with his gun?"

"No, he just drove away."

"Why didn't you take the keys?"

"I was too afraid. He might have heard them jingle."

"Didn't you have to turn off the ignition?"

"No. I left the engine running."

"So you tramped down on the emergency pedal?"

"No."

"Weren't you afraid the pickup would roll into a ditch and wake up the perpetrator?"

"The ground was level I guess. I was in a panic. I didn't have time to think about all these things."

Officer Green puts his headset back on and speaks more code. Maybe he's calling in help, someone to saw the truth out of me. Now I'm panicked. I should have taken criminal law courses or interned at the DA's office. Interrogation not Immigration.

"Look," I tell Officer Green, "this man is dangerous. Aren't you going to take his license number?"

"Have you ever seen this red-haired man before?" he asks.

"No."

"You're sure?"

"Yes."

"Does he know you?"

"No. Nobody in Denver knows me. I told you, he came up to my car and forced me into his camper."

"So you're not from around here?"

"No, I'm just visiting."

"Look, ma'am," the kid says and leans back in his chair, as if he had thirty years on the force, "please don't be offended, but I'm going to ask you something for your own good. Are you sure you want to file a complaint?"

"Why are you asking me that?"

"Well, you're not from around here. Are you sure this isn't a one-night stand or a camping trip that went bad?"

Before I could deny this, the kid goes on, "You see, this is a really strange story. I've never heard one like it. I want to make sure you're telling me the truth before you file an official complaint. You could be prosecuted if this report is false."

"I could be prosecuted? What are you talking about? This is the way rape victims used to be treated. This is insulting. I should report you to your supervisor."

"He's home sleeping right now," the kid says and gets up. He's not wearing a gun, and he's only about 5-7, but he's behind his counter. "You weren't raped. You say you were just abducted for no reason either of us can understand. There's no evidence. I'd advise you to go outside, have some coffee, and think about this story. If you decide you want to file a complaint, I'll call my supervisor."

I went outside. No evidence. I was like Osman. No bruises, no wounds, nothing to show for my imprisonment in the camper. Maybe, like one of Don-O's clients, I should have bashed Osman and dragged him here. Or taken longer to make up my story. The applicants, I realized, have days and weeks to invent or refine their stories. But no matter how long I spent, I couldn't change what I told the kid. And I wouldn't have documentary evidence until I got back to Denver and my laptop. I looked at my watch. Osman was now a hundred miles away, maybe out of the state. Yes, he'll flee as far as he can, then drop his poison. Maybe I have time to go to the FBI. A call would do no good.

I walked down the sidewalk, went into a convenience store, and found out how to get a bus to Denver. Riding the bus, I had lots of time to imagine Osman's victims and think about my story. No scribe or translator or examiner to help me, but hours to rehearse and revise and anticipate questions. My first story lacked future fear. This time I'll be like Professor Malik. I'll have my documents and I'll tell the truth:

"This man Osman is dangerous. I know him. He's my husband. I helped get him into this country. Then I discovered a computer file and confronted him next to the Zaza Cafe. We drove for hours while I attempted to talk him out of what he confessed he planned to do. When I judged this was futile, I slipped away and tried to report him. But the local police wouldn't believe me because I didn't have my computer."

"Please sit down, Ms. Mahan," the FBI agent said and asked to look at my laptop. She was about my age. Ms. Sherrod had long red nails and a gold watch, not the agent I pictured on the bus to Denver. She read Osman's letter.

"Why did you confront your husband instead of coming to us?" she asked.

"I guess I didn't believe the file was authentic. I thought it might have been written by his sister. I didn't believe he could do a thing like this."

"But now you do?"

"Not only 'could,' but 'will.'"

"The only evidence of his intent is the computer file and your word."

I showed agent Sherrod the document Osman left behind.

"What proof do we have it's his handwriting?"

"Fax UNHCR in Athens. Compare this sheet with the writing in his file."

"It would still be inconclusive. The language here is vague."

"Not when it's connected to the computer file."

"Writing is cheap. What we need is hard evidence."

"I suspect he was preparing his poison at the Zaza Cafe. You could check it out, do some tests on the plumbing."

"Ms. Mahan, you're an attorney, right? You must know we can't just barge into private property and conduct a search without a warrant. And how are we going to get one on your suspicion of your husband?"

Partial truth had no more effect than my whole lie to the local dispatcher. I told agent Sherrod about tossing the ricin and my gun. She got up from her desk and took down a book from a shelf behind her.

"Ricin is on the Prohibited Substances list. Very deadly stuff. Can you tell me where we can look for it?"

"The overlook on seventy-two, about two miles south of Wundervu."

"Good. Now, how do you know what you threw over the bank was ricin?"

"From my research in the computer files."

"Did you look inside the bag?"

"No."

"Did your husband say it was ricin?"

"No."

"Then what was inside the jar that broke could have been baba ganoush."

"I don't understand."

"'Baba ganoush?' It's a Middle Eastern dish."

An American. As in the monoglot joke clients told me, I was an American, an American lawyer who had never litigated, never cross-examined or been cross-examined.

"Okay, it could have been apple pie. But if it was ricin, and if it's as toxic as I read, it's worth looking for."

"We will check that out."

Agent Sherrod made some notes on a pad. Writing. Now we're getting somewhere.

"About this pistol you say we're also going to find. Did you use it to abduct your husband?"

"What? No. I just used the gun to defend myself when I got rid of the poison."

"Did you also use the pistol to force his confession?"

"No."

"Why didn't you use the pistol to bring him here after his confession?"

"I thought he would change his mind with the poison gone."

"And that's why you threw away the gun?"

"I wasn't afraid of Osman any more."

"You didn't fear this man you'd been pointing your gun at, a man who said he was going to poison Americans?"

"Not right then. He's very ill. I knew I was stronger."

I pulled myself up in my chair to remind red-nailed agent Sherrod of my height and strength.

"But you were still willing to take that chance with a potential mass murderer?"

"Yes. He's also my husband."

I held up my wedding band.

"Do you have any documents to prove that?"

"Not with me, but you can fax the American embassy in Athens."

"We'll look for ricin. But even if we find the poison, I'm afraid it won't prove your story. It could just as easily be you who was planning to poison wells."

"Me? This is god-damned outrageous. I'm here reporting a public peril and you suspect me?"

"I'm just saying that anything is possible. It's your computer, isn't it? I want to believe you, but this guy Osman may turn up and say he forced you to toss the poison. We may get a missing persons report on him. In two months time, he may be found dead at the bottom of a ravine."

"In two days time, he could kill a family. Jesus Christ, don't you understand that?"

"You may be right," agent Sherrod said, clicked her fingernails on her desk, and stood up to end our interview. "But you have to understand we're hamstrung. It's terrible to admit, but if we pursue your husband before he commits a crime he could charge us with persecution. You say he's a member of a minority. He's legally in this country. His rights are protected here. We're a nation of laws, right?"

"You're the fucking FBI. There must be something you can do to protect

Americans' lives."

"Ms. Mahan, please. We'll look for the ricin and monitor reports of any poisonings. But we can't do anything more right now, not unless a crime is committed."

VI Letter of Recommended Action
(continued)

Chapter 23

"Casey Mahan, now a 34-year-old citizen of the United States, departed Denver in her country of origin on July 27, 1999. Ms. Mahan arrived in Cincinnati on July 29, 1999. Shortly thereafter, she began her application for asylum."

On the road I wondered if the authorities refused to believe me because I secretly—unconsciously, a secret to me—wanted Osman to get away. I didn't believe that, but maybe I'd undermined my stories with my voice, betrayed my intent with my manner. Standing before agents of the law, perhaps I was unable to project myself as a credible victim after tracking Osman, pointing my pistol at him, and facing him down at the wall. I wanted and needed the impersonal objectivity of writing.

My first day back in Cincinnati, I sent letters briefing the facts, evaluating my interviews, and recommending actions to INS and members of the House and Senate Foreign Affairs Committees. Two weeks later INS wrote back to say Osman was now on their watch list. A month later I got the responses from Washington I'd predicted to Osman.

I wrote a letter to the CIA and faxed it to Costa in Athens. He had a channel. I never heard anything from him or Langley.

I faxed UNHCR. Ziba was no longer translating there. Then I called her employer, who said she'd left the family. If I understood his Greek, Ziba was "nowhere."

I went back to work part time. I emailed clients and wrote briefs to the Department of Labor. I never heard from the FBI. Maybe Osman didn't have ricin in the bag. I bought USA Today every day and read its local news from all the states. No "mystery killings" or unexplained poisonings. Maybe I dissuaded Osman or he switched to some other strategy. Or Osman had even less time than he believed.

In the other half of my time, I began writing this book, to record and understand events, to confess a guilty secret, to document my fear. But the events remain inconclusive. Though I understand the connections between events, I still can't quite believe that so small a cause as Ziba's Greek sentence in Lavrion could send me seven thousand miles to the FBI office in Denver. My actions are now revealed, but my motives are still mysterious to me, as tightly knotted but not as beautiful as my Jalali carpet. Those are the reasons why, I suppose, my focus shifted while writing—from the desire for self-awareness and self-punishment to informing and warning and protecting others. But even these motives may have been manipulated, as I was by Ziba. I may be Osman's mouthpiece. Not translating his ideas into action, as he hoped, but transcribing his spoken words—our interviews—into this printed transcript. Fright, flight, fight, write. I've even wondered if *Well-Founded Fear* is what Osman intended. Perhaps he never meant to poison people, just trick me into expanding and extending the essay on fear and refugees I was writing when Ziba walked him into my life.

Despite ambiguities, uncertainties, and mysteries, the examiner has to decide, has to judge and recommend in her Letter. I can tell you this:

> Kurds have a well-founded fear of persecution in any future anyone can foresee in Turkey and Iraq.
>
> Americans have a well-founded fear. Not of Kurds, at least not just Kurds. But Osman is right about America. Despite our economic anxieties and xenophobia, America is now a fearless state. We exercise our power and altruism with impunity, proudly prosecute a televised war and support a state that persecutes its citizens. But a nation without fear, like a tribe without land, is subject to the law of terror in the future.
>
> I no longer fear persecution, Osman's torturing and killing Americans because they're Americans.

And yet, despite finishing this written confession, I still feel persecuted by memory and imagination. Perhaps they were stimulated by writing, recalling events, retelling stories, seeing myself from a distance. "Everyone has the right to seek and to enjoy in other countries asylum." So says the Universal Declaration, but I don't enjoy talking with friends at the water cooler or drinking coffee with my parents. No law will protect me from picturing them poisoned, falling down in their offices, thrashing on the kitchen floor, tortured like Kurds in Turkish prisons. Talking on the phone with Third World computer programmers, I think of Kurds in the Pendeli camp, the Fourth World. Looking out my office window at the Ohio River, I'm no longer anxious about falling, but fear I will never forget what could have happened, my complicity in the bombing of a city's water supply, Americans dying like Kurds gassed at Halabja. Reading documents in my apartment, I don't feel at home, not in my apartment, not in a country that aids the destruction of homes and villages in eastern Turkey. Sometimes I feel Professor Malik's disgust for my government. Lying awake at night, I think about Osman and Ziba, Ziba and Osman, gone, lost, disappeared. I fear I will never be able to flee them and, like them, the hundred thousand Kurds who disappeared in the Anfal. I flick through the cable channels and watch ads for insomniacs. Late-night and early-morning hours are given over to agoraphobics, the home shoppers, and to public service, ads for UNICEF, United Children's Fund, Save the Children. The oversized eyes of little kids in rags peer into my bedroom. They don't speak languages I can't understand. They just stare out at me like the kids at the Pendeli camp, like the dead Kurdish children in photographs. I'm not sure what the live kids are feeling. Surely hunger, probably fear. But these kids aren't asking to leave their countries. They need aid right where they are. Now and in the future. An American attorney with refugee experience, a person willing to relocate, could be useful outside her country of origin. I'm gathering letters of recommendation, writing queries, mailing resumes, filling out questionnaires. If a humanitarian organization asks for a writing sample, I'll send them some of this narrative, a published document. When I'm interviewed for asylum, I'll tell no story. I'll say, simply, "I want to help." I don't know why. That doesn't worry me, not now.

—End—

Author's Note

Well-Founded Fear is a fiction. Some of its documents are authentic, some are doctored, and some are invented. All of the characters are imagined. The novel's UNHCR is a composite of United Nations protocols and some practices of the Greek Council for Refugees, a UN subcontractor in Athens. I want to thank Marion Hoffman, formerly of the actual UNHCR in Athens, for sharing her knowledge of Kurds with me. I also want to thank the GCR for allowing me to read files, observe interviews, and talk with applicants and translators. Many thanks to the Greek office of Medicins du Monde for giving me access to the Pendeli refugee camp.

Thanks also to the editors of *Witness, Fiction International,* and *MondoGreco* for publishing excerpts from the novel and for allowing me to print revised versions here; to the University of Cincinnati Taft Research Fund for their generous support of the project; to Barbara Fields for providing me a writer's colony of one in Athens; and to those who read and re-read some or all of *Well-Founded Fear*: Heather and Wayne Hall, Lee Kellogg, Brad Vice, Alison Russell, Brett Clarke, Cindy Lewiecki-Wilson, and Michael Freeman.

For those who care to know more about the Kurds, I recommend beginning with two excellent books: Jonathan C. Randal's *After Such Knowledge What Forgiveness?* and Susan Meisalas's *Kurdistan,* a remarkable collection of documents and photographs.

Printed in Canada